By Norah Lofts

THE HOUSE
AT OLD VINE

NORAH LOFTS

DOUBLEDAY & COMPANY, INC.

GARDEN CITY, NEW YORK

1961

Library of Congress Catalog Card Number 61-9532

Part One

JOSIANA GREENWOOD'S TALE

Circa 1496

I

Tomorrow the man I love is to die; horribly, and in public. Only two other people ever knew of our love, and they are both dead now; but there are circumstances which make it natural enough that I should spend the night on my knees before the altar in the St. Mary Chapel of the Abbey, praying for him.

I am supposed to be praying that he may recant. They don't like this burning of heretics. A heretic who recants is defeated and finished; one who burns scores a kind of victory. The common people who come to stare go away asking themselves—Would a man suffer so much and die untimely for anything less than a sincere belief? Even the judges themselves must feel a nibble of doubt—Would I face such an end for *my* beliefs?

I wish I could pray.

If I could pray and if prayers were answered, Walter would recant within an hour. He'd be what they call "a known man" and for a time would be obliged to wear a little badge, with a faggot on it, to show how near he had come to burning; but he would be alive, alive to feel the warmth of the sun, the splash of the rain, even the sting of the sleet.

I wish I could pray, and I wish I could believe. If I could believe anything I should believe as he does; then I could go with him tomorrow, certain that once the pain and the dying was done with there would be happiness in Heaven. Walter does not believe in Purgatory. He says there is no evidence for it in the Scriptures. He says that Christ said to the dying thief, "*Today* thou shalt be with me in Paradise." For Walter, that disposes of Purgatory.

I have studied my Bible, too, and have been left with the feeling that men have always been able to believe what they wanted to.

Thousands of men, all through the ages, good men, sincere men, like Walter, picking out what they will believe and what they will not, and making an issue of it. Walter will burn tomorrow because he will not believe that at a given moment the wine and the wafer become the veritable blood and body of Christ—yet he has no difficulty in believing that Christ fed five thousand people on one boy's dinner, and walked about on the sea, and made dead people come to life again.

I see no difference myself. And why go about saying what you believe and what you don't? They're going to burn Walter; if they could see into my mind they'd think burning too good for me. But they can't. And the priests value me as highly as a parishioner as Arthur values me as a wife.

Poor Arthur.

He came with me to the Chapel and helped me to light the candles. This is St. Egbert's Abbey so naturally he has his; Walter was born on St. George's Day and my nearest saint is St. Michael, so they have theirs; Our Lady, in her own Chapel, must have two. They are all tall candles, and thick; I pointed to them when Arthur asked if I should be frightened and offered to stay with me. I needed, tonight, to be alone. Once I was frightened of the dark, of being alone in the dark, but tonight, even if the candles burn out, I shall have no room in me for fear of anything except tomorrow.

I was thinking of it even while we lighted the candles. I held my little finger in the flame of one of them and counted. At three I couldn't bear it any more. A whole body, Walter's body, and a fire greater than a thousand thousand candle flames. Not to be borne. Not to be thought of. Oh, God . . .

It's no good. I believe in God, but not as a kind loving father who cares what becomes of us. How could He have played such a trick on us, if He cared? I believe in God the Grandfather Almighty, Grandfather Greenwood. . . .

What am I doing? This was to be my time to think of Walter. One night, of all my many. I am Arthur's wife; we are regarded as a happy, enviable couple. I have pretended well; and when this is over I suppose I shall go back and pretend again.

Tonight is for Walter, and the truth; not the truth of what I believe, the truth of what I know because it happened to us.

II

Tonight is Walter's and I must face the story that we share, and remember again all the things which turned a cheerful, outward-looking young man into a soul-searching Lollard of such fanatical beliefs that this world counts for nothing. For that change in him I was, in part, responsible but not to blame; the makings of Lollardry must always have been there, just as you must have cream in a churn in order to make butter. You could turn an empty churn, or a churn filled with water, until the end of time and still have none.

It is natural for me to think in homely terms and of practical things; what learning I have came late in life. I was born and spent my first thirteen years on my grandfather's farm at Flaxham St. Mary.

The farm was one of those separate, enclosed ones which were gradually replacing the old open fields. My grandfather had bought it from the loot he had gained in the French wars, and it would be less true to say that he owned it than that it owned him. The work, the care of the soil, the state of the crops and the prices were as much ingrained, as much part of his mind, as the brown earth itself which was embedded in the cracks of his hands, the creases of his neck, the pores of his skin.

Perhaps because he had married late in life, he had but one child, my mother. My grandparents' embitterment may have started with that disappointment, for to land-loving people a son is a necessity. They made the best of a bad job and at an early age betrothed her to the son of a neighbour named Bowyer; they planned that he would be as a son to them and work the farm when their feeble time came. Before the marriage took place my mother had disappointed them again by getting herself with child. Young Bowyer denied all responsibility and backed out of the contract, and my mother, with a stubbornness hard to credit, refused to name any other man.

It is as difficult to believe that in this matter she defied that terrible old man, that grim old woman, as it is to believe that she was once a pretty girl. I never saw her other than meek and timid, as hard-working and patient and almost as dumb as our overworked mare, old Jenny. By the time I was of an age to notice her she seemed like an old woman herself, stooped and bent by burdens, thin and anxious of face, her hair and skin a uniform greyish-brown colour. In resigning themselves to this second disappointment my grandparents had used her hard; disgraced and unmarriageable, she could still be useful; and I, when I was born, could be useful too. My earliest memory—that is the first moment when I became aware of myself as "I"—is concerned with a stumble, a broken egg and a clout from my grandmother's hand.

(I have argued the business of this awareness of oneself as a person with Walter. I believe that it is what he calls "the soul," the part which never dies. In that case surely it would be born with one; and I certainly was old enough to walk, however unsurely, by the time when it dawned on me that I was I. I believe that this awareness grows with the years, that we cherish it, so that even such a small individual thing as a dislike of onions becomes important, a part of us; and in the end we cannot bear to think that death can put an end to this I, this wonderful and unique thing. Therefore, for comfort and assurance, man chose to believe in God and ever-lasting life, even though it meant believing also in Hell. Walter says that even the heathen Turks know better than that!)

Mother and I led miserable lives, but I at least was so ignorant of any other condition that I was not troubled by any comparison. To me it seemed natural enough to rise very early, work all day, to be shouted at and slapped, to get the worst of the food my grandmother's careful housekeeping set on the table. As I grew older I did regret that I was not stronger and had been cursed with a kind of fastidiousness. Sometimes, straining at a heavy task, I would turn dizzy and lose consciousness for a while; and often, set to some disgusting task, I would vomit. No allowance was ever made for these frailties. The work must be done, the lost time made up. Mother was the only one who ever pitied me; she sometimes whispered that she would finish a job for me, but as I grew and realised how heavily burdened she was already I hesitated to add to her load. My grandmother's attitude towards what she called "fancies" was shown, once for all, when I was very small. My piece of meat one dinnertime gave a little heave, and turning it over I found the underside all a-crawl with maggots. Already wise in the ways of my small world, I said nothing, I simply left the meat; but she noticed and asked why I was leaving "the good food." I showed her the maggots. She lifted the slice and roughly brushed the creeping things onto the floor, crushing some in the process and smearing them into the meat. "Now eat it!" she said. And such was my fear of her that I did try; but was unable to swallow and had to run to the door to cast up my stomach. Such pernicketiness, she said, was a sure sign that I wasn't hungry. Whenever she was more than ordinarily cross with me she called me "little bastard" and all the other unkind names for children born out of wedlock. The one kindly word for such, "love-child," she never used. Kind words, indeed, were far to seek in that house; my grandmother must have had a name, but to this day I don't know it. My grandfather always called her "Woman." My mother was "that girl"; I had various names, all hurtful, but was mostly addressed directly as "You." "You, did you feed the pigs?" "You, how many eggs did you fetch in today?" "You, hand me that whetstone."

It was life on an animal level, and looking back on it I wonder why I didn't grow up to be dull and simple-minded. I think the earth itself saved me, the young green breaking out like a shout every springtime, the bugloss and poppies, the daisies and meadowsweet, the wild roses and the honeysuckle trails on the hedgerows. Flowers were my first love, and that was a secret love, too; for my grandmother held that anyone who had time to gather flowers—except cowslips for cordial—hadn't been "rightly busy."

My second love was a great, loud-voiced, black-haired man named Tom Thoroughgood. He also was a neighbour, though not so near as Bowyer; his farm lay beyond the long thin arm which Layer Wood threw out along the river. He and his fathers before him were noted for a special kind of horse they bred, silver grey with almost white manes and tails, and with quiet natures and easy paces suited for ladies' riding. After young Bowyer's refusal to marry my mother there was no neighbourliness between our houses, but there was always a coming and going, if not a great warmth, between us and Tom Thoroughgood's because my grandfather, though he was hard on dumb things, was very knowledgeable about their ailments; he had his secret ways of making liniments and drenches and was a skilled cutter of stallion foals. I'd seen Tom Thoroughgood at intervals all my life and never given much heed to him until one winter morning when I was sent over to his farm with a bottle of liniment. I was eight then, and old enough to be trusted.

He was in his yard, and I handed him the leather bottle and gave him the directions which my grandfather had given me and which I had repeated to myself as I walked. Tom took the bottle and then looked at me as though he had never seen me before.

"My, my, Josiana," he said, "you're going to be pretty. Prettier than your mother even." He said the last words in a funny way, as though being prettier than my mother were nothing to be glad about. While I was thinking that over, he noticed my hands.

"You've got some masterous bad chilblains, child. I wonder your granddad don't brew you up a remedy for them."

I was again surprised. Nobody in our house noticed chilblains. Mine were so much a part of me every winter that I hardly noticed them myself.

"Wait a minute," he said, and he went into his house, leaving the door open, and I heard his great voice shouting about some mittens that had been knitted by, or for, Alice. Alice was one of his three daughters. After a minute he came out, carrying a pair of red mittens in his big hand.

"There," he said, "they'll be a bit of comfort. And the colour'll go well with your lovely black hair."

I hardly thanked him for I was looking at *his* hair. By that time I'd heard enough about a black stallion that had once jumped a fence and worked havoc amongst his precious grey mares, and about a much-sought-after bull at Minsham whose heifer calves gave twice as much milk as any others, to know the stark facts about breed coming out. I had his black hair: and he had just given me the only present I had ever had in my life. He must be my father.

I was too young, I suppose, to feel any resentment against him for bringing me into this unkind world and leaving me to the mercy of my grandparents, or for ruining my mother's whole life. I never gave that side of the matter a thought at that time. I just looked at the mittens and had a hitherto unknown feeling of being cherished and cared for. And I wished with all my heart that I had been one of his proper family and not just a by-blow. I was even pleased, in my silly way, that my father was so big and loud-voiced and prosperous. In fact I fell in love with him, and like everybody in that condition, I felt the need to talk about him.

That evening, as I kicked off my clogs and dropped my dirt-stiffened shift beside them and made ready to climb into bed, I said:

"It was kind of Tom Thoroughgood to give me the mittens."

Mother was already in bed and the light of the dip shone level on her face. I watched her craftily and her expression did not change.

"He's a kind man," she said.

"I wish he was my father."

"And well you may. Hurry now, do this dip 'on't last the week."

We made the dips, Mother and I, every summer, gathering the rushes and peeling them and dipping and redipping them in melted mutton fat; but one of my grandmother's petty meannesses was to limit us to one a week. I got into bed and Mother blew out the light. The darkness gave me courage and I asked in a half-whisper:

"Is he?"

"Is he what?"

"My father?"

She made an impatient movement in the bed.

"Now for Mary's love, don't *you* start that. Thass a thing I kept to myself all this time and mean to go on keeping. The way I look at it thass something that don't concern nobody except me. *He* tried to beat it out of me, there's the marks on my back to this day; and *she* bruk my little finger, squeedging it down to make me tell. But I never did and I shan't now."

"Not even me?"

She made another movement.

"No. What good would it do you? I'm looking out for you," she said, astonishingly, "and do you be a good girl and work hard and bear up, everything'll work out all right for you in the end. So don't go bothering about what don't concern you. Angels guard you while you sleep."

That was her usual good night to me and I had no choice but to make my usual response—"Matthew, Mark, Luke and John, watch the bed that we lay on."

Just before I fell asleep I thought, At least she didn't say that he wasn't!

Since that time I've often seen a homeless pup, pitiable and thin, pick out from a whole crowd of people one person to follow and fawn upon, saying wordlessly, Take me, be my master! The most usual response is a swift kick in the ribs, "Get away, cur!" Occasionally a scrap of something edible is thrown with contemptuous pity. Whenever I see such a pup I think of myself. I must have spent two years or more thinking about my father, always very eager to do any errand that took me to his farm, always making some excuse to show myself when he came into our yard, and most thankfully accepting any scrap he threw me. Once it was an orange. He'd just come back from Baildon market when I arrived with some message from my grandfather, and in the kitchen all his children had gathered about him to see what he had brought them. One of the girls said, "Oh, there's Josiana," and Tom said, "Here's one for you, too, poppet," and threw me a golden globe.

I'd never seen one before.

"It's to eat," Alice Thoroughgood said, pulling the peel from her own. To me it was much more than that; it was a secret acknowledgment. It made me one of them. I never did eat that orange; I hid it away and at last it shrivelled to half its size and became as hard and dry as a stone. To this day, however, the scent of an orange can recall that one and the hopes it kindled in me; for somehow his giving it to me, and calling me "poppet," linked with what my mother had said about all coming right in the end. It was concerned with waiting. For what? For his lawful wife to die. That was all I could think of. I was sensible enough to realise that with people the act of breeding and begetting was not so simple as with the beasts; a married man couldn't—however much he wanted to —take into his home, into full recognition, a child of his born out of wedlock. But the time would come. . . .

After that I began to take a morbid interest in Mistress Thoroughgood's health, which was uniformly and disappointingly good.

When did the change come? And why? I have no answer to these questions. I can only suppose that in people, as in animals, some kind of wisdom comes with maturity. I only know that there I was, one day regarding Tom Thoroughgood as a fine fellow, a father to be proud of, and hoping with all my heart that the time would come when he could openly acknowledge me; and the next day I saw him for what he was, a heartless scamp who had ruined my mother and abandoned me to a life of misery. All this without a word spoken to anyone or by anyone. A pair of red mittens, a dried-up orange, a ribbon for my hair and a silver farthing, a few kind words, what were they worth? I despised myself for ever having placed any value on them; I hated myself for ever having thought Tom Thoroughgood other than hateful. And suddenly, for the first time, I understood my mother's silence; she, too, was ashamed of ever having liked him. Then what, I argued to myself, had she meant by waiting, and everything coming right? That someone would marry me? Who? I was between twelve and thirteen and Tom had called me pretty, but no father from Flaxham or any nearby village had ever come bargaining for me. The word "pretty" might be just as valueless as the other things Tom had given me. I had no means of knowing; there was no glass in our house and the only reflection I had seen of myself was from the distorting round belly of a well-polished pot, or the quivering surface of a bucket of water.

That was the year 1485, the year of great changes in the outside world. Even we, on our Flaxham farm, heard in due time news of the Battle of Bosworth, and how the crown had fallen from King Richard's head and landed in a thornbush, whence Henry Tudor plucked it as though it was a berry, and set it on his own head. To us it was a story of no importance; to us all kings were tax-extorters and one no better than the next. Much more important to us, in the autumn of that year, was the news that Lady Maude Rancon was to set about reviving a dead business and, late as it was in the season, was hunting all over the countryside for wool.

My grandfather had his whole summer clip stored in the barn. Except for perishable goods he seldom sold anything at its proper season. "No profit in plenty," he would say. When eggs were plentiful Mother and I spent long hours in the evenings, rubbing them with wax and storing them away in wood ash, so that in the winter, when no hens laid, we might spend other long hours washing them off and making them ready for market. Our corn never went to the mill until after Christmas, when stocks were low and prices high. On a few occasions my grandfather managed to outwit himself, and this year was one; nobody had come along late in August or in September, crazy mad for a clip of wool to complete a load or keep the spindles working, and willing to pay his price. With October growing old and the roads worsening he was faced with the prospect of not selling his wool that year. And then someone in the market told him the news, he'd gone at once to see the lady and she had promised to ride out next day and see what he had to sell.

He came home in, for him, a jubilant mood and all through supper explained to us how clever he was, and the advantages of his system, miscalling those improvident fellows who rushed their wool to market "still warm from the sheep's back." We had heard it all many times before and gave him no heed. Presently, however, he rambled on to a new subject, Lady Rancon herself. In his father's time, and in his own very young years, there'd been a business at the Old Vine that hadn't its match in all Suffolk. It had gone to ruin because the clever, hard-working old man who had made it had no son to leave it to. (Here he gave my grandmother one of his hard, hateful looks.) So it had got into the hands of women, who'd ruin anything, being senseless, idle and extravagant.

How he could sit there and say it to us, beyond all to my grandmother, passed my understanding; and perhaps in her own dull way she resented it; for presently she said:

"*She* got a *boy* out her marriage, didn't she?" The emphasis was the slightest possible, but it was there, and then, as though to cover her daring, she said quickly, "Why ain't he seeing to the business?"

"Woman, he's dead. Years since. She brung him up idle and good for nowt and he went to the bad and died of the French disease."

He went on to say that Maude Reed, as she was, had married above her so she could be called "Lady" and then wasted all the good hard-earned money buying Sir Henry swords with silver handles, set with shining stones, and great horses that had to be fed corn even in summer when the meadows were full of grass. It was a pleasure to see anybody so wasteful brought to their senses at last; if she ever earned an honest penny, which he doubted, that'd teach her the value of money. He glared around the table as though we, his womenfolk, had also squandered fortunes on frivolity.

Something about that squandering had caught my fancy. Except for the flowers, the sunrises and sunsets, there was little of colour in my life, and except for a rare story told in church by the priest, nothing to fill my mind's eye, either. My grandmother knew some tales, all grisly, about murders and hauntings and ill-wishings, but they made me feel so ill that I turned a deaf ear to them. Now my imagination got busy and pictured swords with handles like the great cross which stood on the church altar, and horses three times the size of any I had ever seen, scorning to eat grass and whinnying for corn at midsummer when, as everyone knew, it was worth its weight in gold. I longed to see the woman who had wasted a fortune on such things and for the first time in my life was glad to be set to clean out the pigsty next morning.

I expected the lady herself to be more than life size, brightly dressed, and her hands all shining with rings like Lady Shelmadine's when she came to church at Easter. And a woman who gave great horses away would surely have bought one of the Thoroughgood palfreys for herself.

I was dreadfully disappointed when, at midmorning, she rode into our yard, a little old woman huddled into a cloak and hood of wool as grey as the sky. And her horse was no better, except that it was fatter, than our old Jenny. I thought to myself that of course my grandfather had got it wrong, Lady Rancon wouldn't go round buying wool; though it was strange to have sent a woman servant. However, there was my grandfather, bustling forward and doffing his woollen cap and all very civil and pleased.

On foot she was taller than I had expected, and once down she did do something that was different. She took an apple and gave it to her horse, which, as it munched, nuzzled her shoulder, drooling spit and bits of chewed-up apple onto her grey cloak. My grandfather would have as soon given Jenny a good apple as he would me a silk dress, and even Tom Thoroughgood, precious as his grey horses were, didn't spoil them that way. I thought to myself, Ah, a woman who would give a horse an apple would give away swords and things, and spoil her son so that he grew up idle. And alas, she would never make a good job of wool buying; if you were soft in business you were always cheated; I'd heard my grandfather say that a hundred times.

However, when they came back from the barn he did not wear his good-bargain look. Far from it. His head was down like a bull's and he was scowling and muttering. Lady Rancon said in a voice that wasn't loud but so clear that every word reached me:

"It's an offer you're not *obliged* to accept. If you change your mind, let me know."

To hear a woman speak like that to a man, to my grandfather of all men, gave me a funny feeling inside me, like a hiccup coming on.

Because he was angry he'd put back his cap and he did not help her to mount. She took her time and I was able to look at her face. It was thin and pale and as heavily marked by trouble as my mother's, but with a calmer look. Mother's face looked as though the worst had happened once and she expected it to happen again any minute; Lady Rancon's looked as though the worst had happened and could never happen again. But then, she didn't live under my grandfather's heel.

She swung the horse's head round and began to ride quietly out of the yard. Before she reached the lane my grandfather called, "My Lady!" and she reined in and waited, not turning her head. He broke into his shambling run and caught up with her. They spoke together for a moment and then she rode away.

He'd sold her the wool at the price she offered, and from that day on he never had a good word for her. "Grasping bitch" was the least horrid name he called her. He swore that he'd never again sell her a handful of wool no matter what she offered; and indeed in the next year, contrary to his custom, he sold his clip in June to a man from Lavenham. Although as a rule anything that angered him was deeply to be regretted, just for once I was glad, and I hoped that she would find all the wool she wanted elsewhere and get her business going again and prosper. I thought of her quite often and the way she said, "You're not *obliged* to accept . . ."

III

In the next year, in the autumn, just before I was fourteen, came the day when Mother and I were sent to market.

There was a market every week and some farmers went to it just for the sake of going; my grandfather never did anything for its own sake. If he had business to do he would go, grudging the wasted hours. If it was just a matter of selling something small, like eggs or butter or fowls, my grandmother went, and little as I liked her I was sometimes sorry for her when she came back and gave an account of her dealings.

"Woman, you hev the gall to stand there and tell me you give three good fowls for that little owd block of salt! They did you. You let yourself be done!"

"No, thass right, Jack. You ask anybody. Wicked, ain't it?"

Meek, meek to him, she would then turn and vent her spite on Mother or me.

To go and do the marketing and face the unfailing grumbling afterwards was the very last thing I would have chosen; yet I was the one that brought it about.

Of all the jobs that sickened me the pig-killing was the worst. I fed the pigs more often than not, and I cleaned them out—another sickening job. I know that people use "pig" as a term of abuse

—greedy as a pig, eat like a pig, live like a pig—but I used to get quite fond of them. They knew me and, even when I wasn't carrying the swill pail, they would run to the fence of the sty and greet me with grunts. I hated to see one of them taken by the hind leg and hauled up onto the killing board and have its throat cut. I hated the blood and the squealing and the death closing down, like black night. But most of all I hated the job which, a few hours afterwards, always fell to me.

First of all the hams were cut off and soaked in the brine barrel before being hung in the smoke hole. The head and the trotters went into the big pot to be made into brawn. One good joint—the best meat we ever had on our table—was hung on the spit and other joints were set aside for sale. But there are other parts to a pig. I always had to wash out the guts so that they could be used for skins for sausages, and the bladder so that it could be filled with lard.

When I was small and sick over this disgusting job Mother used to say that I should "get used to it," "grow out of it"; but I grew, if anything, worse. When I crossed the line between being a child and being a woman I sickened more easily than ever, and on the Monday morning in that October when the pig-killing was to be I felt ill before I started work. The female benefit was on me; I woke with a throbbing head and a pain, and I could eat no breakfast.

Dealing with that pig's innards I vomited three times and fainted once. I must have been senseless longer than usual, for I lost a lot of time, and when my grandmother came into the backhouse to see how I was getting on she was very angry. She called me a lazy young varmint and went to catch me a clout, which I dodged, and in doing so let go the long slippery tube I was cleaning. It fell over the side of the tub. My grandmother came to give me a clout that I couldn't dodge, penned in the corner as I was by that time, and she stepped on the slippery mess and fell. She was up in a moment and I got two clouts for good measure.

Next morning her knee was black and swollen and she had to sit on a stool to make the sausages. My grandfather said it was nothing to make a fuss over, and he fetched his horse liniment and rubbed her so hard that he brought all the skin off. He then went out and wrung the necks of the young cockerels which, with the pork meat and some walnuts and red apples of a kind that didn't keep well, were to make up the load. By evening, however, even he

could see that my grandmother would never be able to walk into
Baildon next day. She'd borne the rubbing with no more than a
squeak or two, now she was groaning with pain.

"Here's a fine to-do," he said angrily. "The load all ready and
me promised to take my plough into Thoroughgood's ten acre!"
He gnawed his lip. "There's no help for it," he said, turning to my
mother, "you'll hev to go this once. And mind, no foolery." He
swung round on me. "You. You'll go along with her and keep a
sharp lookout. Do she speak to any fellow, except in the way of
business, you let me know and she'll be sorry." It says everything
about the behaviour between my mother and me in *their* presence
that he should think of sending me as a spy!

The next morning was crisp, almost frosty, cold enough to set
me thinking about the coming winter, and I was so downhearted
that I could have cried.

"Look how he is to *her* over the prices; he'll be ten times worse
to us," I said.

Dragging at old Jenny's head to get her started, Mother said:
"Well, we know whatever we do'll be wrong, so there's no use in
fretting. We'll see the market and hev a day off."

They were comforting words, and presently the sun came out
and shone on drifting, whirling leaves, and I felt better. I'd never
yet been in Baildon, never been anywhere outside Flaxham, and
when at last from the top of a hill we could look down and see the
town with all its tall towers and huddling roofs, I was overcome by
excitement. From the top of the hill the road ran down in steep
curves and was almost roofed in by trees which by this time had
dropped half their leaves. Piled in the narrow road and sheltered
from the wind, the leaves had turned into a moist, slippery mass
upon which old Jenny slithered. We all arrived at the bottom of
the hill sweating and breathless, and Mother pulled to a stop.

We were just outside a house at which I stared with awe and
admiration; it was so large and had shining glass in its windows and
a door so wide that Jenny, laden as she was, could have walked
straight in. On either side of the doorway there was a narrow strip
of garden, separated from the road by a low wall. There were a few
late roses and masses of starwort, like huge daisies, pink and purple
and white. Flowers were never grown on farms, where there is no
space and no time for useless, pretty things.

Mother said, "She lives there. You know, Lady Rancon, who came to buy the wool."

"How do you know?"

"I've been to market before. In the old days. . . . And once, when I was a bit older than you, I went to the Guild Plays. There was a Devil with real smoke and a smell of brimstone."

I was reminded that, before I arrived to ruin her, she had led an ordinary life. When she was my age she'd been betrothed to young Bowyer, my grandparents had got over their sharpest disappointment and, though she no doubt had to work hard, she wasn't disgraced and enslaved. Oh dear. Why had it all gone wrong? Why had she *let* it go wrong? What had Tom Thoroughgood given, promised her? Or had he just jumped on her one dark night and taken her against her will?

"Come up!" Mother said to Jenny, and we made our way into Baildon town.

We went through a gateway and along a narrow street which turned and opened into a wide-open space set with cobbles. It was right in front of the Abbey gateway and the space belonged to the monks, so anybody who wanted to sell anything there had to pay a due. Once upon a time, Mother said, dues had been paid at the gateway but the town walls were breaking down and people would squeeze in and set up in the market without paying, so nowadays a monk and another man walked around the market all the time. They took two of our cockerels and at least half of the apples and in exchange gave Mother a token, a piece of metal stamped with a pattern, which could be shown if, when they made their next round, they asked for the dues again. All these pieces of metal had to be put into a box when the market was over.

"And it's no use taking it home because they have tokens of different sorts and if you show the wrong one, ever, you can never trade on this market again," Mother explained. Everything had to be explained to me and I asked so many questions that I think Mother tired of me. She told me to run away and take a look round the market, because Heaven knew when the chance would come again.

I ended my wandering, having lost all sense of time, by a board covered with a white cloth upon which was set out a display of gingerbread cut into shapes, little men and women, stars, hearts, true lovers' knots, wild roses and bells. Of all the wonders I had seen that morning this seemed to me the most marvellous. I longed to ask the woman behind the board whether she had tools to cut the shapes, something like our butter stamper, or whether she did them with a knife, but she had many customers, for these were the hot cakes people speak of when they say a thing sells well.

I jumped and turned when someone touched my shoulder. I found myself looking into a man's face, ugly, purple except where grey stubble clung to the sagging jowls. He was so ugly that even when he said, "Are you hungry, little maid? Then which do you fancy?" I heard no kindness in his voice. I thought that he must be the woman's husband, placed there to urge on a reluctant customer.

I said, "I've got no money," and would have backed away, but he held me.

"Go on. Take your pick. I'll stand you treat."

Choosing was hard, I admired them all so much, but at last I lifted my hand and pointed to a true lovers' knot, because that seemed to me the most intricate. He said I had chosen well, and paid the woman.

"Well, go on, let's see you eat it."

"I can't eat it yet. I want to show it to my mother."

He said, "Jill, give her another. There you are, one to eat and one to show. Where is your mother?"

I pointed vaguely.

"And what's your name?"

"Josiana."

"What?"

I thought perhaps he hadn't heard, for I had taken a bite which was quite as delicious as I had expected. I swallowed and repeated my name.

"Josiana what?"

This was my happy day, my free day, and I didn't want to spoil it by even mentioning the name I shared with my grandfather. So I said, "Thank you very much for the gingerbread," and slipped away into the crowd.

Mother had sold all that we had brought and bought the few things she had been told to buy and was ready to go. I went skipping up to her, holding out the knot of gingerbread.

"Look," I said, "this is for you. I've eaten mine."

She asked how had I come by it and I told her. She said:

"Oh dear. I should have told you. You shouldn't take presents from strangers. Still, it's done now. . . . This is a light load. We can ride and tie. You first." She helped me up amongst the empty baskets and the bundles, and when I was settled I looked down and saw, near at hand, the man who had stood me treat.

"There he is," I said.

The man came nearer, smiling.

"Joan Greenwood," he said. "Well, well, well!"

I'd never seen Mother any way but humble and downtrodden. Suddenly, though, she took on what I now know was dignity.

"Good day, Master Hayward. I was coming to look for you. You lent Josiana the price of a sweetmeat or two. That was neighbourly. Thank you."

She dipped into the little pouch she carried, pushed a coin into his hand and at the same time gave Jenny a smart slap, so that she shot forward, not like the aged mare that had trudged into market but so fast that for a moment Mother had to run hard to keep up. When the speed slackened, I said:

"Oh dear! They'll take it out on us for that. I'd never have *looked* at that gingerbread if I'd thought you'd have to pay for it."

"We didn't want to be in *his* debt!" Mother's voice was breathless. "I shall stick the price onto the salt. They'll grumble anyway. It's paid for now, so eat it up."

The price of that piece of gingerbread was higher than we guessed.

Three or four days afterwards I was late for my dinner because I'd been moving the sheep from one pasture to another. I was hot and dirty and panting like a dog. There at the table was Master Hayward, halfway through a great plateful of meat and with my grandfather's own horn mug, out of which nobody else was ever allowed to drink, full of ale at his elbow. He looked mighty pleased with himself, and my grandparents wore their most pleasant expressions. Not so my mother. Her face was whiter than ever, but with two round spots, red as a berry, high up on her cheeks; and her eyes, usually a pale mild blue, looked quite black.

"Here is Josiana!" My grandfather spoke as though my coming had been eagerly awaited. "She've bin tending the sheep."

"So she's handy, as well as bonny, eh?"

"She's as good as two men to me," said my grandfather. I thought he must have gone out of his mind. My grandmother too.

"So good about the house and all. Her butter's as good as my own, and her bread, truth to tell, a mite better."

What lies. I was never allowed to do the pleasant easy inside-the-house jobs.

Mother made a noise, like a laugh, but mocking.

"Nothing like praising up something you want to be rid of. The poor child's dim-witted and prone to fits besides being . . ."

We never heard what, for my grandmother leaned over and silenced her with a clout that rattled her teeth.

"Now, now," said my grandfather, "don't hit the wench. 'Tis but jealous spite speaking. She missed the market herself, poor creature. That go against the grain to see another girl bid for."

Master Hayward pushed his stool from the table, exposing his thick legs clad in moleskin.

"Come here, my lil dear," he said coaxingly. "Sit on my knee. Lemme look into them pretty blue eyes and I reckon I'd take you even if you did hev fits."

My grandmother gave me a push, so that I landed up against him.

"Let the man see what he's getting. We ain't done bargaining yet."

Mother, with her eyes watering and all one side of her face the colour of a poppy where the blow had landed, jumped up and began to shout.

"She's only a child, not ready for any man yet. Wicked. It'd be wicked. He's old enough to be her grandfather and look how he treated his first wife and his second, killed . . ."

"Woman," my grandfather bellowed, "take her in the backhouse. How can men talk sense with that caterwauling in their ears?"

Mother went, meekly.

Then, while I sat rigid on the greasy moleskin knees, trying not to look at the stubbly face, the black teeth, the pig's eyes, trying not to catch the stinking breath of the man who kept moving his hands over me, they struck their bargain.

I was to marry Master Hayward. In return, one of his younger sons was to come and live with my grandparents and work for his keep and one noble a year spending money, and see them both comfortable until they died. In addition Master Hayward would hand over a young horse and a heifer calf.

"And you still got the best end of the stick," said my grandfather.

"She could marry a youngster that'd come here and be more bid-dable."

"Rob'll be biddable. There's four ahead of him. He've got to go for a day labourer or a soldier unless he's settled this way. As for getting a youngster, you might, Jack Greenwood, you *might*. On the other hand, though she's a pretty filly she come from a mucky stable, don't she? Afore you got a offer she might go the way her mother went. No, this is the best way for all." With that he took hold of my chin, tipped my face up and kissed me. That was so horrible that, without even being sick first, I fainted.

Next morning my grandfather went to work at Thoroughgood's again, and because my grandmother's knee was still troubling her my mother was obliged to make the butter, so I had all the outside jobs to do. Overnight Mother had tried to comfort me, saying she'd think of something, she'd make sure I didn't marry Jim Hayward no matter what; but when I asked what *could* we do, she had no answer. So I worked that morning in greater misery than I had ever known before. At noon I had no appetite for the boiled goose-grass root with which we always "made do" when there was no man to feed. Shovelling her own into her mouth, Mother said in a defeated way:

"Jim Hayward'll be expecting a lot of Josiana, the way you talked. And she've never done only yard work."

"What of it?"

"I was wondering . . ." Mother said vaguely.

"What?"

"Whether she couldn't come and help me make up the butter. That seem the least . . ."

"You took the words outa my mouth. I mean she should go fit and able to do what I said. Today she can make up the butter and next week she can churn it. And I'll show her the way with bread and dumplings. I'm no liar."

She then turned to me and told me to wash my hands and put on a clean smock, butter being very quick to take up any stench.

The dairy had only one door, which led off from the kitchen. When I went through I saw that the butter was all neatly made up and stamped. Mother was hanging the cream skimmer and a bucket in the window opening, so that every time the wind blew—it was a gusty day—they hit together with a little thump. I opened my mouth to ask what she was doing and why the butter was already shaped, but she signed to me to be quiet, and then began to whisper. I was to take a bucket and go to the well and make sure that my grandmother saw me go. I was to leave the bucket by the well and run to the orchard. "I'll be there," Mother said. She then told me, in an ordinary voice, to go and get some fresh water.

In the kitchen my grandmother, never one to be idle even when lame, had settled down with her spindle. She would never have admitted it, but it was true that over any such quiet, sitting-down job she was inclined to fall, presently, into a cat nap. I drew her attention to my errand and she said, "Don't dawdle."

Mother had managed to force herself through the narrow opening that served the dairy for a window and was waiting for me under the apple trees. She snatched at my hand and said, "We must run like the wind." I thought for a moment we were making for Tom Thoroughgood's; and what was the use of that? In any case my grandfather was there. Before I could speak, however, she had pulled me off the track that was worn between the two farms and there we were running across a piece of ploughland, heading straight for the main part of Layer Wood. Then she gasped out: "We're going to Clevely."

All I knew about Clevely was that there was a nunnery there, and the nuns kept bees. Tom Thoroughgood bought his honey from them, not liking to have a hive himself in case the bees should sting his precious horses.

"Not to the nuns," I said, and stopped running.

"Just for the time being. Till I can think. The only other safe place I know is too far. I must be back afore I'm missed. Come on."

"I don't want to be a nun." I'd heard some tales about a terrible old woman who had ruled the Clevely House and might, for all I knew, still do so. Some of her deeds figured in my grandmother's grisly stories.

Mother gave a sort of laugh that sounded like a dog's bark.

"Small chance of that! They don't take poor girls! You'll work in the yard, just for a little while. Till I can think."

We ran again. It isn't so easy to think clearly when you are running fast over rough ground, but before we came to the river which here, as near Tom Thoroughgood's, ran alongside the wood's edge, I had it all plain in my mind. I saw why she had hung the bucket and the skimmer up to make a noise like someone working on butter; and sent me out for water. It would look as though I had run away. But that wouldn't save her when the truth was discovered.

"They'll take it out on you," I gasped. "Don't go back. Let's run away together."

She said, "No!" so fiercely that I looked at her in surprise, and then was frightened. She looked so like my grandfather. Then she said, "Careful now, step where I do," and letting go of my hand plunged into the stream which reached halfway to her knees. When we were on the other side and into the trees, she said:

"I shall be there when the breath go out of his body. His land he can leave as he like but I know where he keep his money box and the key round his wicked owd neck. When he give his last grunt I shall be there to take what I've worked for all these years!"

So that was what had held her there through so much ill-treatment and misery. The very same greed that had been to blame for most of the misery.

"Suppose Gran's looking in the dairy this very minute. Then what? Look what they're losing. Think how they'll treat you."

"Thass a risk I must take. Come on now. This is a short cut. Not far now."

I thought of the whip with which my grandfather was so handy; and the way he had used it on her before.

"Look," I said, "I'll marry Master Hayward and ask him to take you to live with us." I held back a shudder. "He's took a fancy to me and I'd ask him nicely. And he'd be glad to have you when he found I couldn't do all the things . . ."

"He only want you for one thing. You don't know what you're saying. You're too innocent."

"I do know." This time the shudder mastered me. "I took our cow . . ."

"The poor beasts are clean by comparison. In my living memory Jim Hayward killed off two, bigger and stronger then you. At his place you'd work harder than you ever did and hev him at you all night as well. I'd sooner see you dead!" She slackened pace a little. "Last night I did think about henbane, for both of us; but we never had nothing, and that way we never should. And then I thought of this, and this is best. We only got to howd on and be patient; our time'll come."

She pulled me forward again, and soon we came to the edge of the trees and could see, across a meadow with a few sheep in it, some gloomy-looking grey buildings.

"Wait till you hear my tale. You keep quiet, act simple like. You're a poor orphan and your name is . . . Jenny Reeve and I'm your friend and we've run all the way from . . . Nettleton. Now, pray God it'll work."

It worked, mainly because the tale she told was so nearly the truth. It was true to say that we had worked together for many years, and that in bringing me to the nuns she risked getting into trouble with the man she worked for. It was true to say that she was all the mother I had. But the lies slipped out as smoothly as the truths and the half-truths. There was no need for me to try to act simple, I just stood there, agape, as the words poured from Mother's mouth.

"Madam, I could not stand by and see the innocent child led into sin by a man three times her age. Bought with beads and ribbons, madam. Jenny, you brought none? Thass right, thass like I towd you. She's a *good* girl at heart. Beads and ribbons and him with a wife too. And, madam, where else could I turn? Night arter night I've laid there, racking my brains and praying for some way to save the child. And last night, madam, the Blessed Virgin herself answered me. 'Take her to the Ladies at Clevely,' she says, 'she'll be safe there.' So thass just what I done."

I was half inclined to believe that the Virgin had inspired her. Where else had it all come from? How had she hit upon exactly the story to appeal to a pious old nun? A story that explained our breathlessness, and her own desperate need to get the business settled quickly.

"I must be back, madam, afore I'm missed. He'd beat me black and blue if he guessed. And she must stay close to the house. When he miss her he'll search everywhere."

"Not here," the nun said; and I knew that Mother had won.

I had early learned the uselessness of tears, yet when the moment of parting came, which it did promptly, I clung to Mother, weeping bitterly. Our relationship had been a strange one, bare of caresses, of loving words, but the bond between us was strong and true, and my fear for her well-being in the immediate future was lively. She sensed that.

"You know how hard it is for me to get away but as soon as I can I'll come and see you. Don't you fret about me. Be a good girl and do what you're told."

She pulled herself free and, with some gabbled words of thanks to the Lady, went scurrying away. Dame Isabel came and put her arm round me and pressed my face into the folds of her robe, which smelt of sweat and onions and wood smoke and something else unknown to me.

"We'll look after you, child," she said in her gentle voice. "You'll be safe here, and happy. You'll see."

That was a true prophecy; my happy years were about to begin.

IV

Walter being a Lollard, and very argumentative, I have had plenty of opportunity of hearing how people of that persuasion regard religious houses. Arguing back I have often said, "But there was none of that at Clevely." Walter's reply to that is that Clevely must have been exceptional.

Perhaps it was; it was certainly a dying House, reduced to eleven Ladies, all old, one of whom was blind and one astray in her wits, but harmlessly. It had always been a poor, obscure House, not the kind to attract the kind of inmate who would bring it wealth and fame. Well-to-do widows who wished to retire from the world, heiresses who for some reason had failed to find a husband, would choose a Convent which offered some comfort and something of entertainment in the way of visitors or passers-by. (And I still believe that very often it was this kind of inmate who was responsible for the "scandals" in other Houses, the love affairs, the fine clothes, the outrageous quarrels, the lap dogs licking cream from silver plates.) The Prioress of whom my grandmother told such shocking tales had, forty years earlier, tried to make Clevely into a fashionable House, but she had failed and much of her later cruelty and strictness may have been due to her disappointment. The Prioress of my day was the Lady whose wits had failed her; all her work and authority had fallen to Dame Isabel; she was the one with whom I had most to do—partly because she was the most active of all, and partly because when I first went to live there she, being Suffolk-born herself, was the only one who could understand what I said, or make me understand. To begin with I thought all the other Ladies came from foreign lands, their speech was so strange.

There is no Clevely now. It was closed by order of the Bishop about eighteen months after I left; by that time the House was deemed to be uninhabitable, it was in such a state of disrepair; the Ladies were deeply in debt for flour and candles and other necessities, and—which the Bishop found shocking—there was no priest in attendance except Sir Roger at Flaxham St. Giles, who visited at irregular intervals largely determined by whether his horse was lame or not.

The Ladies were unfailingly kind to me and I like to think that while I was there they ate a little better and increased their debt a little more slowly. I worked at Clevely harder than I had at Flaxham because I did it willingly, and because I was praised instead of being constantly chidden. I earned myself a new name. Jenny Do-well the Ladies called me; and since, when first asked my name I had gulped out "Jenny" and never mentioned the "Reeve" which my mother had chosen, Dowell became a family name to me.

I was astonished to find how strongly the blood of my hated grandparents ran in my veins; my grandfather himself could not have been more shocked than I was over the mismanagement out of doors, nor my grandmother more grieved over the muddle within. When I went to Clevely the two fields which should have been cultivated, turn and turn about, and made to yield enough corn to make all the flour eleven old ladies could need, both lay fallow, thick with shrivelling weeds. The waste of it! They had no horse or ass, and the plough had disappeared—"I know we had one," Dame Isabel said. "Oh yes, we had one, when Jankyn was alive. He used to borrow a horse, but the plough was ours." It was never found, and during my first winter at Clevely I dug the smaller field with a spade, turning it sod by sod and then breaking each stubborn lump with the spade's edge before passing on to the next. To pleasure me Dame Isabel "borrowed" a few handfuls of seed corn and the same of peas, and I planted them, grain by grain. Careful farmers, even my grandfather, sow their seed broadcast, saying:

One for wind and one for crow,
One to die and one to grow,

but I planted every separate seed and covered it against crow and pigeon and patted the soil down, with a prayer to St. Phocas, who, Dame Isabel said, was the friend of all who grew things.

When I went to Clevely they did not even keep a cow. It was the old story. "We had one, when Jankyn was alive." Jankyn and William were two brothers who had looked after the Convent's little farm; with Jankyn to rule and direct him, William's lack of sense, even of willingness, had never been apparent; then Jankyn had died and William had given up all attempt to manage. Under his slovenly care the cow had died and when the sow farrowed, unwatched, she had eaten her litter; only a few sheep had survived, "And they are going lame, I notice," said Dame Isabel placidly.

I quoted to her one of my grandfather's dictums, "If there's a frog in a field your sheep'll start to hop too." It was just a way of saying that sheep flourish on dry land and go lame on damp.

Moved from the soggy meadow, the Clevely sheep did better and in June, when Lady Rancon made her round, we had a little wool to sell. It was, I realised as I laid it out, of the poorest quality, and I was surprised when, in the evening of that day, Dame Isabel said to me, joyously:

"Now, Jenny Do-well, you shall have your cow."

I had often urged upon her the wisdom of keeping a cow, especially in a House of old women with so few teeth and such weak stomachs, always in need of a comforting posset.

I said, "I should never have thought so little wool would fetch so great a price as to buy a cow."

Dame Isabel and Dame Constance, who was also in the kitchen, began, together, to explain, trying, I think, to show which of them had kept most of her memory. Often I closed my ears to their talking matches, but this time, because of my interest in Lady Rancon, I listened avidly.

Once, as a girl, plain Maude Reed, she had lived in this House; here she had learned to read and write and reckon.

"And unlike many, she has remained grateful, and our friend."

They did not say that she had ruined the business by extravagance or negligence, they said she had followed her husband—a famous knight—as a wife should; but they agreed with my grandfather that she had spoilt her son, allowing him to grow up idle, caring only for playing the lute and making songs, "and," said Dame Isabel, with a glance at me, "other more regrettable pursuits." They always treated me as though I were an innocent child, which in

many ways I was. I had heard my grandfather say that Lady Rancon's son had died of the French disease, which in itself meant
nothing to me, but he had linked it with "went to the bad" and
said it in such a way as to make it sound evil.

Then, as so often with their antiphonal conversations, Dame Isabel and Dame Constance fell out a little.

Dame Isabel said, "Well, at least she learned her lesson and is
doing better with her grandson."

"How better?" Dame Constance demanded. "To my mind his
proper place is with his grandmother, learning the business, so that
she is not forced to ride unattended, like a fishwife, and bargain for
maggoty fleeces. He must be twenty years old. Yes, it is full twenty
years since she had the roof of the chapel mended in gratitude for
his birth. And any young man of proper spirit would be shamed
to have his grandmother so demeaned while he idles in a great kinsman's house."

"At Beauclaire he will not be idle," Dame Isabel said. She herself came from a great house. "There is no training—no, not even
a novitiate—more strictly ordered and disciplined. Only by being
sent away from home can a man child be tamed and tempered—
their own parents are too tender for the task."

"That is rubbish," Dame Constance said. "I had three brothers
who until they married never slept a night under any roof but my
father's. When he said go they went and when he said come they
came, and if they so much as looked amiss he felled them to the
floor."

"Plough horses, without blood or spirit, are easily broken," Dame
Isabel said. "Destriers need more subtle handling."

I could see, by the expression on Dame Constance's face, that
somewhere in that speech a deadly insult lay; so I asked:

"What is a destrier, Dame Isabel?"

"A war horse, a knight's charger, child. And this discourse began
with a cow—a far leap."

"Some people," said Dame Constance, who had been given time
to barb and fledge her arrow, "swear to abjure the world, its pomps
and vanities, and to follow the example of Christ, whose only
mount was a humble ass; yet they hold to their old false values and
reckon those for whom Christ died as easily divided by breed as
animals that have no souls."

For a moment Dame Isabel looked as though she would make a

sharp answer, but she governed herself and asked pardon, admitting her fault. And that little near-squabble was typical of Clevely.
I cannot speak for every nunnery and for monasteries not at all,
but in this small, poor, dying House there was a good spirit. I also
have ever been grateful for what I learned there, and for the kindness with which the Ladies rewarded the work I did, and the advice
I gave.

They had never, for instance, heard of mutton ham. When a
sheep died or was killed they ate the whole carcass while it was
fresh, knowing no means of preserving it. I explained about treating
mutton haunches like pork, almost giving myself away by saying
"My gr . . ." and changing it quickly to "grumpy old mistress where
I used to work always made mutton hams." Next time there was a
sheep to be dealt with I managed it all; and in return they gave me
a string of blue beads, "Mary's own colour, to keep you from harm,"
Dame Isabel said, and a pair of leather shoes. One Lady who could
sew made me a pretty dress to wear on Sundays and Holy days.

Naturally, being of a sensible nature, I kept my new things carefully and worked in the soiled, worn garments, growing small for
me, in which I had run away. I was clad in them when Walter first
saw me. And the yeast of Lollardry must have been working in him
even then, for later he told me that his first thought when he saw
me was that I was some poor orphan child of whom the nuns had
taken advantage.

Nothing could have been further from the truth. But then, everything to do with Walter and me has been obscured, and mistaken.

V

That was my third summer in Clevely, and for a holding run by
one girl and one lazy old man, the place looked well. The low-
lying pasture from which I had moved the sheep was now a hay-
field; my corn and peas were flourishing; we had a cow and her
heifer calf; we had pigs, and though we had eaten several, the sheep
numbered twice as many as I had found there. I reckoned my
achievements with some pride as, on that hot mid-June morning,
William and I went out to cut the hay. After two hours of it he fell
back upon his invariable excuse—a pain in his belly.

"Go tell Dame Constance," I said, unkindly. "She'll dose you with juice of sloes."

It wasn't as bad as that, he said, thus proving that he was not so simple as he pretended to be. He would just lie down for a minute or two and it'd pass off. So he lay down in the shade of a tree and within a minute the pain *had* passed off, for he was sound asleep. I worked on alone, remembering the first time I handled a scythe and the sorry fist I made of it and how my grandfather nagged. That was years ago, when I was really too small to balance the tool; now I was expert.

Scything *is* hard work, but, once you have the knack of it, less hard than it looks because you get into a kind of swing. I was working happily enough, and humming to myself, when I knew that I was being watched from behind. I swung round and there was time, while I made that one movement, to feel terror, to think, "Grandfather!" and "I won't go back!"

At that minute I no more saw Walter than Walter saw me. He saw an overworked waif with a frightened look which spoke of ill-usage, and I saw a fine young gentleman on a big black horse. He'd missed his way and needed directing, I thought; so I laid down my scythe and ran to the baulk which separated the meadow from the track, jumped to the top of it and stood almost level with him, looking into his face and waiting for him to speak first.

People can believe in love at first sight when it is in a song or a tale, but they laugh about it in real life. It can happen, though. It did to me. Before a word was spoken, before he could nod towards the grey buildings and say, "Is that Clevely Priory?" I had fallen in love with the shape of him, and the colour of him, with the idea that there should be people like him in the world. It was all mixed up with the feeling I had always had for flowers and sunrises and sunsets; a sudden certainty that *this* was what they had all been leading to. And I knew with an equal certainty that when he had asked for direction and turned his horse about and ridden away, I would suffer, forever, as long as I lived, a terrible sense of loss.

He asked about Clevely, a question to which, he told me later, he knew the answer already, and asked it for the sake of saying something. He told me that he had stopped his horse and stared at me, with pity and concern because I looked so small to be wielding that great scythe. Then, when I had jumped onto the baulk and faced him, "I was overcome. Never in all my life had I seen anything so beautiful."

(In truth I am not beautiful, not even pretty. What I have, what made Jim Hayward notice me in the market place, and drew Walter to me, and held Arthur in thrall, is a *different* look. I have very blue eyes and straight smooth black hair; you don't often see them together. And my skin, which no amount of wind or sun can ever redden, is unpocked; the cowpox which strikes country people is not so deadly nor so disfiguring as the smallpox they have in the towns.)

Walter put his question and I answered it and then he told me that he had come to buy our wool. That surprised me greatly, for he hadn't a merchant's look.

"You can't," I told him. "Lady Rancon always buys the Clevely wool."

"I am here on her behalf," he said. "I am Walter Rancon."

I told him that I would show him the wool. He asked me, half jokingly, whether I did all the work around the place, and I said:

"Not entirely. I have help from William. That is one of his ways of helping me!" and I pointed to where William lay asleep under the tree. Abruptly we broke into that laughter which has nothing to do with its apparent cause but is, in the right circumstances, a kind of wooing, with eyes meeting and the glance renewing the laughter again and again. Walter was quite breathless when he said:

"I can see, he's a *great* help!" And off we went again, laughing so hard that William woke and reared up and saw us and called:

"What's to do? What's to do?"

I called back to him, "I'm going to show the clip to Master Rancon. That'll give you a chance to catch even with me, if you don't fall asleep again."

I meant to skip alongside the horse, for the barn where the wool was was no distance away, but Walter reached down to me.

"Take my hand," he said, "and set your foot on mine. Up you come. Holy Saints, child, you weigh nothing at all!" And there I was, perched on the saddle before him with my heart beating so heavily and so loudly that he must surely have heard it.

He bought the wool, paid Dame Isabel and rode away. I fell into a curious state of mind. I was entirely certain that I should not see him again until he came to buy the next year's clip; but I was equally certain that he would come again soon. Up and down, like a seesaw, joyful and dismal, but always preoccupied so that the work I did was a mere keeping to habit, quite mindless, and my behaviour so vague that Dame Constance was certain that I was sickening for the jaundice and dosed me with parsley piert and horse-radish; she also suspected an ascendance of the melancholy humour, for which the sovereign cure was a small cup of the wine which she made from honey. That I did welcome, for after a few sips of it my certainty that Walter would return, and soon, was greatly enforced.

Every evening, when the work was done, I washed myself, put on one of the gowns the Ladies had made me, the buff or the grey, and my string of beads and my shoes. I combed my hair smooth and wished that I had a headdress. In secret I tried out ways of knotting my hair, so that all I needed was a net to hold it. I looked older so, older and more important. I knew my true reflection now, for at Clevely there was a looking glass, backed with silver, that nobody owned. It lay propped against the wall under the stone basin in which we washed. Every evening, coming face to face with myself in it, I said to that other self, This is nonsense; this is a waste of time, he will not come until he comes next year to buy the wool. Then I would go to supper; and if the dish—as it most often was—were flavoured with onions, I would pass it by. I did not wish to stink of onions when Walter came.

Ordinarily I shared the Ladies' evening occupations. Dame Isabel was teaching me to read and write a little; Dame Sybil was showing me how to handle a needle; even Dame Constance would now and then ask my help in the pounding of leaves, or the stirring of some mixture. All these pursuits, hitherto so engaging, had lost their charm. Something within me would cry, "Out! Out!"

I made the silliest, most transparent of excuses. Most girls in that state have but one mother to evade; I had six, all the Ladies who were active and shared the downstairs mess. Most girls could at least say that they needed a little air, but I had been hard at work out of doors all day. Still, every evening, for ten days on end, I escaped and walked first to Dame Constance's herb garden where there was a lavender hedge. I plucked a spray and squeezed it, rubbing the rough-feeling juice of it into my hair and skin as I walked on, along the track towards the highroad, the way Walter would surely, would surely not, come. He would come, I knew, while the wild roses were in bloom; he would come, I knew, next year, to buy wool.

Wild roses have a short life span. One by one they opened, sweetened the air and died. Ten days is a long time in the life of a rose. A long time in the life of a girl in love. A long time in the management of a cow whose breeding time, for some unknown reason, has been delayed. Most cows come in heat and are served so that the calves are born in the spring and have all the sweet summer ahead of them to feed and strengthen and build up against the winter, or, if destined for the butcher in the autumn, time to put on flesh. Our cow, that year, had turned awkward, and she was due to calve on the day of St. Peter and St. Paul, two months late at least. But, as my grandfather would have said in such a situation, "There's things you can't order try as you may." We'd have a late-born calf, which, if it was a heifer, might or might not struggle through the winter, or, if it was a bull, would yield little weight in veal when the autumn slaughtering came. However, the lateness worked both ways and I had already decided to take advantage of my grandfather's system of selling on a rare market. Clevely would have milk and therefore butter, when both were growing scarce.

The cow, named Nancy, was staked out by the side of the track leading to the road. I meant to be careful and bring her into the barn on the twenty-sixth of June, her calving date being the twenty-ninth. On the twenty-fourth, which was the eleventh evening that I had walked along the track looking for and waiting for Walter, I found her heaving and moaning, the calf half born and stuck. No wonder, either, for it was wrong way round, hindquarters first.

It was a situation I had never been called upon to deal with before and I knew a moment of frightened indecision; to run back and rouse William or stay and do what common sense suggested. The cow herself turned the scale. She let out a bellow and then rolled her moist bulging eye in my direction, at once appealing for and certain of my aid.

I was wearing my grey dress which had sleeves which were close-fitting from shoulder to wrist and then opened and widened to fall in loose cascades to the hem of my skirt. I ripped it off and threw it aside. When Walter came, as part of me had been sure he would, I was wearing my shift, a string of blue beads and a pair of shoes; and my hands and arms were as red as a butcher's. But the calf was alive, seemingly unhurt by my rough and inexpert handling, and the cow was standing up, licking it.

Any shyness or coyness of the kind which is almost always connected with the first deliberately contrived meeting, I swept away by saying crossly:

"You *would* come tonight and find me so!" And he said that he had been waiting for an excuse to come and had found it at last. The Midsummer Fair had opened in Baildon that morning and he had bought me some fairings.

Dear Walter! I could tell, as he brought out each offering, that he had also suffered from a divided mind. With one eye he saw me as a pathetic orphan child who didn't get enough to eat; for her there was marchpane, a coffer of pastry shaped into a little bucket with a handle, filled with currants in syrup, there were raisins and almonds and rose petals crystallised in sugar. With his other eye Walter had seen me as one who had outgrown childish things; for her there was a pomander ball (most dreadful remindful of that first orange I had cherished), a knot of blue ribbon, smooth and shining, and a flask of painted pottery with a stopper, filled with gillyflower water.

There was a comical side to all this, for I couldn't, with my bloody hands, *touch* anything; and half of what he brought I did not even know the name of until he told me. Since then I have heard many songs and stories about love, and read more than a few, but never in any one have I found anything ridiculous. Yet, with us, there it was. And there was I, laughing and crying at the same time from pure happiness that he should have thought of me.

He was older than I and vastly more worldly wise, yet just then there was something clumsy and boyish, almost touching about him, so that I in a single breath space could be flattered and uplifted by the man's notice and tender and pitying of the young awkwardness. But, oh, who can describe love? And who can bear, at the end of the road, to look back and remember those first few enchanted steps? Not I.

I discovered, again with surprise, that I shared my mother's secretive spirit. It was as though I held in my hand a green leaf and lying on it one perfect plum covered with bloom; to say, "Look what I have," and to have people say, "Let me look, let me smell," would be to lose the bloom which, once gone, could never be restored. I began to understand my mother, too. And I forgave Tom Thoroughgood. I saw how it had happened and why love-child is as true a word as by-blow. I sympathised with her hanging on grimly to the last fragment of her secret, the last bit of bloom.

That was part of it, but not the whole. I had my fears. Walter might love me all the more because I was poor and nameless and, despite all the nuns' effort, still ignorant and uncouth. But he had a family; the grandmother who had taken care to marry above her; a mother who surely must already have picked some suitable girl to wed her son. What would they say?

I feared the nuns, too. Their disapproval. I could hear Dame Isabel saying, "How long has this been going on?" and remembering the circumstances of my coming to Clevely and suspecting the worst. It was all quite idiotic, as I realised later, but this was the first time I had ever had anything of my own. I was like a hen whose eggs have always been taken away as soon as they are laid and who at last slips off and "lays away" in a far hedge or some inaccessible place on a cow-house roof and there broods, secret and solitary.

Walter bore with me for a little time. We met, we kissed, we held hands; there were silences, there were times of talking. That our love remained innocent is wholly to his credit. I was quite mad, utterly reckless of what I did so long as it remained private between us; distraught at any mention of the outside world.

"But, sweeting, they must all know soon. A marriage cannot be secret, so why should our wooing be hole-and-corner?"

I laid my cheek against his and said, "This is so wonderful. The most wonderful thing in my life. I couldn't bear to have it spoiled."

"And what could spoil it?"

"A hundred things. Your mother, your grandmother may despise me and say things that would lower me in your eyes."

"God Himself could never do that. As for my mother—she married again and lives in Bruges; we could pass in the street unknowing. And my grandmother will *love* you." He wrinkled his brow with earnestness, and the wrinkles made two little horseshoes, one inside the other. "In many ways—seeing what is funny where others might miss it, and making the best of things—you are somewhat alike. She'll dote upon you. And even if she didn't, what could it matter to us? You are my chosen one, and the Devil himself couldn't keep us apart. What are you doing now?"

I had crossed my two first fingers and, holding them in front of my face, my eyes turned inwards to squint.

"Blinding the Devil," I said, when I had held the position long enough. "You should always do that when *he* is mentioned disrespectfully."

"Where I was reared, the only Devil anyone feared was Henry ap Tudor and when he was named it was the custom to spit. Much good that did. Now, back to ourselves. I wish to marry you and you say you will marry me. I think the first thing is to ask Dame Isabel's permission and then we'll go and break the news to my grandmother."

"Now?"

"Why not?"

I had no reason. The way he suggested was the decent, orderly, proper way of doing things. So I said:

"Very well. But not Dame Isabel. I have a real mother and she should be the first to be told."

I owed her that; she had been remarkably faithful to me. I'd been at Clevely less than a fortnight when she had come running to see how I fared. My grandmother was still lame, so Mother had been sent to market again and had stolen half an hour to get to Clevely. The news she brought was good. There had been a great uproar over my disappearance, but she had not been blamed; how could she be, working away in the dairy and thinking, when I didn't come back with the water, that my grandmother had given me another task? Nor could my grandmother be rebuked. She had seen me go to the well and then climbed the stairs and spent the afternoon turning cheeses in the attic, which had air holes but no window. My grandfather and Jim Hayward had both fallen into frenzy and gone searching as far afield as Colchester on the one hand and Bywater on the other.

"So stay close to the house," Mother said. "I must go."

I saw her again when it was cowslip time. As in years past she had been sent out to gather a sackful of the fragrant heads and this year she had run to Clevely. I helped her fill the sack as she jerked out the news. Jim Hayward was still hunting for me. He'd heard of a girl with black hair who was serving ale in an inn at Enfield, and he'd gone all that distance, only to find some poor afflicted creature with a harelip. Mother reported that both my grandparents were well. "They'll live to ninety to spite me, I don't doubt," she said. "But I shall still have sap in me, and you and me'll make merry." She ran off, dragging the sack behind her.

She next came in winter, in bitter weather. Both my grandparents had been smitten with the sweating sickness. "I had high hope that it'd carry him off," Mother said, "but he's mending and itching to get down to find fault with how I've managed." She gave one of her long sighs. "Possets and plasters and gruel to make and carry, as well as all else to do. I'm weary to the bone."

She looked older and thinner and more dragged down. I thought, Suppose it's all for nothing; suppose that tough old man bears her down to the grave.

I said, "Stay here. The Ladies would have you, I know. There's work enough, and food too, now. Don't go back."

"No. I must be there. It can't last forever. And one day we'll have a place of our own and eat what we sow." She always made some such promise, straightening her back a little. And the lines would lift in her face, the light come lively into her eyes for a moment. "So long as you're safe and happy; I'm all right," she said, and ran off.

She had come each summer for the cowslips and at least once, on this excuse or that, in between.

Yes, I had a real mother, and she should be the first to hear the news.

I told Walter the whole story. That was easy enough. Had I said that my mother was a strumpet whipped at the cart's tail, my father hanged for murder, he would have been that much more sorry for me, and loved me that much more. When I spoke of Jim Hayward kissing me he put his hands on my shoulders and turned me about.

"Poor sweet," he said. "Forget it. There," and he kissed me hard, "let that wipe out the memory."

It did something else; it started a panic fear in me.

"How can we tell her? If my grandfather should get to know he'd marry me to Jim Hayward yet! Walter, that I could not bear. Not now. It was bad enough, but now . . . now . . ." I clung to him and shuddered.

He steadied me and said, nonsense. He was not a rich man but he could outbid Jim Hayward if it came to that. "If you'll forgive the use of the word, Josiana."

"Jim Hayward has one thing to offer for me that you have not, I *hope*. A great lout of a boy to work the farm." Even in this serious discussion I could not resist the temptation to make him smile.

"I'll hire him a boy. Or two or three. There are boys to be hired, you know."

"It wouldn't be the same. You don't know how people like my grandfather are about bargains. He struck this one and I brought it to nothing. Out of spite, nothing else, mere spite, he'd marry me to Jim Hayward."

"Over my dead body, darling. And Jim Hayward would be dead too. I could kill him for *daring* to think . . ." And he talked about being reasonable; as though my fears were less reasonable than his threats to kill people! In the end I said:

"Very well. Maybe it would be all right—for us. But what of my mother? She saved me; she hid me. Suppose we went there, openly as you suggest, and faced them all with what we have to say; and suppose some word is let slip that shows that she knew where I was all these years; what would her life be, after that? Unbearable. We can't do it, Walter. Not that way."

"Then how?"

"We must catch her alone." I thought hard. There was a tree in the orchard that grew an early apple, red-skinned, very sweet and soft and ill to keep. "Any market day now my grandmother will be taking the red sops to market. Walter, if you could bear . . ."

"For you," he said, "I could bear anything."

"Watch then, for an old woman, lame of one leg, with a very old grey horse, lame of two. . . ." I described them both more fully, the very pattern of my grandmother's summer go-to-market dress, the cut of her apron. He would pick her out, easily enough, on the road that led past his house, I was sure. "Send a man then, as quick as you can, on a good horse, to bring my grandfather to Baildon to look at one of your pack ponies—coughing, or off its feed or some such thing. He prides himself as a horse doctor, his liniment has kept Jenny at work these many years—and he will come out to show his skill, and for a price. Then you come here. I'll wait under the trees and you and I can watch to see your man carry my grandfather past. Then we can go."

On the next immediate market day I found a job for myself, rigging scarecrows in the pea field which was the cultivated piece farthest from the House and nearest the track. I made that the excuse for not coming back for dinner, carrying a noon-piece in a little bag. I wore my working dress, but I had in the meantime washed and mended it. I had dressed my hair neatly and tied a cloth over it.

Although what Walter and I were about to do seemed ordinary enough—two young people in love, politely asking permission to marry—and although my careful arrangements seemed to promise an easy performance, I was so restless and nervous that I was in my hiding place amongst the elms in time to see my grandmother go by; exactly as I had described her, but with a cloud of wasps buzzing about the sweet-smelling load. So far, so good. I ran back to the pea field and hastily reared another post hung with bits of rag and lengths of twine weighted with small pieces of wood and broken pottery which rattled together when the wind blew. The peas were almost ripe and the birds had been busy, and would be again so soon as they became familiar enough with this contraption to know it harmless. Then I must move it, change the rags, add some other device.

While I was busy I heard a horse go past, trotting briskly. I moved back to the trees. It was a warm day but I was shivering; and for the first time since my coming to Clevely I felt sick.

Soon Walter came. He too had thought to bring a noon-piece, enough for two, and far more tasty than mine, small chicken pies with crisp crumbling crusts and sponge cakes spiked all over with sliced almonds which Walter called "hedgehogs." My eyes admired them but I was too dry-mouthed to eat with enjoyment. Walter comforted me and teased me a little. Even when the brisk horse, less brisk now that it carried two, went past towards Baildon and there was nothing left for actual fear, another uncomfortable thought struck me.

"This may not be good news to my mother," I said. "Her dream has always been of us living together in a place of our own."

"Come now. What has she ever done that you should judge her so selfish? She will be like every other mother, glad of your safety and happiness." He took my hands and exclaimed over their coldness. "Is anything wrong? Look, Josiana; are you sure that you love me and want to marry me?"

"How can you ask that?"

"You're very young and you've lived apart from the world. Have I wronged you perhaps . . . taken advantage . . . ?" He broke off and scowled. "Ever since marriage was mentioned you've been different, less happy. If you have any doubts . . ."

"I do love you. More than anything in the world I want to be your wife, Walter. If it could happen, if it could just be done, between us. Breaking the news, hearing what people will say, seeing how they will look—this, I know, is the hardest part, but when this is done we have your family to face, and then Dame Isabel, and all that seems so far apart from us and the way we feel about each other. It's silly, I know."

"No," he said, gravely, "not silly, natural. Nothing in all your life has been calculated to give you any faith either in yourself or in events. But it will all be different now. From this moment on nothing shall ever trouble or fret you again; that I promise. Come along now; I'm with you. In this and everything else, so long as we live, we shall be together."

(This is a fine time to remember that, Walter. With me kneeling here snug in a fur-lined cloak, free to come and go, free to live out my life span; while you lie in a cold dark dungeon in the Bridewell; and two dozen paces tomorrow morning will bring you to the stake and the heaped firewood. And yet, in a sense it is true. Despite everything, we have always been together. We are even now. . . .)

I could have foretold exactly how we should find Mother, for there had been, in the past, just one or two occasions when we had been left alone on the farm. Rare festive hours. We boiled eggs, fresh taken from the nest, for even the most strict accounting could always be evaded with "The brown hen has not laid today, nor the black with the broken tail feather." And Mother always helped herself to a mug of ale, pouring the same amount of water into the cask, while for me there was a tiny cup of one of Grandmother's brews, similarly replaced. We did our work certainly, but quickly and with a light spirit, and then had our little feast. I have no doubt that it was on one of those days that the seed of that "place of our own" had been sown in Mother's mind.

Oh dear. They say that when a great ship goes down with a great loss of lives and cargo, worthless, trivial bits and pieces will come to the surface and float. So, out of that disastrous visit, there remains with me the terrible pathos of the moment of our arrival.

She was in the kitchen, and she had been eating an egg, a smear of yellow glaze lay alongside her mouth. She heard the horse's hooves and thought it was my grandfather returned. She came hurrying out carrying the swill pail and, without a glance in our direction, made for the pigsty. Knowing what I knew I could see that she was swallowing as she scurried across the yard. I called:

"Mother; it's only me," and then she turned.

I had begun to scramble down from the horse and Walter set his hands under my arms and swung me clear. I began to run towards Mother crying, "It's all right. They're both away, we saw to that."

The look of trapped astonishment, such as might appear on the face of a person under whose feet the solid earth has opened to engulf him, did not ease from her face as I spoke my comforting words. We'll grant, I thought, that she believed herself caught idling and eating eggs and drinking ale, and that, on top of that, she is startled to see me . . . but that did not account for her look. Also, she hardly looked at me. Her eyes were on Walter. There she stood, still holding the swill pail and bent slightly sideways under its weight, her other hand held stiffly out at the side, its fingers clenching and loosening as though she were seeking support from the empty air.

"It's only me," I said again. "Me and Walter. I'm sorry we surprised you. There was no other way."

Walter had dismounted and came towards us.

Mother said, and her voice sounded as though someone were strangling her:

"Walter Rancon?"

And Walter—this I shall always remember—he greeted her, in her soiled working clothes, with her dirty bare feet and rough hair and egg-smeared mouth, as though she were one of the grand ladies he had known at Beauclaire.

"That is so, madam. Walter Rancon, at your service."

As though the strangling hand had tightened on her throat, Mother said:

"And what do you want here?"

She'd guessed, I thought. She knew that her dream of our one day being together, of having our place and eating what we had sowed, was over. I knew exactly how she felt. And I knew how right I had been in dreading this moment. Poor Mother.

I broke into a gabble of apology and explanation and promise, a light froth of sound, through which Walter's voice cut like a firm hand moving through cheese curds, "I have come to ask permission to marry your daughter."

Then she went mad. She flung down the pail, the whole precious garnering of buttermilk, wash-up water, bacon rinds, pot-scrapings that nothing could replace, she flung it down and turned to the house wall and beat upon it furiously with her fists, screaming. It was worse than any pig-killing, for just as a pig, being an animal, cries out against death with a human voice, so she, being human, cried out then with a voice that was more . . . more horrible, more protesting than any human voice should be.

I ran to her, put my arms about her and pulled her away from the wall. There was blood on it, where her hands had beaten. As I did so I thought about Walter's words concerning selfishness; I knew it wasn't that. It was just that all through those years when she had shielded me as well as she could, and borne, for my sake, mockery and ill-usage, and had saved me from Jim Hayward, it had all been with one end in view. Thoughts are very swift. I had time to think, Poor dear, it is as though now somebody had come to tell *me* that I couldn't marry Walter because he had a wife already. So my hands, though firm, were gentle on her and I said:

"Don't, I beg you, take it this way. When we are married you shall come and live with us. No more waiting . . ."

I poured out promises, and Walter joined me. She quietened. It was all right. I looked at Walter and smiled, apologetically, because sometimes you must apologise for having been right.

And then she said:

"But you can't be married. The same man fathered you both."

Because I had been, all along, expectant of some disaster, I bore this felling blow better than Walter could. If Mother had taken a sword and run him through he would have looked no worse, turning the colour of tallow and reeling back until he came to a post against which to lean and stare, his jaw sagging.

It occurred to neither of us, in that moment, to doubt the truth of what she said. There wasn't time for a hopeful doubt. Once the seal of her silence was broken, she began to babble, standing there barefoot on the cobbles, muffling her shaking, broken hands in her sacking apron.

"How could I know that this'd be the end of it? My poor little girl. I'd have told! Oh, if I'd only foreseen!" She made a wild, wailing noise, the like of which I never heard before or since. "To think I bore the beating and the finger breaking, to end like this."

Walter spoke as though moving his stiff white lips hurt him.

"He was married then. Did you know?"

"Oh yes," she said, almost eagerly, almost as though it excused something. "He never made a secret of it, there was no secrets betwixt me and him. And he meant to stand by me. When I told him the way I was, he said not to fret, he'd look after me, and he meant it. He would too." She looked at Walter in a curious way, both ashamed and triumphant. "He was married, but that was a fixed-up job, his heart weren't in it . . . though he was fond of *you*; and he wasn't one to want to cause his wife any grief either. Very tenderhearted he was. So he went off to London to settle on a place for me. He said lately he'd been there as often or more as in Baildon and he'd find a place where no questions'd be asked and he'd spend what time he could there and it'd be like being married. All I had to do, he said, was to hold on and say nothing. And we fixed a time to meet in the old place where we always had. I went just as I was . . ." She lifted her hands, clenched into fists, and pressed the knuckles against the lower part of her face.

"We can guess the rest," Walter said. She went on as though she had not heard.

"He never come, and that was one day; and the next, and the next. That never was easy for me to get away, but I did, time after time, a whole month, I reckon. And then in the end Tom Thoroughgood brought the news back one market day. That time the old people wasn't so sour, nor so mean, and Tom stopped by and had bite and sup and he said young Rancon had took ill and died in London, so he heard." She looked at me, and for all she was talking so much, it was a dumb look, far beyond the reach of any words. "If I'd had any sense," she said, "I could have hasted things up with Jack Bowyer and had my baby at seven months, plenty do. But somehow . . . well, I had to get used to the thought of his being dead, that I'd never see him again, or hear him speak. And by the time I'd pulled myself round that was too late. And now . . . You see I kept his name to myself despite all, because that was all I had. He was very openhanded, he was always wanting to give me things, but there was nowt I dared bring home—they reckoned me pledged to Bowyer who'd as soon have ducked in the horse pond as given a girl a fairing. So in the end there was nothing except just his name to hold onto. And who could have thought it'd turn out this way? In a thousand years who'd believe that you two would ever meet?"

"He was rotten," Walter said. "Rotten to the core with selfishness."

"No," Mother said, "you marn't say that; no, not even now. I've lived out my days with selfishness and he was the least selfishest man I ever knew. He was different. I ain't handy with words, but you look at cuckoos! There's sparrers and rooks and pigeons and starlings all behaving according to rule, but do there come a day in April and somebody smile and say, 'I seen a sparrer, I heard a rook?' No, listen to me! Do they? No, they say, 'I heard the cuckoo.' And that was the same with him. He never even looked like other people. You could look at him, in a sheltered place on a still day, and see a wind from far away blowing on him."

"Straight from Hell," Walter said bitterly.

"No. You marn't say that neither. There's no loving-kindness in Hell, young sir. And he had more than his measure of it. That was his trouble, not badness. . . ." She looked at me, pleading for understanding. "Bad though it turned out for us all."

In the silence the pigs set up their impatient squealing and I realised where I was.

"The swill all wasted," I said in a voice that sounded too ordinary to be believed. "Oh, what a row there'll be."

"I'll manage somehow," Mother said, quite calmly; but she was frightened, too. She went down on her knees and began to scratch together the bits of solid stuff that had been in the swill.

I think that action, at that moment, brought home to Walter the truth of all I had said about life in my grandparents' house. He made a great effort, and moved; put his hand under Mother's arm and pulled her upright.

"Leave it," he said. "This has been a bad business from first to last, but what can be put right, shall be. You must both come home with me. Now."

"I can't do that," Mother said. "Not after sticking out all these years."

What seemed strange to me, even at that moment, was that I bore her no grudge. She'd ruined my life, I knew that, though I hadn't yet fully reckoned the damage; but I'd always pitied her and now, having heard her story, I pitied her more than ever, and I understood, because I was in love, exactly why she had acted as she had. So I said, in that same strangely ordinary voice:

"Please, Mother, come away. From now on it'll be you and me together, and I can't come back here, so you must come away with me."

"No," she said. "I must stay here." She turned to Walter. "Take her away and keep her safe, set her where she should be." She made a curious noise, neither laugh nor sob. "The day I took her to Clevely, if I'd had more time and not been in such a maze I'd have brung her down to the Old Vine and made everything plain; that was in my mind; but it was too far. If I had, all this would have been spared. I wish to God . . ." She broke off and began to cry, and crying bent again to gather up what she could of the swill; and I looked down at her and saw her hand, misguided because she was tear-blinded, close on a hen's turd.

My stomach heaved, I turned away towards the wall and walked into a spinning darkness.

When it lifted I was lying flat on my back on the grass by the side of the road and Walter was splashing cold water on my face. Trained from my childhood to regard my weakness as something to be ashamed of, I reared myself and said, "I'm all right now. I'm sorry . . ."

He said, "I thought you were dead. I wanted to carry you into the house but she wouldn't let me. She's mad! She drove me off. All she cared for was that we shouldn't be found there."

I said, "She was right. Out of it all, nothing else matters now. Oh, Walter . . ." I took his arm in both my hands and leaned my forehead against his shoulder for a moment. Then I bethought myself and let go and straightened.

"We're on the road they'll come home by," I said.

"You're safe with me."

"She isn't. Quick, ride me back to Clevely, Walter, please."

"You're coming back with me to Old Vine."

"No, Walter, I couldn't. I know now . . . after what she said, and we know it is true . . . I know that we must feel differently. But I don't yet; I couldn't pretend; I couldn't live under the same roof and not . . . No, you must take me back to Clevely, and we'd best not meet again."

He said, "But how could I rest, with you at Clevely, working so hard and living so poorly? I don't feel differently towards you—

yet, but I must learn and so must you. The one sort of love—the sort we had—is forbidden us; but love has other faces. I swear that I will rule and govern myself and learn to love you as a man should love his sister, and in no other way."

"That," I said, "I well believe. Time after time I have seen how well you govern yourself. I am made of frailer stuff, Walter. The moment I saw you I loved you in one way, and a few words have made no change in me. Suppose she had died, or been struck dumb, or decided to keep her secret to the end. What then? We'd never have known. And knowing something in my head, Walter, makes no difference to how I feel here and here. I can never love you as a brother, never."

They were true words, but sometimes the truth can do as much harm as a lie. I should have held my tongue, and let him take me home, and pretended. How things would have ended then I don't know—but not worse than they did, that is certain.

His love was always less earthy than mine; his wound would have been eased by his taking me home, seeing me provided for; he could have taken refuge in brotherly love. He kept arguing about it, right there in the road along which my grandparents might at any moment pass, and I sweated with terror for my mother. In the end I was pleading with Walter to ride me just as far as the turnoff to Clevely.

"And you must promise to drop me there. Otherwise I shall not ride. I'll run."

He promised, unwillingly. And that short ride was a foretaste of what our lives must henceforth be. Riding out I had leaned against him, lover-like; going back I sat stiffly, holding myself away from him as much as possible, so that we might have been a grand lady riding with a servant, or a gentleman who had fetched the midwife in a hurry.

We reached the Clevely track without meeting anybody and, once off the road, stopped. Walter began to argue again, doing his best to persuade me to go with him to the Old Vine. In the end I frightened him into giving me my way. I threw my arms round his neck and pulled his head down and I kissed him more hotly and roughly and passionately than I had ever allowed myself to do before.

"That's how I love you," I said breathlessly, "and to live under the same roof and see you every day would put me on the rack.

. . . My way is best." I slipped to the ground and thought for a moment that I was free, but instantly he was beside me, holding my hand with gentle firmness.

"It mustn't be decided yet," he said, "and not by you, who are so young and wild of heart. Why throw away the whole apple because of one speck?" His face was still white, and his eyes stricken, but he managed a smile. "Try not to fret. When the first pain has eased we can make plans. Something will be saved."

I bade him goodbye, but he wouldn't say it. As at other times he said, "Until we meet again, sweeting." He kissed my fingers, not my lips.

When he had gone I threw myself down on the ground and cried; I sobbed and I shrieked and moaned. There was no one to hear me, no one in the empty field, nothing in the empty sky. I willed myself to die and in the end reached a state of exhaustion which did, for a while, seem like a prelude to death. But I was sixteen, and healthy, I had a long way to travel to the end of my road.

My mind recovered first. I recognised the need for secrecy. In some bygone age, in another life, I had left the House, supposedly to work in the pea field. I must have some good reason for returning white-faced and trembling and all blubbered with tears. I got up. The track was stony, for it sloped and the rain had washed away the covering earth. I found a large, flattish stone and took it in my right hand. I laid my left thumb on another stone, firmly embedded. I struck my thumb one hard blow and somewhere within the fierce hurt there was a pleasure. I hated myself because of what had happened to me. I hit my thumb again and again.

When I reached the House I said that I had hurt myself hammering in one of the scarecrow posts. Dame Constance took charge of me and, while applying ointment and a bandage, gave me a little homily about bearing pain in the right spirit. I must, she said, offer up my trivial suffering as a contribution towards Christ's agony for the world's sins.

VI

Next day my thumb began to swell and throb, and despite all Dame Constance's plasters and potions it continued to grow worse. My hand became a shapeless lump, my arm puffed up to twice its size and was streaked with scarlet. By the third day I was in such agony as to be almost out of my mind. Only one thing brought me any relief and that Dame Constance used over-sparingly. It was a syrup made of poppies and, after a draught of it, I and the pain would part company for a while. It was still there, grinding and throbbing, but I floated off, sometimes into a kind of daze, some-times into a brief, merciful sleep.

I had been told to keep to my bed, but except just after a dose of the syrup I could not lie still. I walked about, cradling the aching arm in my sound one, and moaning. The room was small, five paces between the bed and the window, six from the window to the door.

I was at the window when Lady Rancon arrived. Walter's grand-mother, and mine. My other grandmother! I guessed that Walter had told her about me and she had come to see for herself. I could imagine how the story sounded in her ears; and suddenly I knew I couldn't face her. I must get out and away; but I couldn't run as I was, in my shift, so I opened the press, awkwardly, one-handedly and groped for my winter cloak. While I was doing that Dame Constance came in.

"Get back into the bed at once," she said. "I came to set you straight. You have a visitor."

"I know. I can't see her. I won't. I'm in no fit state . . ."

"You will be," she said; and I saw that she had brought the poppy medicine with her. She poured me out a generous dose, almost twice as much as I had ever had before. She straightened the bed-clothes, admonishing me to be calm, to be civil.

"From the few words I heard exchanged between Lady Rancon and Dame Isabel just now, this could be a great chance for you, Jenny," she said.

The pain stayed there, with my arm, in the bed, and I began to float upwards and sideways until I hung close to the rafters in the far corner. Then my grandmother Rancon came in and sat down by the thing on the bed and began to talk to it. She stroked its sweat-soaked hair and held its uninjured hand. She called it Josiana, and said that Walter had told her everything.

Her voice was grave, full of understanding and pity. It made me cry in a way I had never cried before.

"I didn't want this to happen," I blubbered. "I didn't wish this on any of us. It's disgusting for you, too, I know."

She said, "No situation is ever quite what it seems at first sight. I am most deeply sorry that this should have happened to you and to Walter; but even after heartbreak something is left, and if we are wise we make the most of it. Perhaps it is selfish of me, but I am glad to have found you."

I went on crying and she continued trying to comfort me, speaking of a comfortable life at the Old Vine and making up to me for all my labours and privations.

I said, "I can't come there. I told Walter that I shall never feel towards him in sisterly fashion, and I cannot live under the same roof with him."

"Walter is not there. . . ." Her clear voice trembled a little. "He has gone to live in Amsterdam, so that you may come home."

"He shouldn't have done that! You needed him."

"I needed a reliable factor in Amsterdam, too. And now I need you, you see."

Floating there where I did, it was the easier to answer her boldly. I said:

"Madam, you need a base-born granddaughter as much as I at this moment need a toothache!"

"I need you," she said, quite fiercely. Then, in a different voice, "The relationship seems to me to be our own business. I have not spoken of it downstairs. To my household and such people in Baildon as are interested in our affairs we can say that you are a kinswoman of my late husband. If you are satisfied with that."

"It is a wonder to me that you accept me at all."

She said, "When Walter, all distraught, began his tale I knew the end of it." She sighed and then said abruptly, "Your mother was to blame, in part."

"She has suffered for it."

"So I understand." But there remained always in her mind some resentment against this unknown Joan Greenwood who had let herself be seduced, and then by her secrecy set the scene for this situation. Later on, when circumstances changed and it was possible for me to go from the Old Vine to visit my mother, my grandmother always saw me off with reluctance and disapproval.

Because she had held me there in conversation and not let me drift and drift away, the benefit of the poppy draught lasted a shorter time than usual; and soon the pain and I were joined again, moaning and tossing on the bed.

"As soon as I heard you were abed, and why, I sent the man from the yard into Baildon, on my horse, to fetch the doctor. He will be here soon. In the meantime, let us try something which I have known to ease a festering wound." She spoke of soaking in hot water.

"Dame Constance says no wound should see water for fourteen days," I groaned.

"I venture to think that I have seen more of wounds than any nun could have."

So the tub of water was brought, and my bandage removed. She was shaken when she saw the state of my arm.

"Poor child. And I have been bothering you with talk, God forgive me."

The hot water added to the pain at first, but each time as the water cooled a little of the agony drew off. We were still busy at it, adding more hot water every five minutes, when the doctor arrived.

He was a stout, fussy little man, like a pigeon, dressed in a robe which marked his degree, though the fur was rubbed almost bald. He did not handle me at all, but standing at a distance said that the wounds in my thumb had closed too soon and the poison which should have run out was stopped up. What I needed was another slitting with a sharp knife. He would send for the barber surgeon.

"But that," said my grandmother, "means another journey to Baildon and back; with the child in agony and in dread of the knife. You make the slit."

He was very much offended.

"Since when has a physician been required to do barber work? No reputable doctor ever did his own cutting, nor ever will."

She beat the side of one hand into the palm of the other and then stilled them. "I could do the cutting, with your guidance," she said. "I have done trickier things in my time."

"The patient should be fortified," said the doctor. "Brandy is best."

Of brandy, which must be bought with money, the House had none; but they gave me the next best thing, a full measure of the honey wine and another dose of the poppy syrup. This time as I floated I spun round and round. But I saw it all. My grandmother took the knife and sharpened it on the doorsill, and held it in the hot water for a second or two. She made the slit, and I bore it, without flinching, and there and then another bond was welded between us.

The doctor cried, "See, how right I was!"

Out of the new slit the poison gushed, green and yellow, very evil-smelling, and streaked with dark blood.

He went away and we resumed the hot soaking, and presently, when the honey wine and the medicine had lost their power and the pain seized me again, its sharpest fangs were drawn. Presently I was sensible enough to say:

"Will the Ladies allow me to go with you?"

"That is already settled," she said. "I told them I was growing old and lonely and had a fancy for a convent-reared girl to companion me. I shall recompense them for what they lose."

VII

At the beginning of my life with my grandmother at Old Vine I was conscious that I had robbed her of Walter and that it therefore behoved me to fill, as best I could, his place. So I worked as hard as I had ever done, without the need. She would have let me be idle or frivolous had I wished. After a while I learned a truth which sounds harsh—the kind of thing my grandfather Greenwood might say—but a truth it is nonetheless: hard work is an easement for sorrow. There would be stretches of time when, busy and struggling to learn something new, I would forget Walter, and my feeling for him, and all our sad story. Only at night sometimes, lying in the soft, warm, goose-feather bed, I would find grief flooding over me again; then I would turn my face into the pillow and cry myself to sleep.

My grandmother—whom now I called my aunt—was careful at first to avoid mentioning his name, or, if it slipped out unwarily, would check herself and look confused; she showed her feelings very openly in the widening of the pupils of her eyes. One day I said to her:

"I can bear to speak of Walter, and to hear his name. I am in no worse case than any woman who loses her lover through death, or his own unfaithfulness."

She said, "Sometimes I wonder whether we were not hasty. You and Walter were brother and sister and neither of you had others. Is it possible that what, being young, you took for the ordinary love between men and women may have been the call of the blood, the sense of kinship?"

I saw what she thought. Plant that notion firmly enough in my head and Walter could come home; a happy family under the one roof, and for decency's sake bandying about the word "Cousin" twenty times a day.

"For him," I said, after some thought, "it may have been. That and pity. But not for me." I added quickly that if she wanted Walter home, I would go.

She said, "It was Walter's own wish that you should come home. And if you left for any other reason than marriage, he would hold me to account."

I shuddered when she said "marriage."

"The very thought of another man is distasteful to me," I said.

"Time may mend that. I hope it will. My grandfather, who was a wise man, once told me that to a woman children mattered more than anything else in the world. I lived to prove it true. Sir Henry and I were fortunate, ours was a love match, and the *love*, the heady thing people mean when they say the word, lasted perhaps five years. Kindness remained, and affection, and loyalty. But in the end his horses and his arms, his tourneys and his triumphs took first place with him, and our child first place with me."

It was the first time she had ever made mention of my father, even indirectly. I was interested in the man who ruined three lives that we knew of, who had left a memory of kindness in the woman he had betrayed, and whose own son spoke of him with hatred. How had he seemed in his mother's eyes?

I said, rather timidly, "What was he like—my father?"

"That no one can say, I least of all. I could say that he was like my own brother—but that would mean nothing to you. To me it did though. The first moment they laid him in my arms I looked down and I knew, and I thought—Oh no, not *that* again. But it was." She narrowed her eyes and looked at me. "When Walter told me about you, Josiana, I was afraid. If you had looked, or acted . . . no, despite my promise to Walter I could not have borne that again."

"Borne what?"

She said, "The charm and the heartlessness, the way they could make magic with music, until you cried and then they would laugh. Something not . . . not quite human, something wild and unaccountable. Dear child, there are no words. Something strange crept into this family—there are queer tales of *my* grandmother—and it crops out now and then, a flaw in the weave. Thank God neither you nor Walter show it."

"Yet my mother," I said, "who is meagre with words, spoke of him, the one time I ever heard her speak of him, like a poet." I told her of Mother's comparison with the cuckoo.

"I wonder," she said, "was it by accident or intent that she hit upon so apt a word." And I knew by her tone that that was the end of that conversation. She was very gentle, very kind, but she could, by a change of voice, a lift of the eyebrow, a set of the lip, issue a rebuke, express disapproval, make a claim to something for which, in her own words, "there are no words." It pleased me to think that I had recognised that quality in her on the day when she had visited our farm and outbargained my grandfather Greenwood. It pleased me to see it in action, again and again, as I followed her about on her rounds. She could buy and sell without losing dignity; in an emergency she could lend a hand with a most menial task and yet still seem fastidious. I watched her, I did my best to emulate her, I loved her.

She was scholarly, and, through her teaching and even more by her example, she made me scholarly too. I had Dame Isabel's rudiments to build upon and the best of all reasons—the wish to escape from my own thoughts—as a spur. In the winter evenings we would often sit, one on each side of the hearth, and read for two hours or more, without exchanging a word. But for our clothes and the comfort about us we might have been two old fellows in a Cambridge cell. At other times we would talk. I learned, with secret delight, that it was not she who had ruined the business which my grandfather Greenwood had called the best in all Suffolk.

"My grandfather," she told me, "made a curious will. He left this house, and some money, on certain conditions to me. But the business and the premises behind the house he left to a young man who had been his secretary and general amanuensis. I think his intent was good, that we should marry and thus combine the house and the business. But I married Henry, and Master Freeman sold the business and the premises behind the house. That led to an awkward situation, because the pack ponies had to run clear through our house. Then Henry went to Pamplona—I went with him of course—and he won the greatest prize of all, a silver cup filled with gold pieces. I was so proud. And he said, 'Now we can buy back our own back yard.' So we did. And there were the lofts and the looms. And then Henry and I had our first real dispute. I wanted to keep the business going, and he made it very clear how he felt about *trade*. He called me a huckster and I called him old-fashioned! Still, it grieved me to see the thing my grandfather had given his life to shut down and made of no account. . . ."

"You've brought it to life again."

She smiled. "I've dragged together a few remnants of a wool business. My ambition to see the looms working again I shall never realise now, I am afraid."

"Because Walter has gone?" I asked quickly.

"You mustn't," she rebuked me, "get into the habit of reading more into a remark than is intended. Ambition dwindles with age, you know, and so does energy and enterprise."

I had been living at the Old Vine for almost a year and a half, when, on a grey December afternoon, my mother arrived. She presented a strange appearance, wearing my grandfather's warmest jerkin and his old woollen cap pulled low over her ears; and she was riding one of Tom Thoroughgood's satin-hided palfreys.

We had not met since that day in the Flaxham yard. Before I left Clevely I had charged Dame Isabel with a carefully worded message for "her." On her next visit I asked that she should be told that I had gone to live with Lady Rancon because her grandson had gone abroad. I thought that if she should, at any time, be sent to market again, she would visit me; but she never had. Since I had lived in Baildon I had seen my grandfather on two occasions, and my grandmother on three or four—both as hale and hearty as ever.

But now Mother, scrambling clumsily from the palfrey, cried:

"He's dead, praised be the saints! He's dead!" I never heard such delight in anyone's voice before, or since.

I chanced to be alone in the house, so I took her in, sat her by the fire and warmed some ale. She looked around the comfortable room, a little timidly at first, then more boldly.

"We'll hev our comforts, too, God willing," she said. "I took the key off his neck and I opened his box. There was more'n I ever dreamed of, both silver and gold. I left a few pieces and buried the rest in the muck heap. So if they come asking did he die rich or poor, they can see for theirselves."

"How did he die?" I asked.

"Just as he should. Yesterday morning it was and he was coming in to market hisself. We'd been out in the bitter cold, loading up, time he ate a bowl of porridge to warm hisself, and when we'd done that was a tidy old load; best part of a pig and a sack of corn to be ground as well as odds and ends. When he was ready he took howd of the leading rein and went to give Jenny a slap on the rump. 'Come up,' he say, but instead of coming up she come down." She broke off and laughed with gruesome glee. "Ah, toppled clean over, she did, pinning him down. He wasn't killed, he laid there groaning and hollering to us to get Jenny off him. But who was we to go lifting a dead horse and all that gear? Your granny *tried*, but she was all of a tremble and she couldn't do it alone. I never tried. I told her not to go pulling and pushing, she'd do more harm than good; I'd go for Tom Thoroughgood, I said. And Josiana, I took my time. . . ."

It was not to be wondered at; he'd used her brutally for years; he was the enemy and could not expect mercy.

"When we did get him out he was like a stove-in barrel and as dead as old Jenny."

"And how is *she*?"

"Gone to nothing," Mother said, "like a spray of old-man's-beard without no bush to cling to. Scared of *me* now, she is. We hadn't got him laid out afore she was telling me all she'd done, ever, was by his order. I told her sweet words now was too late, she could've spared me many a clout in her time, the same as I tried to you, the best I could."

"I know. And for that I shall always be grateful."

She looked pleased, and began again to talk about the money.

"If they knew what he had they'd be after me to give to the poor —and the only poor I care about is me and you, my dearie! They'd want Masses said for his soul—and I hope he rot in Hell forever-more. So I must go slow with the spending for a bit."

"There'll be talk if you go riding round on one of Tom's best palfreys."

"Thass a loan, so-called. Tom'll get his money, little by little. And ain't it natural for a neighbour to lend a horse, specially with ours dropped dead? And I was eager to see you. Thass been a long time." She looked around the room again. "I was glad when I knew you was here, I reckoned you'd feed better and lay softer and not toil so hard. But the first thing I thought when I see him lay there, dead, was that now you could come home."

My heart seemed to drop. There was a bond between us, even the knowledge that she had ruined my life hadn't broken it. She had been kind to me, she had been faithful, she had saved me from Jim Hayward. . . . But I couldn't go back to the farm.

"I can't come back there," I said. "I was too unhappy there. But if you like—if you'll sell it and move away I'll come. We could buy another farm, or a little business, a baker's or something, or we could take a job together."

And then I shall be gone from here and Walter can come home.

"That'd be silly. There's fifty good acres there at Flaxham and I've sweated over every inch. I ain't giving that up now. Where would I find a place in such good heart? You wouldn't hev to work, Josiana. I'm going to hire a man, maybe two. And when I die, that'll be yours and whoever you marry. I'll give you a dower. Tom Thoroughgoood's Peter is a right comely lad."

I said, "I don't want Peter Thoroughgood, or any other man, however comely."

Perhaps purposely she took this in the wrong way.

"You mean you got your eye on somebody?"

My inward eye, which every night strained towards a strange city named Amsterdam, where Walter was. Alone? Not alone? Happy or grieving? His letters to his grandmother, as regular as wind and tide allowed, told nothing of his state of mind.

But I might, with a little pretence, buy a little time for making a decision.

"I'm not sure about that, yet," I said.

And then, through my mother's pale, cold-roughened lips, spoke the old yeoman pride, based on its ownership of land, however little, upon its contempt for any other way of life.

"Whoever he is," she said, "he'll think the more of you seeing you on your own place, that'll be yours one day, than here, a kind of body servant, however glorified."

"It isn't like that at all. I am acknowledged as a kinswoman. I call my grandmother my aunt."

"So you may," Mother said, and this time it was her voice which reminded me of my grandfather Greenwood, "but afore people marry they look into things. You'd do better at home where the truth is known and not took amiss. Tom Thoroughgood know all about us and he never flinched when I kind of put out a feeler for Peter."

Something took hold of me then; after all, bastards are no different from other people; they have their feelings and their pride.

"The man who would marry me tomorrow," I said, "wouldn't flinch at my bastardy either." Was it true? How could I know? I'd never until this moment given the matter a moment's serious thought.

The man existed; I hadn't made him up. His name was Arthur Kentwoode and he lived at Minsham Old Hall. There was a connection of some long standing between his family and my grandmother Rancon's, a connection that I had never bothered to sort out. It reached back to my great-great-grandfather's day and was very involved. Arthur, who was thirty, and rather dull, but honest and good and kind, always stopped at the Old Vine on his way home from market, and talked to my grandmother, of whom he was obviously fond. I knew that he was taken with me, but he was shy, and I had done nothing so far to encourage him.

"Why ain't you married then?" Mother asked.

"Because I am still in love with Walter."

Her elated mood tipped over—helped perhaps by the ale. She began to cry, to accuse herself. . . . It was horrible, especially when I must think that *this* was the happy day, the great day to which she had looked forward, in which she had believed, and which had enabled her to bear everything. And after all, if she had ruined my life I, by my mere existence, had ruined hers. In the end I said:

"I know what I would like to do—come to Flaxham for Christmas."

She cheered up instantly.

"Ah, you do that, and see how different everything'll be."

My grandmother came home soon after Mother had gone and I told her the news and that I was going to Flaxham for Christmas. Too quickly she said:

"This is the fifth. If I wrote at once . . . Walter could come home."

She meant no ill; Christmas is the family season, and Walter had been away for eighteen months. She was fond of me, I never doubted that; but I was something which had been grafted on, Walter was of the true stock, he had smiled at her from his cradle. She wanted him home, she wanted his advice—for to a woman a man's advice has always a special value, she wanted his arm to lean upon. She wanted to see him married, begetting another little true-born Rancon. Any other woman would most surely have hated me. . . .

When, on the day before Christmas Eve, I rode out to Flaxham, I was face to face with my choice. I could go back and live with my mother, or I could get married. One or the other I must do, for everybody's sake.

Before the first evening was spent I knew that I could not live with my mother. She was mad in the same way as a dog which has been chained for years and years goes crazy if by some chance it is loosed. She never stopped talking—except to laugh, and her talk was all of a kind to remind me, horribly, of my grandfather Greenwood in those rare good moods when he had got the better of a bargain. Mother had got the better of Life itself! The urge to spend money and the need to conceal the fact that she had any was in itself enough to dement her. She'd done her shopping for Christmas in Colchester where nobody knew her, not in Baildon where people might talk. She'd bought every luxury available, including a cask of red wine from Burgundy, over which she was sure she had been cheated. "That run very thin," she complained. She had always thought of real wine as being syrupy and sweet. She'd bought herself a velvet gown and a gauzy headdress, which she would only put on when the doors were locked and the shutters fastened; she'd bought me a cloak lined with coney and a ring set with a ruby. But every purchase had some story attached to it. "I said to him, I said, 'Is that the best you got? Then why not?' I said. I said, 'My money is as good as the next man's, surely. I ain't asking for credit, like some,' I said, 'cash down,' I said, 'thass my way!' Just because I was in my working clothes . . ."

On and on, like that, not just on the first evening, but all the time.

And there was my grandmother, suddenly a frail, shuffling old woman, saying "Yes, Joan," and "No, Joan," where formerly she had said "Jack." It was difficult to see in her the tyrant of my childhood, the one who had brushed off the maggots and said, "Now eat it." The memory of that episode stood, I must admit, between me and any real pity for her, nonetheless she was not a cheerful sight.

I stuck out the Twelve Days. On one of them some of the Thoroughgood family came to eat goose with us, and on another Mother and I went to eat goose with them, and it was all very merry in a coarse and boisterous way. The table manners—which had been my own until I went to Clevely—I now found disgusting, and there was but one brand of humour, the bawdy. When, at the end of the holiday, Mother again broached the question of my coming home to live I made her the answer which alone would content her and excuse me. I told her that I was going to be married.

Once it was said I wondered whether I had overestimated myself; all I had to go upon were some yearning faithful-dog looks across the width of the room, but I was soon reassured. Within an hour of my return to Old Vine my grandmother had mentioned Walter four separate times, each time in an unconsciously wistful voice. I said to her:

"Walter would come home for good, would he not, if I were married?"

"He is not waiting for that; he would be willing . . ."

"I know, I know. But I would sooner be away. Nothing will change my mind on that. Besides, I told my mother that I was almost betrothed."

She asked me to whom and I said:

"I had Arthur Kentwoode in mind." And then she took my hand and told me that Arthur had spoken to her, months before, and that she had told him to be patient. She said, "I think you would be happy with him, Josiana. If there were anything for you to hope for, or to wait for I would say 'Wait'; but in your case there is nothing. And many people hold that love comes after marriage, I shall pray that it may be so with you."

I knew that could never be; but I made up my mind that I would be kind and faithful, a good wife.

We arranged to be married during the first week in March, just before Lent began. Walter wrote me a letter which, but for one sentence, might have been that of any elder brother to his sister just betrothed. The one exceptional sentence said that the news had taken a great load from his conscience since he feared that because of him I might go unmarried all my life. For the rest he praised Arthur, saying that if he had had the picking he could not have found me a sounder man. He said that he was sending me a roll of Milan silk which, if it arrived too late to be made into a wedding gown, could be worn at the christening of my first-born.

I have that letter still, the only one he ever wrote to me. It is creased because I crushed it in my hand, and it bears the mark of my heel because I flung it on the floor and trod on it. Its very kindness was a rebuff. But how else could he have written?

Eight days before my wedding I went with my grandmother on one of the last errands I should go on Old Vine business. She owned some pasture land at Horringer which was let on a "make and take" contract; the man who walked his sheep there paid no rent, but every year, when the lambs were all dropped, very formally and courteously, she and he met and saw one lamb marked with a tarred V which was our sign and one with an ochre cross which was his. It had been a good season, with mild weather, losses had been few and the little creatures were strong on their legs. I found myself thinking that perhaps by this time next year I might have a child. For me that was the only love which could come after marriage.

We rode back on one of those evenings that have the whole promise of spring in them; the sky was a clear apple green, streaked in the west with primrose. The trees, though still bare, were no longer winter trees, and the birds were singing. As we rode into Baildon the smoke from the supper fires rose straight and steady into the air, columns of purplish grey.

We rode abreast, with the man who had done our sheep marking following a few paces behind. We spoke of the lambs, of the beauty of the evening, and of my wedding. We came to the road which ran in front of the Great Gate of the Abbey, and there, with no warning, my grandmother's mount stopped, stiff-legged. It was so sudden that, good horsewoman as she was, she was almost unseated. My own horse, holding to its own pace, carried me forward two lengths before I could check and turn it. I heard my grandmother say in a voice of the utmost horror, "Oh no!"

I swung round and saw that she had dropped the rein and was pressing both hands to her face, so that only her eyes showed. She was staring ahead as though she saw something horrible; the horse, too, had the attitude of a horse confronted by something which it will not pass.

I cried to her, "What is it? What is the matter?"

She didn't answer me, but she moved, took the rein and pulled her horse's head round sharply to the left as though avoiding some obstacle, and set off for home at a quick canter.

The manservant came lumbering up.

"What ailed the beast? Like a wasp had stung it, but they ain't abroad yet."

I turned my horse again and hurried after my grandmother, overtaking her just before we reached the Old Vine. She was still deathly pale and looked strange. I asked her again:

"What happened? What did you see?"

She said, as breathless as though she had been running:

"I must write to Walter. . . ."

In the yard she flung herself from the saddle and hurried into the house, making for what we called the old side, where her office was. As she went she pulled off her gloves and threw them on the floor. I followed, and at the door of the office I was close enough to touch her, but she seemed unaware of me, and closed the door in my face.

I went and sat on the stairs which ran up nearby. I tried to convince myself that nothing was wrong; that there was a reasonable explanation. Perhaps—I thought—just outside the Abbey she had remembered something which she wanted to tell Walter, that in remembering she had jerked her rein or gripped her horse with her knees—she still rode astride in the old manner. The clapping of her hands to her face, the horrified "Oh no!" might just possibly have been an aging woman's exaggerated response to her first noticeable lapse of memory. But even as I explained it to myself I knew that there was more in it.

I waited. From the kitchen there came the clatter of supper dishes, otherwise there was no sound. The light, already fading when we entered the house, seeped away. Presently it was almost dark and I thought that if she were writing she must have lighted the candles and a line of light would show around the door, a spot of light in the hole where the latch went through.

I hesitated to intrude, but I remembered her pallor; so I opened the door, and calling her name, went in. In the deep twilight I could just see her, slumped forward across the table.

Afterwards I saw that she had begun her letter. Ordinarily she wrote a marvellous neat, clerkly hand and headed her letters, "Written at the Old Vine, Baildon on . . ." and then the date. There were no such preliminaries on this, her last letter. A violent, unsteady hand had driven across the top of the page. "My dearest Walter, on no account must you . . ." From the final word the quill had rolled, leaving an inky trail which ended in a blot. And that was all.

VIII

It was unseemly to follow a funeral so soon with a wedding, and ordinarily we would have postponed it until after Lent was past; but I was anxious to be married and out of the house before Walter returned and Arthur was concerned for me, left all alone at Old Vine. So, with no wedding finery, no feasting, Arthur and I stood before the priest in this same Church of St. Mary and were made man and wife. Afterwards we went to Minsham Old Hall, and there I settled down to prove once more the virtue of hard work.

Arthur, though he owned more than fifty acres, and was well-born, with the right to call himself a gentleman, was far from wealthy; in order to make his place pay at all he was obliged to be out and about overlooking the work a great deal of the time. With-indoors I was busy too; the house was extremely old, and cold and damp and awkward, and had I not known other homes than the Old Vine the change might have fretted me; as it was I could tell myself that at least I had more space and was not so near the midden as at the Flaxham farm, and that this house was no colder, no damper than the House at Clevely.

I had discussed with my grandmother the wisdom of telling Arthur the whole truth about my birth and my parentage; she had been against it, asking what purpose it would serve. Her motive was the same as had made her conceal our real relationship—a desire to hide the truth about the man who was, after all, her son, and dead. So all I had told Arthur was that I was born out of wedlock, and that my mother still lived at Flaxham; I had the foresight to realise that to conceal this might lead to trouble in the future. Concealing the full truth led to trouble, too, for Arthur was fond of Walter, "our cousin Walter," and naturally eager to entertain him. Our cousin Walter must ride home with him one market day, and have supper and stay the night and tell us all about Amsterdam and his plans for the Old Vine. Our cousin Walter was now, remember, alone in that big house, and probably feeling his bereavement. I deferred the dreaded day of meeting for a week or two, pleading the state of the house, which, left to an old servant for many years, was indeed dirty. But the day could not be postponed forever, and one Wednesday Arthur brought Walter home.

He had aged in some way not to be described in physical terms; his hair had its gloss and colour, his skin was unlined, his body still strong and upright; at first glance he was the handsome young man who had come riding down the track at Clevely and dazzled my eyes; but at second glance one saw the change. Youth had gone. Mingled in the tumult of feeling with which I greeted him, there was pity—I have done that to him, I thought. And the pity ran over to extend to Arthur, so innocent and so well meaning; I must be very, very careful not to do or say, or even look, anything which might hurt Arthur too.

It was worse than even I had expected. I had cherished a secret hope that time, and marriage, might have changed me, that only in my mind had I remained in love with the thought of Walter. But as we exchanged, under Arthur's benevolent eye, a cousinly kiss, the old hunger leaped in the same way and I was sick for love. I said to myself the ugly word "incestuous" and my mind flinched, but not my heart. Nor would it be deterred by the plain fact that he had mastered any feeling he had cherished for me, and could, in every word and glance be, not act or pretend to be, my good cousin Walter.

I was relieved to hear him say, somewhere through the evening, that he must go back to Amsterdam to appoint someone to take his place there and train him to fill it.

He was gone almost three months and when he returned and Arthur began proposing another visit I had a good excuse, for I was pregnant and my never very reliable stomach was queasy in the extreme.

"If you think Walter needs company," I said, "you go and sup with him; and that will give me one evening when I need not even *think* about food."

After that Arthur made a habit of stopping at the Old Vine whenever he went to market, just as he had done in the old days. He brought me back news. One day he told me that Walter had the looms at work again; only six of them in the great loft, but still it was a start.

"He will do well," Arthur said, "for Baildon cloth is not forgotten. They used to say that a coat or a dress of it would last a lifetime."

I thought how happy my grandmother would have been if this could have happened in her day. And but for me it might have done!

But that thought had no power to hurt me, for I had become, as most women do, at such times, a mere brood animal. I was merely the container, the seed pod. It was a blissfully it-and-me engrossed time when nothing else in the world mattered. Walk carefully, eat well, suffer nausea or be free of it, steer this bulk, this valuable cargo, safely through doorways and up stairs, avoid a stumble, a twist or a fall, and in the end the pod will burst, the cup so carefully carried will spill its treasure and there will be new life in the world.

My baby was a boy. When he was about two weeks old Arthur came and sat on my bed and said:

"Would it please you to call him Walter and ask your cousin to stand godfather?"

"No," I said, firmly, "in my family Walter is a name of ill omen."

Arthur blinked. "What do you mean? Walter Rancon is set to be one of the most prosperous men in Baildon."

I said untruthfully, "I wasn't thinking of him. There was another Walter—Walter Reed, my . . . my aunt Maude's brother; I've heard her speak of him. He died young and far from home. There was another, too—I misremember his story but it was a sad one and he died young."

As always Arthur was ready to humour me. "No Walters then. What do you say to Henry? It is the name of the King; and it is also the name of your uncle, Sir Henry Rancon, who when I was small often gave me a ride on one of his great horses. Henry for his name, and Cousin Walter for his godfather."

"I thought he would be named Arthur," I said.

"Two of the same name in a family leads to confusion."

"So will asking Walter to sponsor him," I said, little dreaming that I was making a prophecy. "You have two intimate cronies, Sir Mark Fennel and Mr. Hatton; if you ask Walter and one of them the other will take offence. Why are you so set on Walter, Arthur?"

Arthur said, with a frankness which robbed the words of some of their crudity:

"Because he is going to be a rich man, and will have no children of his own."

"How can you be so sure?"

"He told me so. I was teasing him one evening; I said that what the Old Vine needed was a mistress and why didn't he get married."

"And what did he say?"

"He turned serious. I had spoken, half in earnest, half in jest, but he answered me gravely. He said he had loved a woman once and could never fancy another. I grant you that many men have said such a thing and wedded within a twelvemonth, but, young as he is, there is something *settled* about Walter. My best hawk to a peck of corn he'll live and die a bachelor, and this boy here will inherit a flourishing business."

I would have argued more, but it would have looked strange; also there was in Arthur a stubborn streak where practical things were concerned; also I was still weak. So I gave in, and two weeks later when I was on my feet again and as lively as ever, Walter was asked to visit us and to see the baby.

Over the table Arthur said:

"We would like you to be one of his sponsors at his baptism, Walter."

Walter said, "I am conscious of the honour you do me, but I can't accept." He looked from one to the other of us, apologetically. "It would involve responsibilities which I am not prepared to undertake."

"In God's name, why not?"

"If you want an answer to that question, Arthur, I will answer you. But what I say may displease you. I'd sooner let it go."

Arthur's face had gone dark red. Later on I wondered whether he suspected that Walter had suspected his mercenary motive, for he looked angry in the way men do when they are caught out.

"I do want an answer," he said. "Never in all my life have I known anyone refuse the office of godfather save on account of age. Give me your reason."

"I should be obliged to promise to see that the child was brought up to believe a number of things which I know to be untrue."

"God's blood!" Arthur said. "Are you a heretic?"

"That is the name they give us," Walter said mildly.

"What other name is there?"

"Well, you could call us the seekers after truth."

"But *what* truth?" Arthur demanded. "We know what is true and what we should believe." He stopped eating and folded his arms and leaned forward across the table. "I'm interested, Walter. Where do you get your notions of truth?"

"From the Bible."

"Which, to start with, is a sin to read."

"There you are. Why should it be a sin to read God's own word and to learn at first hand what Our Lord said and did during His earthly life?"

"Can we be sure that that is what your Bible is? If you read it in English, most like it was translated by the enemies of the Church, and might contain anything."

"Mine is Wycliffe's; and he was a scholar and an honest man, and as good a Churchman as ever lived."

"That won't save you," Arthur said, "if you're caught with it in your possession."

Before Walter could reply to this the baby woke and cried his hunger cry; not liking to bare my breast before Walter, I retired, and when, taking my time over it, I returned the talk had swung to ordinary things and it was almost time to say good night. In our room, however, Arthur said:

"I'm worried about Walter. If he speaks elsewhere as he did at our table, he will run into trouble."

Perhaps I looked worried, for he added quickly, "Of course he is young and he has lived in foreign parts; maybe he has brought home new notions as other young men bring home new fashions. We must try to persuade him out of them."

Arthur's attempts at persuasion were painful to me, for they took the form of frequent invitations to Walter, the laying before him of the best that our house could afford, and then a long argument. The trouble was that Arthur *had* no argument; his best bolt had been fired when he made his suggestion that a translation might mirror the mind of the translator; after that he could only contradict whatever Walter said, and fall back upon the phrase, "The Church teaches . . ."

Sometimes I listened; sometimes I made an excuse to slip away to some job in kitchen or dairy, but even when I did that I would carry with me something which Walter had said and mull over it in my mind. Nothing he said seemed to me to be so very extraordinary or wicked. I'd think about this vexed question of Transubstantiation and ask myself how many people really believed in it as a fact. How many people would open their mouths and accept what they were certain was a morsel of a man's flesh, a sup of his blood? Then I'd hear Walter say that the monasteries and nunneries were corrupt with wealth and full of idle self-indulgent people, and I'd think of Clevely, so poor, where self-indulgence was unknown. About pilgrimages, which he decried, I knew very little, never having been on one; I did know that for every genuine pilgrim to St. Egbert's shrine in the Abbey there were four hangers-on, hucksters and tricksters and entertainers, who doubtless got the pilgrims a bad name.

One day I horrified Arthur by asking Walter to lend me his Bible; and then was myself horrified by the sight of it. Even in my studious-eveninged days at the Old Vine it would have taken me years to read from cover to cover. Walter advised me to start on the Gospels. I read slowly and carefully, and so far as the mind's grasp was concerned, I think I could say that I understood what I read, but the thing which had always most puzzled me remained a puzzle still. God the Father, all powerful, had made the world and all that was in it, and He loved the world and its people, yet they were wicked and they were afflicted; God the Son came down from Heaven to save the world—and that was fourteen hundred and ninety-one years ago, but people were still wicked and still afflicted. During His lifetime He had healed lepers and restored sight to the blind; yet we could still hear the leper's dreadful bell and see his sores, and as for blindness one had only to walk round Baildon market place. . . . I just didn't understand. And always, of course, there lurked at the back of my mind the question of how a loving

God could possibly have allowed to happen what had happened to Walter and me.

Once—I was then about two months pregnant with my second child—I made a positive trial of the virtue of Confession, another thing against which Walter railed. I had always been regular at Confession, admitting and asking forgiveness for the usual trivial things, but on this day I said that I had sinned in that I loved a man who was not my husband.

The priest asked me how far I had sinned; had I carnal knowledge of the man?

"No," I said, "but I have sinned with him in my heart." It didn't strike me at the time as being an unusual thing for a woman to say; nor did I, as I said the words, hear in them the echo of what Christ said to the crowd who wanted to stone the woman taken in adultery. But perhaps the priest heard it. For after saying that I had done well to avoid the sins of the flesh, and advising me to eschew the man's company and to cling to my husband, he accused me of my *real* sin, which was, he said, spiritual pride. I must pray, he said, for the blessing of a humble heart, and he would pray that it should be granted me.

I was puzzled again; but when I was about halfway home I thought I saw what he meant. It was, perhaps, a form of pride, to think that what went on in your mind *mattered*. The priest had rather that I had answered "Yes" to his question about the carnal knowledge; then he could have set me a penance and told me to go away and not do it again, like slapping a dog for chasing chickens. My self-accusation was something on quite a different level.

What happened next? Oh, something for which I blame myself bitterly because I was guilty of something far worse than spiritual pride. I made a great blunder.

Arthur hated to see me reading in Walter's Bible, so, although by this time I had begun reading in the earlier part of the book where there were some fascinating stories, I decided to give it back; and before I did so I said, carelessly, thoughtlessly, to Arthur, "Walter's ideas can never make much headway. All but the stone deaf can listen to the priests, and very few can read."

All unknowing I had handed Arthur a weapon. In his next argument with Walter he said:

"You know, Walter, if the soul's salvation depends upon Bible reading, most of us would be in poor case because we cannot read."

Actually he could read, about as well as I could do when I left Clevely, going along from word to word with a busy finger and mouthing. And he could write, his name and perhaps a dozen other words, all connected with his stock. One of the few genuinely *tender* feelings I ever had towards him was when, in the early days of our marriage, he showed me his list of assets up to the end of the previous year. It read, "Cow 6. Hawse 8. Pig 40 and 4. Sheep 50 and 50 and 12." Coming, as I did, straight from the Old Vine where I had helped my grandmother with her accounts, I found this little list touching in the extreme; and equally touching Arthur's willingness to allow me to help him with his reckoning. Many men would have resented the fact that a woman could glance at the sheep column and know the number to be one hundred and twelve.

When he made his remark about being unable to read Arthur looked proud of his skill in dispute rather than ashamed of his lack of knowledge. Walter didn't reply immediately, and Arthur's pleased expression deepened, saying wordlessly—Ah, I had you there. Then Walter said:

"That's very true. And it's the duty of those who can read to spread the truth."

Then Arthur issued his warning.

"What you say at this table, Walter, does no harm; and what you think is your own affair. The Church itself does not go querying what goes on inside a man's skull. But if you start spreading this truth as you call it, then anything may happen. I'll tell you something. It happened when I was eight years old, but I've never forgotten it. My father took me, for a treat, into Colchester. You know, going in by this side, there's a steep hill where you have to walk your horse. Halfway up, on the right-hand side, there was a crowd and my father said, "What's to do?" and we rode close. We could see over the heads of the crowd. They were burning a Lollard— that's the name they gave people with notions like yours in those days—and, Walter, that wasn't a pleasant sight. It quite spoilt my day, and my dinner." He paused, and then said in the most solemn possible manner, "And there's this, too. You're our kin, you're welcome to come and dispute over a cup of ale as often as you like, but an out-and-out heretic is like a chimney sweep, he blackens those he brushes up against. If you're coming into the open with this nonsense, Walter, we must forgo your company."

Walter nodded his understanding.

"That's just enough—if nothing I've said has convinced you, if you go on holding to the old superstitious ways. The point is, if there were enough of us, enlightened and sure, they couldn't burn us all, could they?"

"There will never be more than a dozen of you in any one place," Arthur said. "Heresy will always be stamped out. Don't be a fool, Walter, think your own thoughts, but keep your mouth shut."

I added my pleas to that. Whether he would have heeded had I said, "For my sake, Walter," I shall never know. I didn't say that; I said other things, things that made Arthur look at me with astonishment and say, "God forfend! If this is what Bible reading does . . ."

And then there was a time when Walter visited us no more, which was a relief to me. If he were spreading heresy he was doing it carefully; every time Arthur returned from Baildon I would ask, "Any news of Walter?" and wait with a quickening heart for the answer. Arthur would say "No" or tell me something trivial about the business at Old Vine—another loom at work or something of that kind.

My second child, a daughter, was born, and the seasons followed one another speedily, each with its special activities.

I think that if Walter had lived in London, or even in Norwich or Lynn, his shrift would have been shorter. In small places things move slowly and people are loth to think ill of, or move against, men who are known and respected in the community. Walter benefited by the piety of his grandmother, and of her grandfather. Old Martin Reed had been generous to Flaxham Church; its great bell bore his name and a rhyme cut into its rim. "Pray for the soul of Martin Reed whenever you my tongue shall heed." My grandmother had left her personal goods to the Church. (And if, as my grandfather Greenwood had said, she had been extravagant in gifts to Sir Henry, he had given her several things of value in return. She never wore anything except her wedding ring and another, a thing of no value, base metal and blue enamel, but she had others laid away, rings and brooches, bracelets and belts.) So the acts of the family were taken into account when it was a matter of how many times Walter Rancon absented himself from Mass or failed to visit the Confessional. He had a long run; my little Maude was steady on her feet by the time the next thing happened.

Arthur came home from the Wednesday market and I could see by his face that something had unsettled him. Before I could say, "What news?" he said:

"I saw Walter today. He'd left a message for me at the inn. So I stopped on my way home."

"Is he well?"

Arthur nodded, and dropping down on the bench began to work off his boots.

He said—and he gave me the impression that he was picking his words with care:

"Walter wants to sell the Old Vine."

More than once Walter had said that in the great merchant cities of the Netherlands there were more people who thought as he did; perhaps, I told myself, hopefully, he had decided to go back to Amsterdam.

"Is he leaving Baildon?"

Arthur busied himself with his boots. Then he said:

"Josiana, you're not to take this to heart. We've tried to talk sense into him. Even today I tried . . . but he won't listen. There's trouble ahead and he knows it, and he wants to get rid of his property before it comes."

"Heresy trouble?"

"No less. And if a man is convicted of heresy his goods are forfeit. Walter wants us to have the Old Vine. I told him . . . Josiana, I agreed to buy it."

He looked up then and the unsettled expression was graved deeper. There was a kind of anger, and some sorrow and some shame, even some fear on Arthur's usually placid, pleasant face.

"How can you?" I asked. "Where would you find the money?"

He looked relieved.

"I was afraid that you'd say I was encouraging him; or taking advantage of his plight," he said, with the air of a man throwing off a burden. "He said I could name my own price. And he said that if I didn't take it he'd sell it to the first man who made an offer, however small. So I named a price—every penny we have in the chest."

It was the price of the farm at Flaxham which my mother had left to me. She'd died early in the year, during the hard weather. It was sad to think that she'd borne overwork and near starvation for so long a time, and enjoyed her comforts so briefly. Sometimes I thought that it was her comforts that hastened her end; she ate and drank far too much, and seldom stirred from her chair. She hired a man to do the work, and after my grandmother's death, a girl to take her place and wait upon her. In a short time she grew very fat and short of breath; in an icy February a cold settled upon her chest and she was dead in a week.

Arthur had sold the farm for me and laid the money away. We planned to buy sheep in the summer, when pasture was scarce and prices low. The farm had made a good price and there was still some left of my grandfather's hoard, but in all it amounted to less than a twentieth of the value of Old Vine and the business Walter had built there.

"I couldn't see it go cheap to a stranger, could I?" Arthur asked, defensively.

I said, "Of course not. You did right, Arthur. None of this is your fault."

Not mine, either, though I was concerned, as a tool is concerned with a finished job. If Walter and I had never met . . . but it was no good thinking in that fashion. We had met, we had loved, and we had seen our love turned by a few words into something obscene and loathsome. We'd taken the blow in our different ways, I'd turned away from the God who could let such things be, I'd turned to work, to comfort, to marriage and childbearing, to making the best of a bad job. Walter had turned towards things of the mind and the spirit, and had come, perhaps naturally, to prefer a form of religion that was stark and simple, and which cut out all the offices of go-betweens. He'd once actually used the expression "wrestling with God." I thought at the time, and I still think, that the Church is in error in taking Walter's kind too seriously; for, for every one man who is capable of thus dealing directly with God, there are a thousand who prefer to use the intermediaries, the priests and the pardoners. To people of Walter's kind the Church should behave as I behaved to my daughter, who showed a tendency to be left-handed; I gave her a light slap and said, "Do as your brother does." She tried, but she *was* left-handed and no trying could cure it, so I said, "Then be awkward if you must."

Walter went and hired himself a hovel in the Saltgate; we moved into Old Vine, and very strange it felt to be there again, mistress of the house. Because Arthur was new to the business and I had had at least the experience of helping my grandmother, he relied upon me a great deal in the early days. There were days when I was too busy to spare a thought for anything but practical matters; but I began to dread my bed. Bone weary as I was, I could not sleep and would lie for hours, with Arthur snoring peacefully beside me, and my mind would go over and over all that was past, and shrink in terror away from what might be to come. There was talk in the town now, rumours about meetings in Walter's home, with readings from the Bible, reports of incautious things he had said to this man and that. And there was one thing, small, but sinister to me; when the taxes were due Arthur was asked to show proof that he was the legal owner of the Old Vine; this was most unusual, for ordinarily they were only too ready to assume ownership and grab what was due.

Once I saw Walter, close to in the market place. He looked thin and poor and uncared for, my handsome young man who had come riding to Clevely on his glossy horse. I went home and said to Arthur:

"We must do something about Walter; he looks half starved."

"For that he must blame himself. He spends his money on Bibles and other forbidden books—or so I hear."

"Where do you hear such stories?" I asked in terror.

"The whole town buzzes," he said. "I'm afraid, Josiana, that with Walter it is now merely a matter of time. And for that reason we cannot have him here and feed him. That was what you had in mind, was it not?"

I could truthfully say that it was not so, that I had only thought to take or send Walter a good meal now and then. As soon as I said it Arthur showed his quality.

"It must be taken," he said, "since sending would involve another person whose tongue might wag. Put food in a basket and I will lay it on his step myself, under cover of darkness."

"Is the situation so dangerous?"

"It will be. And we want no part or lot in it."

Yet despite all the rumours and the town buzzing with tales, it was Walter himself who hastened on his doom. And all over what seemed such a small silly thing.

IX

On the road that led out of Baildon, through Clevely and Minsham and Flaxham and on to Bywater, there was a stone bridge over the river. It was old beyond reckoning. My grandmother Rancon, who had been learned in such matters, said that it had been made by the Romans and that there were stories of a lost road which they had also made, now overgrown and forgotten. She also said that for as long as she could remember the bridge had been in poor repair.

The September of 1496 was very wild and wet, with gales which ripped the thatch off houses and floods in many places. Twice during that month, Arthur, trying to get to Minsham to see to his farm, had been obliged to turn back because the bridge was under water. When the river went down almost half the bridge had been carried away. There remained a portion, seemingly safe, wide enough to take a pack horse. Arthur said:

"Now the Abbot will be obliged to repair it, for one side is unguarded and on a dark night a stranger on the road might walk into the water."

The bridge was the Abbey's responsibility because at that point the land on both sides of the river was Abbey property.

Nothing was done, however. People who used the road regularly grumbled, but they had no redress.

Early in November the Bishop of Bywater came to Baildon on his way to London. He was a sufferer from the stone and was unable to sit astride a horse and had to travel by litter. What remained of the stone bridge was not wide enough to accommodate him, and he was obliged to turn aside and cross the river higher up, at Marley. That added several tedious miles to his journey and he arrived in the Abbey at Baildon in a bad temper.

Next morning the Crier was out, bawling a proclamation; any man willing to work upon the bridge, so that it should be ready against his Lordship's return from London in six weeks' time, should have a pardon for all his sins.

It was a cunning and perhaps a necessary move, for business was good in the town and few men except the halt and the lame and the half-wits were unemployed that winter. And bridge building in

November is not work which the ordinary man would choose if he had a choice. As it was, a team was mustered in a short time, and put under the orders of a monk who was experienced in working with stone.

The next evening was one of those when Arthur was due to take Walter some food, and when he appeared to have forgotten it I reminded him gently and he said:

"I'm sorry, Josiana, I've finished with Walter, and so must you."

"What has he done now?"

"Run mad. He went along to the bridge and told the men to work for pay if they liked, but not to be deceived by promises of pardons. Only God could forgive sins, he said. And much else. You know how he talks. . . ."

"The monk will report him if nobody else does," I said.

"I fear so. The wonder is that he has escaped notice so long. This nobody could overlook."

Because I longed to hear my inmost fear contradicted I said: "What will happen now?"

"What happens to heretics everywhere," Arthur said.

My stomach began to heave and I had to run from the room.

Even at this point Walter's story could not be plain and straightforward like anyone else's. He was still at liberty on the next day, and again he went to the bridge. By that time the men knew what they had undertaken, one had been drowned, one had his foot crushed under a stone block; they were in ill-humour, so they turned on Walter in anger and threw stones at him and accused him of ill-wishing the work. Through all the awful time that followed, amongst the common people the charge of witchcraft ran alongside that of heresy. In many people's minds they were akin, both being of the Devil. . . .

When I heard that Walter had been taken and lodged in the Abbey, there to await trial before the Bishop on his return, I fell to the ground senseless and lay like the dead for two hours. That and the fact that my stomach threw up everything I ate convinced Arthur that I was pregnant again. Another boy, he said, like somebody ordering a joint, beef or mutton, at the butcher's, another boy so that there would be one to see to the business and one to look after the Minsham farm in days to come. I think he was trying, poor Arthur, to distract my mind, and to cheer his own, for he, too, had been fond of Walter, in his way.

The poor old ailing Bishop came back to Baildon in mid-December; the bridge was fit to carry him over; he wanted nothing but to get back to his home for Christmas. They said later that he spent four hours trying to reason with Walter and that Walter *preached* to him. That was a private affair, an attempt to avoid the routine examination. Oh, they gave him every chance. But he was obdurate, and on the eighteenth of the month there was a full enquiry in the Guildhall.

I did not attend, being in no state to go anywhere; but Arthur did; and came home, good man that he is, to try to cheer me with a rueful joke. "I'd best go work on that bridge a day or two myself," he said, "for I have perjured myself. I swore on oath that I had never heard Walter express a heretical opinion. But plenty had, and he was the chief witness against himself."

I whispered, "It was good of you to try—and brave, too. Where is he now?"

"In the Bridewell. They found him guilty and handed him over to the secular arm. Now who can that be?" For someone was hammering on our door.

It was the Sheriff's man, to see me. He said that the Bishop was very much put out about this whole affair; there had never been a conviction for heresy in his diocese and he didn't want one now. So, since the convicted man had no family, no wife to plead with him, would I try? Would I visit him and try to persuade him to recant?

Arthur had doubts about my physical state; but this was hope and it strengthened me like wine. My stomach lay quiet and I was steady on my feet. All the way to the Bridewell, which stood in a muddy lane, a stone's throw from the Abbey's great gate, I planned how I'd plead, I'd say, "You loved me once, Walter; recant for the sake of the love I bear you. . . ."

Arthur came with me as far as the gaoler's room and he would have come further, but I stopped him.

"Perhaps if I talk to him alone, Arthur."

"Very well," he said. "Send for me if you need me. And you," he said, turning to the gaoler who stood by with a dim lantern, "carry that stool, so that my wife can be seated as she talks. She is far from well."

Walter lay in a little stone box, deathly cold, foul smelling. He wasn't fettered; he was free to come and take my hands in his.

He said, "Jenny—I always think of you by that name, you know—you shouldn't have come here. This is no place . . . And they'll say you aided and comforted me in my misdoings. *Which is not true.*" The last words were meant for the ears of the gaoler who was setting down the stool and the lantern.

I didn't speak until he had gone. When we were alone I said:

"Walter, they sent me. To beg you to recant. And I do beg you, for the sake of the love we once had for one another. Think what you like, do what you like, so long as it is safe and secret but please, please, Walter, I beg you, don't be stubborn now. They'll burn you, and that I just could not bear. I should go mad, Walter. I'm almost mad already. You're all that matters to me. I'm fond of Arthur, I love my children, but in these last days they've none of them seemed real to me. Only you. . . . Please, Walter, recant, and then go away if you must. Go back to Amsterdam where people think as you do, we'll send you money, we still, in truth, owe you a great deal . . ."

He said, "Dear Jenny, always so practical!" He had kept hold of my hands and his grip tightened. "Just for a moment look at it *my* way. Somebody must lead the way to freedom. I did work in secret —perhaps too long—but the time comes when truth must come into the open. What I said will soon be forgotten, but if I die for the truth, that will not be forgotten. And you're not to grieve, Jenny; it will be horrible, but it will soon be over."

I saw the hopelessness of my errand; the Bishop himself had failed to turn Walter, the threat of a horrible death had failed, too. And here was I, with no argument, with nothing to say except, "For my sake, Walter."

I said it and he answered me.

"Alive, what use am I to you, Jenny? Nothing but a reminder of old sorrow. Dead I may help to unshackle you, and your children, from the chains of superstition." His voice changed. "Sometimes I think that it was all planned, the blow that hurt us so sorely when it fell; that was God's way of calling me and shaping me for His own ends."

He threw up his head as he spoke, and in that foul narrow place it was as though he heard the voice of God and was blown upon by a fresh and fragrant wind.

"You mustn't grieve, Jenny," he said again.

"How can I not, loving you as I do?"

"This," he said, touching his chest lightly with his finger tips, "you must cease to love. We must love with our immortal souls which have no father save God Almighty." He took my hand again. "John Boreman has my Bible; I'd like you to have it. Study it well, Jenny, for the truth is there, and the truth shall make you free, so that when the time comes, as it will, as it must, when the old things are done away with, you will be ready. The seed is planted, soon there will be a great harvest. I and those like me will not have died in vain."

But it seemed to me at that moment that Christ Himself had died in vain, if His object had been the redemption of the world; and He had died in despair, crying His dreadful question, "My God, why hast Thou forsaken me?" Would Walter, likewise, when it was too late, know himself forsaken?

I began to weep and say things without forming them in my mind first. I begged him to recant and give himself time to think things over again, to try to reconcile himself with this world. If he married, I said, he would grow fond of his wife, if he had children he would love them and then his views would change. I even said, "The Bishop's reluctance to carry out the sentence, Walter, mightn't that in itself be a sign that God wants you to live?" He said no, that was all part of the wiliness of the Churchmen and also part of the test of his faith. "And so is this," he cried, moved by my distress. "If they had schemed for a thousand years they couldn't have found a stronger temptation. Your tears . . . more than any argument . . ."

"You do love me," I managed to blurt out.

He said, "Yes. Now I can own to it. I clapped a mask on my face that day, the mask of brotherly love, and I hid behind it. But nothing was changed *here*." He struck himself on the chest. "I was *glad* when Arthur said he couldn't have a heretic in his house. And that is how I know that I was chosen by God to bear witness to the truth—because the fire that finally consumes me and sets me free of this flesh will be as nothing to the fire that has burned in me all these years."

I cried, "So I am to blame for it all . . ." and never heard his answer. One of my fits came on me, and when I was sensible again I was in my own bed.

Tomorrow morning, at ten o'clock, they will burn Walter, just outside the Abbey Gate, on the very spot where our grandmother clapped her hands to her face and cried, "Oh no!" I know now what she meant to write, because she had seen it all. "On no account must you come back to Baildon," she would have written; but then, if she believed that she had been given a glimpse into the future, the warning would have been wasted. Because it was bound to happen.

I don't understand any of it. I'm here on my knees in an attitude of prayer, but I'm praying either to nothing or to something as hard and unforgiving and terrible as my grandfather Greenwood.

I only know that there I was, on a sunny summer day, wielding a scythe, and singing, and there was Walter, riding in to buy wool. How did it end in this?

Now the candles are beginning to burn low; soon, one by one they will fail. For all my fur-lined cloak I can feel the cold creeping in. That is where we all come to—the darkness and the cold of the grave; but the dead don't know how dark and cold it is. I do, for I am still alive. . . .

Interlude

There had never before been a burning for heresy in Baildon—though there were more to come—so, despite the great cold, Walter Rancon's execution was well attended. Save for the actual bridge builders, who in any case suspected more than unorthodoxy, the spectators' attitude was one of sorrowful curiosity and lacked vindictiveness. Walter was, after all, a Baildon man, the Bishop and the Sheriff both in a sense "foreigners."

The sentence was carried out in an atmosphere of unwillingness, and of amateur improvisation. The iron hardness of the frozen ground made it impossible to drive in a stake, so it was decided to use a barrel. The martyr's end was thus deprived of its small dignity; to die at the stake for one's beliefs is subtly different and less ridiculous than dying in a barrel.

After the faggots were placed and the men with torches had taken their position, the Bishop of Bywater, seeming to wilt under the weight of his robes, moved with a feeble step to the open space between the condemned man and the crowd, and in an astonishingly firm and resonant voice offered him a last chance to recant. When Walter, in equally clear tones, refused, saying, "I die for what I know to be the truth, and I know that by God's mercy I do not die in vain," those at the forefront of the crowd could see that of the two his Lordship was the more distressed. He stepped back weeping.

The torches were applied to the wood in four different places and the flames leapt, orange and scarlet in the grey air.

And then Walter Rancon was denied even the poor distinction of being, at his own martyrdom, the centre of attention. Mistress Kentwoode, his kinswoman, whose heretical leanings had hitherto been most cunningly concealed, broke from the crowd and ran forward. Those who were nearest, or had the sharpest hearing, reported that as she ran she cried, "We will be together," or "We will go together."

Her husband, poor man, ran after her and actually had her by the cloak, but it stayed in his hands while she ran forward, straight into the heat of the fire, her arms outstretched as a woman would run to greet her lover, after long absence.

For many years the scene was remembered, in the main as a warning. If Walter had succeeded in persuading anyone else in Baildon to adopt his particular form of heresy, there was no evidence of it. Even the Bishop of Bywater, who had been so anxious for Walter to recant, owned to himself that perhaps things had turned out for the best. There were no other cases for some years.

Time moved on. Arthur Kentwoode, at first distraught, composed himself, and finding, in his busy life, two small children too much to manage, remarried. He lived just long enough to see the heretical notion of his wife and her cousin, if not fully accepted, well on the way to be, for the new King, Henry VIII, under the spell of a pretty face, had broken with Rome.

This move was, on the whole, popular with the townspeople of Baildon; they had always grudged paying Peter's Pence; and the next event—the Dissolution of the Monasteries—was even more welcome. The services which the monks had rendered, the alms they had provided were all forgotten, only their extortions and the rumours of scandal remembered. And the destruction of the great buildings meant pickings for everyone. The lead from the roofs, the gold and silver vessels, the treasures, the hangings and the furnishings went, of course, to the King; the vast estates were sold, or in some cases given away to country gentlemen who embraced Protestantism with the acres; what was left was virtually a stone quarry from which the humblest man with a wheelbarrow could remove what he wanted. There was more building in Baildon during the years immediately after 1539 than at any other time. The Old Vine, which once stood alone, now had neighbours on both sides of the road, and the new houses were built in less haphazard fashion; style and design had crept into domestic architecture.

Compared with its neighbours the house looked very old, so that part of its name was comprehensible. But why Vine? The monks' old vineyard had been long forgotten, and their newer one had vanished.

Bluff Henry died in his turn and during the brief reign of his sickly son the beliefs for which Walter Rancon had died were compulsory, and only a few people, old, or contrary, clung to the old ways. For them there was a short sunset glow during the reign of Mary who, all unwittingly, had done Catholicism a bad turn by associating it with Spanish domination and the fear of the Inquisition. So when, with Elizabeth's accession, the seesaw swung again, it was weighted in favour of the new ways, for could one be true loyal English without being Protestant too? To be Catholic—it was understood—was to be against Elizabeth and for Mary Queen of Scots, against the English seamen and for Philip of Spain, against freedom and for the Inquisition.

It was in such a mental climate that Josiana's son Henry Kentwoode, a hale old man in his early seventies, spent his declining years. He was cheered by the almost constant companionship of his pretty and engaging little granddaughter, Elizabeth.

Part Two

ELIZABETH KENTWOODE'S TALE

Circa 1565

I

When I was almost, not quite, eight years old, a travelling painter, a Dutchman, called at our house and begged to be allowed to paint our portraits. My grandfather, who was very softhearted about beggars or tinkers or anyone on the road for a living, asked the man in and gave him food and said he would like to have a picture of the whole family. "There are three generations of us," he said.

But there were difficulties. One was that the painter, who had to hump his gear from place to place, carried only small pieces of canvas, the biggest only eighteen inches by twelve; the second was that it happened to be shearing time and my father had flocks at Minsham and at Horringer; he said, bitterly, that he was accustomed to being in two places at once, but he couldn't be in three; the third was that my mother was suffering from her seasonal nettle rash and it would be three weeks before her face was its normal size and colour; and the fourth was that nothing could persuade my two small brothers to stay in one position long enough for the man to catch a likeness. So in the end my grandfather said in his kindly, settle-it-easy way:

"Never mind. You make a good likeness of Elizabeth."

It hangs on the wall now, exactly where he hung it with his own hands. He was delighted with it and even my mother, somewhat grudgingly, agreed that there was a likeness. It shows my head and just the tops of my shoulders, enough to show that my blue gown was of velvet, not of Baildon cloth or Kersey. I am wearing the stiffly starched ruff of which I was so very proud; it comes down to a point on my chest, leaving my neck bare, and there was a time when I greatly regretted that I had not then been given my beautiful blue beads. On my head I wear a little cap made of pale lace, crisscrossed with strips of velvet. And between the cap and my ruff there is my face.

Such a true likeness, they said. I wonder. It has such an innocent look. You would swear that no ugly, crafty, angry thought ever lived behind those wide blue eyes, that no cruel word ever issued from those sweetly curved, pink lips. Even my wiry copper-coloured hair must have been smoothed down for the occasion; it waves away under the edges of the little cap in such a meek and demure way.

The man who painted it became very famous later on, and now and again someone knowledgeable expresses surprise that a piece of his early work should hang on the wall of a merchant's house in a little Suffolk town. I remember my grandfather saying to him:

"Make your mark, man."

Our own mark was a black V; it was stamped on every bale of wool, on every roll of cloth, branded on every pack pony, marked on every sheep.

The painter said, modestly, "Your mark, master, has value; mine has none." But, wishing to oblige, he dipped his brush, which he had wiped clean, and painted in the lower right-hand corner an M and a G interlinked.

So it was finished. Portrait of Elizabeth Kentwoode. What a sweet little girl!

I thought so too, at the time. I thought I was perfect and that my grandfather who indulged me was in the right, my mother who criticised me, all wrong. The child was never born who could seriously sit down and think—My mother says I am bad-tempered and a liar, and spiteful to my small brothers, therefore I must be. It was so much easier to run to my grandfather and say, "My mother is angry with me again," and give him, not a completely untruthful account of what had happened, but a carefully biased one and then bask in the sympathy which he never failed to show. I think he knew how I felt about my brothers, particularly about Harry, the elder of the two, because when he was a little boy himself his mother had died and his father had married again. The new wife soon had a son of her own and my grandfather's young nose had been put out of joint—just as mine had been, with Harry's birth. He'd hated his situation so much that when he was twelve he'd run away to sea and stayed away for twenty-five years.

He told me that he knew now that his stepmother had not been wholly to blame. "I was as bad as a boy could be, and there came a day when there was nothing my poor father could do except give me a hiding. So then I ran away and went to sea and I very soon learned what a *real* hiding was."

"Why didn't you come home, then?" I asked.

"Well," he said, "for one thing, child, it's far easier to get onto a ship than off it—one day I must take you down to Bywater and show you the sea and some ships—and for another thing there was pride to consider. I'd vowed to myself that I wouldn't come home until I'd made my fortune. I planned to come home with jewels in my ears and on my fingers, and with my pockets sagging with gold. I'd *show* them, I thought."

(It was a feeling that I understood only too well. I had already experienced it when my mother rated me. One day I'd *show* her!)

"And did you?" I asked. "Show them, I mean."

"No," he said. "No." He laughed a little. "I came home very much as I'd left, with the clothes I stood up in. I'd made money, but I'd spent it all—not on jewels, mark you. And I had worked, like a slave, but never for myself."

"Then why did you come home?"

"I was homesick," he said simply. "In a way I'd been homesick for twenty-five years. . . . But my father sent for me, you see. My half brother died and my father was getting old, he wanted me to come home and help with the business."

I thought this over. My mother often slapped me, but she had never beaten me—though she threatened it often enough.

"I wouldn't have come back, not if I'd been beaten," I said.

"Dear child, within a week I realised how light my father's hand had been. He'd beaten me a little because I was bad; my shipmates beat me often, just because I was *there*. But there I was, and with all the world to see, and, as I said, with my pride to consider. So I stayed away until I was sent for."

"How did he find you?" I asked, when I had thought this over. Though I had never seen the sea I pictured it in my mind, like a horse pond but huge, going as far as you could see in all directions, and then on and on, the way the fields did in the country; and I could picture too, my grandfather, in a ship, in the middle of all that water.

He laughed. "He had men on the lookout for me—over half the

world in the end. It was at Tenerife in the Canaries they caught up with me. 'Have you one Henry Kentwoode aboard?' they asked. Our captain thought the law was on my heels. A ship out from Plymouth had left a message that I was to be enquired for, a good six months earlier. All in all it was two years between when he started to hunt for me and the finding."

"So you did show him, didn't you?"

"How do you mean?"

I knew what I meant, but it was a little difficult to put into words.

"Well, he wanted you back, and then had to wait so long. Perhaps all the time he thought you were angry still and wouldn't come."

"Oh," he said, "I'd got over being angry long before that—before I got down to Bywater, I reckon. That's one thing I can tell you, Elizabeth, because I learned it myself, the hard way, when you do things in anger you're more like to hurt yourself than anybody else—in the long run."

He spoke as though he regretted having run away and stayed away so long; but I was glad he had, for it was that which made him different, I thought. If he'd stayed at home he might have been as dull as my father, who never thought about anything except the business and never spoke of anything except matters concerning it. You would have thought that just on one day he'd had just one single moment of absent-mindedness, and during it gone out and fitted himself up with a wife and family. My mother suited him exactly; her devotion was to the house and my young brothers, to seeing that the table was well spread but no crumb wasted, to seeing that holes were patched and weak places darned over, windows washed, moths and spiders chased away. Life without my grandfather would have been too dull to be borne.

I was the eldest of our family; between me and Harry there had been three children who had died very young. I was too old to spend all my time with the babies and yet not old enough to be left to my own resources; I therefore fell naturally into my grandfather's company. Even our paces matched, for he had had, some time before I was born, a slight stroke, which had left him lame in one leg, so he walked with a great blackthorn stick; and from as far back as I can remember we had walked together, his great brown hand holding my small one.

I never annoyed him for the simple reason that he never

demanded anything of me that I didn't want to do, and never
denied me anything that it was in his power to give. He'd answer
any question I asked him as well as he could and he was always
willing to tell me stories. My mother often said that he spoiled me
and would ruin me and make me good-for-nothing, and I hated
her when she said such things. He would soothe her down, saying
you were only young once, saying little girls so soon grew into
women who had to be busy all the time, saying that when Harry
was of an age to be spoiled no doubt she would spoil him, young
Arthur too, in time. Once he said:

"Children can do with a bit of spoiling, Margaret. I'd have been
a better boy if I'd been spoiled a little."

On the other hand he was fair, and always admonishing me to
be civil and obedient and affectionate to my mother; to have a
mother was a blessing, he said, a blessing he'd missed.

"Why? What happened to your mother?"

"She died young," he said.

I thought that was a curious thing to say. No mother was young,
the two words simply didn't fit together. Perhaps it was because he
was so old—much older than most children's grandfathers—that
anyone under fifty seemed young to him. He'd even call my father
"Boy" at times.

I look back now and it always seems to have been summer, with
the sun shining; or very rarely, an exciting winter day, with snow
falling, or the roads so frozen that the pack ponies could not go
out. In summer Grandfather and I would walk a little way into the
country and find wild flowers or blackberries; or we would go into
the town and do the household errands, which I loved to do because the people in the shops or at the stalls knew that the way to
please him was to praise me—"Oh, the pretty little maid," they'd
say, or, "How much for one of those sunny curls?" or even comment upon how fast I grew as though that were a virtue. Such a
remark pleased me less, for it chimed with my mother's constant
nagging that I was a big girl, big enough to look after the babies
for an hour, big enough to learn to sew and help with the mending.
I had no desire to grow up. I was happy as I was.

On fine days, when we walked into the town, we often turned
aside into the place where the Abbey had once stood. Having
walked so far my grandfather would welcome the chance to sit down

on one of the broken walls. When I was very small I, too, was glad
to sit down, but by the time I was seven I was less easily wearied
and would move about amongst the ruins, only willing to sit still
if he began to tell me a story. Often, of course, in those surroundings he would speak of the Abbey as it had been; and the words he
spoke and my own imagination would combine to give me a picture of a wonderful place, of a church in the centre, for instance,
that was as much larger than the still existing one of St. Mary's as a
house is larger than a shed, of St. Egbert's tomb, all aglitter with
jewels, of an altar that was furnished with gold candlesticks and
vessels, and of a screen that was of solid gold with twelve pictures
laid upon it in colour, a miracle of the goldsmith's art.

Now all gone, and the walls and the towers brought down to
heaps of rubble and stretches of wall upon which an old man and a
child could sit, to little enclosures in which certain privileged people kept geese or goats.

Always, when he spoke of the vanished glory, my grandfather's
voice would take on a sad tone; but even then he would put in,
here and there, one of his just remarks.

"Mind, I don't say it all went into the King's pocket. He built
some good ships and they were sorely needed at the time."

Or, "It wasn't all wasted. There's many a good house in Baildon
that would never have been built but for the free stone. That was
a sight, child. People who had donkeys would load up and go off
with the panniers breaking; real poor people'd bring a bit of sail-
cloth and heap stone on it and drag it away."

I asked if our house was built of Abbey stone.

"No. We didn't need it. Whoever built Old Vine built it good
and strong and big enough for one family's needs. But our stables
are Abbey stuff. They were wattle and daub before. And once the
thing was done and the flint there for the taking away . . ." His
voice trailed off, and he added as though talking to himself, not to
me, "It'd have looked odd to hold back, just then."

I knew, without knowing how I knew it, that he hadn't much
enjoyed the rebuilding of our stables.

When he had no story to tell I used to hunt about for pieces
of coloured glass which had once—he said—been in the Abbey
windows. I'd rub off the dirt and hold them to the sun, deciding
that this, no, this, or this was my favourite colour, ruby red,
hyacinth blue, leaf green or sunset yellow. My mother said picking

up bits of broken glass was a silly pastime and dangerous besides, since I might cut myself. But that didn't stop me and at home I had a boxful.

One day, in a deep rut which a cart laden with stone had made in the ground, I found a piece that was different, bigger than any I had ever found before, and instead of being flat and thin, thick and curved. Against the light it was a dark, most vivid green and it was flecked with gold, tiny smears of gold brushed off onto my fingers along with the dirt. I took it back to my grandfather and held it out, saying, "Look."

"Where did you find it?" he asked me. I showed him the place and he began grubbing in the soil with the end of his stick. Soon we unearthed another piece, even larger and with a thick, out-turned edge, like the rim of a bowl, and after that a third piece. We fitted them together and they made an almost whole bowl which must have been very beautiful when it was complete. We hunted for a long time for another piece, but failed to find it.

"Whoever smashed that was a fool," my grandfather said. "There're scores of Johnny-come-latelys who'd give good money to eat their porridge out of a Venetian glass bowl even if it had been an aspersorium."

If he used a word which meant nothing to me during the full flood of a story I would let it go, not wishing to interrupt, but now I asked:

"What's that?"

"A bowl," he said, "used for holding holy water." He gave me one of his serious looks and sighed. "Sometimes I feel that I'm failing in my duty to you, Elizabeth. But it's difficult, the way things are."

"What things?"

He didn't answer that; he asked:

"How old are you now, exactly?"

"I shall be eight on the twenty-third of June."

"St. John's Eve. Well, that's not so far ahead. After that, maybe . . . We'll see."

"Are you thinking about my present?"

"I wasn't, just then. But I will." He spoke more cheerfully. "Have you something in mind?"

"I want a string of blue beads, please," I said promptly.

He smiled. "Well, knowing exactly what you want is halfway to getting it."

That from him was as good as a promise, I knew. I could safely leave that topic and return to the one in hand.

"These pieces won't go in my box," I said, "but they're too pretty to throw away again, aren't they?"

"Much too pretty. I'll keep them for you, shall I?"

It was unlikely that I should have been able to get them into the house unobserved, so I was willing to let him have them for a time. But I still regarded them as mine; after all I had found the first piece.

Soon after that the painter came and did my picture, and a few days after it was finished was my birthday, and my grandfather gave me a string of the most beautiful beads I ever saw. When I had pictured a string of blue beads I had no notion of anything so wonderful. They weren't just blue, in places the colour shaded into purple, in others into green, and where the blue was blue it was such a deep rich colour that there was nothing to which one could liken it. My grandfather tried; slipping them over my head he said:

"They match your eyes." It was a nice thing to say, but it wasn't true; no eyes could be so beautiful.

The trouble was that when they were around my neck I couldn't see them except when I looked in the glass, and Mother didn't like me to look in the glass too much; so she said some sharp things about what with having my picture painted, and being given such a present, I was in danger of becoming vain and frivolous.

"And to me they look valuable," she said, as though that were a fault.

"They're lapis lazuli," my grandfather said.

"For a child of eight, who will break the string in a week, or put them down somewhere and forget!" That was unjust, for I was, even then, extremely careful with my possessions. But the next thing she said was worse—they must be worn only on special occasions.

I cast a pleading look at my grandfather, and he, as always, came to my aid.

"Oh, let her wear them, Margaret. In Cath . . . In Spain and Italy all children and most donkeys even wear a string of blue beads. They're held to be a protection against evil. Mary's own colour," he said.

"Sheer superstition," Mother said. "And not a thing to say aloud these days may I remind you."

"I know," he said. "But so is the green bough at Christmas, and that you always have."

The beads stayed round my neck and were a comfort to me later in the day when Mother gave me one of her talks. It was so like her. In the morning I was eight, too young to be trusted with a string of beads; in the afternoon I was "a great girl of eight," and it was time I mended my ways, became responsible, sensible and helpful. In future I was to spend more time learning to cook and to sew and tending Harry and Arthur. What a dismal outlook. But for the beads I should have wished to be seven again.

II

A week or two after my birthday, on a hot Wednesday morning, my grandfather and I went out to do the marketing. Betty, the maid, came with us to carry the basket. Butter was one of the things we had to buy, and it being such a hot morning we left it until last. While we stood by the stall, and I was admiring the sight of yellow butter laid out on cabbage leaves that had been sprinkled with water, all silvery drops, a man came up and in a peculiar sly way, without speaking, laid hold of my grandfather's sleeve. A friend or a business acquaintance would not have had such a secret look, a servant or a beggar would not have made so bold, so I looked at the man with curiosity and waited with interest to hear his first word. But as soon as my grandfather turned and faced him, instead of asking what he wanted, he looked down at me and said:

"You and Betty go and take your pick from the gingerbread stall. You can have two pieces each and I'll be with you before they are eaten."

I felt that we were being got out of the way. Also I was offended because he gave the money for the gingerbread to Betty, which was an insult to me after I'd gone to such pains to learn the value of coins and how to take the price you had to pay from the worth of the coin you proffered, so that you knew what change to expect. It was the first time that my grandfather had been careless of my feelings in just that way and I resented it.

So I dragged my feet as we went to the stall, and once there refused to eat, though the gingerbread was fresh and fragrant and my mouth watered for it.

"I've got a loose tooth," I said.

That was true, but I'd had it loose for a week, and others before it, I was perfectly accustomed to eating on one side of my mouth. Betty began to gobble and I stood and sulked, watching my grandfather and the man who had now drawn away from the butter stall and stood a little apart from everyone else.

I'd never seen the man before. There was nothing remarkable about him; he was fairly old, rather small, rather shabby, but not dressed like a servant. I gathered that he was speaking quietly, for my grandfather, who was a fine tall man, leaned on his stick, bringing his head down to hear better. The stranger did not speak long, but he spoke very earnestly. Then my grandfather nodded and came to join us.

"Who was that man?" I asked.

"A servant."

"Then he should learn how to approach his betters," I said. My voice startled me, it sounded so like my mother's. It startled my grandfather too and he gave me a sharp look.

"Plucking you by the sleeve, like that," I explained.

"Did he so? Well, his message was urgent. We must forgive him."

He said no more and I judged it unwise to ask what the message was. Amiable and just and mild as my grandfather was and much as he indulged me, he had a way of letting his will be known, often without wording it. So it was not until we were all at the dinner table that I learned anything further.

"John Arbour," my grandfather said, "has asked me to sup with him this evening."

"John Arbour, Father. He lives at Marley. How did he imagine you could travel so far just to sup with him?"

"He is staying overnight at the *Hawk in Hand*, and it is there that we shall sup."

"At an inn!" said my mother in a horrified voice. "And he married to my cousin twice removed. Have we no empty bed? Why didn't you bring him here?"

"I didn't see him, Margaret. His servant brought the message to me in the market."

"Then one of ours can carry him a message in return. He will sup here. I have a saddle of mutton with samphire, and a hare pasty, good enough for anyone."

"That nobody doubts, my dear. But John brought in his own supper, a sucking pig which Doll Webster will cook. And . . . and he has other guests, among them Chris Hatton."

"Then there's no more to be said. I will not entertain Chris Hatton and it passes my understanding why John Arbour, decent man that he is, should have any doings with that gambling heathen." She made it very plain that my grandfather's willingness to sup in such company was also beyond her understanding.

"Chris Hatton may gamble," my grandfather said, "but he always pays his debts."

"*And* his fines for absenting himself from church on Sundays," said my mother.

My father changed the subject.

"You'd be wise to take a man to lean on, Father."

"I'll do that. Which one?"

"Jack Plant, I think, is likeliest to wait about an inn yard and stay sober."

"What we need is a coach," Mother said. "How useful it would be on such an occasion! But I suppose we must wait till the blacksmith has one, or the chimney sweep."

Father said, "I wouldn't have one if the Vestry gave them away like Poor Relief. Great clumsy things, needing four horses and a driver and always breaking down. I'm told the Fennels' coach stuck fast in a miry patch in the road not long since and Lady Fennel, in all her finery, had no choice but to ride home on one of the horses, with no saddle and the reins twelve feet long."

Their attention had been distracted; and they had believed the story about the servant and the invitation. But they hadn't seen the man. I had, and I was sure that he did not look like, nor act like, a servant. Also I had noticed that slight hesitation before my grandfather named Chris Hatton and so ended all my mother's plans for altering his plans. There was some mystery here. What my grandfather could have to hide I couldn't even guess at; I was only eight and I had no idea of what grown-up people might have to hide. What concerned me was the fact that *I* had also been shut out from whatever the secret was, and that was something new in the relationship between me and my grandfather. New and very distasteful.

Not long after that he did another thing which hurt me.

There was a man in a village a fairish way from Baildon who made pots, crocks and jugs and bowls and pipkins, and every summer his two thin brown boys, with a heavily loaded donkey, came round to sell their wares and to take orders. My grandfather had once told me that in the old times that particular pottery had been famous for making images—little brightly painted figures that were in every church and every home, and that being obliged to make plain things for use in kitchens had soured the potter's temper so the boys had a bad time if they went back with goods unsold.

This summer when they came round Mother bought a crock and two jugs, all reddish brown in colour, with yellow rims. I stood in our big doorway and watched the boys drag the donkey along to the next house. As always I noticed their feet; they had no shoes, and the soles of their feet had a thick polished layer of something like horn and their nails curved over and downwards, like a dog's claws.

As I stood there my grandfather came out of the door on what we called the old side of the house and into the passage, and, without speaking to me at all, hurried after the boys. Without thinking I fell in beside him and for once he did not seem to welcome me.

"I'm not going anywhere, Elizabeth. I just want a word with those boys."

Again I was conscious of his unvoiced wish, so I stopped.

"You go and get the baskets," he said, "and I'll be back in just a minute to pick the raspberries."

He set off, faster than he usually walked, digging his stick into the ground ahead of him and heaving himself along. I ran across the road and squeezed myself through a gap in Mrs. Clipstone's hedge. Even as I did it I could hardly believe that I was doing it, it was such a brave thing to do. Mrs. Clipstone had a son who was an idiot and fearful to look at. Hers was one of the new houses, but it didn't seem new because all in front of it there was a tangled shrubbery, people said it was to stop folks from looking in at her window. I crept along amongst the dusty leaves until I was opposite the gate of the house on our side of the road where the boys had stopped. I was in time to hear my grandfather say:

". . . white, glazed inside and out and with these set into it." And he held out to the thin brown boy the three pieces of gold-speckled glass which we had found amongst the ruins of the Abbey.

"That'd be a job after me dad's own heart, sir," the boy said. "He love anything fancy."

"When would it be ready?"

The boy screwed up his face, thinking hard.

"That ain't easy to say; depend on how we unload. We might hev to go as far as Kelvedon. If we do we'd be home about the middle of September, then, if you wanted it special, me dad'd do it and I'd bring it back. About Michaelmas."

"That would do very well. And when it is done," my grandfather sucked in his cheeks as he did some hard thinking, "take it to Mrs. Webster, at the *Hawk in Hand*. It was a bowl she cherished. Some pieces were thrown away, but I thought that if your father *could* work what was left into a new bowl it would be a present that would please her. It will be a special job and I don't know what he will charge, but take this now and if there is more to pay, I'll arrange with Mrs. Webster to give it to you when you bring the bowl."

He must have given the boy a good sum of money, for he almost pulled his forelock out by the roots as he took it.

I was at once mystified and shocked and angered. Lie upon lie upon lie! The only other time when I had dimly suspected that he wasn't speaking the truth, it was only a suspicion, I had no proof. The man in the market, despite all appearances, could have been a servant, and Chris Hatton, despite that little hesitation, might have been a guest at John Arbour's supper table. But here were lies that I knew were lies. Mrs. Webster's cherished bowl! Those pieces of glass were mine. Why should he lie? I lied, so did Betty and all the other servants; we had to, to protect ourselves. There was no such excuse for him; he was master in his own house. Why hadn't he stood at his own door and given the boy his order? Was it because he realised that the pieces of glass were rightly mine? But he must have known that I'd have given them to him if he had asked. Why Mrs. Webster?

In all my previous moments of misery or bewilderment, for as long as I could remember, I had had him to turn to. This—unless I were prepared to own that I had sneaked out and spied upon him —I must not mention.

We picked raspberries together in an unusual silence. I wanted to cry to him across the loaded, sweet-smelling canes, "Why do you have secrets from me? Why don't you trust me?"

III

I always thought of the year as an up and down curve, with Christmas in a hollow at the bottom and the Lammas Fair at the top. The bowl had been given to the potter's boy just before the top of the year, and as we went downhill again towards Christmas some of the smart and sting had worn off, though I had not forgotten, nor ever should. The weather was turning colder and it grew dark early.

One evening I was sitting sulkily in the parlour with my parents at a time when, in former winters, I would have been in the office with my grandfather. Mother had kept her threat and I was slowly and painfully hemming round a patch in a shift. Mother herself was stitching away at my new winter gown and my father, who had not long been in the house, was half dozing in the fire's warmth. We heard the bell of the great door ring and Father jerked awake saying:

"Who can that be at this hour?"

Within two minutes Betty was in the doorway saying that there was a man asking for Mr. Kentwoode. My father buttoned his doublet, my mother glanced round to see that the room was tidy and then said:

"Bring him in."

The man who entered was the man who had taken my grandfather by the sleeve on that summer morning. When he saw Father he looked more dumbfounded than I ever saw anybody look, as though he had gone to feed a calf and found a bull in the stall. He pulled himself together quite quickly and said:

"I'm sorry, sir. It's the other Mr. Kentwoode I must speak to."

"If it's a matter of business . . ." Father began.

"Oh no. Nothing to do with business. And I was told most particular to see the elder Mr. Kentwoode. I'm sorry, sir, that I didn't make myself plain. Mr. Kentwoode has a name for being very charitable. Besides, he knows the family."

His aim being to get to my grandfather, he was doing his best to defeat himself; Father was not charitable and often deplored the fact that Grandfather was. He asked briskly:

"What family?"

"A poor woman, sir, left a widow with several children, in sore straits."

"What name, man? What name?"

"The widow? Oh, Tomkin, sir, Tomkin."

"What parish?"

The man hesitated for half a breath and then said:

"Nettleton."

"My oath!" Father said. "Has it come to this? Not enough that we must care for all the poor and afflicted and idle of our own parish but must be cadged from at a distance of ten miles. Let your Widow Tomkin apply to her own Vestry for Poor Relief."

The man said, with a little show of spirit, "Sir, I am not asking *you*. Mr. Kentwoode might think otherwise."

"My father is an old man who goes to bed early. I am not disturbing him on behalf of the Nettleton poor. This is the kind of thing that happens when a man gets a name for putting his hand in his pouch."

"I must seek another occasion, then," the man said. It was plain enough that he wished to leave.

"Not so fast," Father said. "I'm waiting to hear why a widow doesn't ask her own parish for relief."

"She isn't of Nettleton parish, so has no claim."

"Then let her go to her own parish."

"That is near Yarmouth and she has a babe in arms and two children so small that they could never make the journey, especially now when they are weak with hunger. That was why we hoped . . ."

Mother stood up and interrupted, saying that she didn't like to hear of children being hungry. She'd give him a jar of mutton broth and some cold dumplings. Father began explaining that he wasn't in favour of children being hungry either, but genuine cases were all taken care of by the Poor Rates and that he paid these in three parishes. I slipped out of the room behind Mother. Mischief had got into me and I thought it would be interesting to see my grandfather and the man brought face to face under my father's eye. I went into the office and said:

"There's a man in the parlour asking to see you."

"What man?"

"I don't know. He asked for you."

He reached for his stick and stood up. We went across the passage and into the parlour where Father was still explaining about Poor Rates and the law as it applied to paupers.

I was sorry that I couldn't get into a position to watch both faces at once. For the first second or so I could only see that of the stranger, whose cheek twitched. He said quickly:

"It's about the Widow Tomkin, sir."

"Ah yes, poor soul," said my grandfather in his ordinary voice. I'd edged farther into the room by then and could see his face, which looked ordinary too, except that his eyes, usually grey, had gone dark.

My father said, "You can't legislate for hard cases. The Poor Rate is iniquitous high and if you give to everyone who asks, you might stand at the door and give your nose away for a whistle. There're plenty who would take it."

"My dear boy, I'm not so easy a mark as you suppose. I know something of this case, and I shall know more before I part with a penny, never fear. Will you come this way?"

My mother came bustling in with her contribution for Widow Tomkin and my grandfather, when he saw her purpose, said, in a voice I'd never heard him use to her before, "God bless you, Margaret." Then they were gone. I intended to go too, but I had to leave my work neatly. While I was folding it my father said:

"My dear woman, they don't want food. They don't want work. All they want is good coined money to take to the alehouse."

I said, "I will go to bed now. Good night, Mother. Good night, Father." I made my little bob to each and escaped.

Ours was rather a strange house, cut into two parts by the wide passage which the ponies used. One side was called old and one new. The parlour and the room where my parents slept, and the room where Harry and Arthur were, were on the new side; the room which I shared with Betty was on the old side, and the stairs ran up from just outside the office door. I stopped there, and with very good reason; I was lighting my candle from the one that stood there on a little shelf. I listened as hard as I could, but the door was closed and they were speaking very softly and I was unable to distinguish one word from another. Their talk was brief. At the first twitch of the latch of the door I went scuttling up the stairs and was out of sight, but not of hearing, by the time they left the office for the little passage that would take them into the large one. I heard my grandfather say in a grave and solemn voice:

"Rest assured, I shall do what I can."

And suddenly I found myself believing in the Widow Tomkin. It was astonishing how, once given a firm peg upon which to hang belief, everything else fell into place. She was one of my grand-father's secret charity cases and he hadn't wanted my father to know anything about it. The man who seemed so mysterious was prob-ably a relative of hers, or a neighbour, and he'd begged for her in the summer and now again tonight, when my father's attitude had fully justified my grandfather's secretiveness. And the bowl? Yes, I could even work that in. When we picked up the pieces my grand-father had said that it had some value as a porringer, and perhaps he had arranged with Mrs. Webster to buy it and give the money to Widow Tomkin.

There I did pause, for it seemed a little awkward and round-about, since he could have given the widow the money he paid the potter's boy; still it was explainable, if the bowl was going to fetch a good price.

Having settled all this to my satisfaction I fell asleep.

In the morning, as soon as I woke, I realised that if my overnight thoughts were right and my grandfather was interested in Widow Tomkin's welfare, I deserved a word of thanks because but for me her messenger would have been sent away with some soup and cold dumplings and nothing more. As soon as the chance came I asked my grandfather:

"Would you have been sorry not to see the man who asked for you last night?"

"Well, yes," he said, less positively than my thanks-seeking mind would have liked. "Yes, I suppose I should."

"Father would have sent him off with a flea in his ear."

"I know, my dear. There are some matters upon which people do not see eye to eye."

"I'm glad I thought to come and tell you," I said.

He gave me the look and the smile I desired and put his hand on my shoulder.

"I'm grateful to you, Elizabeth," he said.

We hadn't finished with Widow Tomkin; she came up again as a topic of talk at the dinner table that day. My father said:

"I suppose you gave him money, which he took straight to the *Hawk in Hand.*"

My grandfather's eyes went dark again, but he spoke lightly.

"Why should he—if he were a rogue—walk so far, with the *Rose and Crown* so much nearer?"

Father said irritably, "Oh, what matter? *Rose and Crown* or *Hawk in Hand* or *Smiths' Arms*, the principle is the same. Haphazard charity leads to abuses. The man who pays his Poor Rate has done his duty; and anyone can look in the Beadle's book and see how the money was spent."

"Well, at least we can be certain that none of the Nettleton Beadle's money ever went to Widow Tomkin. But some of mine did. And as you say, it may have been wasted. I know what I'll do. To make amends I'll do that job on my clothes closet myself instead of calling in Tom Woodman as I planned to do."

"What job?" asked my mother, instantly alert at the suggestion of something being amiss with the house and she ignorant of it.

"Worm in the pegs," Grandfather said. "Also when it rains the damp comes in from the chimney. The other day when I took out my winter clothes they were all of a mould."

"Good gracious! You never told me. Did you air them off?"

"I did. I lit my fire and aired them well."

"You should have told me," Mother said.

"I believe that at the moment of discovery you were feeding young Arthur. But I made a note in my mind to call in Woodman before the weather worsened. Now, having been rash with my charity," he grinned at Father, "I'll do penance by hammering my thumbs."

My father looked up and said sharply, "Father!"

"What now, my boy?"

"Watch your words. There're ears pricked everywhere for the careless 'Holy Saints!' and 'By Our Lady!' To talk of penance at this moment is to invite a suspicion of Popery."

My grandfather said mildly, "I'm in my own house, in the bosom of my family, and if I let slip an old-fashioned word or two, what harm? And I still think that 'By Our Lady' has a pleasanter ring than the 'bloody' that has taken its place nowadays. Still, if you like it better, let us say, 'make amends' by hammering my thumbs."

"It isn't what I like," said my father, sticking to his point in his dull, dogged way. "It's the way things are now between the Queen and that French wanton, Mary Stuart. Everybody as nervous as a scalded cat and ready to pick on a blown straw. People in our position can't be too careful."

"And what do you mean by people in our position?"

Even more irritably Father said, "The damned priests get into the country somehow, don't they? That place in France manufactures them and exports them, as we do cloth. And somebody smuggles them in. People like us, who do business abroad and have pony trains going to and fro to the coast, are bound to be watched closely. And we *are* watched, let me tell you."

"Oh yes, I see. I suppose they think it would be *easy* to smuggle in a Jesuit disguised as a pack whacker, or out, smothered in a wool bale."

"That's the size of it exactly. So we have to be careful."

I had listened to this conversation as I listened to everything, but in the main it meant nothing to me. I did see, though, a chance to do something more interesting than hemming or minding the little ones. So, meekly, because I was in my mother's presence, I asked:

"May I help you, Grandfather? I could hand you the nails."

"Yes, you may. So long as you promise not to touch anything."

"Then I can't hand you the nails, can I?" I said, and waited for the laugh with which he always received any joke from me.

"Now that," said my mother, "is the sort of saucy back answer that I can't abide."

"She meant no harm, Margaret. It was good logic. *You* know what I meant, you imp; no touching of sharp tools."

If we had been alone I should have asked did he intend to use *blunt* nails. But I thought it wise to stay quiet.

It was always a pleasure to me to get into his room, to stare at and finger the things he had brought from faraway places. On the shelf over his fireplace there was a piece of coral, a lovely pink colour and shaped like a little branching tree. On either side of it was a great shell, lined with the same pink colour; when you held one of them to your ear you could hear a roaring which he said was the sound of the sea. On one wall, set in a frame and glassed over, was a beautiful fan, painted with flowers; its sticks were made of ivory, so finely carved that they looked like lace. Below it on a table was a head, cut out of black wood and almost life size. Its nose was wide and flat, its lips very thick. On the same table was a red flower which had once been alive, and then held in a well which turned everything to stone, which would have been hard to believe except that you could see that it had been a flower and could feel that it now was made of stone; and there was an oyster shell with a pearl in it, not a shining pale pearl like the ones in Mother's earbobs, just a bump in the shell, covered with the same many-coloured stuff as the lining of the shell. There was also a box containing a substance called tobacco which in some place which my grandfather had visited people put into pipes and set light to and drew the smoke into their mouths; he had tried it once and it had made him vomit, he said.

Grandfather's room was in the old part of the house, and all that part was built around an enormous chimney. The fireplace stuck out into the room; the space on one side of it held a great chest with brass handles, and the space on the other side had been made into a closet for clothes. The back of it, where the pegs were, was not plumb back against the wall because had it been the closet would have been so deep that you would have wanted an arm twice the ordinary length in order to get at the clothes.

I helped him to clear the closet, keeping a wary eye on the pegs as I did so; I hated garden worms and expected that those he mentioned to be much the same, brown and wriggly. I was at once relieved and surprised to see, when the pegs were empty, no signs of worms at all. I mentioned this.

"They're not earthworms," he explained. "They're too small to see, but they do great damage. And they spread, so we'll put these in the fire as soon as I get them down."

They made a fine blaze.

Then he began to remove the boards from the back of the closet, and when the first one came away a horrid stench came with it.

"Ah," he said, in a pleased way, "no wonder my clothes moulded. Look at that!" He pulled away another board and then I could see into the space behind. The wall was clotted with what looked like dirty wool. The stench grew worse; there was the smell of soot mixed with it, and something else, very sad as well as nasty. He drove a knife into one of the boards.

"Quite rotten," he said, "soft as butter!" And again he sounded pleased. "Slip down into the yard, Elizabeth, and lay hold of the first man or boy you see. I want these out of my room before the stink settles. And bring back a brush so we can sweep the wall clean."

By dusk, when he finished for the day, all the rotten wood and the mould had been cleared away; the new timber for tomorrow's work had been carried up and its fresh clean scent mingled with the lingering smell of soot and decay and sadness that came from the cleared space behind the closet.

Over supper my mother, who had seen the state of the old boards, expressed her concern; she'd had no notion, she said, that such things could go on, unnoticed, in a well-kept house.

"But then," she said, "all that part of the house is so old. Too old." She glanced at my father. "If I had my way," she said, with the air of knowing very well that she never would, so she could make whatever wild statement she fancied, "I'd have it all down, and some new rooms built; and I'd make an entrance for the pack ponies at the side. How many other women, I wonder, if they want to go from their kitchen to their parlour, must stand and wait while twelve ponies trot clean through the house?"

It was one of those questions to which there was no answer, and the subject lapsed.

All next day we worked on the closet. My grandfather kept me busy; when I wasn't holding nails for him I was beating his clothes with a little cane, or polishing every bit of woodwork in the room, for fear that the worms which were too small to see should have spread into other places, or wiping the dust from the inmost crevices of the little coral tree. For a good part of the time he entertained me by telling me a story I had never heard before.

It began with the black head. I asked:

"Shall I polish this too? It is made of wood, isn't it?"

He said yes, polish it well; and drifted into a tale about a place called Africa where the people were all black and had faces like the one carved in the wood. They were always having quarrels amongst themselves, and fought, not to kill, but to take prisoners who were then sold as slaves and taken a long journey by sea to work in the Sugar Islands. My grandfather had made three voyages on a slave ship.

"Once would have been more than enough for me," he said, "but we went back and forth without touching a European port at all; and if I'd deserted in Africa I should have been killed, and if I'd deserted in the islands I'd most likely have ended on a plantation myself. It's a sad, bad trade and I was glad to be out of it."

He then went on to say that there were white slaves as well as black. In another part of Africa there were some brown men, called Barbary pirates, who would attack ships and capture white men and make them into slaves. "And their fate is worse than that of the blacks, I'd say."

"Why?"

"Because they have known freedom, my dear. The Negroes never have, not as we know it. What with their chiefs and their witch doctors."

I asked what was a witch doctor, and off we went again. That day soon passed. Once he sent me running to ask my mother if she had a few sprigs of lavender and rosemary to spare; he said that now his closet was so clean and fancy it might as well be sweet-scented, too.

When dusk fell that evening all was in order again, and his clothes were hung back on the sound new pegs.

IV

Two days later came one of the days which I shall never forget. It began badly; the wind was howling and throwing sleety rain against the casement when I woke, so I knew that I should have to stay indoors all day, and sooner or later be forced to look after the boys. That, like learning to cook, was one of the things Mother was strict about, a training for later life. I'd never even liked playing with my doll and I liked playing with Harry and Arthur even less, but of course I had to do what I was told.

Arthur wasn't much trouble; sometimes he crawled about the floor, sometimes he sat in a little chair my grandfather had made for me, with a bar across the front. Harry was able to run and reach things and be a nuisance, and he was always much naughtier when I was left in charge, and did things he wouldn't have done with Mother or Peggy, who was the woman who helped to look after them.

One thing I had been told was never to let either of the boys go near the fire, but fire fascinated Harry and he was always trying to get near it and throw things on it to see them blaze. He had a little hobby-horse, with a bit of real mane on its head, and on this particular morning he'd pulled the mane off and went to throw it on the fire. I hurried to pull him away. He was two and a half years old and a very headstrong little boy, and when I pulled he kicked and struggled and we had quite a tussle. When at last I did get him pulled to the side of the hearth he suddenly went limp, and then very quickly took hold of my beads in both hands and tugged with all his might.

I took hold of his hands and tried to pull them away. He wouldn't let go. I shook him and still he tugged. The beads pressed, quite painfully, into the back of my neck, and then the string snapped and they began to clatter down to the floor, like hailstones, and went rolling all about. I let go of Harry and hastily put up my left hand to catch some of them and with my right hand aimed a slap at Harry; truly not a hard slap, for I had lived with babies all my life and knew how easily they could be hurt. I only meant to tap him and teach him not to break strings of beads. But he saw the slap coming and stepped back and lost his balance and fell against the basket that held logs for the fire. It had just been brought in and was piled high, so two logs fell and one hit him on the head, just where his hair grew, and goodness, within a minute there was such a great bump that he looked like a bull calf just growing a horn.

He screamed and screamed, and Arthur, in his little chair, screamed too. Mother and Peggy came running, and Peggy trod on a bead and almost fell over.

Harry wasn't very good at talking; I'd heard my grandfather say how slow he was compared with me at the same age, but he could make himself understood if he wanted to. He said:

"Lizbet hit me. Lizbet hit me."

Mother thought I'd hit him hard enough to raise that bump, which just shows how silly women can be; even my clenched fist couldn't have done such damage. She shook me and boxed my ears. I cried and kept trying to explain, and I said "Beads"; so then she looked down and said I was vain and spoiled and she'd teach me not to be. I was to pick up every bead and she would put them in the fire.

The bump went on growing and Harry looked deformed, almost like Mrs. Clipstone's boy. Peggy was sent to get a bit of raw meat to put on it and Mother took him in her lap and rocked him, speaking soothingly to him and chidingly to me in the same breath, while I crawled about the floor collecting the beads. I held up the edge of my skirt to make a kind of pocket for them, and cried myself silly, thinking of them being burned and Harry being an idiot and Mother angry with me forever. But out of it all I meant to save my beads. I would run to my grandfather; he'd understand and believe that I hadn't meant to hurt Harry.

I went on pretending to search for and find beads long after they were all collected. Then Peggy came back with the piece of meat, and when she and Mother were both busy laying it on, I stood up and rushed out of the room, down the new stairs, across the passage and into the office where I thought my grandfather was sure to be on such a rough morning. He wasn't there, so I ran up the old stairs, quick as a weasel, and pressed the latch of his bedroom door.

It was barred on the inside.

I went into a frenzy. Although in fact nobody pursued me, I had a hunted feeling. Mother wasn't the woman to sit there and let herself be defied. My only hope of saving my precious beads was to get to my grandfather quickly and tell him my story. After all, he had given me the beads, he had a right to say whether they were burned or not; besides he would see the unfairness of it. I beat on his door with my free hand and kicked at it with my feet, screaming:

"Let me in, let me in."

Calmly, unhurried he called back:

"Just a minute, Elizabeth." And I learned just how long a minute can be.

At last he opened the door, and his first words should have warned me; he said:

"What on earth is the matter?" in a testy way.

I threw myself at him, and sobbing and gulping and hiccupping got out my tale. He didn't say anything, just sat down and took me on the knee of his good leg and listened. When I had finished he said:

"Dear me. What a pity."

He wasn't *with* me; not properly sorry for me, or properly angry with Mother. He was like a man with a raging toothache being bothered by a fly.

"You won't let her put my beads in the fire, will you?"

"Elizabeth, you put me in a very awkward situation. Your mother is your mother. She has a right to be mistress in her own house."

"But I didn't hit him. It isn't fair."

"We can't always expect things to be fair in this life. I think the threat to burn the beads was made in a moment of anger, and the best thing you can do is to go to your mother and explain calmly—not with a lot of crying and shouting—exactly what happened."

"But I did. I did."

"Shouting like that and scowling like that—you look just as though you might have hit Harry in a temper. You *must* control yourself. Then she'd listen to you."

I doubted that; but perhaps there was something about crying. It was all right and got you what you wanted until you were eight; after that you were too old to cry, and if you did, you simply annoyed people. I drew some deep breaths and mopped my eyes and blew my nose and tried again.

"Please," I said, "will you keep the beads while I talk to Mother?"

"No. I don't think that would be wise. I don't think I should take sides. You go and explain as calmly and nicely as you can. And then please her by being agreeable to Harry and Arthur for the rest of the day. Yes, that'll be best."

I jumped off his knee. All my life I had relied on him and now, in the moment of need, he had failed me. For the first time in my memory, I was entirely alone.

And I had my beads to save.

"All right," I said. And that wasn't just an acceptance of his advice. It went much further than that. It was the casting off of dependence and a friendship which, though it had been selfish, had been fond. I can look back now and see that I was, at that moment, like a jelly, made of good stuff, capable of setting very firmly into any mould. And with that "All right," I was put into the mould and shaped. In the face of any disaster, any challenge, forever after, I could say "All right!" and go my own defiant way.

If Mother or Peggy had been waiting to snatch me outside my grandfather's bedroom door I should, without doubt, have been a different woman. The beads would have been taken from me and I should have learned that "All right!" is not the answer. However, they were not, and I was able to slip into my own bedroom and, once there, I knew where I could hide my threatened treasure.

Betty had a bag of coarse brown linen which hung on the back

of the closet door. I had been forbidden to touch it. It was connected with something which I should one day understand. Clean
clouts; bloody clouts, an occasional nasty smell. I loosened the cord
that held it closed and shot in my beads. Mother, even if she
searched, would never think of looking there, and Betty I could
trust, for I knew one or two things about her which I had promised
never to tell, and she was very much afraid of losing her place.

Then it occurred to me—Why should Mother search? Couldn't
I fox her? I could but try. I ran down into the yard and gathered
as many pebbles as I had had beads in my skirt; then I went back
into the boys' room and, with a meek and sorrowful look, said:

"I am sorry, Mother. Shall I put them in the fire?"

She said yes, and she was glad to see that I had come to my
senses. The pebbles rattling into the fire made exactly the right
noise.

Even so, Mother did not forgive. All that day, whenever she
looked at me, her eyes went cold and her lips went thin, and towards the end of the afternoon she set me to the task which, after
looking after Harry and Arthur, I liked least—sewing a long, long
seam. She sat opposite me, stitching away at her embroidery, so
there was no escape for me. I was very glad when Sir Richard Drury
arrived.

He had never been in our house before and Mother was flustered,
wanting to make much of him, yet at the same time wanting not
to seem to. He asked for my father and she said:

"My husband is at Minsham, but he will be back any minute; he
is always home before dark at this time of year." She then sent me
running to the kitchen to ask Alice to mull some wine, saying that
in any case Father would welcome it when he came in. Sir Richard
stopped me, saying:

"I've been out all day, Mistress, and would appreciate something
to eat, if it wasn't putting you to too great inconvenience."

Mother, looking delighted, said it was no inconvenience at all.
She had a game pie, made yesterday and uncut.

Sir Richard said, "Splendid!" and rubbed his hands.

Mother had made the pie herself. Alice did all the ordinary
dishes, the stews and roasts and cloth puddings, but special things,
like saffron cake, syllabub or pies, Mother held could only be prop-

erly made by the mistress of the house. She would don a big apron and cause considerable confusion in the kitchen with her, "Hand me this," and "Fetch me that," and her "Slut! Do you call this clean?" Since I should one day be mistress of a house, I must stand by and watch and lend a hand by doing the more tedious jobs like beating eggs until my arms were fit to drop off. I had already decided that when I was mistress of a house I would never go into my kitchen, except to give orders and see them carried out.

These special dishes, intended for the family only, were always set in one place, on shelves near the larder window. The window was small and heavily barred, so the larder was never very light, and on this day dusk was falling, so while Alice set about mulling the wine, the girl who helped her, Jill, took a candle and went to fetch the pie and after a long time came back and said:

"I can't find no pie."

Alice snorted.

"You! You couldn't find a pack pony in a pickle barrel. Here, howd this and give me the candle."

She was gone even longer, but came back empty-handed.

"Well, thass a mystery! I know it was there. I set it away meself." She went into the pie's history, where the venison, the hare, the partridge and the pigeon that had gone to its making had come from, who separated the bones from the meat, how it was seasoned and what fancy shapes my mother had laid on the crust in the way of decoration. All very helpful as proof that the pie had existed, but no aid in finding what had become of it.

"And who's going to break it to the mistress? Thass what I want to know."

Not I, I thought. Bearers of ill news are never in favour and I was in disgrace enough already. I slipped away and up to my bedroom. It was cold there, and the chilliness and the loneliness brought home to me what it meant to be on bad terms with my grandfather. Ordinarily, at such a moment I should have sought him out. That made me think of my beads. I unhooked Betty's secret bag, and diving into it with some distaste I brought out the beads and laid them in a little heap on my quilt. They looked sad and useless that way. I let the bag fall to the floor, and sitting on the bed I began to rethread them. I was hard at work when Betty came in and at first she was angry with me too.

"I towd you over and over never to touch that!" she said. "Meddlesome!"

I had no wish to fall out with her as well, so I explained:

"It was the only safe place I could think of in a hurry. I didn't meddle, I didn't even look. I just put them in and took them out again."

"If you was towd to burn 'em, burn 'em you'll hev to," she said.

I told her about the pebbles and her anger changed to amusement.

"You're a one!" she said. "But you've done yourself all the same. Whass the good of threading 'em up again, so careful? You'll never be able to wear 'em, will you? Not till your ma's dead, or you're married and out of this house."

I hadn't thought of that. My fingers went weak and stopped working. Then they moved again.

"I can wear them at night; and keep them by day in your bag."

"If I let you. Thass for me to say. And I don't want nobody messing about with my things. I've a good mind to tell your ma."

This was my day for falling out with people; a bad day from beginning to end. And if we were to be out, Betty and I, we might as well do it properly.

"You tell her then, and I'll tell her about that night when I left my cough stuff in the parlour and asked you to go down for it and you wouldn't and you told me all about the ghost. And I'll tell her how you told me about the baby born with the pig's head, and how you broke our jug and we said the frost did it. I've got plenty to tell, too."

She looked at me, and the fright showed in her face; fright and something else—almost as though I had suddenly grown a pig's head.

"Keep 'em where you like," she said. "Not that your ma'll look for 'em, thinking they're burned."

That was true, and so far so good. Not good enough, though. I wanted to wear those beads all day, openly. My neck missed them, and my fingers missed them, and when I could bring myself to look in Mother's glass my eyes would miss them most of all.

I threaded them, all but two, which I had to leave off in order to have enough thread left to make a firm knot. By that time I was chilled to the bone. So I hid them again and went down, and into a troubled house.

Mother had just managed to keep herself on rein while Sir Richard was in the house, and then she let herself go. I had never seen her in such a temper.

"The unfairness of it," she cried. "There I was, all yesterday afternoon, making that pie and it was fit to set before anybody. Yes, fit for the Queen, though I say it myself, I shouldn't have been ashamed to offer it to Her Grace. Then, just when I need it, because some sly-boot thief guzzled it down, I have to serve Sir Richard, his first visit to the house, too, a slab of cold beef like any farmer's wife."

"He ate with zest," said my father, in his way of using the fewest words.

My grandfather, who had by that time come into the parlour, tried harder to comfort her.

"You go to Rushbrooke one afternoon unannounced and see how much pie you get, my dear. He was lucky to get good beef and not be fobbed off with cheese."

"I felt *ashamed*, and it isn't fair. I do keep a good table. The crust alone took me an hour and was as pretty as a picture. Well . . . now I'm going to find out. . . ."

She stormed out of the parlour and into the kitchen. I followed. It hadn't occurred to Mother to suspect me; I had what she always called a "pingling" appetite and it would have taken me several days to eat that pie. So, blameless, I could observe and take a certain pleasure in the scene in the kitchen.

Nobody had touched that pie. Everybody cried. Alice did more. She went purple in the face and shouted:

"God strike me dead if I laid a finger on it except to set it away."

She didn't fall dead. Instead she went into a hysterical fit, and flung two wooden spoons and a rolling pin the length of the kitchen before throwing herself down and beating her heels on the pamments of the floor. Mother told Jill to douse her with water straight from the well.

"And then to Woodman's for me. Tell him to bring his tools and a good strong padlock."

She saw now, she said, where her folly had been; she'd been too easygoing; too trusting; but all was to be different in future. There was going to be some order in this household. Any food that wasn't actually being prepared, or eaten, would be safe behind the locked larder door. Now she came to think of it, this wasn't the first time;

a batch of oatcakes had vanished marvellous fast and she remembered a goose carcass, with two meals still on it, which Alice had *said* had gone into the broth pan. Mother had had her suspicions at the time.

Fortunately all this commotion did not interfere with the preparations for supper; in the kitchen they would eat what Sir Richard had left of the cold joint; in the parlour—where the family supped alone—there was beef dumpling, which had been bubbling away in the pot all through the scene.

When we were seated at table my grandfather asked the question which, but for the loss of the pie, would have been asked much earlier:

"What did Sir Richard want with you, Arthur?"

"Some advice," said my father, with a glance at Jill who was setting the beef dumpling before him. When she had gone he busied himself ladling out portions. Then, pulling his own plate towards him, he said:

"It's reached us now, this Jesuit invasion." He spooned food into his mouth and champed heartily.

"You mean they've found one?" my mother said.

My grandfather said, "Lost one, more like," and reached for the salt bowl.

"That is so. Lost somewhere in Baildon or near." This was one of those few occasions when my father knew that he must explain, go into detail, muster his words. He braced himself by taking two quick spoonfuls of the dumpling.

"The fellow was at Abbas Hall, holding his Popish Mass last Sunday. A serving wench informed on him. She'd had her ear to a keyhole and said he was coming here, to the *Hawk in Hand*. And that rings true. Doll Webster is known for a backward-looker; every Easter she serves up her buns with a cross on them; she said they wouldn't rise else."

"What nonsense," my mother said. "Mine rose, light as a feather."

My grandfather said, "You mentioned advice, Arthur."

"I'm coming to that. Taking the serving wench's word, they searched Abbas from roof to cellar. There is a chapel there, but it was used as a duck pen. Cunning. The duck stink would hide the incense. . . . Too late there, anyway. So on to the *Hawk in Hand* where, by some close questioning, they learned that there was one more dirty platter than there had been places at table. But they went through the place from roof to cellar and found nothing. So they gather that he's been passed on."

"And Drury asked your advice as to where it might be," said my grandfather.

My father fed himself hastily.

"The advice he wanted was on policy. Whether it was better to send the Crier round with the news, or move secretly. There's a lot to be said on both sides."

"There always is."

"If you send round the Crier, ninety-nine out of every hundred will be all agog to lay the fellow by the heels; but you warn the hundredth, who is the one who matters. And you start a scare. Every old dame running to the Constable to report a Jesuit in her chicken shed."

"Under the bed, Arthur! Under the bed," said my grandfather with a smile.

"It's nothing to laugh at," said my mother. "If I lived alone and heard that a desperate man was on the run, I should be nervous and look under my bed, I swear."

"On the other hand," said my father, "keep quiet and there's a chance you may surprise the traitor. I said, and I think I was right, that it'd be best to say nothing until watch had been kept for a day or two on Chris Hatton."

My mother said, "That heathen!" and my grandfather said:

"Chris Hatton. Why, Arthur, I'd say he'd be the last man to be a Papist. His father, old Barnabas, bought Mortiboys at the Dissolution. It's Church property. Restore the Church and where would he be?"

"In good case. Hatton's a gambler who would wager on how many peas in a pod. He'd gamble on the Papists being grateful; he'd sit there with his Mortiboys while thousands of other people were chucked out. That's reasonable, isn't it?"

"You're always reasonable, Arthur. And how do they propose to watch him?"

"Rather cunningly," said my father, with a note of gloating in his voice. "Lady Drury is . . . er . . . unable to ride just at present. Tomorrow, first thing, she's sending both her horses to Jane Hatton. A bit of flattery—nobody else she can trust not to harden their mouths or spoil their tempers. And the groom goes with them. He's a Pope-hater. His name is Boreman and his grandfather was burned at Colchester in the same year . . ."

"As my mother. I see. Somebody in ancient times said that the blood of martyrs was the seed of the Church. Nowadays it is a certificate of anti-Papist reliability."

"Well, you can't be too careful. Look at them, hand in hand with Spaniards; plotting against the Queen; wanting to put that murdering wanton, the Queen of Scots, on the throne." My father took a mouthful and chewed, and went on. "It isn't their nonsense I mind. As far as I'm concerned they could worship Diddicoy's donkey, and welcome. It's the company they keep."

"For all that," said my grandfather, in his calm way, "I wouldn't suspect every Catholic of treachery."

"You'll see," my father said darkly. "Once the war with Spain comes into the open, you'll see that these shorn pates haven't been over here from Douai just to hold a Mass. Oh no! Spying and organising is their business."

"How terrible," said my mother. "And to think that there's one hereabouts."

"No nearer than Mortiboys, I'll warrant," my father said.

My grandfather asked, "Have they a description of the man?"

"They have. That servant girl had her wits about her. He's tall; what hair he has is reddish and his face is badly pocked."

"*He* shouldn't be hard to find," said my grandfather, laying down his spoon.

"A Jesuit, remember; and the Devil is said to look after his own."

I had long since learned the way in which a child could make itself unnoticed and thus overhear grownups' talk, and I was following that way now; keeping my eyes on my food, moving my spoon quietly. Nevertheless, I was being noticed; I could feel an eye on me. I did not look up; I went on spooning my gravy. So I was surprised to hear that it was my grandfather who had noticed me.

"Elizabeth," he said, "you'll remember that you're not to chatter about anything you hear in this room."

I raised my eyes then and looked straight at him, as sadly as I could.

"I wasn't listening. I was thinking about my beads."

"If you're going to sulk," said my mother, "I know a good cure!"

He could have stood up for me then; too late, but better than nothing. He could have said that I had been punished enough; or shown some sign of displeasure that the beads which, after all, he had given me, and which must have cost a good deal, had been so spitefully and wastefully treated. At the very least he could have said that I was downcast, not sulking; he had said that kind of thing many times before, just to show he was on my side. Tonight he said nothing, but turning to my father remarked:

"Oh, by the way, Arthur, Hopkin sent his money this morning. So that's all right."

"And he'll never have a moment's credit from us again. Cash on the nail in future."

When Betty joined me in our room she gave me another proof of a thing which I had remarked often, the impossibility of keeping anything secret. First of all, she opened our clothes closet as though it were a jack-in-the-box and felt about behind the clothes; then she looked under my bed. Her own was too low to make a hiding place for anything larger than a mouse. Then she told me that there was a priest on the run; he'd been seen at our end of the town.

"So now we know where the pie went. Alice is gonna show your ma in the morning. Alice showed me and Peggy and Jill and Jack Plant tonight. You can stand outside the larder winder and put your arm through them bars and take things off the family shelves as easy as easy. Alice say that make her see red, decent honest English people being said to steal pies, and be shouted at, and locks put on doors, and all on account of a dirty thieving Spanish rogue. Alice say lose her place or no, she'll hev something to say about this in the morning, Alice say."

I had taken my beads, on their mended string, and put them around my neck, and lay, as I had done every night since my birthday, with the fingers of my right hand hooked over them because the feel of them pleased me almost as much as the look. I wasn't sparing a thought for the runaway priest or the stolen pie. I was slipping off to sleep thinking about the happenings earlier in the day, the breaking of the string, my mother's rage, my cold reception by my grandfather . . .

Suddenly, in a flash, I remembered something that I had seen with my eyes, but not noticed with my mind at the moment because I was so upset and crying; now, in the remembered scene, that thing took its place. It was one of the kitchen platters, with some crumbs on it, and it had stood on the table near the Negro's head. At the time it had been without significance, but now . . .

Wide awake again, I thought—The priest; the pie; the locked door; my grandfather's inattention to my tale. Suppose!

It was rather like taking a walk after a heavy rain when you could walk along so far and then have to jump over a puddle. My mind had to make many jumps; but between them there were patches of firm ground. Leaping from one to the other it was easy enough to reach the conclusion that my grandfather's mysterious visitor had come to tell him that the *Hawk in Hand* was no longer a safe hiding place for the priest, and to ask him to find another. And he had promised, "Rest assured, I shall do what I can." Next day he had set about the work on his clothes closet, behind which, if some boards were left movable, there would be a good hiding place. I remembered how pleased he had seemed by the evidence that the work was needed; and the way he had invented little jobs that would either engage my attention or take me out of the room. I remembered those fragments of a glass bowl which had been used in the old times, and how when they were made into a new one it was to be taken to the *Hawk in Hand*, where Doll Webster was a backward-looker who put crosses on her Easter buns.

It could all be made to fit.

Then I recoiled. So did it fit that Harry had broken my beads and said, "Lizbet hit me," and had a great bump on his head. Mother also had put certain things together and had been entirely misled.

I saw that what I needed was just one more scrap of evidence, something that had nothing to do with what had gone before, nothing to do with anything remembered or anything supposed.

Given that, I could save my beads. Lying there in the dark I smiled as I thought of a cunning way to deceive Mother if once I could demand Grandfather's support.

All I needed was one small thing to convince me that I was right.

Within twenty-four hours I had it, or so I thought.

Our supper next day was boiled bacon and peas. Father carved and gave us our nicely judged portions; one slice, almost without fat, for me, two for Mother, for Grandfather three cut thin with plenty of fat, for himself three cut thick. My grandfather, as usual, mashed his peas and cut his first slice very small; his teeth were bad.

Mother had been doing some thinking too, and she gave us the results of them, over the meal.

"I see very well what happened," she said. "Jill brought in the dumpling and then hung about, hoping to hear what Sir Richard had come about. And she heard about the priest on the run and told Alice. Alice seized on it. She's soft as grease about Jack Plant—and him married with a sick wife and four children. They had that pie, I have no doubt. No doubt at all. But like all liars, she overlooked one thing."

"Oh," said my grandfather, "and what was that?"

"The dog, old Wolsey. You see she said to me, saucy as you please, 'Try it yourself, Mistress,' so I went outside and put my arm through the bars, and true enough, the shelf where she *said* the pie was was within easy reach. I took a piece of cake, and then I turned to the dog and said, 'Here, Wolsey,' and he came and took it from my hand, *with his chain slack*. The whole of that wall is well in his reach and it's clear to me that if any Jesuit stood there reaching in old Wolsey would have had him in pieces."

"So he would," said my father, "and I'm glad to think that our pie didn't go into a Spanish belly."

I looked at my grandfather's plate. It bore the one slice, finely chopped and hardly touched at all, and his mashed peas. There had been no time for the other two slices to be chopped and eaten.

My heart began to bump. My bacon lost its flavour and I had difficulty in swallowing, my mouth was so dry. I thought of my blue beads, hidden all day in Betty's bag.

We came to the end of the meal. My grandfather took his stick in his right hand and with his left pressed against the table and so heaved himself to his feet. His pouch came into view.

It was fashionable, at that time, for people of our kind to have pouches which matched the doublet, made of the same material, stiffened, quilted and sometimes embroidered. Poorer folks had one, mostly of leather for hard wear, and the truly rich and fashionable had theirs worked with gold and silver thread and set with jewels. My mother embroidered well, and both my father and my grandfather had several pouches with the Old Vine mark, a big black V worked on them, and their initials done smaller at the point of the V.

My grandfather was wearing his tan-coloured doublet and pouch that evening, and to this day I can see how the fat from the hot bacon had seeped through the stuff, darkening it, even making a dark patch on his doublet where it touched.

"I'm going into the office for a moment, and then early to bed," he said. "It's the warmest place on a night like this."

"Would you like a hot brick in your bed?" Mother asked.

"God bless me, no. Not till there's ice on the pond. Though it was a kind thought."

I followed him, as I had on so many evenings before, but tonight I was not welcome. As we crossed the passage into the old part of the house, he said:

"I meant what I said about going to bed, Elizabeth."

"I'm going, too. I just wanted to ask you something."

"Ask away then," he said. But it was far too important and secret to be dealt with in the passage. I skipped ahead of him and opened the office door. The candle had burned very low, but the fire was still bright, and when he followed me in he brought a fresh candle from the shelf outside and lit it from the old one. He went to the chair behind the table and lowered himself carefully.

"Well now, what is it, child?"

"You remember yesterday? My blue beads."

"Blue beads? Oh yes. Yes, of course. What about them?"

"I didn't put them in the fire. I only pretended to. I threw pebbles into the fire, but Mother thought it was the beads, so now I shall never be able to wear them again."

"No," he said slowly, "I'm afraid you won't."

"Unless you help me," I said.

"My dear child, how can I? You've put yourself very much in the wrong. Your best plan would be to confess to your mother, and leave it to her to decide whether she allows you to wear them again or not."

"We know the answer to that. But you *can* help me. I've threaded them again, a little shorter than they were before. I want to give them to you; then you could say that you felt sorry the others were burned and you got me a new string, as much like the others as you could find. Please, Grandfather, will you do that?"

He gave a look very much like the one Betty had given me when I threatened her. That cheered me, because she had given in and let me have my way.

"Elizabeth, you almost frighten me. Do you seriously suppose that I would aid and abet such a deception? You deceived your mother yesterday, but that wasn't planned. What you're suggesting now would be *wicked*. Don't you see that?"

I said, "I did *not* hit Harry. It wasn't right that I should be punished at all. And I want to wear my beads."

"Not that way. What I will do, I promise, if you go and make a clean breast of it to your mother, is to buy you a new string presently. Perhaps at Christmas, or New Year."

"I don't want to tell Mother. And I don't want to wait. And I don't want a new string. I want my own."

"Then, my dear, want will be your master."

I didn't want to threaten him, I wanted to stay friends. So I gave him one more chance.

"Please, Grandfather, do it my way."

"I can't. And there's an end of it. I can't encourage you to deceive and tell lies."

I went close to the table, and I said:

"You deceive people, and you tell lies. And if *you* asked *me* to help you, I would. I'd tell a lie for you."

"What *are* you talking about?"

"The Jesuit hidden in your clothes closet!"

He gave me a dreadful look. I thought he was going to hit me, so I stepped back quickly. His face went purple, like a plum, and then it slipped sideways, horrible, horrible, worse than Mrs. Clipstone's idiot boy. I said, "Don't look like that. I won't tell, I won't tell," but the words didn't make any sound. He sagged against the arm of his chair, and it tipped over and crashed with him to the floor.

I tried to scream, but no sound came; I tried to run but my feet were heavy. It took me a long time to get to the parlour on the other side of the house and when I got there I couldn't speak. I could only flap my hands about and point. . . .

They made rather a fuss of me, because I had had such a shock, and been, for all they knew, struck dumb. Mother said maybe they had been unwise to let me and the old man spend so much time together; he'd had one stroke and was bound to have another someday, but how could she know, she demanded, that we should be in the office together that evening, I was supposed to be on my way to bed. That remark put a thought into my head to be used later.

They gave me a dose of nasty-tasting medicine to make me sleep, and a hot brick for my feet, because they and my hands were cold as stone. I slept until midday next day, and when I woke I could speak, which pleased even those who had formerly said that I talked too much.

When I was dressed I took my beads out of the bag and put them around my neck. As soon as Mother saw them she changed countenance but before she could speak I said:

"Grandfather believed that I didn't hit Harry and he didn't think my beads should be burned, so he got me a new string, as much like the others as he could find. It's a little shorter; there were twenty-six on the other string and only twenty-four on this. He was giving them to me when he . . . died."

"The last thing he ever did," Mother said in a sad voice. I knew that she had accepted my story and that my beads were safe.

Once I was sure of that I could think of other things, and eight years old or not, I cried. Now that he was dead I wasn't angry with him any more. All I could think of was how kind he had always been to me, and how we should never walk together any more, and how he would never tell me another of his tales. And the look he had given me just at the last.

I certainly wasn't going to shame his memory by giving away his secret. I *hated* that hidden priest. He had caused all the trouble. If he hadn't been there behind a barred door, gobbling pie, just when I most needed my grandfather's help, none of this would have happened. I liked to think of him, stuffed away there in that dark, ill-smelling place, wondering what had happened, and slowly dying of hunger and thirst.

Two or three nights later Betty woke me and said she could hear some faint tapping noises. I persuaded her, easily enough, that they were of ghostly origin, and that the best thing that we could do was to stay still and put our heads under the bedclothes.

Interlude

Mrs. Kentwoode, good manager that she was, lost no time in going through her father-in-law's clothes, carefully deciding which, if any, could be used by her husband, and which given away to the men in the yard. The discovery of two slices of bacon hidden in the old man's tan-coloured pouch, since it came after the funeral, was not associated with the supper dish of the evening of the tragedy, but it did call to mind the loss of the game pie and other things from the larder. Just, as well as strict, she mentioned the matter—not to Alice, to whom the apology was due—but to her husband.

"Maybe I wronged Alice, and Jack Plant," she said. "I believe your father was a secret eater. I found one of his pouches with food in it, and ruined with grease. It grieves me to think that he felt he must eat on the sly; and at the same time I am sorry that I made such a to-do about the few things I missed. It must have made him feel badly."

"More like it made him laugh. Old men are like children, of whom they say 'Stolen apples are sweetest.'"

"I hope it was so," she said, ready to seize upon the comfortable thought. "I mislike the notion that he felt anything grudged."

She decided to give Alice a pair of shoes as well as a petticoat for Christmas.

Henry Kentwoode, in contriving the hiding place, had been mindful of the fact that a man needs air, as well as food and water. During one of Elizabeth's absences on an errand, he had stepped into the space and held his hands to the brickwork of the chimney, and was pleased to find, in more than one place, a definite draught. All through that winter as the smoke went up into a sullen or a shining sky it carried with it what, in other circumstances, might have set the household at Old Vine hunting for a rat under the floor boards.

The years passed. In Baildon, where memories were long and entertainments few, today's gossip tended to become tomorrow's legend. It was not forgotten, for instance, that once before at the Old Vine a woman had revived a moribund business, and when, in the year 1587, another woman, Elizabeth Kentwoode, emerged from a self-imposed seclusion and saved—by cunning innovations— the business which her brother Harry had ruined, it seemed as though history were repeating itself. It seemed strange that at the same place more or less the same thing should happen.

The secret of Josiana's parentage had died with her; nobody knew how closely the Kentwoode family and the Rancons were connected. Had the blood tie been visible they would have understood better why it was that Harry Kentwoode, gay and irresponsible, extravagant and profligate, was so much like one of the Rancons who had come to a bad end in London, and one of the Reeds who had come to a bad end somewhere far away in the West Country.

Between Lady Rancon and her descendant Elizabeth Kentwoode there was this difference; the former had been loved by those in close contact with her and everywhere respected as a woman of great integrity; for the latter, and with ample reason, few people had a good word. She had no friends; and although for many years there had been close ties between the Old Vine and the Hatton family out at Mortiboys, when she made her first visit to that house in the year 1618, she came as a stranger.

Part Three

BARBARA KENTWOODE'S TALE

Circa 1620

I

I was born Barbara Hatton, and between my sixteenth and my nineteenth years I was afraid that I might keep my maiden name and my maiden state forever. I had four elder sisters and my mother stuck stubbornly to the old-fashioned notion that marriage should go by seniority. The sister ahead of me, poor Avice, had come badly out of the smallpox; her eyelids had thickened, which gave her a crafty look, most ill deserved, for she was the soul of simplicity. She was twenty-one and unbespoken, I was eighteen and getting frightened, when my father, who—like his father before him—was a reckless gambler, had an unusual run of bad luck and, looking round for something he could sell quickly for a good price, hit upon the big tapestry that hung in our hall.

In truth it wasn't a very good idea, because anyone who wants to buy a tapestry must come into the house and see it, and neither my father nor my mother could stomach the thought of anyone riding out to Mortiboys and going away unrefreshed. By the time it was sold, the hospitality had cost a good deal. However, immediately afterwards Father's luck changed again. And I had found a husband.

My mother was a match for most people. Walter Fennel had wanted my sister Annabilla, but Cecily was next to be married and when Mother had finished with Walter he was married to Cecily. In Elizabeth Kentwoode—Madam Elizabeth as everyone called her —Mother met her master for stubbornness. Madam Elizabeth wanted me as wife for her nephew, John, and she got me.

Unlike most people who showed interest in buying our very famous tapestry, Madam Elizabeth sent a servant ahead to enquire, first whether it were sold already, and second would the next morning at eleven be a convenient time for her to inspect it in the event of it still being for sale. When the man had gone away with his answers, Mother said:

"That is a good time; a glass of wine and a slice of cake will suffice."

Father said, "A very good time. I needn't be here. After the way she treated Harry, I doubt if I could be civil to her."

"Who was Harry? A friend of yours?" Father had hundreds of people whom he called "friends" and Mother would have been happy to see most of them hanged, drawn and quartered.

"Harry was her own brother, as good a fellow as ever wore shoe leather. She stripped him down to the buff and threw him into the street."

Mother had a very literal mind; it showed as she said, on a note of bewilderment:

"How could a woman do that to a man?"

"I don't mean she took his clothes away. Harry wasn't much of a man of business and when the slump in wool came, some long time before the old Queen died, he was in trouble. He'd have weathered it if his precious sister had lent him the money her grand-dad left her. But she wouldn't; she bought him out, instead."

Mother knew, as I did, the kind of man whom my father would call a good fellow; so she said:

"Maybe she knew that to lend him the money would be to lose it. Maybe she knew she had a good head for business."

"We know she had. It wasn't the buying so much as the way she treated Harry afterwards. Worse than a servant, till he could bear it no more and went off to Colchester to work for Barrowby."

"Oh, I see now," Mother said with an air of enlightenment. "I always wondered why you went all that way for your wine."

"I liked Harry. He was worth a hundred of that creeping, toe-kissing Arthur. Anyway, sell it to her if you can."

Next morning Mother wore her second-best dress and her ear-bobs, and, thus armed, awaited the customer. If the person expected had been a man—any man, or a woman with a marriageable son, Avice would have been dressed up too, with elder-flower paste powdered over, hiding the worst of her pocks, and I should have been told to keep out of sight whatever happened. As it was, neither of us was to make an appearance, so we stood by our bedroom window, eager to see what we could.

Madam arrived in a coach, a very fine one, all gilt-stamped leather and cords and tassels. It was drawn by two horses, black and nicely matched, and the servant who rode on the left-hand one, though he was older and stouter than the one who had come on the previous day, was dressed the same blue, slashed with tawny. But for that I should have jumped to the conclusion that this was an unexpected visitor, not Mistress Kentwoode at all. My father had spoken of her taking over a business some good time before the old Queen's death, and this woman, stepping from the coach, looked no more than thirty. She was upright and, within her voluminous gown of blue-green silk, slender. Her hair was uncovered and shone saffron yellow in the sunshine, which also struck sparks of light from the jewels in her ears and on her fingers.

She walked into the shadow of our deep porch and was lost to sight.

I said, "How very grand!" and poor Avice showed where her thoughts were by saying:

"Now why didn't she ever get married?"

"Perhaps she didn't want to."

"Everybody—every woman, I mean—wants to get married."

"I don't," I said.

"You! Barbara, how can you stand there and tell such a lie. You're always on and on about it."

"I want not to be unmarried," I said, trying to explain something that would have been difficult to make clear to anyone, leave alone Avice, who had a very unsubtle mind. "If I could be rich and have all my own way, without being married, then I'd choose that. The way it is now, you get a man you may not like very much, and you have to be dutiful . . . and always having babies. Look at Clarice!"

"I envy Clarice from the bottom of my heart."

"I don't," I said.

"I know what your trouble is. You'd like to choose for yourself. Jeremy Freeman."

I willed myself not to blush. But I did, as always. Whatever it is that works that shameful, tormenting rush of colour to the face had now, with me, got beyond control. I even blushed if Father said, "Coming through Nettleton my horse cast a shoe." I'd reached the point where the word "farm" or "farmer" could set me off.

Generally I was kind to Avice, it wasn't her fault her looks were spoiled, but I was angry with her for making me blush, so I said:

"Well, you get yourself married, and then maybe Mother will be tired, or contented, and let me go my own way."

She looked so hurt my heart smote me. I took her by the hand and said:

"Let's go out onto the gallery and see how they are getting on."

Mother and Madam stood at the far end of the hall. Mother had a loud voice, used to giving orders; the other woman's was soft, indeed very soft, but it had a cutting edge to it, and that made it carry.

". . . handsome piece. And the right size. The subject I can't say I care for."

I thought—Oh dear me, another glass of Canary, another slice of plum cake wasted. Yet I agreed with her. I had always, from my earliest, nervous days, disliked that tapestry and been a little frightened of it. In our family, however, it would have been blasphemy, or worse, to say such a thing. For that tapestry had once hung in an anteroom in Whitehall Palace, and had been given to our grandfather, Barnabas Hatton, by His Grace King Henry VIII.

It was all long ago. Our grandfather was a leather merchant, a very powerful Guildsman, and the King was wanting to divorce his wife and marry Nan Bullen. At a meeting of his Guild my grandfather had said, "And what's wrong with that? Get rid of the Spanish woman, I say, and have an Englishwoman, born and bred, for Queen." Word of that speech had been carried to the King who was, just at that moment, a bit anxious about how the people of London were taking to his plan. He sent for my grandfather to go to Whitehall, and he was set to wait in an anteroom where the tapestry hung. When he went into the audience chamber the King said he was pleased to meet a representative of sound good English sense.

"I'd like to give you a handsome present, but *my* sound good English sense informs me that your pocket is probably heavier than mine at this moment, Master Hatton."

My grandfather said, "Your Grace, I never match pockets, only wits." They had laughed together. Then, so the story goes, the King had offered to knight my grandfather, who said, "That wouldn't do.

Some of my shy customers would be at a loss how to address me, and I'd lose trade."

The King laughed again and said that for those words alone, so typical, so English, he must give my grandfather something. And my grandfather, who hadn't got where he was by being diffident, said that there was one thing which he would accept with great pleasure because he did so much admire it.

That was how the tapestry came into our family. And when the King had his divorce and had broken with the Pope and taken all the Abbey property and sold it off, my grandfather bought Mortiboys and married a lady who counted amongst her forebears one of the Norman nobles who had come over with the Conqueror, and an even more noble Saxon who had defied the Normans to the end.

But, interesting as the tapestry was, it was ugly. It was Flemish, and woven at a time when the stories of the Old Testament were becoming popular. It showed the battle between David and Goliath—or at least, I should say, the result of that battle. There was Goliath, at least ten feet from head to toe, clad in a full suit of armour, as worn by knights about two hundred years ago, but without a helmet and with a great red hole in the centre of his forehead. Standing over him and looking down with an expression of smug satisfaction was the boy, David, wearing the clothes of a shabby page and fingering his sling. Immediately behind them was a range of hills, dotted with sheep; massed to the left were the Philistines and to the right the Israelites.

Mother started to retell the history of the tapestry; Madam cut her short, not rudely, but decisively.

"I know its story. That is its interest for me. But it could have hung on ten palace walls and still be ugly."

With that she swung around so sharply that Avice and I had no time to withdraw. She tilted her head and regarded us steadily, and then said something to Mother, who immediately called:

"Girls; you may come down. My daughters, Avice and Barbara. . . ."

As we made our curtseys, she added, "All that remain of five." And that was to say that though, with us, she may have failed, she had known her triumphs too.

Close to, there was no doubt about Madam's age. The white paste, something much thicker in texture than the elderberry that

Avice used, was laid on heavily from the edge of her yellow hair to the low edge of her bodice; her cheeks were just touched, her lips bright, with carmine. These were the colours of youth, and they blotted out the lines and wrinkles of age; nothing could hide the sagging of the jowls, the hollows under cheekbones and around the eyes. Her eyes were very blue.

For a moment I was too much engrossed to notice that she was studying me just as closely; when I did I would have looked down, but her stare held me. It was uncomfortable. Nobody spoke; and although had we been in her house I should have waited for her, as my elder, to make the first remark or ask the first question, I felt that here, in my father's hall, I might risk breaking that staring spell by saying something. And all I could think of to say was:

"Avice and I have been admiring your coach, madam."

She did not answer immediately, and my discomfort grew. The blush started, this time without reason. Then she said:

"I like pretty things about me. That is why I am dubious about the hanging. But behind my chair . . ." She made another of her sudden turns and faced Mother. "There is another small matter I should like to discuss with you, Mistress Hatton."

Mother dismissed us with a movement of her hand and led the way to the table where the cake and wine were set ready.

When it came out, which was not until two days later, after much discussion behind closed doors, Avice cried and Mother said, very crossly:

"I did my best for you. I said that from every point of view you were worth three of Barbara any day of the week." That only increased Avice's woe, and Father, whose mind in many ways was livelier than Mother's, caught my eye and then said:

"I doubt whether your mother did try very hard, Avice. I think when it came to the point she broke her own rule because she didn't want to part with her favourite—and mine."

My feelings were mixed. I was glad enough that Avice's eyes hadn't put St. Catherine's cap on my head as well as her own; and I told myself firmly that my dream about ever being allowed to marry Jeremy Freeman had only been a dream, a wild one at that. But I had meant it when I told Avice that I didn't want to marry just anybody: I had plenty of doubts and fears. I felt rather bitterly, too, about Father; when it was a matter of selling a tapestry he disapproved of Madam Elizabeth so much that he couldn't trust himself to be civil to her; when it was a question of marrying off a daughter, he could trust himself to be not merely civil but downright affable.

We met at the Old Vine, whither we were all bidden to supper. Madam Elizabeth, more resplendent than before, received us; standing on her right hand was a thin, grey old man, stooped and anxious-looking; on her left an extraordinarily handsome man of about thirty with black hair and eyes as blue as Madam's own. As we entered the room, Avice, being older than I, walked ahead of me, and as I swept my glance over the three Kentwoodes and then allowed it to rest upon John, I saw his face take on a look of horror which changed to pleasure when we were named.

At that moment I felt the first twinge of . . . what? Doubt? Suspicion? Understanding? Mother had thought it uncommon civil of Madam to invite Avice. Had it been done with a purpose? The thought was gone almost as soon as it came, for I, in turn, was engulfed, giddy with relief to see that my future husband was handsome, had good teeth, an amiable look, and seemed disposed to be pleased with me.

At supper—which was more like a banquet than a simple supper—which we took in a long narrow hall, at a long narrow table, capable of seating twenty people, I sat by him, and he said:

"My aunt promised me that you were pretty, but men and women see through different eyes. I agree with her heartily."

I took the compliment greedily, with a smile and a blush. It never occurred to me to wonder why he should still be unmarried at thirty, or that he should so meekly have taken his aunt's choice—even if it were poor Avice. All of my three brothers had had their marriages arranged for them, and Walter Fennel, whose parents had at least allowed him to state and show his preference, had, in the end, fared no better. It did come to me that John Kentwoode could hardly have reached his present age without being offered several brides, and sitting there I entertained the pleasantly romantic thought that perhaps he had been difficult and stubborn—young men could be that so much more easily than girls—and had then succumbed to his aunt's description of me.

I was, in fact, thoroughly well pleased. I looked at the table, so richly appointed, with Delft ware and Venetian glass, the salt bowls silver-gilt, and I thought that not even Cecily at Ockley Manor, Cecily, who would one day be Lady Fennel, for Walter's father was one of the new baronets who could hand on their title to their sons, not even Cecily had nicer things or was better served. I was a lucky girl; and I would do all I could to merit my good fortune. Under that thought—with a funeral feast of shrimps in wine jelly, sucking pig with fresh peas, a salad composed of twelve ingredients all well dressed with oil and vinegar, suckets, figs and Portugal oranges, the whole washed down with the best Rhenish—I buried my true love, Jeremy Freeman, yeoman farmer of Nettleton parish.

I have a little blemish, a brown mole the size of a barleycorn, just below the outer corner of my left eye. Sometimes I rubbed it with Avice's elder-flower paste and powdered over it; tonight, wishing to appear my true self and not, on my wedding night, have any damaging thing to reveal, I had left it bare. Towards the end of the meal John Kentwoode said:

"You have—in addition to all your other charms—that most entrancing thing, a beauty spot, a kissing spot. I long with all my heart to kiss it."

I was so simple that I truly did not know what he meant. I said so. He laughed and, lifting his hand, touched the blemish with his little finger.

"I never heard it so called before," I said. "Mole. Brown blight. And once, when somebody was angry with me, Devil's pawmark."

"You've lived," he said, "with unappreciative people. Wouldn't you agree that 'beauty spot' is a preferable term? No plain woman ever had one. They're set there to call attention to a pretty mouth or beautiful eyes."

"Nobody ever said that to me before."

He said, "I am sure there are a thousand things that nobody said to you before. I shall say them all."

He gave me a look which melted my bones, and under cover of the laden board took my hand. Then I was aware of being looked at. Mother, I thought, all-seeing and disapproving. I recalled, with some dismay, the lecture she had once given to Clarice on How to Make Your Husband Respect You. I looked guiltily towards the head of the table where Madam Elizabeth sat in a chair, higher-backed than the others and more gilded, with our David and Goliath behind her on the wall. Mother was listening to Mr. Kentwoode, who was explaining something to her, setting a spoon, a salt bowl and a comfit dish into a pattern that made plain what he was saying. Father and Avice were counting orange pips, "This year, next year, sometime, never." Avice, I was sure, thinking about marriage, Father about making his fortune at the gambling table. Only Madam Elizabeth was looking our way. And she looked as pleased as I felt. When she caught my eye she lifted her glass and, with a smile and a nod, drank to me . . . to us. . . .

As we jogged home, through the hawthorn-scented dusk, Mother said:

"Well, don't you think you're a lucky girl?"

I said, "I am indeed. And grateful, too."

"Such style they keep," Mother said. "I confess I was astonished."

Father said, "Ah, it was a shrewd move, dropping wool and taking up silk, just when every woman in England but the poorest looked to have one silk dress for Sunday." Then, aware that he had spoken in Madam's favour, he must justify himself. "You girls drop back, the road is too narrow for four abreast." We did so, but listening hard, I could still hear. "She told me something about Harry that I did not know. She'd asked him tonight and he had said he'd come if he could bring his woman. It seems that there, and not the business, was the cause of the split. I always thought she was his wife; she passes as his wife in Colchester, that I do know. I always thought Harry hard done by, and there the scamp is, living out of wedlock."

He seemed to find something amusing in the thought. Mother did not. She said somewhat stiffly:

"I never knew there was a scandal of that kind in the family. It's not the kind of thing one wishes to discover at this late hour."

"It makes no difference. Black sheep crop up in the most respectable families; and Harry at least has stuck to his light-o'-love."

"Why didn't he marry her?"

"How should I know? I thought he had. Till tonight."

"I should have thought that on such an occasion it would have become her better to keep silent on such a subject."

"Maybe I provoked her. I mentioned Harry and how we used to hawk together at Minsham in the old days."

Beside me Avice said, "He's a good deal older than I had expected." I knew what she meant and what lay behind the remark; just at that moment of sourness she would have been comforted had my man been in his dotage, harelipped, crook-backed. To any-one else I should have retorted—Who wants to marry a raw boy? But to Avice I simply said:

"Yes, I was surprised, too." I tried not to make it sound as though the surprise had been altogether pleasant.

"Just the difficult age, I should say. A girl would stand more chance of getting her own way with one younger or a good deal older."

"I agree," I said. But I touched my mole as I spoke and recalled with gloating what he had said about it. For a moment I wished that any one of my other sisters had been riding there alongside; I could have told them that a mole was a beauty spot, a kissing spot. . . .

"There was something to be said for the old days when girls afflicted like me could go into a Convent and stay out of sight, instead of having to dance at their young sisters' weddings," Avice said.

"Oh, come," I said, "you're not *afflicted*, Avice. People don't notice your eyes after the first minute or two. You have the sweet-est smile; and your hair is much prettier than mine."

"I saw his face," she said.

I didn't know whether to pretend that I didn't know what she meant and thus give her the pain of explaining, or to show, by staying silent, that I understood all too well, and so increase her hurt. And the uncertainty—as uncertainty always did with me—made me feel peevish. I thought—Well, in a month I shall be free of her complaining. I must be patient until then.

I said, "You know what I have always said, Avice. Somewhere there's a man who thinks thick eyelids the very perfection of beauty. Look at Clarice's nose and how often she went to bed with a linen-peg on it to make it more shapely, and then Philip, when they were betrothed, called it tiptilted and tantalising."

But nothing that I could say could comfort her and in the end, I lost patience, thinking—This is my evening, it shouldn't be spoiled in this fashion. And then I was sorry again.

I could have spared my pity.

Father, with the price of Goliath in his pocket, was able to sit in and play deep, and his luck changed, so once again money was plentiful and I was to have a fine wedding. Guests from a distance began to assemble a good week beforehand, and one of them, Sir Robert Randolph, arrived soaked through by a sudden thunder shower and next day had a heavy cold which kept him to his bed. Mother and I were far too busy to give him any attention; Mother indeed was resentful of his staying in bed. "Coddling himself like an old woman!" she said; so it was left to Avice to tend him, and this she did most diligently, saying to me that she hoped she would take his cold and thus have an excuse to be absent from the wedding. Sir Robert, who had been a widower for some years, was so grateful for her kindness that the moment he recovered his voice he used it to ask for her hand. This cast the whole family into a state of high jubilation and Avice was beside herself with excitement and joy. On my wedding day she might easily have been taken for the bride; indeed my sister Annabilla—always the outspoken one—told her pretty sharply that this was Barbara's day, hers would soon come.

It came indeed a bare three weeks later, so that guests from far away, and my sister Clarice, pregnant once again, did not bother to go home. Three weeks of acting hostess to such a company had worn Mother to the bone and when, on the morning of Avice's wedding, we met for the first time since mine, I looked at her with dismay and said:

"You look tired out."

She said in her brisk way, "Nonsense!" and then added, "You look pretty peaky yourself, my dear." I could see all manner of well-meant, maternal questions beginning to form themselves in her mind, and braced myself to give stout, deceptive answers. Fortunately some demand was made on her attention and I was spared.

I told myself for the thousandth time that I was a fool to have taken a few careless words so seriously and, which was worse, to have allowed them to influence my behaviour. But as I watched Avice being married, I thought to myself—Your man is old and stout and bald, but nobody is going to take you aside in a day or so and explain that he only married you because he wanted a nurse! And there I was, once more looking back at what had happened to me. . . .

My wedding night had surprised and delighted me. Girls at that time were strictly guarded and supposedly locked in ignorance from which release could only come through the marriage bed, but the youngest member of a large family would have had to be stone deaf or dim-witted not to know what to expect, and also have some inkling of the strange things which could happen. (Cecily, my sister who had married Walter Fennel and lived at Ockley and therefore within easy reach of us, had taken a month to lose her maidenhead, and was first amused, then sad and then furious about it, saying to us, in a temper, that Mother might just as well have let Walter have Annabilla for all the good he was to *her!*) So I was prepared for almost anything, and what I found was that John was a skilled and expert lover; none of the whispered talk had given me any notion of the joy and wonder; perhaps this kind of thing happened to only a few people, perhaps only to us two. I rose in the morning as a bride should, satisfied with my man and with myself, feeling sleek and cherished, altogether different.

I spent three days in a kind of dream; helped by the fact that at the Old Vine, Madam Elizabeth, some seventeen years ago, had laid out a proper garden, quite unlike any I had ever seen, and therefore the right and proper place in which to indulge in dreams. About other houses, even Ockley, the gardens had grown up haphazard, the rosebushes jostling the gooseberries, lilacs and onions side by side. The Old Vine garden was laid out to pattern; close-shaven grass paths running between borders of sweet-scented shrubs, paved paths bordered by roses, flower beds bright as patchwork with hems of clipped box. At the very end was a lawn, sheltered on three sides by a high yew hedge, solid as a wall; there was a stone seat there, and some stone figures, and a little carp pool.

It was beautiful weather and every day I walked there, snuffing the sweet scents and hugging my secret joy.

On the fourth morning, when I was only halfway along the first grass walk, Madam Elizabeth's body servant, an old woman named Betty, came hobbling after me. She looked as though she had been crying, and her always surly expression had hatred in it.

"Madam wants you, Mistress. In her chamber."

Through the blindfold of my dream I had observed that Madam was never present at breakfast; her meal was carried to her bedside and after it she spent a full hour on her toilet. She then went straight out to the sheds where the silk was made, and from there to the office where she stayed until dinnertime. After that she retired, to reappear, freshly gowned, in the late afternoon. On two of my three days at the Old Vine, people were waiting to see her, by appointment, in her office; and on all three evenings there had been guests at the supper table, with music afterwards. Consequently I had seen little of her and our talk had been confined to polite exchanges of remarks.

I knew her room; it was immediately over the parlour, and, like it, had been subject to alteration and improvement during the last few years. John had taken me—holding me by the hand—over the house on my first day, telling me things which sank into my mind without my noticing. The long narrow dining hall, where the Goliath tapestry now hung on the wall behind Madam's chair, had once been a passage which cut the house into two parts; at the end opposite Goliath, now a great square-bayed window, had been the main entrance through which, when the Old Vine dealt in wool, the pack ponies had trotted. The parlour and the chamber above had always been fine and large, but Madam had thrown out two more great windows, adding space and light.

I had never been into her bedroom, and although I was now accustomed to the elegance of everything in the house, the beauty and luxury of the room surprised me anew. The hangings at the window, and about the bed, were all of silk, the colour of the sky, patterned in a darker shade. On the glassily polished floor were sheepskin rugs, combed very fine. The toilet table, long and wide, stood in the embrasure of one of the great windows; it had a silver-framed looking glass and many other silver objects on it.

Madam sat before the table; she was fully dressed and her false face was there, ready to meet the day, but her yellow hair hung about her shoulders. She did not turn when I entered but watched in the glass, and as I took a place behind her and slightly to one side, she smiled at my reflection; I returned the smile and she said:

"You look as bright as the morning."

In the glass I saw the hot colour run over my face. I felt that she *knew*. Annabilla had once told me that the cure for blushing was to think about something else, quickly. It had never worked for me, but I went on trying, and this morning the thought that came most quickly to my mind was that sometime, surely, Madam must herself have been in love, been loved. She could still, at a slight distance, give the impression of beauty; in youth she must have been lovely indeed.

She said, "Will you dress my hair for me? Betty grows very heavy-handed. And as the youngest of five sisters you must have had a great deal of practice."

I told her the truth, smiling as I spoke.

"Avice was always the one called upon. They called me ham-handed after I cut Clarice's ear, trying to make her some cheek curls."

She did not smile. Out of the depths of the glass her very blue eyes looked back at me and I noticed how cold they were. Her voice, when she spoke, was gentle and pleasant.

"Is that a polite way of telling me that you do not wish to help with my hair?"

"Oh no, on the contrary, madam. I was . . . warning you not to expect any great skill."

"We'll see," she said, and handed me the brush. "After Betty's almost any touch would seem light."

I took the brush in my right hand and slipped my left under the yellow hair and was instantly filled with a sickening repulsion. It looked so bright and shining, waving prettily down its length to the ends where it curled slightly, but it felt all wrong, dead. . . . It reminded me of a dead kitten I had once handled, just as light and just as soft as it had been when alive, but with that difference.

All nonsense, I told myself sternly; there the hair was, growing out of the head of a woman who was alive, who was, in fact, watching me in the glass, and I could only hope that my face had not betrayed me. I brushed away steadily.

She said, in a light, chatty way:

"And how do you like being married? No, don't answer. It was a prying question and one which, in ordinary circumstances, I should not have asked. But in this case there is more at stake than you can possibly imagine. You have—or at least I trust that you have—the power to save John."

I had no notion what she could mean. I just gaped.

"Oh come," she said. "Does gossip stop short on the boundary of Minsham All Saints?"

We stared at each other in the glass.

"Other women, child. Women, women. Exactly like his uncle Harry. And so perverse with it. Dozens of women, then Harry must settle his fancy on a woman whose husband is in Bedlam and John must do worse, for the man in Bedlam at least makes no threats, extorts no blackmail. John's passion for the tavern-keeper's wife led to a pretty scandal."

I shall never quite understand why I minded so much. I was

neither silly nor innocent; I knew that few men went virgin to their marriage beds and when they did—like poor Walter Fennel—their brides weren't altogether to be envied. I knew that what was past was past, and that I hadn't the slightest reason for feeling so smitten. Unless it was the touch of squalor, Bedlam and tavern-keepers, coming so abruptly into my shining, flower-scented dream.

I suppose I turned pale, for Madam said:

"Sit down, Barbara." I walked past her and sat down on the velvet-cushioned seat which ran around the big window. I put the brush on the table as I went by and she lifted it and went on with the brushing. I could now see her face, but she did not look at me, she went on staring into the glass.

"I thought everybody knew," she said. "Dan Webster raised a howl that could be heard in Bywater, or so I would have said. He looks simple, but he laid a very neat trap. John just escaped, but he left most of his clothes behind. Webster is a big man and he has two brothers. They armed themselves with great cudgels and shouted to Heaven that at the first opportunity they'd beat John to pulp. We had no redress; you know how Puritan everybody is these days; adulterers and fornicators are frowned upon. For three weeks John dared not set foot outside the house. At the end of that time Webster, who after the first flush of interest was losing custom, and his brothers, who were missing their wages, offered to call off the siege—in return for a considerable sum of money." She changed the brush to the other hand. "John has always been well paid for what he does, but women are an expensive hobby; he had to come to me. I said I was willing to accommodate him in return for his promise to get married immediately. You see, I had always been sure that if my brother Harry could have been persuaded to get married, he could have been saved." She paused, stopped brushing, and leaning forward examined her face earnestly in the glass. "Now I am not so sure. God knows, Barbara, I have no wish to discourage you, but it is never wise to underestimate one's task. That creature has sunk her hooks very deep. I had such hopes; I thought he would find you as charming as I did; but that evening, after you had gone, he gave vent to a most curious complaint; he said you were so like her in appearance that it hurt him to look at you." She moved her glance to me. "I hadn't noticed, of course, but there is a resemblance. She is more buxom, and older, but you could pass for sisters. Still, though that may trouble him at the moment, it could be a weapon to your hand, if you use it properly. That is why I am telling you all this so frankly."

I heard my voice, coming from high up in the far corner of the room, ask:

"Has she a mole on her face?"

A trifle startled, Madam said, "Why, yes; I believe she has. Between the corner of her mouth and her chin."

Beauty spot. Kissing spot. "I long with all my heart to kiss it." Stale, secondhand and *false*. I could, I think, have made an effort and dismissed the past, the sordid episode of the blackmail and the bargain, if, once having seen me, he had liked me enough—as he had seemed to. As it was, I felt shamed and disgusted, and the memory of our nights together sickened me. It was like having greedily and delightedly eaten a dish and then been told what nauseating stuff had gone to its making. Never again, I thought.

There was another feeling, too, at the very back of my mind. A womaniser's expert flattery at the supper table, a lecherer's masterful way with my body in bed, had made me, in my heart, betray my true love. In that hot, lustful encounter I had not even reserved a tiny wish that my partner in joy had been Jeremy Freeman. I'd gone over, given myself absolutely to a man who looked on me as a sorry substitute for a tavern-keeper's wife, a poltroon who had run from a cuckolded husband and then bargained with his aunt to buy his freedom. For that alone I should never forgive myself; and although I did not realise it then, people who cannot forgive themselves are unable to forgive anyone else; forgiveness, like charity, starts at home.

"I had no idea," Madam was saying, "that you would take this so hard. Was I wrong to warn you that you had a task ahead? If you had been a green girl, the fifteen-year-old that John, in his heart, wished, hoped I should find for him, I should not have taken her into my confidence. A young girl would have been dazzled, could never have understood. I think you do, Barbara. You—if you wish your marriage to be a success—must beat Mistress Webster at her own game."

Left alone, blindfolded in my dream, I might have done so. I realised that when it was much too late. There is the world of the flesh, and the world of the mind, forever in combat, forever striving for mastery. With me, for three nights the flesh had known a victory; allowed to go its own way it could have known others. But

now the mind, where pride and resentment and spite and senti-
mentality dwell, was prodded into action—by a few words, the
spurs of the mind—and came, fully armoured, into the fray.

I am so like his loose-living tavern-keeper's wife that it hurts him
to look at me, am I? I asked myself as I climbed into bed. We'll see!

I was compliant, as a wife must be, but stiff and cool, not re-
sponsive any more. He sensed the change; he asked was I tired,
feeling unwell, upset about something. No, I said, and No, and No.

He should have taken me then; or shaken me and asked what
was the matter. Instead he turned away with a little outlet of breath
which could have been a sigh. I lay there, thinking; at least my
pride had been saved.

Now that the years have taught me wisdom I can look back and
see how silly it was; silly, and sad, too. If there had been a grain of
genuine affection between us, if one of us, no matter which, had
loved the other, the situation could so easily have been righted.
There lies my rooted grudge against arranged marriages. There we
were, John and I, pushed together, with no fondness to draw upon
in time of need. We weren't real to one another. For three nights
he had been to me a masterful, satisfactory lover whom a few words
could diminish; and I had been to him a new plaything whom a
moment's coolness could turn into a wooden doll. Our three nights
together had left us strangers, too polite to quarrel, even. A quarrel
might have cleared the air, made us say things which demanded
some explanation, which might in turn have brought healing.

And yet I do realise that all my thoughts on this subject may
be wholly wrong. Whatever I did and however I acted, it may be
that he would have tired of me quickly. Then I might have been
more deeply hurt.

My withdrawal did not prevent my being curious. The same lack
of reason as makes one probe a once aching, momentarily easy
tooth with the tongue tip made it needful for me to see this Webster woman. There were several taverns in Baildon, and I had to
move discreetly, so it was a day or two before I knew that the one
her husband kept was the *Hawk in Hand*. Every time I went into
the centre of the town I walked slowly, two or three times, past
the place, and one morning I saw a woman placing a bowl of mari-
golds on the ledge inside the window. I stopped and looked in,
just as she, having placed her bowl, lifted her head and looked out;
and so we stood with the windowpane between us. It was true; we

were very like; our faces just a little too wide at the cheekbone, a little too narrow at the chin, so that our mouths seemed too large. And we both had eyes and hair that were of the same chestnut colour. We both had our Devil's pawmark.

I walked on to the end of the street, took a left turn, and another, and so came back to the market place. She must have walked straight there after placing her flowers, for there she was, just ahead of me, making for the butter stall. What she was showed in the way she walked, in the slow indolent swing of the hips, in the un-mended stockings and the soiled torn flounce of petticoat exposed by the cunningly lifted skirt.

Like the tooth prober, I had what I asked for; pain. Because I could see it; give me another four years, unlimited ale, some sly love-making, and you'd hardly tell us apart!

The food at the Old Vine was exceptionally good, Madam liked exotic and expensive dishes; but now I set a curb on my hearty appetite. I was not going to grow voluptuous, like the Webster woman. I took to walking so primly that when I next saw Annabilla, my outspoken sister, she asked me if my shoes pinched me. I be-came overly particular about washing my underlinen; I spoke care-fully and if I laughed did so sedately; I creamed and powdered over my mole twice, sometimes thrice every day. After a short time John gave up asking what ailed me. When we coupled we did so as I imagine people do who have been long married, and for no other reason than that we were married and there side by side in the big bed.

His part of the work at the Old Vine took him away a good deal, for it was he who dealt with the silk mercers in Norwich and Lynn, in Colchester, Cambridge and London, so he was luckier than most men tied to a woman they do not fancy much. The high standard of dignity that I had set myself forbade that I should notice too closely the lengths of his absences. There was, in any case, no need; Madam did that. As the days went on I could see that she knew that I had failed in my work of reclamation. I was grateful that she seemed not to hold me to blame.

II

Having come out of my dream, I began to take more notice of my surroundings and the people about me. Even in those early days I found that I tended to see everybody in relationship to Madam Elizabeth. She and her brother—whom everyone called Master Arthur, never Mr. Kentwoode—appeared to manage successfully that difficult thing, maintaining in one department a relationship of friendly equality, in another a master-and-man relationship. No one could be in that house for a full day without seeing who was the head of the business; failing all other evidence there was Arthur himself, always ready with it. "It's your business, Lizbet," or, "That is for you to decide." They seldom talked serious business in public, there was an office for that purpose, but she did often ask his advice or opinion on some trivial matter. Always with the same result. That he was in awe of her was evidenced by the way he would preface certain remarks: "I don't know how you'll like this, Lizbet, but . . ." or, "I assure you, it wasn't my fault . . ." I never heard her say a word to him that was not amiable. She called him "Dear Arthur" and often said, "What should I do without you?" In the main she was pleasant to John too, but brisker: "My dear boy, I'm not going to last forever, you know. What will you do when you're on your own?" She often said things like that, and his answers varied from a frivolous, "Sell it all and buy a ship and sail to the Spanish Main," to a sulky, "When I know that my decisions are final, I shall find them easy to make." More often than not she would laugh, but I have seen her give him a hard cold look, and him return it, though they seldom pushed a difference to the point of bickering. And if it came near, there was always Arthur with his "Now, my boy," his, "John, mind your manners." One day it struck me, rather comically, that they were like two sheep dogs, the one old and so well trained that it never merited rebuke, but was patted and praised, the other only half broken and likely to be nipped by its elder as well as checked by its master.

One day, towards the end of August, on a very hot afternoon I went into the garden and found my father-in-law there before me, sitting in the shade on the cool stone seat.

"We're lucky," he said, hitching himself along to make room for me. "At least, I'm lucky, people don't expect pretty young ladies to work. But I was thinking just now of all the poor devils standing behind counters or in stuffy workshops, perched on stools in counting houses. While here I sit, eating plums. Have one." He bit into his and nodded appreciatively. "I'd have been one of those poor devils but for my sister. Ah, she's a wonderful woman."

To encourage him I said, "My father says she has a rare head for business."

He nodded. "That certainly. But much else. Foresight and courage and . . . and . . ." He failed to find the word, looked at me with his gentle smile and bit his plum again. "You see, Harry and I, we weren't . . . I think my father was to blame; he loved the business, he never seemed to want us to interfere; little jobs he'd give us, I had my music, and I'm afraid that when Father died we went on in the same way, and the business was like something that had been well wound up; it ran, for a while. And we never noticed when it began to run down. When it came to a standstill, it gave us a jolt."

"Had Madam not noticed?" I asked.

"In those days she hardly came out of her bedroom, except for meals. She'd got in the habit while our mother was alive. Mother and Lizbet didn't . . . get on very well. You know what they say about two women in one house." He offered me that gentle apologetic smile again. "And then there was that dreadful day when Harry said to me, 'Arthur, we're ruined.' That's what he said. 'And only Lizbet can save us.' So she did, but not the way Harry looked for. Poor Harry, he was set in his ways and masterful, he couldn't take to the new things. . . . You know, there're those who'll still say that Lizbet was hard and unkind and turned Harry out. That isn't true. I was here. I know. She said to him, one day, 'We're like a cart with shafts fore and aft and one horse pulling that way and the other the other; we'll never make progress.' So she gave him some money, enough to buy a quarter share in Barrowby's. And she sent me to Lyons—that's in France, you know—to learn French and the silk weaving. We had started the silk by that time, but as she said, we hadn't the knowledge, or the language, we could be fooled."

She had sent him and he had gone; he had cast in his lot with hers; so, on this stifling afternoon he could sit in the shade and eat plums, while Harry served customers in the Colchester wineshop.

I thought that. I also thought about that day, long ago, when Madam—and she must have been in her late twenties, no girl—had emerged from her bedroom and taken charge. How had she known that the day of wool was drawing towards its close, that it had meant too much easy money to too many people for too long? I had heard my father speak of those times when there was too much wool on the market. He'd seen the change coming and at Minsham had reared sheep for mutton, not wool, and bullocks for beef. As he said, "One woollen garment can last a lifetime, but meat's gone when the plate is clean." Our acres were profitable and it was only his passion for gambling that led us into lean times occasionally. A lean time, the sale of a tapestry, and here I was.

"I've been wanting to ask you something," my father-in-law said. "I'm afraid it's rather an intimate question. Would John take notice of anything you said? No, that doesn't sound right. Of course he would. What I meant was . . . could you influence him?"

"I don't know. I've never tried. I don't think that I am a person who would have much influence."

He regarded me gravely, kindly, sadly.

"No," he said, "perhaps not. I was only going to ask you, if you had influence, to use it to make him . . . a trifle less truculent. There've been one or two occasions lately when he has seemed to me to be going the way Harry went . . . sharp answers, sullen looks, you know what I mean. You must have noticed. We don't want another disaster, do we?"

"You mean that she might . . . send John away?"

"If he tried her too high. She cannot bear to be crossed, you know. I've talked to John again and again but . . ." He shifted a little on the seat. "People don't get sweeter-tempered as they get older and they are both getting older, Lizbet and John. You could at least point out one thing which wouldn't come well from me. . . ."

"And what is that?"

"That he's only got to be patient, my dear. Threescore years and ten, so it says somewhere in the Bible, and few of us reach that age these days."

I made the mistake of thinking that he was older than Madam; certainly he seemed so with his grey look, his muted voice, his self-effacing manner. I thought—Poor old man, perhaps his threescore and ten are almost tallied; thirty-two of them spent in saying, "Yes, Lizbet," "No, Lizbet," "You know best about that." Still, there was no need to pity him; he certainly did not pity himself; sitting in the shade and eating the purple-bloomed, golden-fleshed fruit, he thought himself lucky, and maybe he was. . . .

I had been married three months when I began to feel queasy first thing in the morning. I said nothing until one morning, brushing Madam's dead hair, I turned dizzy and almost fell. Instantly she was all kind interest and attention, as eager as my own mother would have been to lay down the do's and the don'ts. I was excused the hairdressing, and Betty, reinstated and exultant, softened in her manner towards me, for which I was thankful, for she was a formidable old woman, feared by everyone except Madam, who exploited her devotion quite shamelessly. Betty was also interested in my condition and missed no chance to talk about it.

With the start of the cooler weather, a wave of sickness, cold accompanied by fever, struck the weavers and Madam ordered good nourishing broth to be made and carried out to them regularly. Grumbling about this one day Betty said:

"She's too softhearted, thass what she is. And will they be grateful? Not them! Ungratitude and Frenchies go together. Look at Master Arthur's wife." I had never heard her mentioned before and had concluded that she had died so long ago as to be forgotten. Had I loved John, I should have been more interested, and asked a question or two.

"She was a Frenchie. Master Arthur brung her back with him when he went overseas to learn the silk weaving and the outlandish lingo. A fine dance she led us and all. I never see such a flibbertigibbet in all my days."

"Was she pretty?" She must have been, I thought, comparing Arthur's plain hangdog face with his son's dark good looks.

"If you fancy them black-visaged sort. To me she allust looked as though she could do with a real good wash, though she had the cheek to call us English dirty. Madam took her in, as nice as nice, though not a word of warning had he sent on ahead, and she started making trouble the minute her foot was over the threshold. You can believe this or not," Betty looked at me challengingly, "thass as true as I stand here, she wanted the best bedchamber! Hers by right, she said, a man's wife counted afore his sister, specially a spinster. Get into her head that this was Madam's house and Madam's business she just would not. Rows from morning to night, who would take the head of the table, who should say who was to come to supper. Mind, she never got her way, not once! But she went on trying. Why, she even went out to the sheds and tried to make trouble there—she could talk to them, you see. Towd them they was overworked and underpaid—they wasn't so settled then, some of them listened. They'd know better now. There was one in particular, Jacks was his name, not Jack like good English, Jacks. They," Betty lowered her rough voice dramatically, "carried on. That'll show you the sort *she* was."

Having made this accusation she seemed content to leave the tale.

"What happened?" I asked.

"Oh, Madam bore with her like a angel. She'd laugh when she could, and say breeding women was known to act queer at times. Things'd be different once the baby was here. And so it was. So it was!" She laughed raucously. "Master John was weaned at eight weeks and his ma was sent packing. In a nice way. Madam said being's as Françoise—that was her name—didn't like the weather nor the food, and everything was done so much better in France and she was fretting about her religion—she was a Papist, of all things to be—best thing she could do was go back home with enough money to keep her comfortable for the rest of her days, enough to hev the best bedchamber wherever she went. Jacks went too—but there was never no scandal about that. I was the only one that knew, outside the family."

"How did Mr. Kentwoode take it?"

"Master Arthur? Ask me, he was glad as glad. That'd gone on more'n a year, you know. Him like a bone with two dogs pulling at it, and trying all the while to keep the peace. He could see what he'd got, a scold and a hussy, he was thankful to Madam for getting rid of her so neat."

I remembered his groping for a word; "foresight and courage and . . . and . . ." Was it of this long-past episode he had been thinking? And what exactly was the word he wanted?

Betty was wrong in condemning all the French as ungrateful. I had several times accompanied Madam on her morning rounds of the sheds and it was plain that the workers adored her. They were all Huguenots, or the children of Huguenots who had come out of France, at some time to escape religious persecution. Great numbers of them had settled in London in a place called Hospital Fields, and the Spitalfields silk was Baildon's greatest rival. Madam held her own, even in the London market, by undercutting the price. She was able to do this because at the Old Vine she had something more than a wage in coined money to offer. She had space, fresh air, clean water. There was a row of neat little cabins, called for some unknown reason Squatters' Row, and there were the stables, which had once housed the pack ponies; these, divided off and freshly whitewashed, made pleasant dwellings. Decent people—and most of the Huguenots were decent, clean-living people—preferred a small wage in such a place to a higher one in the stews of London. The arrangement gave her a strong hold on them, for a silkworker sacked from the Old Vine would not find another loom just round the corner, and he would be homeless as well; but there was no resentment in their attitude towards her. They had given her the title of Madam; their faces lit up with welcome when she entered the sheds, their eyes followed her when she left. With the workpeople, I saw at once, she was different, far less cool and stiff; she knew them all by name and which children belonged to which parents; she adopted a hearty, unladylike manner, would slap a man on the shoulder or pat a woman's hand, and was always ready with a joke, speaking a mixture of badly pronounced French and baby English to the older people.

More than once, as time went on, I thought that the word Arthur Kentwoode had needed was "imaginative." It was that quality in her which enabled her to be kind to me at this time in just the right way. There was her coach; take it and visit my mother at Mortiboys, my sister Cecily at Ockley; make an early start and spend a night or two, and even a visit to Clarice at Bures was a feasible plan. She said:

"I don't suppose, being your sisters, they would tell you any horrifying tales. If by chance they should, don't listen. Bearing a baby is the biggest thing that ever happens to most women, so they make much of it."

For every visit she sent me off in fine style, bearing gifts. Just coming off the looms at Baildon was some silk which showed one colour and then another as you moved it in the light. A dress length for Mother in lilac and heliotrope; for Cecily green and gold. For

Clarice, who now had three daughters, yards and yards of beautiful ribbon. And I, of course, was a wonder to behold, all beflounced and bejewelled, with a cloak of double silk, lined with miniver fur.

They said I was thinner and looked older. They asked was I happy. I could say "yes" truly; for once I was with child John didn't matter any more, his work was done. I think that if Madam had not, with a few words, severed the slight bond between us, it would have broken of its own accord as soon as I was with child. What I saw and heard of my sisters' married life did nothing to alter this idea. Their husbands fed and clothed them, got them with child. I was in a slightly different position. Madam fed and clothed me. Sometimes I could, in my mind, catch a glimpse of something different; a love match, a relationship in which the children—though loved and wanted—would be appendages. But love matches are few and far between. I was every bit as well off as any of my sisters, as any woman I knew. Clarice said that Avice's husband had turned out to be close-fisted.

It was after I had come back from my visit to Clarice that Madam one morning eyed me up and down and said:

"Barbara, are you still wearing your stays?"

I said, "Yes," and not without pride. They weren't comfortable, but they held me together; what with them and my careful eating I still, four months gone, did not look blowzy.

"Throw them away," she said. "I've seen what stays can do."

Without thinking I looked at her waist, much smaller than most young girls'. She laughed.

"They were my stays, clapped round Betty's waist. Heavens, I had almost forgotten; yet how important it was at the time. I was seventeen . . ."

I had sometimes wondered upon what hook that surly, independent old woman had been snagged and made into a devoted slave.

"Betty and I shared a room in those days," Madam said. "By my Mother's reckoning that kept us both safe. I had stubbornly refused all offers of marriage, and to Mother's mind that argued a secret lover. Maidservants are naturally always suspect. So we were supposed to spy on one another, but we had our own arrangements. When Betty fell into trouble she was terrified of discovery and of being sent home—anyone who had seen her home could understand that. She had no stays; but I had, a fine pair, not iron, the new whalebone. I laced her into them every morning. I did something else, too. . . ." She broke off and laughed, almost the way she did in the sheds. "It was silly enough to have ruined us, because I had always hated to sew. I made a new kind of working apron, with a big pocket, divided into pouches on the front of it; there was a place for the jar of beeswax or whiting or wood ash, whatever the wench was using, and for rubbing on rag, and polishing cloths. I had the wit not to give it to Betty—I gave it to another girl and Mother thought it such a good notion she asked me to make more. For months all the girls in the house went about looking very pregnant."

At seventeen she had done that!

"How clever," I said.

"Helpless people have to be clever to survive, Barbara. I was an unmarried daughter, completely dependent, Betty had no friend but me, and my mother was a very strict woman—except with Harry. But I was speaking of stays. Betty's baby was malformed and born dead. In the circumstances it was a blessing, though we had a plan . . . so throw away your stays; we want a live, healthy child." She reached for the box in which she kept her rings and slipped them on, with little clinking sounds. Then, with a last look in the glass, she twisted slightly on her stool and faced me.

"People shouldn't interfere between husband and wife; I know that. But you're young and I'm old—though unmarried. Do you mind if I ask you a question?"

I minded, because I guessed that it would be a difficult one to answer; but there was no escape.

"No," I said.

"Do you think you're handling him rightly?"

"In what way, madam?"

"Don't you think you give him too much rein? I know—at least I have heard it said—that a woman having a baby, especially her first, tends to lose interest in her husband. And most decent men are more attentive than usual at such times. John, on every journey he has made lately, has been away a night, or two, even three more than was necessary. Without a question or a remonstrance from you—or so he says. I charged him; 'What do you think Barbara feels?' I asked him. Do you know what he said? He said, 'Barbara is indifferent to me and to my whereabouts.' Dear child, that will never do. You must cajole, nag if necessary." She put out one long white hand and tilted my chin. "You're still pretty enough to cry with good effect."

Perhaps it was because we were in her room again, in almost the exact positions as we had been when she first spoke to me about the Webster woman; the two occasions seemed to link and become one. Despite my childbearing muffling of emotion, a prick of the same disgust made itself felt. I said in a voice whose cold haughtiness surprised me:

"Madam, I was not reared to be a mummer." She was surprised too, and looked at me without speaking. I went on, in a more ordinary way:

"I have never knowingly failed in my duty to my husband. I am always here when he returns, I greet him amiably. I am carrying his child. What more can be required of me?" Even as I spoke I remembered the wild passion of those nights before the dream was shattered and I knew the answer.

Madam said, "You mustn't upset yourself, Barbara. Of course you have been dutiful, and very sweet-tempered and forbearing. Any ordinary man would value you very highly. The trouble—and perhaps that is too serious a word for it—is that John is not quite ordinary. Like my brother Harry, he should have been born a Turk."

I knew nothing of Turks except the saying "Cruel as a Turk," and in fairness to John I said:

"He isn't cruel, madam."

She laughed. "I was thinking of their domestic arrangements rather than their natures. Turks have, I understand, as many wives as they can afford to feed; at least one for every night of the week."

I thought that over while she straightened, with deft light touches, the things on her toilet table.

Then I said, "I don't think that is quite fair to them, either. From what you said I gather that Mr. Henry Kentwoode has been very faithful to . . . to the woman whose husband is a lunatic; and I think that, in his way, John has been faithful to . . ."

"His moll," she said, spitting the word.

"Her name is Emma," I said, wondering, as I did so, how I knew. She laughed.

"You delight me," she exclaimed. "So cool. So fair-minded. But I think you are a little mistaken, even so. It is the element of the forbidden, the outlandish that holds them to their paramours. A case of the grass being greener on the other side of the fence. I'll warrant that if the Bedlamite died tomorrow Harry wouldn't marry his trollop, or, if he did, he'd have a new one within a fortnight. And if . . ." She checked herself sharply, looked away from me and twitched at a bow on her bodice.

"If I died in childbirth and Dan Webster fell down his cellar steps and broke his neck," I said, "you think John would have done with her?"

For the first time in my knowledge of her, she showed what she felt—other than amusement or irritation—in her face. She jumped up and came to me and laid both her hands on my shoulders.

"For God's sake," she said, "don't say such things. Die in childbirth, of all things to mention at such a time! Women do die, because they are ill fed, or have been careless, or get up too soon, or haven't been properly attended, or are worn out. You're young and strong, you shall have the best care. Wasn't I just telling you to throw off your stays? As for John, don't worry about him. Let him go his own way. *We shall have the baby.*"

III

The weather grew warm again. In May, John went to London and came back saying that the plague had shown itself there, not gravely, and so far only in the mean streets. Madam said that he was to make no more visits to the capital until after the first frost of autumn.

"Then the Spitalfielders, on the spot, will get the business."

"They'll get the plague, too, maybe," she said. "And we are not so hard pressed that we must risk our lives for orders."

At the end of June, which was an exceptionally hot month that year, and which I, with only four weeks to go, found very trying, a pedlar came into Baildon, visited about forty houses and lodged at the *Hawk in Hand*. He went to bed early, saying that he had outwalked himself. In the morning he had the plague signs on him, and they dragged him out into a stable, put a pitcher of water nearby and shut the door.

The news ran through the town like water flowing along a gutter. Madam Elizabeth took immediate action. On one side of us lay the country, uncontaminated yet; she sent out her emissaries; this one to buy a dozen sheep; this one a dozen pigs; a third to Flaxham mill for flour. As soon as they had returned, she closed the great gates. Once upon a time the main entry to the Old Vine had been through the house; but when she made that gate into a window and the passage into her dining hall, she had made a new entry on the far side of the house, tall wooden gates set in a high wall, and fastened by iron bars. When those gates were closed, she ordered the bell whose ringing marked the end of working hours to be rung, and every man, woman and child who was employed at the Old Vine was gathered into the yard. Madam climbed onto a mounting block and addressed them, very simply, very forcibly. A single case of plague had occurred in Baildon, she said, and it was nothing to worry about. There could be more. Until we knew, the Old Vine would be isolated. Nobody would go out, or come in. Anyone who had any obligation to another person, outside the Old Vine boundaries, could go, now, if he or she so wished. Such a person would not be readmitted until all danger was past. There would be food for all, she said, work would go on as usual and wages would be paid. Anyone who wanted to leave could leave now.

There were a few of the oldest weavers who had, for one reason or another, taken houses in the town; sons or daughters had married and parents had gone to live with or near them. One or two of the original families, now with several grown children all in work, had saved their money and bought their own houses—a wise precaution, for those who ceased to work at the Old Vine were turned out with no ceremony. Almost all the women servants had homes in the town. For them, at a moment's notice, it was a choice between family ties and work with wages.

The making of such a decision, coming hard on the heels of the news that the pestilence was so near, whitened still further the always pale faces of the weavers and set the girls weeping. It was a frightened, haggard-eyed crowd which Madam addressed in her cool, clear voice.

"Those who wish to leave, go now." She turned her head. "John, could you quickly reckon the wages due for those who wish to go?" She turned back to the people. "For those leaving, pay, reckoned until the end of this day, will be ready in the office, immediately. The rest of you, back to work."

Some of those about to leave paused by the mounting block, anxious with their excuses.

"Thass like this here, madam, me owd mother, she might get sick."

"I understand that, Phyllis."

"Madam, my wife, my little ones . . ."

"Yes, Pierre. You have a duty to them." She said again, "You do all understand; you are free to go, but you cannot come back until the town is clean again. It may be six weeks, or more." And then she put both hands to her mouth and said, "God in Heaven; six weeks!" and looked at me as I stood by the yard door.

"Go," she said, to those who still stood helplessly about the yard. "Go, and God spare you and yours. Arthur, your hand." He held it out and she took it and climbed down from the block, moving for the first time like an old woman; she had skipped up on it nimbly as a girl. "Agnes Fuller was bespoken," she said, turning to me in the doorway and drawing Arthur with her by the hold she retained on his hand. "There are plenty of women about the place capable of assisting, I have no doubt; but Agnes is skilled—and lucky, and I promised this child the best of care. I think we must risk one outing. Have my coach made ready, Arthur, please."

"Where are you going?" he asked.

"Don't be stupid! To Agnes Fuller, the midwife's. If she is clean, if she was not in the tavern yesterday or the day before, I shall bring her back with me."

"Let me go," Arthur said.

"She might lie to you. I know when people are lying. Have the coach made ready."

She brought the midwife back with her; satisfied that she had been far from the source of danger, having been called two days earlier to a woman in a house at the extreme end of the Saltgate. The labour had been long and difficult and was only just ended.

By the time the coach returned, all those who were leaving the Old Vine had gone, and once the coach was inside the gates were closed again. It was a little like being in a besieged town in the old times when a whole town could be sealed off as easily as the Old Vine now was. Madam Elizabeth certainly had all the qualities that would have made a good commander of a garrison. She had swiftly organised the necessary material things, and now she turned her attention to what was, after the plague itself, the worst enemy—fear.

It was impossible not to be frightened of the plague, whose ways were so secret, so mysterious and so baffling. In London and in other large towns it was said to strike every summer, so that all through the warm weather people were sickening and dying, but in small numbers. Then there would be the exceptional year when it spread like wildfire, abandoning the poor, overcrowded hovels which were its constant dwelling place, and stalking into palaces and mansions and even into country houses standing aloof in their own acres. Nobody knew how it spread, or why. There were those who said that it passed by touch, that it was possible to catch it even by touching something that had been touched by one sick of it; others held that it was conveyed by the breath; yet it was known for a wife to be stricken, her husband stay healthy; for a woman to hold a dying child in her arms and live to mourn its loss. There were cases so isolated that for lack of other explanation people said that it rode on the wind, or was carried by birds, rats, fleas. People also said that the moon ruled it, that it gathered strength as the moon waxed and weakened as it waned. What every-one—even those who like myself had been lucky and never seen a plague-stricken person—knew for a surety, was that it brought death in a loathsome form, and that there was no known cure.

Madam left me to show the midwife to the room she would occupy during the waiting time, and herself went out to the sheds. She was gone a long time and when she returned had a grave look—and her own theory about the plague.

"The fools will frighten themselves sick," she said. "There're the empty places and already they're looking at them in such a way you'd think their owners were in the graveyard, instead of home, on holiday. Those that are at work, you'd think their fingers were candles, half melted. This won't do at all." She twisted her rings thoughtfully. "We must have a feast. John, go and pass the word quickly. We'll roast a sheep and have plenty of ale. And some music, Arthur, good merry music that people can dance to. That will put everybody in good heart."

It was a warm pleasant evening, just right for an outdoor feast. From over the high wall that divided the garden from the yard came the scent of flowers, to mingle oddly with the odour of roast mutton and of burned fat that fell from the turning joint onto the fire beneath. Some old trestle tables and benches had been dragged from some dusty corner and hastily cleaned and spread with the white, beautifully embroidered cloths which were the pride of the weaving women's hearts. The bell to cease work had rung early, so that everyone had time to wash and don best clothes. When the sheep was ready for eating and the company assembled, the mood was moderately cheerful, though still a trifle uneasy. It showed in an unusual restraint, even the children were subdued.

The good roast meat and the ale soon altered things; voices reached normal level, laughter was heard. Madam nodded, satisfied.

"They'll all sleep well tonight and by tomorrow will have learned to live with the fact that a plague case reached Baildon. Twenty years ago it would have been taken for granted; but times change and we grow soft. I think I shall make a little speech."

She stood up from the velvet and gilt chair which had been carried out and placed by one of the tables. The movement attracted the attention of all present, and within five seconds there was silence. She spoke without effort, and with complete calm.

She mentioned the Bible story of the Flood and Noah, comparing the safety of the Old Vine with that of the Ark. She mentioned the healthful qualities of a cheerful heart and hard work, and ended:

"Six looms will be unmanned because those who worked them felt that their duty lay elsewhere. If by working harder, or longer, those of you now listening to me can do any part of their work, it shall be measured and paid for double. Now we will have some music and I hope that those who can will dance."

Arthur moved to his virginals which had been brought from the music room, and his little group of picked musicians put fiddle to cheek and pipe to lip. Madam stood and watched for a moment and then turned to me.

"I think you should go in, Barbara. I'll come with you. It has been a long day."

Inside the house it was cooler and almost dusk. We went up the wide stairs together, moving slowly, two women, one burdened with the new life within, the other with years and responsibility; sharing the relief of the coolness, the escape from watching eyes. We reached the landing, and near the window which overlooked the yard paused to say good night and part, she to go to her great chamber, I to mine. And at that moment the music trailed raggedly away and a single voice, pitched high, reached us, a blurred, wordless sound.

Madam went to the window and opened it.

". . . a time to eat and drink and make merry, to feast and dance and sing? Is it not that we should be on our knees, imploring God to spare us and forgive us our sins? Of Noah and his Ark, yes, the Bible tells us; but it tells of the sins of the people, and why those who were saved were chosen. Those who feared God and kept His commandments . . ."

I recognised the speaker; he was an old weaver, one of the first, whose name of Bonhomme, John had told me, had become Bonham in the next generation. His sight was almost gone now, he lived with his sons in Squatters' Row and did little tidying-up jobs about the sheds and the yards. His shoulders were stooped, and although he was thin he had the soft bulging paunch that came of long sitting at the loom.

John, from his place near the musicians, had jumped up, and shouting angrily, "Man, you're drunk!" was bearing down upon Bonham.

Madam leaned from the window and called:

"Let him speak!"

The last of the day's light shone in the eyes of the people, as their gaze shifted, upwards to the window, back towards Bonham. The fear and uneasiness which had lain like a spell on the place all day, and which the feasting had just dispelled, was back, reinforced. Madam, through her teeth, said:

"Just what I feared. The very worst thing. Wait here."

She had come up the stairs with the weary tread of the aging; but she went down them as a cat goes, her feet seeming not to touch the treads. I heard the slam of the kitchen door. I looked for her to appear in the yard, wondering what she would do, what she would say; even wondering for a second that she should have abandoned the advantage that the position at the window would have given her, if she intended to speak again.

The man had started again, his manner becoming wilder, his words more incoherent and biblical. Flinging his arms wide to include all the company—who had, after all, only enjoyed a moderate issue of ale—he spoke of winebibbers. Then, with a pointed finger, narrowing his accusation and looking at my husband, he accused all fornicators and whoremongers. The names of old lost cities gave a flavour of poetry to his outpourings; he spoke of Sodom and Gomorrah, of Jerusalem and Babylon.

Madam was back at my side, her right hand clenched and held close to her bodice, as though a stitch in the side troubled her, or her heart beat too hard.

She leaned from the window again and called, still in that voice which, without straining or shouting, made itself heard clearly above or through the man's heavier tones.

"Come closer, Bonham. I want to hear you."

He obeyed, stumbling his careful way until he stood under the window. There he raised his head and demanded:

"Can ye touch fire and not be burned? Can ye touch pitch and not be defiled? Woe to this generation that has lost all sense of sin. Hearken to the voice of God. As I live, saith the Lord God, surely with a mighty hand and with an outstretched arm and with fury poured out will I rule over you. Now the vials of His wrath are opened and the plague is poured out upon us as the plagues were poured out upon the Egyptians in the time of Moses."

Little flecks of foam formed at the corners of his mouth and flew into the air with the force of his speaking. Behind him the people clustered in little knots, as though seeking comfort from nearness, some of the children and one or two women were beginning to weep. I saw John and his father lean towards one another and speak and look upwards to the window; I saw John shake his head and his beautiful teeth shone in something that was not a smile. Arthur came forward and hurried into the house. In a moment he was at the stair foot.

"Lizbet, he must be stopped. He's mad, he's starting a panic. John and I could take him . . . and the rest are not all with him, *yet*. But they . . ."

"It's all right, Arthur. I'm biding my time."

Outside the frenzied voice went on.

"Cry and howl, son of man, because you have made your iniquity to be remembered, your transgressions are discovered . . ." The words reeled out, almost meaningless in their confusion, and yet ominous. In the end, for lack of breath alone, he stopped. Under his shirt his thin ribs moved with the short sharp gasps of a dog that has been running.

Into the silence Madam spoke.

"We are to repent, eh? Bonham, I know my Bible, too. It says—in sackcloth and ashes." She made one of her lightning movements, the clenched fist shot out through the open window and released, into his upturned face, wide-eyed, gape-mouthed, a handful of ashes from the kitchen hearth.

"There you are. And you'll find a sack in the barn!"

For just a second the tension in the yard, poised on the very pinpoint of hysteria, balanced and trembled, and then fell over on the side of mirth. I must admit I laughed myself. There was something irresistibly comic in the sight of the man who, a second before, had been a prophet, denouncing all and sundry for their sins and foretelling doom and judgment, rubbing ash out of his eyes, spitting small cinders from his mouth. Those who had been most frightened laughed the hardest, cleansing themselves. One of Bonham's sons, roughly, because he was embarrassed, took him by the arm and led him away. Madam turned to Arthur, still at the stair foot, and said:

"Now go and play!"

I looked at her, and there was some awe mingled in my admiration.

"Madam, how *did* you think of that?"

"How else could I have discredited him—so quickly? What worries me is that most of those shafts were aimed at John. Huguenots are strongly Protestant, and Protestantism all too easily becomes Puritanism. You can see that today, wherever you look. If the country goes Puritan and I am in my grave, God knows . . . Well, never mind, we'll think about that tomorrow."

First thing in the morning, Bonham came and asked permission to leave the Old Vine. There were sinners outside who must be warned, he said. Madam said he could go, and welcome, it'd mean one less mouth to feed; and anyone who shared his view that the Old Vine was a stronghold of iniquity could go with him. Nobody appeared to. Outside, free of all restraint, he gave his lunacy full rein; clad in sackcloth, with ashes on his head and carrying a pine torch, he ran about the stricken town, his tirade reduced to a manageable parrot-cry, "Repent ye, repent ye, the day of judgment is at hand."

Later in that day, my father came riding in to ask me to go to Mortiboys. Finding the great gates closed, he jumped to the conclusion that we were already afflicted, and when he came into the parlour he was deathly pale and the flesh quivered on his face bones. It was the only time in all my life that I saw Father out of countenance. In his relief at finding himself mistaken, he extended the invitation to Madam, to John and Arthur.

"Barbara must please herself," Madam said, "though she would be well advised to consult with her midwife. I must stay here. I think the Old Vine is as safe as Mortiboys."

Father was one of those who thought the wind carried the plague. He said so. "We're off the main road, with the whole of Layer Wood between us and the wind. You never hear of plague where there're trees to act as a windbreak."

"In that case, we may have been blown upon already," Madam said.

"That I'll risk. What I can't have is Barbara sending for her mother once she's brought to bed. The pest may then be running strong."

They both looked at me to decide. I was torn both ways. The plague had no place in my calculations, except as a side factor; I had that certainty, common to women in my state, that nothing could touch me. Madam's foresight and care in installing the midwife a full four weeks early seemed to commit me to staying where I was; on the other hand I looked ahead, saw myself safely delivered, anxious to show off my child, and still isolated here. At Mortiboys I should have Mother and both my sisters who were within riding distance, and two of my brothers and their wives.

I said, "If Agnes thinks it advisable, I would like to go."

Instantly I knew that I had made the wrong choice; women in my state, happily married, or making a pretence at it, didn't make such decisions on their own. They clung to their husbands.

Father said, "It isn't for long and it isn't far; John can ride out and see you." He was saying what I should have said.

Madam said, "I'm afraid not, Mr. Hatton. I have given the order and it applies to everyone, to me myself, and to the stable sweeper. No coming and going until this thing is ended."

I said, "In that case, I think I should stay here." And having said it I could have burst into tears, thinking that for outward show, to make something look well, I had sacrificed what I really wanted.

When Madam said, "Nonsense! At times like this surely a mother matters more than a husband, who at best can only stand about and wring his hands and say how deeply *he* is suffering—is that not so, Mr. Hatton? If Agnes agrees—we'll send for her now and hear her verdict—off you go. The coach can drive at walking pace." I wanted, for the first time in our acquaintance, to throw my arms around her and kiss her painted cheek.

Agnes, whether she believed in the virtue of trees as a barrier, or simply felt that the further away from the centre of trouble the better, decided for Mortiboys. So there was hurried packing, the horses were harnessed to the coach, and we rumbled away.

Before I left, they had tactfully arranged that John and I should be in a room together for a few minutes, and a curious little scene had taken place.

He came in and said, "So you're going to Mortiboys. I think that is very wise." Then he said, "We could be taking leave of one another forever."

What a thing to say, I thought.

"You mean . . ." I said, placing my hands on my swollen stomach, "that I . . . that I might . . ."

"God bless you, no. You're young and healthy, and Agnes Fuller's boast is that she has never lost a mother yet. No, I was thinking of the plague. Barbara, I'm sorry I haven't been a better husband to you. I mean that, if it is the last thing I ever say to you. At first I meant . . . and I thought . . . that things would be different. It seemed . . . I shall never know. . . . You were very sweet," he said. "I blame myself entirely."

"Wrongly," I said, able now, full and ripe, passive, unfeeling, to speak the truth. "I was to blame. I took offence at something. . . ." Even now I found it hard to bring myself to the point of saying what had offended me.

"You were young," he said. "I should have handled you more gently, with more restraint. But you were very sweet and I . . . I had had little experience with inexperience."

"It wasn't that. It was hearing about Emma Webster and . . . yes, now I will tell you the truth . . . and what you said about me the first time we met. Don't pretend you can't remember! That I was so much like her—to look at—that it hurt. And she *is* like me, only fat and down-at-heel, and a trollop." I added the last word with spite.

He looked at me, and I realised that all the lines in his dark face, usually set in an expression of mockery—of himself or others—could be sad too.

"I never saw her so, you know. And the words you minded so much—they were a compliment. Though you couldn't know that, the way they'd be repeated to you. If ever the Devil took human form . . . There's no time now. If we come through this, we'll try again."

I was in no state to think quickly, or clearly. The dark, inner meaning of what he had said did not strike me then. All I knew was that the remark which had spoilt it all, stopped up my natural feelings, changed me, hadn't been meant in the way I had taken it. I even overlooked the significance of that "I never saw her so." I reached out both hands and said, "We'll do better."

Madam and my father came in; it was the sound of their steps and voices outside the room which had made John say there was no time. Madam had made an excuse to get Father away, saying she wanted him to see the place she had made ready for the isolation of anyone at the Old Vine who had so much as a headache or a sneezing fit. They had left me and John to take leave of one another as a fond couple should; and they found us as Father, anyway, might have expected, hand in hand. Our final leave-taking kiss as I was helped into the coach left nothing to be desired either. I shall carry the memory of it to my grave.

I never saw John again.

IV

Of what took place at the Old Vine while I lay snug and safe under my father's roof, I only know by hearsay and the stories don't always run together.

In Baildon the plague spread rapidly; the Old Vine, with its good well of water, its store of sound food, the high standard of cleanliness which Madam's desire to have everything look well enforced, remained untouched. At the end of the first week, two thirds of the absent weavers' work had been done by the others, and to celebrate this Madam ordered another feast. Years after, in Baildon, they would tell tales of how, with death stalking the town, we at the Old Vine feasted and made merry and escaped the sickness. Bonham, now regarded as a holy man of God, had denounced us and been expelled—so the story ran—and all this feeling, together with old jealousies and dislikes, mounted up into a form of madness. On the evening of Madam's second feast, when the scent of roasting meat and the sound of music drifted over the wall, a gang of louts gathered stones in the road and broke every pane of window in the house. By the end of the next day, by setting every man on the place to the work, Madam had stout wooden shutters barred into place behind the ragged teeth of glass that the stones had left.

Presently, to the ever present fear of death, the loss of loved ones, the constant tolling of the church bell, the many interments every day, hunger was added. The miller died of plague and the mill stood idle. The country people, upon whose market stuff the town so largely depended, stayed at home on their farms and in their villages. Poor people always live from hand to mouth, and in these modern times, in a thriving town like Baildon, even the better sort of household was not so well stocked as in the old times. The people were hungry, and there was the Old Vine, stuffed with good things. The sheep announced their presence by bleating, and anybody, walking by the wall at the rear of the premises, could smell the pigs.

On the fourth, or fifth, of Madam's feasts—nobody seemed certain which—the same lawless element as had smashed the windows, but now greatly increased, planned a raid. They brought a ladder and swarmed over the back wall, crept up past the deserted dwellings of Squatters' Row, and appeared suddenly in the yard, just as the pig was lifted from the crossbars over the fire and being carried to the trestle on which it was to be carved. The intruders were armed with knives and cudgels, and looked—as Betty told me afterwards—very wild and frightening, but all they demanded at first was a share of the food.

"Madam could see there worn't much to be done, our folks took by surprise like that and with nowt but table knives. So she say, pleasant-like, 'Help yourselves,' and to us near her she say to run round the trestles and tell everybody to go in the house, quick, the thieves might hev the plague on them. Most of us did like she said. Only Master Arthur took off to turn the beasts loose, he was a farsighted man for all he was so quiet. And Master John, he stood by the meat with the long carving knife in his hand. He lost his temper. I was running for the house door, with the rest, but I heard him say, plain as plain, something about armed robbery and 'Touch it at your peril,' he say. Maybe that'd hev stopped them a bit, armed robbery being a hanging matter and them only out for a bit of a prank like, then. But somebody else say, 'Thass the whore-monger!' And then they set about him and beat him to mash."

They ate the roast pig and the freshly baked bread and drank the ale, so to the plague wildness there was drunkenness added. They wrecked the looms and pillaged the silk store. It was said that in the following days corpses went to the graves shrouded in Mad-am's fashionable new shot silk. Somebody set fire to the place where the thread silk, which was imported spun and dyed, was housed. It was worth hundreds of pounds, the Old Vine's biggest single asset, aside from the looms themselves.

Despite Arthur's efforts, the livestock was rounded up and driven off, and what exactly happened to Arthur nobody ever knew. He was found lying senseless near the pigpen with no more than a bruise and a scratch or two, and died, without speaking, next day. Whether the excitement had been too much for him, or one of the bruises more serious than it seemed, there was no means of knowing.

Of all this, at the time, I knew nothing. When I reached Morti-boys my legs were swollen; Agnes said it was due to water and that by lying in bed, with the foot higher than the head, I should even it out. So to the normal discomforts of my state were added the thrumming in the ears, the sense of the heart beating behind the eyes, which result from such a position. Then, in due time, I went through the gateway of agony and learned how apt is the expression "to be delivered." With my son in my arms and my family about me, I was very happy. I shared Madam's confidence in her pre-cautions; the plague would end, I should return to the Old Vine, and John and I would complete our reconciliation. At that moment, lying there in the milky, cherished idleness of the recently delivered, even the loss of happiness during the past year seemed a small thing, measured against the years which lay—I thought—ahead. As my body knit, I began to remember those three nights when I had given myself without reserve, and the warmth of the kiss when we parted, with all its promise.

I saw nothing sinister in all the care and petting I received. Even when Father one day stood by the bed and said that I knew I was welcome to stay at home as long as I liked, I was unwarned. Wrapped in another dream, I made the progress back to ordinary life, the first sitting out in a chair by the window, the first venture downstairs, a few steps into the sunny garden. And then, when all danger of milk fever, or white leg, or afterbirth melancholy was past, Mother told me.

They all said that I was very brave. The truth was that my grief— which was genuine enough—was mixed with a furious rage, and rage is a bracing thing. I cried, thinking of that wasted year, of the reconciliation which would now never flower. Then anger would dry the tears. Madam had ruined my marriage by a few carefully chosen words, and I had been fool enough to let her. I was angry with myself too; but not nearly so angry as I was with her. I could see through her now, see all her cunning, her lust for power. By keeping people separate and unsure of themselves, she could rule them. If John and I had gone on as we started, sooner or later we should have combined against her domination. It had probably been the same with poor Arthur and his Françoise.

Into my hatred came the memory of the way in which she had once said, "We shall have the baby." Well, there I could take a small revenge, I thought. She'd share no baby of mine. His father was dead; she was only a great-aunt; she had no claim at all. We'd stay under my father's roof, my baby and I, and never set foot in the Old Vine again. That would punish her.

V

Madam came out to Mortiboys on one of those tempestuous days which disturb the golden calm of September. This time she came unannounced, alone, riding in the wooden cart ordinarily used for the transport of flour, pig meal and the like. Mother and I were sitting in the hall when we heard the sound of wheels; Mother jumped up and looked out of the window, and said, "It's Elizabeth Kentwoode. In a cart!"

"I won't see her," I said, getting up as quickly as I could with the baby in my arms.

"Oh, there hasn't been a fresh case for three weeks now," Mother said. "She wouldn't have come had there been any risk."

"It isn't that," I said, making for the stairs.

"What do you fear then?" Mother began to ask, going towards the door and getting ready her welcome look.

Safe behind my bedroom door I found myself trembling so much that I had to lay the baby down for safety. I sat on the bed beside him, gripping my elbows with my hands and willing myself to be calm and strong. In a few minutes Mother came.

"She wants to see you—and the baby. That's natural enough, surely. Come along, Barbara; brush your hair back and bring him down."

"I don't want to see her. I don't want her hands on my child."

"Have you gone mad?" Mother asked, almost crying with impatience. "I should have thought that at a time like this . . . John was her nephew, but as dear as a son . . . a shared grief, even if you have had differences . . . should bring you together."

I hadn't thought of that. And without telling a long, involved story—a story that I could never tell anyone, and one that no one would ever understand—I couldn't explain. Also, to stay hiding here was really a confession of weakness.

"All right," I said. I picked up the baby and went downstairs.

She was wearing a black dress, as plain as a dress could be, woollen. The saffron-coloured dead hair was as elaborately arranged, the false pink and white complexion was in place. Behind it the face had aged by twenty years, grooved, carved, chiselled into something terrible, an All Hallowseen mask. Not of grief . . . nothing so soft and passive as grief. In fact, in that one moment, as we faced one another, the anger and hatred that was in me looked out and recognised its fellow, only a thousand times greater.

Once, after a night of hard frost, I touched an iron door handle and it was so cold that it burnt, as though it had been red hot. Her look was like that; so cold that it scorched.

She said, "I would have come before, Barbara, but I wanted to be quite sure that it was safe. When they broke in, they brought the plague with them. Several of our people have died. So I waited. I hope you didn't think me unkind."

"I understood," I said.

She bent her head above the baby.

"He's very beautiful. I think he is the most beautiful baby I have ever seen."

And I thought—Ha! You won't catch me on that worn old hook.

But, bless my soul, it is always the hook that you are not expecting which snags you.

There were a few moments during which civil words were exchanged, and Mother was busy with the spiced buns and the wine—Rhenish this time, because Father was once more riding the crest of his perilous wave. And then Madam said:

"In addition to my wish to see Barbara and my great-nephew I have another errand. I wondered if your husband would care to buy back the tapestry, for the price I paid for it. I must let it go and I thought it only right that he should have the first refusal."

"He hated to sell it," Mother said. "I think he might be glad. But of course it's not for me to say."

"It is one of the few things that can be spared," Madam said. "All I have left, really, is the house; and it would not be wise to strip it too much. It has a certain . . . reputation, and I hope that sheer curiosity will attract a certain amount of custom."

Mother and I lagged behind, like two very slow hounds while the foremost make the kill. What was she talking about?

"Custom?" Mother repeated on a questioning note.

"Custom," Madam said. "You see, my looms are wrecked. Silk looms are very fine, very intricate and expensive. Thirty years ago, when I began with two, rigging them and buying the silk to start off with, cost so much that poor Arthur and I lived like paupers for three years. But we were young. I can't," she said, with the air of one confessing to a grave fault, "at my age, go through that again. Arthur understood the process—as I never did, and John travelled and knew the mercers. Without them . . . No, it is impossible. So I am left with the house. I could sell it and go to live in a cottage, and wait for death, I suppose. But I choose not to do that. So the house must set to work and earn a livelihood for me. I intend," she said, "to open it as a hostelry."

Mother said, "Oh!"

"Not a *tavern*. A place where decent people, compelled for any reason to travel, can find the same comforts and refinements as they have in their own homes."

"Well," Mother said, "I'll not say that that wouldn't be answering a need. When we went to the christening of my daughter Avice's first child, we were two nights on the road and the accommodation was unsavoury to say the least."

"I considered the need. I also remembered something that my grandfather told me when I was a very little girl. He was speaking of the old days, when the Abbey was in being. Travellers of quality were then accommodated within its walls and in return were expected to make gifts. If it is properly conducted there is nothing humiliating, so far as I can see, in the provision of hospitality for travellers."

"Well, no," Mother said, dubiously; and then more firmly, "No, of course not." She looked vaguely about our hall, and up towards the gallery off which the bedrooms opened. "Myself," she said, "I wouldn't care for it—keeping open house for all and sundry."

"That," Madam said, "I shall never do. The Old Vine will still be my home and I shall reserve the right to pick and choose who sleeps under its roof." She went through the familiar gesture of twisting her rings, but her fingers were bare. The only ornament she had was a simple string of blue beads, and they were half hidden by the close, prim neck of her bodice. She looked at me. "I came to see the baby," she said, "and to ask about the tapestry; but I also wished to talk to Barbara—about the future." Mother, not always the most tactful, and certainly not the most pliable of women, took this as dismissal and rose. "Please, Mrs. Kentwoode," Madam said, "there is nothing secret or private in what I have to say. I have to confess that I never *saved* money. There seemed no reason for me to do so. To instal a new loom, or lay in a stock of raw silk, that seemed good policy; for the rest, why spare? I had a thriving business."

She stood up, and still twisting those invisible rings, began to walk up and down.

"I mean to have another," she said, "but it will have to be made." She swung round and faced me.

"You can stay here if you wish and every month I will send you what I can afford. The amount I cannot predict, for I am going into this business blindfold, as once I did before. I prospered then; I may again. If you sit here, waiting for pennies to drop into your lap, when I die there will be no more pennies. If, on the other hand, you throw in your lot with mine and help me, the house and all that is in it, and all that I intend to make of it, will be yours, and your child's."

Mother said, in a flustered way, "She shouldn't be bothered by such matters yet. Having the baby and being widowed . . . This is no time. Presently, presently."

"Oh, I agree. It is not a matter for hasty decision. I would like to point out that no menial work would ever be asked of you, Barbara. Betty is active and loyal and there are several others. But I can foresee situations in which I shall need more help than any hireling can be expected to give. As my father used to say, a man can be in two places at once, but not in three. But I hope that I have made it clear, I am not asking for your help, I am offering you a business proposition."

She was offering me a challenge; and that made me her equal, for one does not challenge one's inferiors.

I said, "You don't have to be clever with me any more. Talking about what will happen when you are dead, like an old bedridden man cajoling a basin of broth from a grudging daughter-in-law!"

Mother said, "Barbara!" in a shocked tone, but I was past caring about such things as respect to one's elders or civility to people under one's roof. I looked at Madam Elizabeth and I did not forget the wrongs she had done me, what I did was to find it possible to see them in proportion, as a part of a whole. So I looked at her with fury and hatred, and respect and admiration which was painfully near to love.

"God knows how you do it," I said, "but you always strike the right note. You're old," I said brutally, "old and ruined, beaten to your knees. Anybody else would be done for. But you're struggling up, ready to fight again. What else, by the flames of Hell, *can* I do but come in and fight alongside?"

Mother said, "The poor girl's gone hysterical."

Madam said, "Oh no. You underestimate your daughter, Mrs. Hatton. That is a mistake I never made."

Interlude

As it had done when Martin Reed started wool chandling, and later when Madam Elizabeth turned it over to silk weaving, the Old Vine in its new guise as a hostelry started off well. Its position was in its favour, for it stood on a main road; every other inn in Baildon was in a narrow street, easily reached by riders on horseback, but more difficult of access to the goods wagons and the coaches which appeared in increasing numbers upon the roads as the seventeenth century advanced.

It had another advantage too, one of which Madam Elizabeth, and after her, Barbara Kentwoode, was sharply aware and determined to exploit in every possible way. It was a new inn and it was different, divorced from the old idea of inns being drinking dens, rough places which respectable people avoided as much as possible. To stay in the Old Vine was very much like staying in a well-run private house.

All over England, especially in the East, Puritan ideas were in the ascendant; the old inns, where men drank themselves stupid, and the chambermaids were notorious for their complaisance, were out of favour. The Old Vine neatly filled a gap which had yawned ever since the Dissolution of the Monasteries which had regarded hospitality to travellers of a decent kind as one of their duties.

Elizabeth Kentwoode was as well equipped to run a respectable inn as her house was to become one. Nobody, guest or servant, trifled with her. The honest merchant's blood which ran in her veins made it natural for her to give good value for money; her boundless egoism made it natural and necessary for her to have her own way at every turn. Most people she could quell with one glance of her cold, completely fearless eyes; the few who attempted to bandy words with her seldom came up for another bout. Upon the very few, hardy enough to defy, she used another weapon, one she did not name even to herself. Hatred, wholly concentrated, and properly directed, can be a powerful striking force.

To Barbara, her niece-in-law, who had so surprisingly thrown in her lot with hers, and to the child, Christopher, she was consistently indulgent.

She lived into her seventy-ninth year, an age not often attained in her day, and when at last she took to her bed, it seemed for a little time that she was about to impose her will upon Death's self.

To Barbara she said, "I shall not get out of this bed again. You came to my aid when I was alone, and I'm sorry now to leave you alone. You have a soft streak. Master it if you can, for there are hard times coming. Only the very strong and the very weak will survive, the strong because they always do, the weak because they don't matter one way or the other."

Seven years were to elapse before the Civil War broke out, but the shadow of its coming already lay heavy and dark on the land.

Barbara, with her soft streak dominating, urged the old woman to lie back in comfort on the soft down pillows, not to worry, to try to rest.

"I shall manage," she said.

"If you trim your sails to the prevailing wind—always remembering that prevailing winds blow themselves out, in time." Suddenly, and surprisingly, since she had never in her life had anything to do with sheep, Madam Elizabeth began to speak of shepherds. "He'd be a shortsighted fool," she said, "who, because the wind happened to be blowing from the west on the day when he built his lambing pen, set it open to the east, when for every spring within man's memory the real wind has blown from that quarter."

"What are you trying to tell me?" Barbara asked.

"All along, in England, we have been loyal to our kings, good or bad, just as, in spring, the wind here blows from the east. There may be a freakish day, but such should be ignored. There was a freakish day in my life, a day when the wind blew all wrong and I let it change my course. If I'd waited, and not been so set on a string of blue beads which were suffering no damage . . . Hasty, that is what I was; it's always a mistake to be hasty, Barbara."

Soon her words became wilder, less coherent; it became evident that she, who had feared nothing, feared death and the hereafter.

The weakness which had made her take to her bed and say that she would never leave it again seemed to recede as her dementia mounted. She rose from the bed and tottered about the room, sometimes speaking in terms of fierce accusation, sometimes pleading force of circumstances, but always in words so disconnected and vague that Barbara, her constant companion through four terrible nights and days, never understood either the accusations or excuses.

"Why should I wish to harm my grandfather?" the old woman would demand. "My one friend. The one who loved me, the only person I ever loved. It was his fault, he knew how I loved those blue beads."

She would switch to the subject of her brother Harry.

"Why should I lend him money? He'd wasted all his own. And he was my enemy from the beginning, always my enemy. I was wearing my blue beads the day when he came to my room and said, 'Lizbet, unless you help me, I'm ruined.' Twenty years or more I'd waited for that day. I thought—How little you know, for all your worldly ways."

She had spoken of her grandfather often, Harry was mentioned occasionally, Barbara knew who they were. But who was the priest who shared with them the haunting of the old woman's last hours? Priests had left, had been driven out of England long ago, though it was rumoured that the Queen, Henrietta Maria, a Frenchwoman, had one or two in her household. It was a fact that the stern, wife-dominating Puritans in the country held against their King.

"You have no choice, no choice at all," Madam Elizabeth said, addressing some invisible presence. "You must hide and starve, because wherever you go you bring trouble."

In the end Death came and quietened her.

Barbara Kentwoode had admired her aunt-by-marriage, and the admiration, though founded upon an old hatred, had grown with the years. Left alone, with a business to run, and feeling herself fundamentally ill equipped for the task, she fell back upon an almost slavish emulation. The strict rules laid down by Madam for the conduct of the inn were still in force; in manner and, so far as physical differences would allow, in appearance, the new hostess of the Old Vine was a copy of the old. The only person who ever saw her softer side, knew her as a person in her own right, was her son Christopher; and when in 1642 the Civil War broke out, he rode away and was lost to her for a time. Two years later, when Antony Flowerdew came to Baildon on his secret errand, it would have taken a very perspicacious person to see, behind the manner and the mask, anything remaining of the girl who had been born Barbara Hatton.

Part Four

ANTONY FLOWERDEW'S TALE

Circa 1645

I

When the Civil War broke out I was thirty-four years old, which is somewhat too late to go soldiering for the first time, unless you are fired with great enthusiasm for a cause. I went unwillingly, and from loyalty to my master, Sir Henry Saxham, rather than from conviction.

Sir Henry had been a Member of Parliament and was a staunch supporter of Pym and Hampden, but he was no Puritan. Once the war was under way, and even more so when it was over, people began to reduce it all to the oversimplification which makes history —so called—easy to remember, and now there is a general belief that the King's men were all clad in velvet and lace, drank too much, used oaths every time they opened their mouths and were devils with women; while the Parliamentarian forces consisted of stern, upright, sober men, plainly clad, all bearing names like John Oh-Lord-Arise-Scatter-Thy-Enemies Smith.

It certainly wasn't so in the beginning. When we, whom Sir Henry always called "my little lot," rode north from Alchester on a warm August morning, we were as gaily dressed, as well mounted and on occasion as foul-tongued as any similar party of Cavaliers could be.

There were sixteen of us in all; Sir Henry, two of his nephews (he had no son), his daughter Katharine's husband, sons of neighbours and of tenant farmers, these last superbly well mounted, and some yokels straight from the plough's tail; and there was myself, who since the age of eighteen had been employed by Sir Henry in a capacity which defies exact description. Sometimes he called me his secretary, sometimes his scrivener fellow. I wrote his letters and kept the estate accounts; I dealt with complaints and requests from tenants and escorted Lady Saxham whenever she went anywhere where her husband scented boredom. I lived in the house, was always called Antony by the family and Mr. Flowerdew by everyone else, and was paid so little that I was still virtually dependent upon the tanyard which I had repudiated when I was about twelve years old. Luckily for me my father, in *his* youth, had known a moment of rebellion, quickly quelled, so he understood and assisted my efforts to escape into sweeter-smelling air. When he died and it became my property, I hired it out on a make-and-take basis and my share made more than adequate pocket money.

When I realised that I was to make one of "my little lot," I ventured a halfhearted protest.

"Sir," I said, "do you think I shall be worth my room as a soldier? I've never handled a weapon in my life."

"You'll learn," Sir Henry said. "When you see some damned great fellow bent on lopping your head off, you'll make an effort to whip his off first, I'll warrant. Besides, there'll be drill; all my Johnny Hodges have a lot to learn. And every four-five days you can write a letter to my lady so she'll know we're alive."

Like many men who have never bothered to master the arts of reading and writing, my master had an ambivalent attitude towards those who had; at once contemptuous and respectful; contemptuous because a quill was not really a man's weapon, and respectful because the whole thing had a faint flavour of magic. Lady Saxham was a great letter writer and during those times when she was left on the Lincolnshire manor and Sir Henry and I were in London, I would read her letters to him and he would sometimes say, with a kind of childlike wonder, "All those miles away and it's as though I'd seen the thing happen with my own eyes. Now you write back and tell her . . ."

He was—to put it mildly—easygoing in the matter of morals, but at the same time extremely fond of his wife, and I believe that he did take me to war with him as a means of communication.

It is hard to credit now, but when the war broke out the great mass of the ordinary people in England were, like me, committed to no cause. As it went on people were forced, for this reason or that, to take sides, and when it was won of course all the waverers declared that they had been for Parliament from the beginning; but in 1642 there were more people on the middle of the seesaw than at either extreme end, and if the King had played his cards a little more cleverly and been less ruled by his French wife, the whole sorry business might well have been avoided.

I disliked soldiering every bit as much as I had expected to, though Sir Henry, in his offhand, mocking way, made things as easy for me as possible. It wasn't until he was killed on Chalgrove Field that I had any real heart for fighting, and ironically in that same skirmish, my usefulness as a soldier ended. A wound, I thought at first of no consequence, stiffened as it healed. It was in my right shoulder, and I never again had the proper use of the arm on that side, never again dressed or undressed without difficulty. From shoulder to elbow my arm was clamped rigidly to my body; from elbow to finger tips I had full movement. Having now a death to avenge, I became overnight an anti-Royalist, and tried very hard to become a left-handed swordsman, but without success.

By that time it was clear that the war would not, as had been said, be over by Christmas, not even the Christmas of 1643. The King might be a muddler, Prince Rupert a reckless hothead, their followers lacking in every virtue, but they were a superb fighting force, with a courage and dash and unity of purpose which we then lacked. It wasn't until the following year that Oliver Cromwell, the plain Huntingdon squire, started remodelling Parliament's army around the core of his East Anglian Ironsides and produced something which could stand up to Rupert's "velvet-clad frippets" in the open field.

While I was nursing my wound and my desire for revenge, Colonel Humphreys sent for me. He was a cold, hard man with whom, in private, my master had several times fallen out. When he asked me what I intended to do now, I thought I saw the point of his question and gave him the answer which I imagined he wanted. I said that my first move would be to return to Alchester and see if Lady Saxham had any use for me.

"That," he said sarcastically, "will be a great help towards winning the war."

"What else can I do? If you doubt the extent of my disability sir, I beg you—try to lift my elbow." As I made the suggestion the sweat broke out of my forehead in anticipation of agony; several people from curiosity, or spite, or in simple fun had tried already.

"Your elbow," he said, as though it were something only just mentionable, "concerns me not at all. Your wits are unimpaired. Sir Henry Saxham thought very highly of them—and of you."

"I have just learned how much I esteemed him, sir. And if . . ."

He interrupted me. "If you could handle a sword with your left hand you would. To what other length would you go to further the cause for which he—and a great many other good men—have died?"

"Any length, sir."

"You're sure?"

"As sure as I am of anything."

"Well," he said, "every battle isn't fought in the field. . . ."

That was how I came to join a secret organisation, known to themselves, and the very few people who ever heard of them, as the Rahabites. The name was taken from the Old Testament story of the two spies sent by Joshua into Jericho "to view the land." Rahab, a harlot of the city, helped and sheltered them.

Our headquarters were in London in a dark narrow street just north of the river, called Tuns Lane. It was a printing shop, always with some bit of work in hand, open and innocent as a place could be. Behind the shop was a room where all the real work was done, and from that room a long narrow yard ran back to a big stable, apparently a separate establishment, in quite another street. You could hire a horse there if you were one of the three first applicants; after that, though your ears might inform you that the stable was not empty, you were out of luck; the remaining horses were all "bespoken." There were six of them, corn fed and in prime condition.

This was the centre of an infinitely complicated and delicate spider's web whose filaments reached out to Scotland, France, Holland and Ireland. A rumour, something observed or guessed at, hundreds of miles away, would set the frail thing aquiver; and there, at the heart of the web, wearing a woollen nightcap on his head and slippers on his feet—I never once saw him dressed otherwise—sat the spider, a little pink-cheeked, sleepy-eyed, miserly fanatic named Enoch Bellson. Nobody will ever know the whole story of the part he played in the war, or even guess at what was stored up behind those sleepy eyes, the secrets he knew, the schemes he had forestalled, the deaths for which he had been responsible.

All I know about him, personally, is that he hated kings. When he was a boy he'd sailed with Sir Walter Raleigh on his ill-fated expedition to the Orinoco. Raleigh had failed to find the gold he had been sent out to look for and James I had had him beheaded. For that reason Enoch Bellson, who had had a boy's passionate hero-worship for Raleigh, hated not only the idea but the very word "king." Once he said to me, "Mark my words, when this is over, some fool is going to think that Oliver's ugly face'd look better under a crown. Over my dead body will he take it. I know enough to discredit him with his own wife. And I'd use it sooner than see another king in England."

Later on, when the prophecy came true and Cromwell was offered the crown and to most people's amazement refused it, putting it, as they said, "steadily from him," I wondered whether a little pink-faced man, in nightcap and slippers, with printer's ink on his fingers, had had any part in that decision.

Working for him was far from easy; he trusted nobody; he set traps even for us; he was mean and utterly ruthless. It says a great deal for the perspicacity of whoever selected the Rahabites that he wasn't murdered, twelve times over. He knew every man's weakness and he was never satisfied. Once he said to me:

"Your trouble, Flowerdew lad, is that you think this is all a game. I've watched you. When you first came you were still waging war; now you're solving puzzles as an intellectual exercise. And that won't do, you know."

I'd just come back from York with some important information, obtained at the price of some danger and a deal of discomfort.

"I get results," I said.

"So far, I grant you. But one day you're going to run into somebody who is playing a game too, but better, and you'll take time off to think—What a clever move! and in that minute you'll be done for. You have your points, you don't drink, women don't bother you and you've got the knack. But you ain't deadly enough."

"I do my best."

"There you are. Your best. I don't want your best, or Tom Noddy's best. I want *the* best. And don't you forget it."

II

One day, very soon after that conversation, he sent for me and said:

"Boy, I've got a real plum for you. You don't even have to get your feet wet or miss a meal." He stirred about in the horrible confusion of papers on his table and eventually a map came uppermost.

"Look here," he said. "Little place called Baildon. Somebody there, or thereabouts, is raising money for the King and getting it to him. Not all, mind, not all. There've been two interceptions, and the second time the carrier had his tail twisted till he squealed. Baildon came out, but no names, and the tail-twisters are satisfied that he didn't know any names. There's your quarry, boy." He ended with the stale old joke, words with which he had more than once sent men to their deaths, "Nothing to fret about in this one. It'll be a holiday—with pay."

"Does it rate a horse, or must I hire?"

His miserliness was a byword; to one of his men who had pulled off the biggest single feat of the whole organisation—the uncovering of a plot to take and hold the port of Lynn for the King—he administered a rebuke over an unnecessary shilling in his expenses; he liked to keep the horses in their stable, where, if they ate their heads off, they weren't wearing out their shoes, and his behaviour towards paper savoured of dementia; he would use one piece over and over again, writing between the lines and then across, and all round the edges.

He said, "Strictly speaking . . ." and then relented. "York was a neat job," he said. "You can take Meg."

Meg was a little red mare, my favourite, gentle as a lamb but with the heart of a lion and amazingly light-footed when the going was heavy. It was October, and though at the moment sparkling clear weather, mire had to be expected.

By the middle of the next afternoon I reckoned I was within eight or nine miles of my destination when I met a man who looked as though he were undergoing some mediaeval form of torture; he was carrying a wheel in such a way that his head went through a space between two spokes and the hub of it rested on the point of his shoulder. As we drew nearer I saw that two spokes of the wheel had broken. When we were level he hailed me, waving one arm and gasping out, "Sir!"

I reined in. It was a second or two before he could speak, he was so breathless.

"Will you be going another four mile along, sir?"

I said yes to that, and he freed himself of his burden, stood it down and leaned on it.

"Would you do a Christian kindness for me then? It wouldn't take you an inch outa your way nor waste you a minute and it'd mean a lot to me."

"What is it?"

"I'm broke down, and I'm carrying the wheel back 'stead of for-wards because thass the nearest wheelwright's. But Annie, thass my wife, she'll be coming to meet me. You'll see her, about four mile on, sir. She pick sticks as she come, so she'll hev a bundle, and she wear a red shawl. If you'd just tell her not to fret, to go back home and I'll be in sometime, soon as I can."

"I'll do that."

"God bless you, sir. She'd get frantic when dark come down."

"Now," I said, "maybe you could tell me something. D'you know Baildon?"

"Like the palm of my hand."

"Then which is the best place to put up at? I'm told there are two inns, the *Hawk in Hand* and the *Old Vine*. Which is better?"

"*Bunch o' Grapes*," he said, "thass what we call it. You'd be com-fortable there. The *Hawk* used to be all right, too, but now Webster make the war the excuse for bad food and ale so weak it can't hardly waddle outa the tap. He wouldn't keep no custom but that Mrs. Kentwoode she hev a lotta rules and she ain't very fond of carters and such. Gentleman like you, sir, you'd be real welcome."

He wiped his sweating face on the back of his hand, shouldered his wheel and went off. Very soon I passed his broken-down wagon, and presently I met his wife and relayed the message. Only later on did I realise that this had been one of those chance encounters which turn out to be momentous.

The *Old Vine* stood outside the closely packed, once walled town, in a new wide street lined with fine houses. Except that it stood so, divided from the roadway by a low brick wall and a narrow space set with clipped shrubs, instead of in a park, it was very much like Alchester; built, I should say, at about the same time. It announced itself by a sign—not the crudely painted wooden board, but an admirable example of ironwork, fixed to a post in the wall and jutting out over the road, broadside on, so that travellers from each direction had a full view of the single vine leaf and the bunch of grapes.

Access was gained by a wide gateway at the side, and this led into a yard flanked on one side by a large open-sided shed for carts, wagons and carriages, and on the other side by stables. My trained eye noted that above the stabling, instead of the usual rough loft, there was a storey, properly built and lit by those wide windows known as weavers' lights. It was plain that sometime in the past this had been the home and the workshop of a prosperous cloth-maker. The wide windows were now boarded over and around their edges, and in some other parts of the stable block, there were signs of fire damage.

As in most other places at the time, the work in the yard was being done by ancient men or striplings. To one of the former I handed my horse, one of the latter took my saddlebags and led the way into the house. As soon as I entered I understood why the landlady was not over-fond of carters and their like. The *Old Vine* was a magnificently appointed house in which only the most necessary concessions had been made to fit its present purpose. Two large mats of woven rushes lay end to end just inside the door, beyond them was the shining floor of the ordinary well-kept house; there was none of the dirty sawdust or sand or chopped straw of the average inn.

Between the foot of a fine staircase and the wall, a table had been set in such a way as to make an enclosure in which an old woman sat knitting. At the sight of us she laid her work aside and, having said "Good day, sir," bent, with a little sigh, over something that looked like a game, small squares of wood of differing colours. Having studied it she sighed even more heavily and said:

"I'm afraid there's nothing for it, sir, but for you to lay in the Great Chamber and there's four there already, with more to come."

In York, on my last holiday—with pay, it had been necessary for me to lie in the gaol for a week and I had only just rid myself of the lice and the stench thus acquired. I thought—Good dame, if only you knew! I said that I hoped to be staying for a few days and perhaps she could do better for me tomorrow. She studied her plan again and looked up with a toothless smile and said yes, to-morrow I could have number seven, all to myself.

The Great Chamber was rightly named; it held, without too much crowding, four beds, two of them capable of holding four sleepers, the others ordinary double size. I had slept in communal rooms often enough and found that the hardship lay less with the bedding than with the other appointments; here there were four basins and ewers, two small looking glasses, plenty of clothes pegs. Very comfortable, I thought, and blessed the man with the wheel. I noticed that both the great windows of the room had hangings, a little frayed and faded now, but of silk. At some time in its history this had been a lordly room.

On one of the double beds a man lay flat on his back, seemingly asleep, but as the boy set down my bags he stirred and eventually raised himself on one elbow.

"Both these is took. On the big 'uns the best place is by the wall, so if you get crammed you can brace yourself against it and heave outwards."

For this sensible and practical suggestion I thanked him, and as I washed and donned a clean shirt we talked. He told me that the men who had already established their claims in the room had gone to drink at the *Hawk in Hand*, there being no taproom at the *Old Vine*.

"There's ale—or wine if you can afford it—with your supper, and you can set and drink afterwards if you like, but Mrs. Kentwoode she don't like no guzzling."

The number of things for which Mrs. Kentwoode had no fond-ness mounted, I noticed, as his talk rambled on; spitting, bad language, fumbling the maids, getting into bed in your dirty clothes. The picture of her built up in my mind a typical Puritan, lean and stringy, her hair hidden by an ugly linen cap, mouth turned down in perpetual disapproval. I began to cherish doubts about the food; such women seldom kept a good table. It was there-fore with enhanced pleasure that I presently sat down to a meal the like of which I had not seen since I rode out to the war.

There were three tables in the dining room. I took a place at one of the two larger ones beside my new friend, whose name I now knew to be Simon Green and who was a cattle dealer. The smaller table, I noticed, had a silver salt bowl, and glasses instead of mugs. The only two ladies in the company were seated there.

I heard of another of Mrs. Kentwoode's dislikes. The man on my left spilt some ale and made a tiny puddle. He pulled out his sleeve and wiped it up, saying somewhat shamefacedly, "Mrs. Kentwoode don't like no slop."

The meal ended with an apple pie in which cloves had not been spared, and as soon as it had been served the door opened and a woman entered. When my neighbour said, "There's Mrs. Kentwoode, now," I didn't know which to disbelieve, my ears or my eyes. She was rather small and plump; the kind of woman of whom I have heard men say, "a nice little armful"; she wore no cap, and her dress was the reverse of Puritan, a bright tawny silk, very tight in the bodice, very full in the skirt.

She stood for a moment surveying the room and then, in a leisurely, stately way, made a progress round it, stopping at intervals to speak and smile. When she reached the place where I was she said:

"Good evening, gentlemen. I trust everything was to your satisfaction."

I noticed that although everyone hastened to acclaim the meal, the cooking, the service, there was no hint of the familiarity found in similar circumstances in other places.

To me, singling me out, she said:

"I think this is your first visit to the *Old Vine*."

I found myself yielding to the pressure of this pretence that she was our hostess and we her invited guests. I told her that this was the first time I had been in Suffolk. She hoped that I should have a pleasant stay, and gave me a smile, as tight-laced as her figure; then she moved away, her skirt rustling like a dry leaf. A faint, pleasant scent remained for a moment on the air.

When she was out of hearing an old man, two places along the table, said:

"I bin coming here now, four-five times every year for fifteen year, and every time Mrs. Kentwoode get more like the old woman; but she still got a good bit to go."

No one nearby remembered the old woman.

"Ah now, she was a Tartar. In her time folks didn't know about minding their manners, but anybody do anything she didn't like she'd got a tongue like a knife and a look that'd freeze your marrow. But mind, she was built for it; straight up and down like two boards clapped together. Mrs. Kentwoode do her best, but she ain't the right shape."

In his simple way he had voiced a truth of some profundity; that icily pleasant manner, the smile that never reached the eyes didn't go with those curves, that warm colouring, that heart-shaped face.

"Show you what old Madam was," said the ancient, making the most of his audience. "One time a chap come in, a bit drunk to start with, and he took all he was allowed and got tipsy. He went to bed in his boots. Nobody know how she knowed, but she did, and in the morning she set about him good and proper. He'd got a sour belly, so he sauced her and said he'd sooner lay in a ditch than stop at a place run like a dame school. Wonder she didn't keep a cane, he say. She say she don't care where he go, he'll never darken her doors again and bad luck go with him wherever he go. Know what happened?"

None of us did, naturally.

"Now this is true; see it with my own eyes, I was out in the yard fixing my pony's panniers. 'Twas a hard frosty morning and he come out, still angry, and go stamping out, straight onto a puddle that was froze over, and he fall down and bust his leg. He holler blue murder and two chaps take him up and bring him in. Madam, she meet 'em at the door and say not ten minutes since she told him never to come back here. But they say to her, 'His leg's broke, see how it dangle.' And dangle it did. She say she don't care if every bone in his body is broke. 'Take him to the *Hawk in Hand*,' she say, 'they'll be glad of his custom there.' Thass the sort she was. And this I will say for her, gentle or simple was all the same to her, you stuck to the rules if you wanted to be welcome here."

III

On the whole I would say that women have bothered me less than they do most men. When I went to Alchester, young and silly, I fell in love with Katharine Saxham. I did it thoroughly; lost my appetite and my sleep and wrote a vast amount of bad verse. She never knew, and it remained a thing of the mind. Once I had recovered from it I was rather like someone who has suffered a severe bout of cowpox and is thus immune from the great pox. No other woman had ever taken possession of my mind. The hungers of the flesh are far more easily satisfied, and no man with one coin to clink against another in his pocket need deny himself. I had never seen any woman—apart from Katharine—whom I wished to spend an uninterrupted week with, leave alone a lifetime, and I had had the salutary experience, before I left Alchester, of seeing my virgin Diana, the young silver moon of my verses, suffer a change of role and become Ceres; bulgy, florid, extremely matter-of-fact. A large number of men witness this change across their own table, in their own bed. I think that the majority remain blissfully unaware of it; or, like Sir Henry, they chase down other glades after new Dianas and go to bed warm and comfortable with Ceres once the chase is over. On the whole I counted myself lucky.

Yet that night I dreamed of Mrs. Kentwoode. I was sitting in a small, cosy room which I did not recognise. I had lately eaten my fill and had loosened my belt and my buttons. She came in, as neat and erect and strait-laced as I had seen her at suppertime, and it bothered me that I did not know her name. I wanted to call her by name and all I knew was Mrs. Kentwoode, which just wouldn't do. So she spoke to me first. She said, "You look easy. I wish I could be easy for once." Then, with one of those sudden changes, possible only in dreams or stories of magic, she *was* easy. Her body, soft and uncorseted, was clad in a loose silk wrapper, her copper-coloured hair streamed down over her shoulders. She leaned towards me, her eyes half closed, her mouth half open in the very attitude of a woman ready to be taken. Desire such as I had never known in a waking moment laid hold of me and I reached out and took her into my arms. For a moment she leaned against me, melting into me, all warmth and softness and fragrance. Then there was another change. She turned cold and flaccid, like a dead woman; but her voice came crisp, deliberately unfriendly. She said, "You should go to the *Hawk in Hand* and ask for Emma Webster." There I woke up.

I am no believer in the significance of dreams. I know that there are a few, prophetic and informative, recorded in the Bible; but then there are miracles there, too; and just as I never expected a miracle to happen in my waking life, I never entertained the idea of having an important dream in my sleeping one. I regarded dreams as the muddled, mixed-up product of what had gone on in one's head recently, or in time long ago, maybe even back to time forgotten. Like the scrapings of all the plates one had ever eaten from going into one enormous swilltub.

Of this dream I could account for everything save the one name Emma. In all the conversations of that day I could not recall Emma Webster having been mentioned. Nor could I remember any Emma who had mattered enough to have retained a place in my mind. My mental swilltub seemed to have received a scrap from someone else's plate. . . . I lay and smiled in the dark at that fantastical notion. Far more likely that, as a tiny child in the Leicester house that always smelt faintly of the tanyard, I had been tended by a female of that name.

IV

At fairs you may watch a man swallow fire, walk a slack rope five feet above ground, wrestle with and throw another man twice his size and weight; and if you are cunning and patient you may get him to tell you, with every appearance of frankness, how the thing is done. You're no wiser; you're no nearer being able to swallow fire, walk a slack rope, or throw a bigger man. You hear some words, but the secret remains a secret, something learned with pain and patience over a period of time. And so it was with us. Rahabites didn't always come home from their holidays—with pay. A steady stream of new recruits passed through that room at the back of the printing shop, and at least three quarters of them had been dismissed by one of Bellson's routine phrases. "No knack!" You could have the nose of a ferret, the single-mindedness of a hound, a fox's cunning, the patience of a cat at a mousehole, but "No knack," and out you went. Knack is that secret part which cannot be described.

Conversations—or monologues—can be.

In the morning I idled about the yard for a while, watching the travellers move off. Then, beyond the open-sided shed, I found a gate in the high wall and went through and found myself in what had once been a very beautiful garden. It still had the charm of a place planned to please the eye, but it was neglected and overgrown. Across one flagged path the unpruned rosebushes threw out branches, bearing the year's last frail blooms, that almost met. Beyond another wall, in which was another gate, there was a herb and vegetable garden, as neat as a well-kept parlour. There an old man was tearing down dead bean vines and throwing them onto a fire. The fine morning, the size and excellence of the onions served with the boiled beef on the previous evening, served as opening subjects. I received, with an appreciative nod, the information that any year when peas were bad and maggoty, the onions were good.

"Stand to reason," he said, "you can't hev it both ways."

Presently a question seemed safe and I asked it. Had he worked here long?

"All my life. Soon's I could crawl I was grubbing weeds outa that path between the roses. You been there? Pity, ain't it? This year I must stretch myself a bit and get in there with the shears. There used to be three of us, and we was all busy then. Now there's only me and I don't get no younger. There's all I can manage this side of the wall."

"I suppose the war has made you shorthanded."

"War? Oh, you mean this bit of a scuffle. War to me mean that time when we set to and give the Spaniards a hiding. Before your time that was. Long before your time." He gave an old man's sardonic laugh. "Mr. Kentwoode, he was alive then, and he had us all a-drilling with cudgels and pitchforks."

I was glad the conversation had come around to the family, and intended to keep it there. I said that Madam Kentwoode seemed to have been highly thought of; and that evoked such a tangled story that I gave up trying to follow it since it concerned the past and my problem was in the present. I did notice the sentence, "That was the night they broke in and burned the silk and killed poor Master John, him that was our Mrs. Kentwoode's husband."

Good. Now I could ask:

"And has she any family?"

Now that, of a married woman, is usually taken to refer to her children; but the old man said:

"Oh aye. She's wonderful well connected, Mrs. Kentwoode is; she's one of a big family, the Hattons; got relations all over the place."

"I meant had she any children?"

With marked contrast to his former garrulity he said:

"A boy." He ripped up a beanstalk and turned towards the fire. "I gotta get on," he said.

The old man at table on the previous evening had said that he'd patronised the inn for fifteen years; and it hadn't been an inn, according to the gardener, until catastrophe had overtaken the silk business at the time of John Kentwoode's death. So any son of his must be fifteen, and was very probably more.

I went back into the house. Mrs. Kentwoode and the old dame had their heads together over the table and as I entered the old woman looked up and said, "There is the gentleman, now."

Mrs. Kentwoode gave me her professional smile.

"We've had your bags taken into number seven. I think you'll find it comfortable."

I thanked her. The old woman handed me a key and then moved one of her little coloured squares.

I now saw the purpose of the "game" and ventured a comment upon the ingenuity.

"Fanny cannot read or write, and it's difficult to remember which beds are taken, night after night."

This morning she was wearing a lilac-coloured dress, very plain with a narrow linen collar. Ignore that, I said to myself.

Behind her, on the wall, there was a picture, rather small, set into a massive carved frame far too heavy for it. It was the portrait of a little girl, dressed in the fashion of the old Queen's day; but since when has a mere man been expected to be aware of fashion?

I said, "What an exceptionally pretty little girl. Your daughter, ma'am?"

"That? Oh no. My husband's aunt, as a child, eighty-five years or so ago. You'll hear mention of her, if you haven't already. She was always called Madam."

The professional part of my mind made a note that most women would have said, "Oh no, I have a son." The other part made me step closer and look at the picture.

"I have indeed heard of her. Last night over supper. How strange," I said, "she seems to have been a very strong character. Whoever painted this missed all sign of that."

She came and stood just behind me; so close that I could smell that fragrance again. She said, rather slowly:

"That is true. But I think characters are made . . . or altered by circumstances. Don't you? Or are you a Calvinist?"

"No. A cheerless creed, I always feel."

"Oh. Now I always regard it as rather enviable—to think that whatever you do has been predestined. So easy. . . ."

It was like the magic word in children's stories. It took me straight back to my dream, and something happened that had not happened to me for many years. I blushed. There is no other word for the stinging heat in the face, the inability to meet the other person's eye. Furious with myself I was obliged to look down and my eye rested on the V shape made by the points of her white collar on the lilac dress. And then I saw that above it the plump round neck, strangely girlish for a woman of her age, had turned bright scarlet. This further disconcerted me. I was horribly and deeply ashamed. It was as though we had been caught in flagrante delicto—and we were two middle-aged people who had never even looked at one another with personal recognition nor exchanged a wholehearted smile. I turned away abruptly and mounted the stairs, already dreading the moment when we should come face to face again.

A little later I set out, on foot, for the centre of the town in search of the *Hawk in Hand*. This was reached by taking a turn off the wide market place and then another, into a narrow street. It was an ordinary inn, with a taproom, for which I was grateful. It was in charge of a ruinous mountain of a man with grievances about which, with the minimum of encouragement—or, I suspect, none at all—he was disposed to talk; the very man for my purpose.

One of his grievances concerned wheels, which were going to be the ruin of him. In the days of pack horses, he said, the two sharp turns meant nothing, but now that there was this craze for wagons and carts and carriages, his trade was falling off.

"They go to the *Old Vine* which is easy to get into, all but a few with sense, that'd sooner make a coupla turns than bear with the airs and graces. Thass a funny thing, this ain't the first time that place done damage to us Websters. I remember my old grandfather telling the tale he'd had from *his*, of how a Webster that was a wool merchant was ruined by the new business there. And there've been damage since then, apart from their taking our trade." He scowled at his mug and then began again.

"There's food too. That ain't so easy to come by, with the army wanting so much and paying high prices."

I said that that applied to all places alike, didn't it?

"Not a bit of it. Them Kentwoodes allust had their roots in the country. Her brother got a great place out at Minsham, and her sister hev another at Ockley. They see she don't go short. Great garden too. Look what that mean in vegetables when we hev to buy in the market. Make a difference, you know. Folks'll go where they get a full belly, even if it do mean wiping their boots."

Then he reverted to the subject of the war.

"Time was when you could look on soldiers as good customers. Not now; oh no! Not that I hold," he said, denying the evidence of his own red-netted cheeks and nose, "with heavy drinking. But a mug of ale never hurt nobody, specially in summer when the water get so muddy. Them that make the rules, no drinking for soldiers and so on, don't think how people like us feel the pinch." He emptied his mug and I made sympathetic and encouraging noises.

"There was a chap in here a day or two ago, pedlar he was, straight from London. He said they was aiming to close all taverns and drinking places and give them that kept 'em ten acres of land to be took off them that favoured the King. All very well if you're young, but I don't fancy meself out at Merravy at my age." He gave a derisive snort. "Not that I think it'll come to that, folks wouldn't stand the interference."

I agreed with him; little thinking that as we stood there we were within measurable distance of the time when not merely drinking, but dancing around the Maypole—surely the most innocent of diversions—and the keeping of Christmas were to be forbidden.

A carter, carrying his whip, hurried in and demanded ale without delay; he had left his team in the street two turns away rather than negotiate the corners. Webster turned the tap and this time the cask yielded only a trickle.

"I wouldn't want that muck even if you had a pint of it," the carter said. Without moving from his stool Webster opened the door behind him and shouted, "Emma!" A flat, defeated voice called back:

"What now?"

"Bring a mug outa our cask in the larder and look sharp."

So there actually was an Emma, and I was about to see her.

She came in with the plodding tread of an overworked animal, carrying the brimming mug with exaggerated care. She had once been plump, but her flesh had lost its firmness and now sagged on her bones; her hair was coarse and lustreless. Her expression was hopeless and sullen. Yet I could see a marked resemblance to Mrs. Kentwoode, a Mrs. Kentwoode shorn of all grace and pride, blowzy and run to seed. Their eyes were the same colour and perhaps their hair had been—though Emma Webster's was so heavily streaked with grey, so greasy and tangled, that its original colour was hard to determine. There was another likeness too; looking at this woman and seeing a small brown mole distinct against the doughy skin, I remembered that Mrs. Kentwoode had one, too, near the corner of one eye.

Webster growled, "Took your time, didn't you?"

She ignored him, set down the mug and said:

"There you are, Jack. Nice morning." She smiled as she spoke and the smile was still there when she turned to me and said:

"Good day, sir."

Her smile had everything that Mrs. Kentwoode's so conspicuously lacked, real warmth and friendliness; it lit up her ravaged face, lifting all the sagging lines and brightening the dull eyes. Once she had been young, I thought, and if then she had been clean and tidy and happy she must have been very charming indeed. Just as Mrs. Kentwoode must have been charming before something froze within her.

I toyed with the idea of their being related in some way. The old gardener had said that Mrs. Kentwoode was well connected; that was difficult to believe of this poor creature. The wrong side of the blanket, perhaps. . . . Then a glimmer of truth pushed that idea aside. The physical resemblance was there but it would be visible only to the eye which saw beyond the exterior; but for my dream of Mrs. Kentwoode ungirt and yielding I should not have seen it myself; and it was a resemblance of type, not of blood and bone.

Seeing resemblances between two women was no part of my job; but drinking in taverns was, since, owing to the fear that Webster had mentioned of the Puritan element gaining the upper hand in the Parliamentarian policy, most innkeepers were Royalist in sympathy at least; also their places straddled the lines of communication. So I looked at my empty mug and intimated that I should like it refilled.

Webster shouted again through the door, "Jim." A boy came running and this time Webster left his stool and between them they carried out the cask.

The carter took a noisy sloop of his ale and said:

"Lord! This got a bit of body. Thass better than what you sell, Missus."

"Don't you go thinking that was a *gift*," she said, and laughed.

It was the kind of remark which, made before several men, all with drink in them, would have passed for wit and made them say, "That Emma Webster, she's a one!"

She settled herself, leaning her arms on the counter. Her sleeves were rolled to the elbow, and though her arms were fleshy the bones in them showed because the flesh was so soft and loose.

"You're a stranger in these parts, sir?"

("I think this is your first visit to the *Old Vine*.")

Troubled by the likeness; troubled by the memory of my dream, by the word Emma; (through what door had that name slipped into my mind?) I said yes, and made a remark about Baildon being a pleasant town. And then, because I should almost certainly want to come here again and it was obvious that I must be staying somewhere, I said:

"I'm afraid I'm staying at the *Old Vine*. It was directly on my road, you see. And how could I know that it had no taproom?" I risked it; at worst they could but refuse to serve me. "I daren't tell your husband," I said in a conspiratorial way, "I was afraid he would tell me to look for ale where I had my bed. He seems to have a grudge against the place."

"Oh, him! Take no notice of him. He got a grudge against most everybody."

The carter slapped down his money and hurried away.

"Your husband," I said, "certainly dislikes the Kentwoodes. So far I've only seen Mrs. Kentwoode. How many are there?"

"There's a son."

"Does he help to run the place?"

"He ain't there. She's alone, and managing right well, so I hear. I don't know her, 'cept just to see at a distance, but she's a lady I always had a . . . a admiration for. There was no call for her to set to and earn a living for herself and the boy. She could hev set out there at Mortiboys and folded her hands in her lap, but she never. And the old woman was horrible. One way and another she hain't had it easy, Mrs. Kentwoode hain't."

Webster and the boy came blundering in with the new cask.

He said, "Move your fat arse, woman, and make way!"

The dull look of defeat which had lifted as she talked settled again, leaden on her doughy face. I thought that she, also, hadn't had things easy. . . .

I went away carrying the one word "Merravy" as carefully as Emma Webster had carried the carter's mug of ale.

That was a concrete thing, like a hard round pebble one could grip; but I carried something else too, flimsy and shapeless—the silly, inexplicable certainty that between these two women, so much alike, so entirely different, there was a link, something hidden and fascinating, human and strange.

Then I remembered that I was a Rahabite, and I clutched my pebble.

Halfway along the street that led back to the market place there was a cookshop, very sweet-smelling, with dishes of tarts and saffron cakes and gingerbread in its narrow window. I went in and found behind the counter a woman who, except that she was small, very much resembled my overnight image of Mrs. Kentwoode, severe-looking, dressed in dark grey and wearing an ugly linen cap. I said that it all smelt so good that I was overcome by greed and could I have a square of gingerbread and did she mind if I ate it there and then. She was much less strict than she looked; and she, too, had a grievance, a small, but rather engaging one. She said that when you made cakes and sold them all day long, you couldn't bring yourself to eat one.

"When I was a little girl I used to stand outside this very window and sniff and stare and long for a penny to spend. And when Joe asked me to marry him, do you know what I said, I said, 'I'll ruin you, love, in a month. I shall eat more than I sell.' And I had the run of my teeth for a fortnight, after which I couldn't eat a cake to save my life."

"That is hard," I said. "You miss so much. I've never tasted such gingerbread in all my life." Then I slipped in my question about Merravy.

Oh yes, of course she'd heard of it. It was out at Nettleton, Sir Rawley Rowhedge's place.

"Funny you should go and ask that. Seeing you bite so hearty made me think of Master Charles. In the old days he'd come in sometimes on his pony and set out there and rap the window with his whip. I didn't have to ask what *he* wanted. Lemon curd tarts. Lemon curd tarts he had a passion for; I've known him eat eight straight off. Once I say to him, 'Master Charles, I'll give you the recipe, then they can make you some to home,' and he say, 'Oh, Mrs. Bun'—he always called me that, though Platt is my name— 'Oh, Mrs. Bun, don't do that, that'd spoil it.' You see, he *knew*. Poor little chap."

Why "poor little chap"? Had he died young—of a surfeit of lemon curd tarts?

"Has he, like you, outgrown his liking for goodies?"

"I don't know. I never saw him after he went off to Cambridge. But to me there's always something sad about the way little boys grow up and alter. Somehow girls . . . well, there ain't all that difference between a girl with a doll and a woman with a baby, not like the difference with boys, eating tarts one day and soldiering the next, seemingly. . . ."

Dear, dear Mrs. Platt!

The next thing that happened was an accident, neither planned nor foreseen. Handled in another fashion it could have meant nothing.

I am, by nature, a tidy man. The boy who had moved my saddle-bags from the Great Chamber to number seven had set them down on the floor by the table that held the basin and ewer, and I suppose that nine out of ten men would have left them there. But there was, on one side of the fireplace, a wide, deep cupboard in which, when I had hung up my few clothes, there was still ample room for the bags; so I picked them up and slung them in, and as they struck the lower part of the back of the cupboard the part they touched receded and the upper part tilted forward, so that the peg fixed into it was at such a slant that my heavy cloak fell off and enveloped me. Despite the fact that I had myself hung the thing there so recently, I was seized with the idea that someone concealed in the cupboard had dropped the cloak over my head and I wrestled with it furiously for a wild sweating second or two. Then, seeing what had happened, I laughed. And then I thought to myself—Here is my chance to make history at the *Old Vine!* A customer is going to make a complaint.

As a matter of fact I was feeling a little annoyed with Mrs. Kentwoode, the annoyance being compounded of a number of other emotions. All day, whenever I thought of it, the memory of that moment at the foot of the stairs had embarrassed me and the thought of meeting her again, face to face, had been an uncomfortable one. Since it could not be avoided I faced it boldly; at suppertime I had seated myself at the table with the silver salt bowl and ordered wine to drink from my elegant glass. When she entered and made her round, following a custom prevalent in many inns I had invited her to drink with me. The shutter of her professional amiability had lifted just long enough to allow surprise to peep through, then it closed again and she accepted the invitation willingly enough. We then exchanged a few remarks, as cautiously as two players, each of whom has been warned that the other is a skilful cheat, might lay down the first cards in a game. Sitting bolt upright, taking her wine in delicate sips, armoured with graciousness, she was far more at ease than I was. I resented that. I resented also the fact that she never wasted a word; she told me nothing. Even when, with the feeling that I was placing a barb, I told her that I had visited the *Hawk in Hand* that morning, she said placidly, "Many people do. A taproom does attract custom, but it has disadvantages in proportion."

"The woman there," I said, "seems to think highly of you."

"Indeed? Did I know her, the feeling might be reciprocal, but she is unknown to me."

After a few more sterile sentences she excused herself, leaving in the glass more than half the wine for which she had thanked me so prettily.

So now I pulled the leaning board into an even more dangerous position, intending to tell her that it had struck me so heavily that it might have done me serious injury. . . .

It came away so cleanly that it seemed to me that it had been designed to be removed. I lighted the shuttered lantern that was part of every Rahabite's equipment and examined the board more closely. There wasn't a nail hole in it. A glance at the back of the board showed me its secret; the peg on which my cloak had hung went through and was attached to a tapered wedge which could be swivelled by a firm turn of the peg. When it was in its correct position, a good three inches of the wedge was firmly hooked behind the horizontal timber at the top of the closet. I experimented, placing the board upright and turning the peg. The opening was then indetectable and the board as firm as a rock. The hanging of my cloak, heavy as it was, wouldn't have turned the peg. Either the board had been taken out recently and insecurely fastened when replaced, or over a period of years every piece of clothing hung and then removed had twisted the peg a little, until at last my cloak had broken its last hold and the throwing in of my saddle-bags had tilted the board. In any case it was a cunningly contrived hiding place. For what? All Rahabite now, I turned the peg, lifted out the board and looked into the space behind the closet's back.

I locked my door behind me and went downstairs. Fanny was at her post, telling two late-comers that there was no bed left, the house was full, and proving her point by reference to her little squares. They could sleep in the stable loft if they so fancied. When that was settled I asked her where I should find Mrs. Kentwoode.

She'd be in her own little parlour, with her feet up, she hoped; and what did I want; wasn't it anything anybody else could deal with? I said no firmly, and was grudgingly directed towards a room at the rear of the house.

Mrs. Kentwoode had her feet up when I entered and she was reading a letter which looked as though it had been read many times before. That is the kind of thing that a trained mind notices even in moments of preoccupation. She folded it in a manner too deliberate to be secretive, and at the same time lowered her feet from the stool and smoothed her skirt demurely. She then looked at me in a questioning way.

The movement of her skirt had loosed that same faint fragrance on the air, and the candlelight, coming from one side and slightly behind her, cast a soft shadow on her face, a bright sheen on her chestnut hair. I remembered my dream again and was aware of the woman behind that manner, the whalebone, the stiff silk. The thing I had come to speak about seemed suddenly horrible. For a moment I thought of making some trivial excuse for having disturbed her, and then going back to my room and pushing the board back into place so that it could keep its secret still.

But to do that would get me no further. It would be a stupid, sentimental action, a throwing away of a weapon unexpectedly placed in my hand. For, as is well known, in mental warfare as in physical, a flanking action can often do more than a point-blank attack.

So I said, "Mrs. Kentwoode, I think it only right to tell you . . ." and having got so far, I stopped. She was a woman, and I knew how they felt about such harmless things as mice and spiders.

She said, "Do sit down. I'm afraid I hardly tasted the wine you so kindly offered me, I was so busy. Will you take a glass with me now?"

I murmured that she was very kind. She rose and went to a cupboard in the corner. I watched closely out of habit. I should still have watched had she been an ugly old crone with unpleasing movements. The cupboard door, when open, revealed two shelves and a drawer. The shelves held wine, and glasses. Any unskilled observer would have thought her busy with these; in fact she moved so cleverly that it was the sound of a lock clicking which revealed to me that one of her hands had not been occupied with movements of hospitality. When she turned and walked towards me with two brimming glasses in her hands, she no longer had the letter.

But there are of course—and this we were always taught to bear in mind—a dozen innocent explanations for every guilty one in any action.

I said, "Mrs. Kentwoode, I have good reason for asking you this. Is there any man about you to whom I could address myself on a somewhat unpleasant matter?"

"Ostlers," she said, "serving men. Otherwise I am all alone. But I am accustomed to dealing with anything that crops up. What have you to tell me?"

She spoke with calm dignity, but she had the look of a person who is wary, almost to the point of fear. Betraying my training I said in a soothing way:

"It sounds more horrible than in fact it is. It must have happened many, many years ago."

"Oh," she said, and there was relief in her voice and in her manner. "What is it?"

I told her, as delicately as possible, about what I had found in the recess behind my clothes cupboard—a dead man, a mere heap of bones and clothing, with a rosary lying across a skeleton hand.

She put her hand to her mouth and turned very pale.

"It probably happened long before your time; in fact I am sure of it," I said.

"A rosary? You are sure of that?"

"Quite sure."

"And the clothes?"

"Of antique sort, the breeches padded, the jerkin short and un-skirted." I could in fact date the garments to within a few years, for Enoch Bellson's most cherished possession was a portrait of Sir Walter Raleigh, copied by someone who had little skill, from an-other. The bones in my cupboard were those of a man who had lived in the old Queen's time; of that I had no doubt. "But that wasn't all," I said. "His head rested upon a roll of sacking. In it were a robe, and a stole and a basin. I think," I said, and I watched her with two sets of eyes, the man's, the Rahabite's, "that the man, in his time, was a priest."

There was a kind of rough rule of thumb, not always applicable, but applicable often enough to be worth consideration, that families with Catholic leanings were Royalist; the Queen, after all, was a Papist.

I was at that moment two men; there was myself, regretting the necessity to speak of hidden bones, the remains of a man who must have died in hideous circumstances, to a sensitive female; and I was also an already half-unwilling Rahabite, on the lookout for any sign of confusion or denial.

She confounded me. She said, "I think I understand. A priest, you say. That might explain. She was very old. She lived in the Queen's time. Yes, that might be it. 'Hide and starve,' she said."

"Who said it?"

"My husband's aunt, Madam Elizabeth. You remember—the lit-tle girl in the picture. She lived to be nigh on eighty and we thought, I thought, that she would die peacefully, as the very aged do. But her end was horrible. Horrible." She reached for her glass and emptied it in one long, desperate gulp. "She raved," she said. "Oh, I know that many old people, just before the end, revert to their childhood; but this was different. When she talked about her grandfather, and her brother Harry, and her string of blue beads, which she always wore, although I didn't understand it all, I knew, at least, what she was talking about. When she spoke of a priest, then I could not understand. You won't understand either. I expect you wonder why I am telling you all this . . . things I've never said to anyone."

"It's often much easier to say things to a stranger," I said.

"I suppose I am talking to myself, really. I'm sorry. It was just that I was so puzzled at the time. Her talk of a priest . . . I even wondered whether, all the time, her apparent indifference to the Church had been because she was a secret Papist. I sent Christopher . . ." The name rebounded against some sounding board in her mind and warned her that she was becoming over-confidential. "He was one I could trust, very loyal, to a family known to be Papist, to ask if they could put us in touch with a priest. But they could not help."

Deliberately, before my eyes, she donned her innkeeper's mask.

"I am sorry that such a discovery should have been made in your room, Mr. Flowerdew. We'll move you at once, of course." She then said, in a manner I found touching, "This is not the kind of thing that will do the house any good. Rumour always favours the most dramatic story and innkeepers have a bad name. Before I know where I am, the body will be that of an innocent traveller, done to death for a bag of gold. They'll even say I put the outdated clothes on him in an effort to hide the crime." She gave me a cautious look. "I'm not decrying those who wish to put an end to the abuses that go on in inns and taverns and such places; but there are extremists who wish to do away with such places altogether; and in their efforts to sway the common people to their side, no stick is too dirty to beat us with."

"And how will they get hold of this particular stick?"

"It'll be a matter for the Coroner," she said. It was a statement, but it held the faintest hint of a question.

I asked myself who would benefit by having the thing made public, and who would be harmed by keeping it secret. Even if I argued the need of Christian burial, it might not be conducted in accord with the dead man's beliefs. Everything pointed to his having been one of those courageous, if mistaken, people who had come into an anti-Papist country to keep the Catholic faith alive and to prepare for the counter-Reformation. Some words said over his bones by a Protestant cleric, out of a Protestant Prayerbook, would be almost a mockery. On the other hand, here was a chance for me to ingratiate myself.

"Is it? I should have thought that burial would suffice. And if it would do you any service *I* would bury the bones. No one else need know."

She gave me one of those searching looks which women turn upon a bargain that seems a little too good to be true.

"I don't know why you should go to so much trouble."

"The trouble will be small," I assured her. "And I feel a certain responsibility. If I had not thrown in the bag so clumsily, the board might have stood there balanced for a long time yet."

"Then if you would, I should be most deeply indebted to you." She spoke earnestly, and seemed to find some explanation necessary. "It isn't that I wish to be furtive, or that there is anything more sinister in this discovery than I have told you. I merely wish to avoid the gossip. The garden would be the best place; at the very end where no one ever goes now, a peaceful resting place, at least. And we must wait until everyone is abed."

"I can do it unaided. There's no need for you to concern yourself at all."

"Oh no, I must come. I know the garden well—well enough to find my way in the dark."

"I know where the garden is. And I shall have my lantern."

"We must show no light, no light at all, until we are deep into the garden, out of sight of the upper windows of the house. You never know nowadays. Spies are everywhere."

She spoke the word "spies" as though it referred to some most repulsive and obnoxious form of life.

"Spies? What spies, and why are they spying?"

She gave me that searching look again. Then she said in a voice of irony, "Surely, Mr. Flowerdew, you realise that every inn and tavern in the Eastern counties is a nest of Royalists. Night after night we drink ourselves senseless and then sit down to *plot*. One in ten of the covered wagons that leave our yards is crammed with gold and silver, or with French troops, in layers three deep, packed head to toe like herrings in a barrel. You were unaware of this? I'll warrant that if you had the skill to move noiselessly, or to conceal yourself with sufficient cunning, you could find a spy at work in the yard tonight, lifting the covers of every wagon, examining every horseshoe, because smithwork varies from place to place."

"They sound very thorough. How much do they discover?"

She laughed. "You think I exaggerate; I assure you that I do not. Not long ago a man came to this inn, for the purpose, he said, of finding himself a small house in the town, or near. A likely enough story, but somehow I felt suspicious of him from the start."

"Why?"

"Well, he was too anxious to tell why he was here, if you understand that. He told Fanny when he asked for a bed; he told me when I first saw him, and he told everybody at the supper table. Ordinary people do not behave so; if one has nothing up one's sleeve it is unnecessary to say so so insistently."

"That is true. So you suspected him."

"I did, and I had *him* watched. Every night he went down to the cart shed and the stables and conducted his search; and every night a man I could trust watched him. One night there was a wagon loaded with boots which had been made in Norwich and were destined for the barracks at Colchester. He helped himself to a pair. Tom had the sense to come and rouse me at once. I was very angry. Out of a load one pair might not have been missed, on the other hand army property is likely to be strictly accounted for, and there would have been another cast-iron instance of innkeeper's knavery. So I acted immediately."

"What did you do?"

"I sent one man for the constable, and another for a magistrate, Sir Walter Fennel, who happens to be my brother-in-law. The man told a specious tale; he said that he suspected the boots of being intended for the King's army, and that he needed a pair as evidence. Evidence of what, they asked him, beside his own dishonesty? He was very reluctant to say any more; but when he saw that there was no other means of saving himself, he said that he worked for an organisation in London which was engaged in preventing any sort of supply from reaching the King. He said that he would name the organisation if he could speak to Walter alone; he swore him to secrecy, but naturally Walter told my sister, Cecily, and she told me. The man's name was Bodkin and he said he worked for someone named Benson or Bellman; he gave the address and said that if Walter got in touch with this man, he would confirm his tale."

Poor Bodkin; how could he have been so naïve?

"And did he?"

She said, "That was a most difficult time for me. My family has always been loyal to me, but unwillingly, if you understand that; they regard innkeeping as something . . . regrettable. And Walter is very partisan; he has been against the King ever since ship money was first levied. He carefully explained to me that he believed me innocent of smuggling boots to the King, but the affair must, in justice to Bodkin, be fully investigated; and that probably as a result this house would be closed and I could go home and live in my father's house. That is what they think I should have done, long ago. So he went himself to London, while everything here, including the load of boots, was held up. And what do you think he found? Enoch Bellman, or whatever his name was, did actually exist; he was a humble little printer whose only connection with the man Bodkin was that once he had had him as an apprentice and been obliged to cancel his articles because he was so extremely stupid!"

Enoch would have said that with an innocent look, but he'd be aware of the irony, and grin once he was back in his room. Stupid was so apt a word; we'd been warned, over and over again, that Bellson would disown us, must disown us, in any such circumstance.

"Did he hang?" I asked.

"No. Nor was he whipped, or stood in the stocks. I think he is still in gaol. My brother-in-law was far from satisfied, and I must say that I believed part of his story, though it would be preferable to suppose him a simple thief. I believe somebody sent him, and will send others. It's a waste of time, of course. We innkeepers know that we exist on sufferance. Besides, how could French soldiers land, with all the ports so closely watched? Yarmouth, I believe, is Royalist, but it is surrounded. Any French landing there would not get far inland."

"I discount the French soldiers. About other things I should not be so sceptical. The fact remains that though the Parliament has all the resources and the King should have been starved out before this, he isn't. Supplies and funds reach him somehow."

"I suppose so," she said, a trifle vaguely. "I've never given it much thought. I have such a to-do making ends meet myself, I've never considered his problems."

I saw an opening, and took it.

"The tavern-keeper at the *Hawk in Hand* said that he had been told by a pedlar that if a general closing down of all such places ever takes place, their owners will be compensated with ten acres of land, land that has been taken from Royalists. For young men, or men with sons, that might be some compensation, but for the old, or for you, Mrs. Kentwoode, it would be cold comfort, would it not?"

She was well guarded. She did not say, "But I have a son." She said:

"We must live from day to day as best we can, and not look too far ahead."

"Webster thinks his ten acres will be at a place called Merravy."

That reached its mark. At any other time, in any other circumstances, I should have been jubilant. As it was the draining of colour from her face seemed to affect my own heartbeat. And when she managed to laugh I was filled with admiration.

"I think it was his wish speaking; the land there is very rich and productive. If I am ever compensated with ten acres of land I'd like it in that direction, too. And do you know what I should do with it? Put it all down to potatoes. They're becoming more and more popular. We grow them here, and serve them when we can, and everyone likes them and pleads for a handful of seed—but they don't grow from seed, you know." She glanced at the pretty little clock which stood by the candle. "I think I might go and make my nightly round now."

She stood up, brisk and straight, but for all that she looked small. "What does that entail?" I asked.

"Oh, I see that all the fires are out, the doors locked, the gate barred. I've found that hired people, however good, grow slack in time on something that is a daily routine. Tom, for instance, would stay awake three nights in succession to catch a spy, but he couldn't be trusted to look to bolts and bars three hundred and sixty-five times in the year."

I thought of the open-fronted cart shed, full of looming shapes and dark corners, of the long range of stables.

"Don't you mind making the rounds all by yourself?"

"I'm used to it, now," she said. And she had something of the air of a brave child, refusing to be frightened.

And I thought of all the people who went in awe of her. "Mrs. Kentwoode don't like no slop," the carter had said, wiping the table with his sleeve. How much more perceptive that broken-down trollop—Emma—at the inn. "She hain't had it easy, Mrs. Kentwoode hain't."

On impulse, I said, "I'll come with you."

"Better not. We ought not to be seen together until I have made sure that the coast is clear." She paused. "Would . . . would a basket serve, a big basket?"

"You can leave all that to me," I said, feeling seven feet tall and protective.

"We can pick up a spade as we go. Shall we meet here, in an hour?"

Spade! "I'll bury the bones for you," I'd said, "no one else need ever know." I hadn't, as Enoch Bellson was always insisting that we did, weighed my words, taken into account every possible development of any given situation. In short I hadn't visualised myself handling a spade. How well could I dig? That was the question. Was a spade as awkward a thing to a left-handed man as a sword had proved to be?

It was a still, cold night with a breath of frost in the air. The old man who tended the garden had been burning leaves and the scent lingered.

She had spoken truly when she said that she knew the garden. We walked in darkness for a while, her left hand holding the sleeve of my right arm. I had placed the poor bones in my saddlebag and slung it from my left arm; in my left hand I held the spade. She had insisted upon carrying my lantern, lighted, but with its shutter closed.

We walked thus to the very end of the garden, far beyond the point where I had talked to the old gardener.

"I think it would be safe to show a light now," she said. "The trees screen us from the house. How does this work?"

I laid down what I carried, took the lantern and adjusted the shutter. Swinging the beam of light around I saw a stone seat, and around it some tall dark trees. Yews, planted to be a windbreak, like those around a similar seat at Alchester, but untrimmed for many years.

"I thought here," she said, and lifted a bough. "The ground should be soft under the tree."

"And then the bough will fall back and hide all sign of our digging."

"That too. I'm acting foolishly. This could have been another Bodkin to whom, being in disgrace already, I feared to call the Constable. . . . If they wanted to condemn me the fact that the bones had no flesh could be easily ignored." She made a curiously muted choking sound. "I've been thinking as I made my round. *You* could have been sent to trap me; you could have brought these

. . . bones with you when you came. It may be my grave that you are about to dig. *Is it?*"

A perfect example of Enoch Bellson's admonition to take into account every possible development of any given situation.

I said, "Can you think that of me?"

"I find it difficult. But in the terrible state that things are in now almost anything is possible. That is the most hateful thing—that people aren't just people any more; they're dummies, with labels, Royalist, Parliamentarian . . ."

"I give you my word—which may be suspect—that at this moment I am merely a man who happened to find these remains in his clothes closet and volunteered to bury them. And that was a rash offer, because, although you may not have noticed it, I suffer a disability, my right arm is half crippled. Still, I'll do the best I can. Will you hold the bough aside?"

She did so and I made the best shift I could at digging. The ground was damp and soft and I brought what pressure I could on my left hand, the right making a niggling motion as though it were wielding a toothpick.

"What I can't understand," she said, "is why you should do this for me."

"Handicapped as I am, I still think that I am probably a better digger than you are."

I managed, not a grave, but a shallow space, sufficient. In it I laid the bones, the clothes, the robe and stole and the bowl. The bowl, at which I had taken a closer look after my talk with Mrs. Kentwoode, was a strange one, about one third plain white pottery and two thirds green glass, flecked and traced with gold. Before I laid it in the grave I held it into the lantern's beam and asked:

"Would you have a mind to keep this?"

"No. I want nothing to do with it."

I replaced the soil and smoothed it down with the flat of the spade. The end of us all, I thought, a few bones, covered with earth. Bellson's idol, Raleigh, had said it all, when he wrote of Death drawing together all man's greatness and pride and ambition and covering them over with the narrow words, "Hic Jacet."

She let the dark bough drop into place as I moved away.

"Ought we not to say something?" I asked.

"If he were, as you think, as I think, a Catholic priest, I'm not sure that anything we might say would be acceptable to him."

"Some things are true of all men, whatever their beliefs. 'Man that is born of woman hath but a short time to live. He cometh up and is cut down like a flower, and never continueth in one stay.'"

She repeated the words very softly and in a voice that told that tears were not far away.

"And rest in peace," I said. "May he rest in peace, whoever he was."

I stepped back.

God knows that by that time I should have been hardened to death and resigned to the knowledge that all men are mortal. Why it took a handful of long-dead bones to enlighten me, I cannot say. I only know that as I stood there, clutching my aching arm, I saw all men as pitiable creatures, bound for a common doom, like beasts in the shambles. Once that was seen clearly, we seemed to make too much of our differences. Catholics, Protestants, Parliamentarians, Cavaliers, how could we attach so much importance to such things? It was as though cattle, on their way to slaughter, quarrelled amongst themselves about the colour of their hides, the length of their horns. Why should we hurt and kill one another because of opinions, not one of which had any sanction outside the human mind? The most firmly held belief could be nothing but a guess. We were alive, and soon we should be dead—that was the whole sum of our knowledge of fundamental things.

Standing there I forgave the man who had killed my master, and I ceased to be a Rahabite. I was just a man of no convictions, alone in a dark garden with a woman who was weeping. I moved forward, put my arms about her and pulled her close.

"Don't cry," I said. "His troubles are over and he is safe with God. So are we all." I added irrelevantly, "And you are safe with me."

She was as warm and soft as she had been in my dream. And she did not, like the dream woman, change. She gave herself to my embrace with a home-coming gesture. When I tilted her face and kissed her, her lips were salt with tears, but beginning already to forget, welcoming.

A love story in a book would end there, on the principle that a kiss solves everything. In life it may solve nothing and be a beginning rather than an end. The warmest, closest night of love has its grey daybreak.

I watched the dawn from the window of my own room, for mindful that travellers and servants rise early I had dressed and stolen cautiously away, leaving Barbara still asleep. There'd been one moment, when I closed her door behind me, when I had wished that this had been just another casual affair, one of the line of "love 'em and leave 'em," and that I could go down, mount Meg and ride away. That was partly the natural rebound, like the drunkard waking thickheaded and vowing to be abstinent in future; and partly it was cowardice. I shrank from the thought of all the explanations that must be made—on both sides; from the memory of the way she had said the word "spies"; and from the magnitude of the task facing me in regard to Enoch Bellson.

Enoch had sent Bodkin to Baildon, and although he had lifted no finger to save him, he must have believed that Bodkin had been hot on a trail. I had been sent to follow it up. For me to go back to Tuns Lane and say that all was well in Baildon, and please I would like to resign, would concentrate suspicion not merely on the town but on me. I'd seen a few examples of Bellson's behaviour to those he suspected of double-dealing. If I wanted to sleep easy in my bed and walk in safety past dark alleyways for the rest of my life, it was essential that I should break with the Rahabites in such a manner that there was no doubt, no resentment left in that narrow, one-purposed mind. And how could that be done?

I'd shovelled some ancient bones into the ground and known a moment of revelation. I wasn't at war any more; but Enoch Bellson most certainly was; Barbara Kentwoode might well be. And there I stood between them, miserably neutral, and yet committed, on the one side by fear, on the other by love.

By the time the house was astir I had a vague glimmer of a plan in my mind. I went down and breakfasted, without great appetite, and then set out, on foot, for the middle of the town. There I asked a passer-by to direct me to the gaol and he said, "You mean the Bridewell?" and pointed to a narrow lane, at the end of which stood a grey stone building with small barred windows and a nail-studded door which was locked. There was no bell and the rapping of my knuckles made little impression. The first sign of life came from behind me, a rather pleasant, husky voice asking:

"What was you wanting, sir?" I turned and faced an old man,

stooped but sturdy still, carrying a cudgel and a bunch of keys. "I been home to me breakfast," he said, and jerked his head towards a neat cottage on the opposite side of the lane. A young woman stood at the doorway, throwing scraps to some hens but keeping her eye on us.

"I wanted to ask about William Bodkin. Is he still here?"

"Should be. He's locked up safe and sound, so he's here, if he ain't dead."

"Is he in danger of dying?"

"He's getting a bit low. Nothing to wonder at. Stranger in the place, nobody to bring him a bite. Rare funny case, William Bodkin, and not fair to nobody, not to me, nor to him. You a friend of his?"

"Yes, I think you might call me that."

"Then you'd best hand over and I'll see he get something real to eat."

I fumbled an angel from my pouch. The old man took it—not greedily, thoughtfully.

"I'll get him something real good. You see, sir, that stand to reason, anybody left high and dry like he is, is bound to clem. You can't hold me to blame. My job is done when I bring 'em out alive to be *tried*. I always done that; nineteen year I been gaoler here and never once in all that time did anybody waiting trial go hungry or cold till the Justices come round to empty the gaol. Never once. But when you get a chap like poor Bodkin, what is tried and is found guilty, but ain't delivered from gaol by way of a whipping or the stocks, just left, what can I do? I don't run a free lodging house, do I? Porridge, and a bit of bread now and then, is the best I can do, and at that I'm out of pocket."

"I see your position," I said. "Should I be allowed to see Bodkin?"

"Surely, surely. Cheer him up a bit. You mean now?"

"Later on would suit me better."

"Me too; and him. We muck out today. There's another thing— straw! Cheap, but it ain't free. But nobody that wasn't downright hardhearted could let a chap lay on bare stone this weather. Tell you the truth, sir, this case, Bodkin, been a eye opener for me. You clump down your good money to be gaoler year after year, and you make just enough profit to keep yourself alive from them waiting trial that can afford to pay for comforts. Then you get landed with a Bodkin and you're sunk."

I remembered my experience in York gaol and spoke from my heart.

"You've been very generous; and I'll see that you don't lose by it. Buy him one good meal. And I'll be back tomorrow. Reckon out, will you, what he has cost you, over and above the ordinary, and I'll try to see that you are repaid. Oh, and by the way, don't say anything about me. I'd like my visit tomorrow to be a surprise for him."

The old man nodded and said yes, he understood. Then he said:

"Would you be this Mr. Bellson he talk so much about?"

"No. My name is Flowerdew. Who is Mr. Bellson?"

"Ah! Who is he? According to what come out at the trial he's the one employed Bodkin to nose round and find who, around here, was for the King. And there was the mystery. Sir Walter Fennel, his very self, and there ain't any man more set against the King than he is, looked into that and said it was rubbish. But every now and then Bodkin he have a funny turn, and then what he is going to do to Bellson, if ever he get free . . . make you laugh, if you didn't feel so sorry for him. Just for a minute I did think that maybe . . . it all was true, about the boots being meant for the King and everything. You see, I'm used to liars. Nineteen years of it and nobody yet ever went in this door that was guilty as charged; think of that. But I never knew anybody stick to the same tale—daft-sounding as it might be—like Bodkin stick to his. I do reckon that is what mainly keep him alive; Bellson got him into it and sooner or later, in his own good time, Bellson'll get him out." His red-brown face creased in a grin. "That's how it is. One minute he's going to wring Bellson's head off his shoulders and the next, Bellson is going to get him out. Make what you can of that."

I said that I could make nothing more of it than he could, and that I would be back tomorrow. Then I said:

"You've lived here for nineteen years, you say. Did you ever hear of a family called Clitheroe?"

Standing by my window in number seven I had racked my mind for unusual but not impossible names and had hit upon that one.

"Never heard of it in my life. It ain't local, nor I never met with it in my seafaring days. No, never heard of it."

So I went back to the *Old Vine* and had my mare saddled and rode out along the road to Bywater. In that direction lay the sea, the house called Mortiboys where Barbara had lived as a child, the house called Merravy which belonged to Sir Rawley Rowhedge, and Ockley where Sir Walter Fennel lived. Something, some instinct drew me that way, asking, all along the road, at every turn, every tavern, every village green for this family called Clitheroe, and every time saying, "Of course they may have moved away."

It was midafternoon before that statement brought anything but a blank look; then a man ploughing in a field with a pair of oxen gave me the answer I longed for.

"Nubbudy moved from these parts lately, 'cept Mr. Helmar."

"Oh, then," I said with exaggerated joy, "I can't be so far off. The Mr. Clitheroe for whom I am looking had several friends whose names I know. Mr. Helmar was one, and Sir Rawley Rowhedge and a Mr. Hatton, all neighbours."

"I know all them, but no Clitheroe. . . . Still I reckon the best thing for you, sir, is to ride on to Merravy, Sir Rawley's place, and ask there. He know everybody."

"I've ridden a long way. Would this Mr. Helmar's place be nearer? Somebody there might know."

"Thass nearer, but that wouldn't be no help. The place is all shut up, the land let off and the house going to rack and ruin. I know. I used to work there, in the stables." He gave the oxen a venomous look. "Pity, too," he said, "and all on account of a ailing woman!" I said nothing; just gave him a questioning look and waited.

"Mrs. Helmar," he said, as though that explained everything. "A foreigner," he said with hatred. "Come from some place where they make wine."

"Burgundy," I said helpfully. He shook his head.

"Madeira."

"No."

"The Canary Islands."

"Thass it. She come from there and she never liked these parts; allust shivering and ailing. Pretty, mind, and him in the hollow of her hand. Then there's the war and that she never cared for neither. So in the end, off they go; and bad luck go with her. Not him, he was a right nice gentleman Mr. Helmar was, till she got howd of him."

"And you don't like working with oxen?"

"Too slow. Still, there soon 'on't be nothing else, horses being took off the way they are now, to the war. Mr. Helmar never sent none." As he spoke, a twinkle came into his eyes and I guessed that he was remembering a good story or two of how Mr. Helmar, helped perhaps by himself, had avoided the army's demands. "No, hung onto his horses, Mr. Helmar did, right to the end. Much good that did me the way things worked out."

Only yesterday at this time, this would have been enough for me; now I was scrupulous.

"He'll be back," I said in a cheerful, consoling voice.

"Not time she's alive; and all she ailed was the grizzles. She'll never come back and he wouldn't come without her, you can lay to that."

Fairly safe, I thought.

"And you still can't remember anyone around here named Clitheroe? Then I think I'll ride back to Baildon and try in another direction."

He went back to the oxen and prodded them into motion. I turned Meg and went back to the *Old Vine*.

I wanted our first meeting after the night's events not to take place in the public eye; so I went straight to Barbara's small parlour. She was not there. I asked the old woman by the stair foot where Mrs. Kentwoode was likely to be and she said in the kitchen; she was always in the kitchen until the last supper dish was on the table, everybody knew that.

"I had something rather important that I wanted to discuss with her."

"Mrs. Kentwoode don't like no disturbance with the meal getting under way, sir. But if thass all that important—there's the kitchen passage."

No wrath was going to fall on *her* head; if disturbance there was to be, let me make it and take the consequences. The kitchen, I thought, would be as public as the dining room; so I muttered that I would wait, and went upstairs. When it was time to take our places at table I carefully seated myself so that my back was to most of those in the room.

She came in towards the end of the meal, and I might have been a boy again, eighteen years old and in love for the first time. My heart made such a thunderous commotion that the front of my doublet shook.

She paused, aloof and amiable, and said:

"Mr. Flowerdew, last evening you kindly invited me to take wine with you. May I ask you to drink a cup with me in my little parlour, presently, when I am at leisure?"

I said, as though I were being strangled, "I shall be honoured, ma'am."

My neighbour at table, as soon as she was out of earshot, said: "God stab me! Did you in truth do that?"

"Do what?"

"Ask Mrs. Kentwoode to drink with you."

"Is that so remarkable? In most inns where I stay, if the supper has pleased me and the host and hostess are amiable, I do the civil. . . ."

"God love me, so do I. But not here. Well, well, what are things coming to? Tell me, did she sit down to drink with you?"

"Naturally."

"I shouldn't have thought it possible. There's a joke about it. They say she can't sit; they say she's ironclad from the knees to the tits."

To show anger would only lead to gossip, so I controlled myself, and merely said in a flat way:

"A woman alone, in a place like this, does well to be on her dignity."

"Aye, that is so," he said.

By the time that I stood by the door of the small parlour I was all eagerness again, my morning mood might have been another man's. So when she bade me enter I went in quickly and crossed the room to where she stood by the fire and would have taken her in my arms. She evaded me, reached out and took my hands in hers, which were deathly cold and, holding me so, said, in a hurried, somewhat uneasy way, her fingers clenching and then loosening on mine:

"There is so much to be said. I've been thinking about it all day. Wouldn't it be best to . . . to leave it? To let things be as they were yesterday at this time?"

I almost laughed, it was so exactly how I had felt in the early morning. I lifted one of the cold hands and kissed its fingers, lightly, briefly.

"Since then you have said that you loved me, and I have said that I love you. Can that be so easily disposed of?" I asked.

She pulled both hands free.

"We're too old," she said, "to think that love settles anything. Last night I was very grateful." She brought out the word with a curious emphasis, as though it were the name of a strange disease which excused any kind of behaviour in its victims. "Grateful and upset. I wasn't myself."

"You mean you weren't Mrs. Kentwoode; you were Barbara, and she happens to be the one I love?" I spoke the more firmly because I was in truth delighted to find that she had shared my doubts and was clear-sighted enough to see that a night's love-making was not a solution for everything. We would not be, I thought, one of those crippled couples who can only communicate in bed.

"Last night," she said, "was a night for ghosts; and I'm afraid Barbara is one of them—a girl who died long ago."

"Oh no," I said. "A girl who set herself to play the part of Mrs. Kentwoode. And played it very well, too. But I was never deceived. I saw through you from the start."

"What do you mean by that?"

"Merely that you aren't cold and hard and stiff and self-sufficient."

She sat down.

"It is as I said. You know nothing about me. I know nothing about you. All the things that should have been known before . . . before we behaved as we did last night. Not that I regret it," she said quickly; "but in the circumstances it was . . . unwise, and I think the best thing to do would be to forget it."

"What circumstances?"

She spread her hands in a vague, inclusive gesture and looked at me with what I can only call a helpless stubbornness.

I said, slowly and deliberately, "I see. Last night you were grateful and allowed your gratitude to take a certain form. And that is the end of that?"

The colour began to run up her neck again.

"It isn't that, and you know it. In fact I think you understand perfectly well what I mean."

"Let's see." I pulled a chair close so that when I sat down we were face to face. "I'll tell you what I think you mean and you can correct me where I'm wrong. What you shrink from explaining is that you have a son who is fighting on the King's side, along with Charles Rowhedge of Merravy. You and Emma Webster—both so careful to deny being acquainted—and Sir Rawley Rowhedge and a few others are all in an elaborate scheme to send aid to the King. It probably started with letters; somebody offered to smuggle letters back and forth; and then the letters began to ask, can you send, can you lend, can you borrow, beg or steal? Isn't that the way it went?"

The tide of colour had turned and now she was very pale.

"Now I'll tell you about me. Up to last night I was one of your creeping spies! You were quite right about William Bodkin; I was sent to take on his job. Last night I had what they call a change of heart. It happened before I kissed you and had nothing to do with you, so you needn't fear that if you send me about my business you'll be in any danger. In fact I spent the whole day inventing a story that will divert suspicion from you and everybody else concerned. Would you like to hear it?"

Long years of self-control bore fruit at that moment; apart from the pallor she gave no sign that anything I had said had touched her at all.

She said, "It *is* true that my son is with the King. His cause happens to be the one which appeals most strongly to high-spirited young men. And it is true about the letters." She fumbled in the little pouch and took out the key of the drawer. "All the letters which Christopher has written to me are in that cupboard drawer. You may inspect them, if you wish. I assure you that you will find only one request—for a warm knitted garment to wear under his shirt. I sent that, as any mother would, and that I would admit to Oliver Cromwell himself. But that is all."

I said, "Darling, I was frank with you."

"About yourself. You didn't involve a lot of other people. I have been frank with you, about myself. . . ."

"You don't trust me," I said reproachfully. "I trusted you."

She smiled, and this time the smile, amused, rueful and wise, lighted her whole face. "So you did—with the information that you were working for the Parliamentarian side; right here, in the very centre of the East Anglian Association, where everybody in his right senses is of the same persuasion! What risk did you take? Now supposing, just supposing, all your other wild accusations were true and I—because I like you, and because of last night—said, 'Yes,

yes, yes,' look at the difference. The stakes are too uneven; on the one side immunity; on the other arrests, trials, deaths."

It was curious, I thought, that she should mention stakes, as though referring to a game; and I remembered Enoch's words about my weakness, his prophecy that I might one day meet a better player and miss a trick through admiration. It would have been true, but for last night's experience which had made me, as it were, throw in my hand. The admiration was there, though. A woman in a million, I thought. . . .

I said, "Didn't I tell you that last night I had a change of heart?"

"You mean you changed sides?"

"No. I mean that when you let the yew bough fall . . ." I told her briefly what I had felt.

"It affected me, too. In much the same way. The same way, but different. That is why . . . I thought of how short a time we have, and age and death, creeping on, and you . . . I knew from the moment I saw you and then yesterday morning . . ." She paused and frowned. "Was it only yesterday morning? It seems so long ago. When we spoke about Calvinism and everything being predestined, I said it would be so easy. Actually I was thinking then . . ." She paused again and said rather forcibly, "I know my occupation argues against me but I have led an entirely chaste life—for more than twenty years. I should hate you to think . . . otherwise. So last night meant a great deal to me." She leaned forward and looked into my face. "In a way it was a betrayal. . . . We both had a moment of neutrality, a kind of truce."

"Mine lasted," I said. "I'm still neutral."

"I'm not. My son is very dear to me. Where he is my heart is. And if he should be killed, then it would be doubly important to me that his side should win, so that it would not have been in vain." She threw me a straight, challenging look. I said, keeping my tone light:

"So that is the truth of it; the thing so difficult to explain that, sooner than do it, you would treat last night as though it had never happened?"

"If you had lived through the war, so far, Royalist in an anti-Royalist community, you wouldn't treat it so lightly. It's almost like being a leper."

"So is being a spy, whichever side you are on and wherever you are. Do you feel a distaste for me on that account?"

"Oddly enough, I don't. I suppose I should . . . but I don't." She considered for a moment. "Perhaps last night, if I had known before I began to think about time passing . . . yes, then I think it might have tipped the scale. And now it makes no difference at all."

"Then I think we have said all that there is to say. Except that I should, very much, like to marry you."

They were words which I had never imagined myself saying to any woman; but I had retained some instinctive masculine notion that any woman so addressed would be flustered and flattered. Barbara, assuming her Mrs. Kentwoode disguise, said:

"Oh, that would need a great deal of careful thinking over. Have you ever been married?"

"No."

"I have. Not very happily. A great part of the failure was due to my fault; and the part that wasn't was due to circumstances. Ours was the ordinary arranged marriage; we knew one another so little that there was nothing to fall back on in time of need. I wouldn't want that to happen again."

I said, "I seem to have known you for a very long time. And surely last night . . ."

"That," she cut in swiftly, "means nothing at all—as a basis for a marriage, I mean. Anything can topple it. Oh, believe me, I *know*." Suddenly she was distressed again, and pitiable. "Please, let's leave it, until we are sure."

I said, "I love you. I want everything to be as you would wish. I'll wait as long as you like. And remember that, whatever your answer is, I shall always love you."

V

Next morning, having visited a cookshop and bought what my brief experience of gaol informed me would be the most acceptable offering, I went to see Bodkin.

Friendship, even good-fellowship, amongst Rahabites was not encouraged and would, in the circumstances, have been difficult to achieve; and of my colleagues Bodkin had never been a favourite.

Still, I should have been sorry to see any man not a confirmed criminal in such a situation. He was confined in a small stone cell which owed its meagre measure of light and air to the slatted door which gave upon a dim passage. As a consequence it was in semi-darkness, even at midday, and despite the mucking out that the gaoler had mentioned the stench was appalling.

Bodkin, wasted down to skin and bone, so that his head with its overgrown hair and beard looked enormous, seemed not to know me, and when the door was opened and closed behind me cowered away, for all the world like some timid wild animal in captivity. For one dreadful moment I was afraid that he had lost his wits; and my plans depended upon him. I told him my name several times, evoking no more response than a wild-eyed glance, at me, and away. Then I said, coaxingly:

"Oh, come on, Bodkin, you know me. Thread of scarlet—Tuns Lane."

Then he sprang at me, bringing his own stink with him, and clawed at me with bony fingers.

"Bellson," he said. "Bellson. Oh, thank God. Thank God. I knew it. I knew he wouldn't leave me here to rot. That's t'one thing that's kept me alive and in my right mind." He was a North Country man and it showed in his speech.

I disillusioned him promptly.

"Bellson didn't send me. I came of my own accord. I was disgusted when I heard how you had been served."

He began to whimper and babble; only Bellson could save him now; Bellson had deserted him and it was a shame because he was only carrying out instructions. Whining, repetitious, the complaints poured out.

"Look," I said. "I bought you a meat pie. And you should have had a meal yesterday; it cost me an angel." Snatching the pie he began to break it and cram it into his mouth, talking all the time.

"Yesterday, yes. Pigs' trotters. But when you're in a place like this one good meal just makes things worse. Starts you hankering. Thanks anyway. Now, what was't about getting me out of here? Man, if you only could . . ."

"I can try. Now, listen carefully. Enoch sent me to take over where you left off. And I've found who was responsible for all that went on. A man named Helmar. Enoch won't be able to do anything about it because he has now left the country; but there you are, that is what you were sent to find out and *you* did it. Not me. I haven't found anything, I arrived on the scene too late. Do you understand?"

"Go on. Go on. How does this get me out?"

"I'm going to write a letter to Bellson, tell him I'm ill—as a matter of fact my wound has been giving me trouble. I shall say that I found nothing but cold trails and that *you* have all the information he needs. You know him. Curiosity alone will make him move. In no time at all he'll have pulled the right string and you'll be free."

I was prepared for anything, even tears of joy and relief. Bodkin swallowed the last crumb, licked his fingers and said:

"I never heard of this Helmar."

"I daresay not. I did. I'm making you a present of him."

"How'd you lay nose to him?"

"Oh, in my own inimitable fashion; but I can give you details enough to satisfy Bellson. And you'll be out of here."

There was a momentary, surprising silence; then he said:

"What are you up to?"

"Me?" I said, all innocence. "If I'm up to anything it's getting you out of this stinking hole."

"Why?"

"Because I'm sorry for you. I spent one week in York gaol and that was bad enough, though I had a pocketful of money."

He said, "I lost count of the weeks I been here. But here I am, and here I'll stay, sooner than go out with a tale put into my mouth by all them that set out to prove me a liar."

"What do you mean by that?"

"You've been fooled, lad. That's what I mean. Somebody's rolled you out a yard of the same old cloth they muffled me in. And a right bonny laugh they'd have if Bellson fetched me out and I handed him a tale about some chap called Helmar." He laughed, and the laugh turned into a cough. He beat his bony hand on his chest. "You've been had, proper, but I don't blame you; she'd outwit the Devil himself. I did reckon, though, that when that door shut behind me, she'd have been satisfied. Well, well, well . . ." He laughed and coughed and hit himself again. "That beats all. Out of my own mouth I'm to go and say I was wrong. Flowerdew, I'd sooner die!"

I said, "I don't understand."

"No. How could you? Sit down. This is a long tale—and the straw was changed yesterday. Now listen. I take it you been told why I'm here. Stealing boots. Well, what else could I do? Get evidence, Bellson said, and t'boots was evidence. There was a load of them, all nicely tucked under a tarpaulin; and they were never meant for our fellows. Oh, I know that the maker in Norwich, and the chap who drove t'wagon, swore they were going to Colchester but, Flowerdew, they were Cavalier boots, platform soles and fancy tops. One look'd tell you who they were meant for. I'd no power to confiscate t'load or arrest t'driver, so I did the one thing I could and took a pair—as proof."

"Yes, I heard all that." I fitted it into place in Barbara's story. "The magistrate, Sir Walter Fennel, he's staunchly anti-Royalist and he wanted to believe your story, I understand. Why didn't he make more of the *kind* of boot, when you came to be tried?"

"You'll hear. Give me your hand. Feel that! Gently now, it ain't properly healed even yet." He took my hand and guided my fingers to a bumpy ridge in his skull, under the matted hair. "Knocked senseless and shoved into a shed I was, and when I came round I didn't know what day of the week it was or anything. And there was a wagon load of boots, tidy solid stuff for decent men to wear, and t'pair I was said to have taken, same pattern. See?"

"Somebody had swopped them."

"Somebody! She did. That Kentwoode bitch. If she'd had her way I'd be dead. She hit to kill. I just happen to have a thick skull."

"She hit you . . . a woman?"

"She hit me—that's how she give herself away. You see, there was no need. I wasn't obstreperous; I'd got what I wanted; I reckoned on the Constable coming and everything being orderly. This man of hers—she called him Tom— popped up and said, 'Got you!' and took me in t'house, and being in t'right, as I thought, I went, with t'boots in my hand. He called her and she came down—pretty as a picture, I will say—in a soft sort of wrap and her hair all loose. The man started to say he'd caught me red-handed and I said I wasn't stealing; and she said then maybe I'd tell her what I was doing. And then she said to this Tom that maybe other folks had been disturbed so would he walk round and, if anybody was, tell them everything was all right. So then I began again to tell her what I was about and she said something about it being cold and she'll just stir up t'fire. She must have taken t'poker. There was t'crack and t'pain and t'blood running into my eyes and next thing I knew I was in t'shed."

I moistened my dry lips and asked:

"You are sure she hit you?"

"Who else? There we were, alone in the kitchen. And here's t'point, Flowerdew. Clear through t'trial all this was said to have happened on t'Saturday night; but it was Wednesday. Even Tom, he was t'one who took me, started to say Wednesday—but she made it out he was too simple to know what day of t'week it was, and then he said it was market day and in this place they have two, Wednesday and Saturday, so that was accounted for. But it give her just the time she needed."

I tried to imagine Barbara creeping up behind an unsuspecting man and hitting him with a poker. The shocking thing was that, though Barbara couldn't have done it, it was just possible that Mrs. Kentwoode . . .

I said, "If she wanted you dead, why didn't she have you . . . killed when you were lying senseless in the shed?"

"Any number of reasons. First there's this Tom. You see, her story is that the minute we two were alone I tried to escape, so she clouted me. But Tom, dim-wit as he is, was honest according to his lights; he wasn't *in* with them; he hauled me into t'shed, he thought Wednesday, she said Saturday, I reckon she kept him well aled. But if anything more had happened to me, time I was in t'shed, he'd have been bound to wonder. Besides," he leaned nearer to me and his death's-head face took on a sly, knowledgeable look, "there was more to it than that. Granted if that one swipe had killed me she'd have been thankful, but soon as she had time to think she could see I was more use alive than dead. My case made everybody that'd had any suspicions look mighty silly, didn't it? Even Sir Walter Fennel, who'd believed my every word, he was left without a leg to stand on, once Bellson disowned me. My trial was a sort of washday and all the fingers that's been in t'pie looked cleaner at the end of it than they did at t'beginning. And that was how she planned it." His voice rose, becoming at once shrill and hoarse. "And now she's planned that I'm to say t'real one to blame was somebody I never even heard of. I'm to say that everything I said before was lies. Not me. I won't do it, I tell you. I'd sooner stop here and die."

"Don't be ridiculous," I said. "You're still a long way from dying and the next part is hardest. I've worked like a ferret to unearth this Helmar and I offer him to you—a key to freedom. He's gone, so nothing would ever come of your report. All these other people you think guilty would never hear a word of the matter, so why all the fuss?"

"Now I'll ask you something. Why don't you turn to and put the finger on the rest of them? Why only Helmar? Where're you living?"

"At the *Hawk in Hand*." The instinctive Rahabitic lie.

He made a derisive sound.

" 'Nough said. There's many a good tune played on an old fiddle, and in the dark willingness is all."

"You think that I . . ." I began, raucous with disgust.

"You've been got at, lad. She'd have had me too, if I was to be had. I thought best to move; and at the other place I run into the other sort of bitch, to my cost! But I know what I know and if ever I stand out in the light of t'sun again it'll not be with Mrs. Kentwoode's lie in my mouth. You go back and tell them that!"

The raised voices had attracted the attention of the old gaoler. He came shuffling along the passage, asking anxiously:

"You all right, sir?"

I called back reassuringly. Then I said:

"Look here, Bodkin, be reasonable. You've borne up wonderfully, that I will say, but you've been here a long time in the half-dark with nothing to do, and half starving all the while. You can't think straight just now. I want to get you out of here. Apart from everything else, you're an experienced, trained man; it's a waste for you to be locked away here."

"That was Bellson's doing. He threw me out like an old shoe. Oh, I know the rules and I wouldn't have broken them or mentioned his name except that I could see I was going to hang."

I said softly, "You minded that; yet now you talk very glibly about dying. . . . Where's the difference?"

"I didn't mean to hang as a thief and a liar. Bellson could have cleared me."

"He didn't. So if you don't take advantage of my offer you'll die here, as a thief and a liar. I ask you again—Where's the difference?"

"Here!" he said, and struck himself on his bony chest. "Here, man, here! When you're as low as I am, you're alone with God. I lay here in the straw sometimes and my one comfort is that God knows that I was right. He can see all; He saw t'first load of boots and t'pair I took, and He saw t'others. And His hand was over me—I didn't hang, did I? I been preserved for some purpose, and that being His, it certainly couldn't be that I get out of here by way of a lie. T'Devil is the father of lies."

I said, "Oh, come, Bodkin! Nobody could be a Rahabite without telling lies. They're the tools of the trade."

"I was," he said simply. "A Rahabite I mean, and I don't recall ever telling a lie."

Far away at the back of my mind I recalled Barbara saying that one reason why she had suspected him was that he told everyone why he was in Baildon. Ordinary people didn't do that, she said.

"I lie twenty times a day," I said. "How did you manage? For instance, what reason did you give for being in Baildon at all?"

"I gave the right one. I said, and it was true, that I was looking for a house, sound and cheap. And so I was. . . ." He made a choking sound. "I found it, too. Snug as could be. In what they call the Saltgate. Had its own well, and an apple tree and room for a couple of pigs. . . ." Abruptly his voice broke.

There is something—oh, what word can I use?—unnatural, terrible about a man crying; I have heard them scream in agony, groan, roar with pain, but simple crying, like a woman or a child, is worse. And there was Bodkin, so lately willing to face death sooner than tell a lie, crying over a little house with a well and an apple tree and room for a couple of pigs.

I was almost unmanned myself. Unmanned—there's the truth of it; a screaming, groaning, moaning man is still a man, but a man who *cries* is unmanned. I said:

"Bear up, Bodkin. The house is still there, or if not there are a dozen like it. I'll write my letter to Bellson and he'll get you out. You shall have your house. And if money is any difficulty, I can lend you what you need. You shall have," I said deliberately, "your own well, your apple tree and your two pigs."

I thought—with thankfulness—that I had found his weakness; the vulnerable point which all men have. The horrid sobbing sound, like the rending of cloth, ceased. I saw him brush the backs of his hands over his eyes. Safe, I thought. Safe!

And then he spoke. He said:

"Get thee ahint of me, old Scrat!"

I said, "What did you say?"

He said, "You wouldn't know. You'd say, Get thee behind me, Satan. And that I say to you, Flowerdew. Don't tempt me. You've been got at and you've gone over, God forgive you, but don't come here tempting me. I got enough to bear."

I made one more effort.

"You've had a hard knock on the head, Bodkin, you're underfed and have had nothing to do but brood; you're not in a condition to take such a serious decision. There's no hurry. I'll ask the gaoler to find you a place with some light and air, and I'll see you have some decent meals. I'll come back and see how you feel in a day or two."

"I shall feel the same as I do now. I'll stay here till I get out on truth made manifest. It's only a matter of time. They're clever, that I'll grant you. They got me shoved in here, they've bought you, but they'll go on with their jiggery-pokery and sooner or later Enoch'll send somebody who can stand up to them. Or maybe Sir Walter Fennel'll get what he's on the lookout for. Everybody'll know then that I was no liar."

"Much good may that do you," I said bitterly.

He flung himself down in the straw and did not answer. I called for the gaoler, who came and opened the door and let me out. At the last moment, when I was some way along the passage, Bodkin shouted:

"Flowerdew!" I thought—Ha, he's seen sense, and turned back eagerly. He was by the door, clutching the slats with his skeleton hands.

"You'd better look to yourself," he shouted. "You've failed in your errand; they'll be after you."

"Sound right lively, don't he?" the old man said conversationally. "Mostly he's quiet and low, 'cept when he talk about this Mr. Bellson."

"I think that, with one thing and another, he's no longer quite right in the head," I said.

The old man stopped.

"Now there's a notion," he said, "thass a way out I never thought of. Bedlam!"

I was horrified; I had merely intended to guard against anything Bodkin might say about me and my visit, to imply a very slight derangement of the wits. And now what had I done? I had a horrid vision of poor Bodkin surrounded by screaming maniacs. Before I could say that that was not at all what I meant, the old man said it for me. " 'Twouldn't work though, not unless he went violent, and he show no sign of that. Melancholy, thass how he'll go when he *do* go."

I tried to tell myself that there was no need for my conscience to be uneasy about Bodkin. It was by the purest chance that I had discovered where he was. In the ordinary way I should have come and gone and he would never have even been offered a chance. All the same I did feel uneasy about him. So, though I recognised him as a potential danger—to Barbara, and by implication to me— I dipped into my purse again and asked the old gaoler to make things as easy for him as he could, and I left him well content, babbling about a cell with a grating in an outer wall, and boiled beef and dumplings.

I found myself curiously reluctant to return to the *Old Vine*; I thought about the *Hawk in Hand* and rejected that, too. Walking slowly across the big market square I looked towards the great stone tower which dominated its eastern side and saw, through its gateway, what looked like a peaceful retreat. I crossed over and entered, and found myself amongst the ruins of one of those great Abbeys demolished in the middle of the previous century. Tons and tons of dressed stone and flint must have been carted away; in some places the walls had been removed to ground level, elsewhere they stood knee, thigh, shoulder high. Ivy had begun to sprawl about, grass and nettles grew everywhere. In one place there was a group of tall trees, quietly shedding the last of their yellow leaves. I walked towards them and found myself in what had been a garden. It had suffered a longer and more complete neglect than the garden at the *Old Vine* but its atmosphere was exactly the same, full of the sadness which falls on any place upon which the hand of man has laboured and then been withdrawn. I found a piece of low wall and sat down, put my elbows on my knees and my chin in my hands and gave myself over to thought.

People who seldom indulge in abstract thought and people with single-purposed minds may find it impossible to view two mental pictures simultaneously, and that disability—if it is a disability—is enviable.

I sat there in the sad quietude, with the yellow leaves spiralling noiselessly down, and found myself unable to concentrate.

I saw myself—I must do it, since Bodkin had taken such an intransigent attitude—riding back to Tuns Lane and telling Bellson the tale about Helmar. And side by side with this picture there was the one of a man sitting, all unsuspecting, with his back to the hearth, and a woman lifting the heavy iron poker and smiting him —a blow meant to kill.

Then I saw myself having a serious talk with Barbara. I would explain that I had managed to fob Bellson off but that this secret traffic must stop forthwith. That talk would take place in her little room and she would sit in her chair, with her hands in her lap. But alongside it was the picture of a man sitting, all unsuspecting, with his back to the hearth and a woman lifting the heavy iron poker and smiting him—a blow meant to kill.

There was no getting away from it; it was like one of those ill-conditioned dogs which will sometimes run beside you for a mile, snapping at your horse's heels. Their ribs show, they are covered with sores and you hesitate to take your whip and aim one more hurt . . . but in the end you must.

So I faced it. She had lifted that poker and dealt that blow. Why was I so shocked? The moment Bodkin told me, I had admitted to myself that it was an action well within Mrs. Kentwoode's capacity. And to regard this one small woman as two different people was the action of a silly boy, seizing upon one aspect of the adored one and ignoring all the rest—Her mouth is ugly, but her eyes are beautiful! It was as stupid as that.

Face it then, Flowerdew. She hit a man who was not, at the moment, offering her any physical menace; by your rule-of-thumb code a woman may only be violent in self-defence, or in defence of her young. Well . . . so he sat there, Bodkin, seemingly harmless, confidently awaiting the coming of the Constable, sure that he was in the right. But he wasn't harmless; inside that skull of his there was the knowledge and the tongue which could say what he knew. So she took up the poker and did her best to smash that knowledge, silence that tongue. In defence of herself, those who were working with her, and, in the ultimate issue, her son. You could, in fact, see it as an admirable action, prompt and sensible. But . . . but somehow I gagged on it, as upon an inedible piece of rancid fat. I even found myself wondering how many years it would take to turn a dead man into a skeleton; wondering whether, for some good and admirable reason no doubt, she hadn't struck an earlier blow, meant to kill, upon someone with a thinner skull than Bodkin's. . . . These are not thoughts to entertain about a woman who makes an appeal to your flesh and to your imagination, a woman to whom you have said, "I shall always love you."

I sat there, and once again I contemplated the easy way out. Go get the mare saddled and ride away. Make a clean break. And then I remembered a boy, wounded on the same day as I was, a simple pike stab through the hand which went wrong; and the surgeon, seeing the ominous red streaks running up the arm, said, "If you want to save the arm you must have the hand off." The boy said, "What's the use of an arm without a hand to it? Leave it alone, it'll heal or rot of its own accord and by God's will." And I saw that I was in the same position as that boy. If I made the break I should go maimed all my days. I must wait, and see whether this wound healed or rotted.

When at last I stood up, I had sat there so long and so still that falling leaves had settled on my head and shoulders and thighs and my feet were buried. Brushing them away, and thinking of all that there was to do, I realised that I was no longer young.

Interlude

In Antony Flowerdew the aging process continued so rapidly that his wife's eight years' seniority was never noticed, and might well soon have been on the other side of the scale.

The period immediately following his marriage, with the fluctuating fortunes of war, the defeat, trial and execution of the King and the establishment of the Commonwealth in England, was an anxious time for many people; to these common worries Antony Flowerdew must add those of his own.

Perhaps foremost among them was a sense of guilt concerning William Bodkin. Before returning to London to face Bellson, hand in his untruthful report, and leave the little red mare in her stable, Flowerdew made two more visits—both abortive—to the gaol. Despite improvements in his accommodation and feeding, Bodkin's condition had deteriorated, but his stubbornness remained unimpaired. He'd never heard of the Helmars, he knew what he knew about Mrs. Kentwoode, and sooner than gain his release by a lie, he would stay in Baildon Bridewell until he died. All the way to London Flowerdew was devising a scheme by which Bodkin might regain his freedom and at the same time be discredited so far as his story about Barbara was concerned.

In Tuns Lane he had a long session with the man who had been his master. He laid all the blame for the Royalist activities in and around Baildon squarely on the shoulders of the Helmars, who were safe and far away. Enoch Bellson accepted this story as he accepted all reports, giving no sign either of credulity or of disbelief. Finally Flowerdew said, "And of course I found William Bodkin."

"That fool," Bellson said. "He came nearer to discrediting t'whole organisation than any man I have ever employed."

"He was not entirely to blame. He'd suffered a blow on the head which had addled his wits. He'd done good work, he was hot on the trail; then somebody hit him on the head with a poker and now all he can think of is being revenged on *her*. It has become a mania with him."

"Where he is his mania is harmless."

"So, I think, would it be if he were set free. The woman who hit him—thinking him a thief—and against whom he now makes most comprehensive accusations, is the sister-in-law of Sir Walter Fennel, as stout a Parliamentarian as there is in those parts."

"And a magistrate, if I remember rightly."

"Bodkin," Flowerdew said, after a pause during which it became plain that Bellson had nothing to add to his comment, "will die unless he is soon released."

"Men of better sense die every day for less reason."

"He is pathetically certain that you will come to his aid."

"He should remember his Bible—'Put not thy trust in princes nor in any child of man.'"

"You will not help him?"

"Have I ever?"

Forcing himself to speak in a more casual way, Flowerdew said:

"Well, I thought I would mention the matter. The other thing I wanted to discuss with you was the question of my own retirement."

"Yes?"

"I'm too old and my wound is troubling me again. I find riding painful and I have sleepless nights. Then by day I am dim-witted, and it may be only a question of time before *I* make a slip and incur your anger."

"And end like Bodkin. Is that it?"

"His plight certainly bore home to me the penalty of failure."

"To put it briefly, you've lost your nerve and—perhaps—your desire to be of service to the cause?"

"Say rather that I think I might give better service in another way." He spoke of the tanyard in Leicester, doing of late less well than it might; of his idea for going back to it and trying to increase production, of the army's need for boots and harness.

Bellson said, "I told you, not long ago, you lacked summat. You always did. Mebbe you'll make good leather. Tanning's a softening process, I understand." He grinned. "You're soft, Flowerdew. Clever, I grant, but soft. I knew that from t'moment I first set eyes on you, and to tell you t'truth, never once have I set you a job without praying to God that t'one you were sent to ferret out wouldn't be white-haired and venerable, or t'father of four squalling brats. Aye, you'll be of more use making boot leather."

It was an easier dismissal than Flowerdew had hoped for. But it was not to be accepted at face value; nothing Enoch ever said or did could be so accepted. The next moves were cautiously made. He left for Leicester, and at Bedford halted on account of illness, not entirely feigned. Bedford was the nearest place to Baildon along any accepted route to Leicester and from there he sent Barbara a letter, scrupulously noncommittal, lest it should be intercepted, a simple statement that he was ill in a Bedford inn. When, in the shortest possible time, she came to him, saying, "I left the *Old Vine* to fend for itself," he knew that he had been right. They went on together to Leicester, and were married there; and amidst the odour of hides and tanbark they decided upon their future. The man who had hired the place was now anxious to buy it; and Barbara confessed to a liking for the *Old Vine*.

"There is Christopher to consider, too," she said, "and I think he would not take kindly to the tanyard." So it was sold, and the *Old Vine* at Baildon became their home.

There was another source of worry, Christopher Kentwoode coming home to the *Old Vine* at the end of the war, and no whit grateful to his Parliamentarian uncle, Sir Walter Fennel, and his Parliamentarian stepfather, Antony Flowerdew, for making it possible that he *could* come home and not be, like so many of his kind, exiled so long as the Commonwealth lasted. He was a sick man, afflicted with what was known as a "graveyard cough," his heritage from forebears he had never heard of. It was attributed to his having slept in wet clothes while in the King's service.

It was from the best of motives that Antony Flowerdew suggested the turning of the *Old Vine* into a school for boys. It forestalled, by a few weeks, the official closure of "drinking places," it provided for two comparatively well-educated men, the one with a useless arm, the other with a graveyard cough, a prospect of employment. But the change brought its own problems. The man who, in a flash of enlightenment, had once seen all men as cattle driven to the slaughter, was bound to see boys, the young of the doomed species, as pitiable things whose innocent pranks and gambles should be regarded with tolerance; his younger partner, with his sensitive ear, thought them noisy, bothersome young rascals. The truth, lying midway between the two extremes, escaped them both.

For a while, standing between them, soothing, emollient, was Barbara, Barbara Hatton, Barbara Kentwoode, Barbara Flowerdew, so skilled in trimming her sails to the prevailing wind that she did it without conscious thought. Explaining her husband to her son, her son to her husband, and the boys to both, she maintained a tenuous peace. Husband, son and boys all adored her.

Two of her sisters had died of a disease, the symptoms of which, eventually, she recognised in herself. "Me too!" Mastering her horror and disgust, proving, although she did not realise it, the fallacy of Antony's comparison of men as beasts to the slaughter, she set about arranging affairs as well as she could so that after her death the situation might not become too intolerable to either man. It was evident by that time that the school would never do more than just pay its way; Antony had sold his tanyard and spent the proceeds; the Old Vine needed a steady income, however small, derived from some other source; and it needed someone capable of assisting Antony if, once her control was removed, Christopher put into action his oft-mentioned threat of leaving the school and trying his hand at business. The person she knew who came nearest to meeting both these needs was her favourite brother, Edward, a Canon of Ely Cathedral, a man of such sound good sense and such small religious prejudice that changes in popular method and ceremony had never injured him, merely annoyed him. He had a little money and had sometimes said that he would like to retire and devote himself to his hobby, which was delving into and recording ancient customs and what he called "curiosities." Whether a piece of Church furniture was called an altar or a table, whether an officiating cleric faced this way or that were matters of indifference to Edward Hatton; a piece of pottery believed to be Roman, an un-Anglicised word on a yokel's tongue, could set him all agog.

Edward, she thought, would be company for Antony, would fill a little of the gap her death would make. Best of all, Edward would supply something which Antony lacked nowadays, something difficult to define. You could say of him that he was too kind, too unworldly, that he had no sense of self-preservation, was vague about money, stupidly indulgent to naughty little boys . . . but all these facts, though each was evidence of what was wrong with him, left his spiritual ailment unnamed. He was no longer equipped to deal with this world, and she, who loved him, recognised the fact.

Her complaint was painful, but in its early stages not disabling. One of the things made in the Old Vine kitchen as regularly as the blackberry jelly or the dried apple rings was a concoction of poppy heads, known as Clevely Cordial because the stuff had first been made by the nuns at the Priory. It was an opiate and a pain-killer. Boys with toothache or belly pains that lasted more than a couple of hours were dosed with it. For months Barbara took it, secretly. Madam Elizabeth's end was never, for more than a few minutes at a time, absent from her mind and she was determined, in this one matter, to do better. When she knew that her state could not any longer be concealed she wrote her brother Edward a long letter, and as soon as it was despatched, racked her brain for some excuse to make a little celebration. It was October and she said to Antony in the morning, "Do you remember what day this is?" He said, "No. Unless it is some boy's birthday."

"It is the day when you first came to Baildon, to this house."

"I thought it was later in the month."

"Men never remember anniversaries," she said.

And that evening there was roast goose and wine on the table, and nobody thought it strange that she should embrace Christopher and say, "Bless you, my dear!" Later, in their bedroom, she said to Antony, "I think I have a cold starting. One of us should sleep next door in the Cough Room. Which shall it be?"

"By rights you," he said, jokingly, "for coughs go with colds. But it is a hard, narrow bed, and I shall sleep in it."

A hard, narrow bed, she thought. And she embraced him too, and said, "Bless you, my dear," and settled herself in the wide bed, stuffed with feathers, and when she was alone drank down the vast quantities of the Clevely Cordial that she had put ready to hand. She knew that a dose excessive but not lethal had results that were in every way unpleasant, and when she felt herself sinking into sleep almost her last conscious thought was that she had managed this neatly.

Her death gave her last letter to her brother great weight, and since the suggestions in it accorded well with his own wishes, he was soon, with his little bit of money and his good sense and all else that comprised his personality, installed at the Old Vine. He was still there in the year 1670 when Ethelreda Benedict came to join the household.

Part Five

ETHELREDA BENEDICT'S TALE

Circa 1670

I

I was born and lived for the first fifteen years of my life on an island in the Fenland, to the north of Ely. When I came out into the world I soon found that what I said about life on our island was disbelieved. People said that if I had been speaking about foreign parts, yes, then they could credit it, but not in England, not right here in the late seventeenth century. Impossible! But they never saw the Fens before the draining began.

Our island was called Mons, and stood up out of the surrounding marsh like a blister on the palm of the hand. The whole of it was very little bigger than the Old Vine, including the yard and the stables. All around it stretched the marshes, in places flat black mud, in places green with rushes, here and there dotted with a clump of willows, and everywhere threaded through with a network of streams, so slow-flowing that they seemed to be stagnant.

We had no neighbours. South of us, and perhaps not very distant as a bird flies but a long slow journey in the boat along the intricate waterways, lay Ely, which Father visited about twice a year; in the other direction was another, bigger island called Withy, which Father went to once a year, always in the spring; he bought two piglets and two lambs. The young pigs went into the pen at the side of our hut and the lambs were staked out every day. They couldn't be allowed to run free because of the danger of their stepping into the bog. Lambs jump and frisk even when they are tied to a stake.

People say to me, what a horrible life; they say, how dull. Knowing no other life, I was completely happy; I can look back and say with truth that they were happy days. Perhaps it was worse for Father, for he had lived on Mons when there were more people

about; he'd been one of three children; and, of course, he had had
a wife. At least one day when he went to Withy for the beasts he
had brought my mother back with him; but she died soon after I
was born. And one of his sisters went to Withy and the other was
drowned; and his mother and father died because they were old.
So in the end there were just us two. Where a lot of people live
together they make very strait differences between male and female,
probably because they can afford to. When there are only two of
you nobody cares about the difference. Father could cook as well
as any woman, and he soon taught me to handle a boat or set a
snare. I think he forgot that I was a girl. The first time I went to
Ely with him, when I was about twelve, I went wearing a pair of
cut-down breeches and caused quite a sensation.

When I was thirteen, what happens to girls happened to me and
I said to Father, "Look! I'm bleeding to death!" But he said no, and
showed me what to do.

It all sounds very rough and barbarous, but in truth it wasn't.
It was just different. We didn't do what other people did because
we didn't know any other people. We weren't even Christians, but
that didn't bother us, because we didn't know. We had our own
religion.

We had a name and it was Benedict. Father was Peter Benedict
and I was Ethelreda. Father said that his father had told him, and
his had told him, and so on, back into the shadows, that once upon
a time a monk of Ely had done something wrong and run away
and somehow reached our island. Father didn't know what a monk
was; I asked him and he said he was telling me just what his father
had told him, and he hadn't asked so how could he know? What he
did know was that that was where we got the name Benedict, and
some very stout woollen cloth—some garment that the monk had
been wearing and which had been made into breeches and jackets.
And there was the thing we called the Touchwood. I know now
that it was a Crucifix. It hung on a nail in our hut and was the only
single thing there that wasn't plainly useful. We always touched it
before going fishing or snaring, or on a journey. The bottom of it
was worn quite smooth with all the fingers that had touched it.

The Touchwood was one of our ritual things; but we had many
more. On the night of the fifth new moon of the year we had the
Beltane Fire and cooked a cake of barley bread in the middle of it.
The fire was always made of last year's rushes and burned very

fiercely; if the cake of bread was cooked through when the fire died down, then that was a good sign; if it was still doughy, then the fishing and everything else would be bad.

They laugh at me; but it is true. I can remember ten Beltane Fires; six times you could eat the bread, all but the black crust, and they were good years; the other four the bread was doughy and they were bad.

Then there was what we called Pleasing the Water. You could do that at any time. Birds—and they must be ones you could eat so that giving them away was a real sacrifice—had to be killed by having their throats cut and their bodies thrown into the water. Sometimes the water was pleased with the gift and returned a good harvest of fish; sometimes a bird would be rejected, thrown up against the muddy verge and left there, and then the fish, especially the eels, would be hard to catch, and small.

It is all very well for Edward to say that these are pagan things, nonsensical and superstitious. I *know*. When you live so close to the bone as Father and I did, and at least three parts of your spending money depends upon whether you please the water or not, you do notice very sharply. It is stupid and narrow-minded to call a thing pagan when you mean different. It is like those people in Ely staring and jeering at me because I was wearing breeches. Most of the time Father and I were walking about on stilts. How could you stilt-walk in a skirt and three petticoats?

When Father took the boat and threaded his way into Ely he always took a good load. There were the rush mats which we had woven in the long winter evenings by firelight, and in the summer evenings as the sun lingered. There were the smoked eels which could only be properly prepared over a peat fire, and luckily at one point our island joined onto an outcrop of peat. In my time I have smoked thousands of eels and they are a very salable commodity because, properly done, they will keep almost forever. We made something else on our island, too; far more troublesome, but very marketable. You took and plucked every kind of bird you could lay hands on, the more varied the better, and boiled them together; then you removed all the skin and the bones and beat the flesh in a mortar until it was a smooth paste. It was put into crocks and sealed away from the air by a thick layer of mutton fat and, properly prepared, it would keep for months. In addition to these things, when Father went to Ely he took behind the boat great bundles of reeds, strung out along a rope and floating. There was a ready sale for these, too, for making and repairing the thatch on houses.

When he came back he brought the things we needed and could not produce for ourselves, flour and salt and pepper and honey. We had all we needed and wanted nothing that we didn't have, and I still think that is a good way to be.

Father never brought any news back from Ely and after my one shameful visit there I understood why; even our talk was different; we used many different words, and even those that we had in common with the people of Ely and the outside world we pronounced in our own way. But the people on Withy spoke more like us, and it was from his yearly spring visit there, in the year when I was fourteen, that Father brought news of this draining.

Edward once asked me how I knew my age. We weren't savages; Father could count and he taught me to; and he remembered the year of my birth because it was the year of the most doughy cake on the Beltane Fire and a bad year all round; bad for fish and bad for birds, and my mother died. I was always a year older ten days after the Beltane Fire day.

The draining was something that was being done to make the soggy ground firm, and when we first heard of it we were pleased and so, Father said, were the people on Withy. If the marshes could be dried out, then our islands would get bigger; then on Mons perhaps there would be room for some flowers, so that we could have our own bees and not have to buy honey; perhaps we could keep more than two sheep. But it didn't work out that way for us. Water pushed out from one place must go to another, and very soon it was plain to us that our island was getting smaller, not larger. Its fringes grew more marshy every day; our peat ridge began to disappear and our special stretch of river, which we always called the Flumen, grew wider and deeper.

Father got into his boat and went downriver to Withy and found that the same thing was happening there. And they told of other places where it was the same. Withy wasn't as lonely as we were, they had only one stretch of marsh between them and the big river. In a way they were worse off than we were because they had built their houses to one side of the island, four houses for the two dozen or so people who made up the tribe, and the wetness had risen so much that it had almost reached their doors. The man who had "married" my father's sister, and another man of the tribe, said they were going to go to Ely and make a protest; my father said he would go with them. They thought that if they explained that draining in one part was drowning islands in another, it would be stopped.

But it wasn't any good. Somebody very important, called a Duke, and a good many other men with a lot of money had started the draining and they didn't care about little islands being swamped. They said that the same thing had happened in other places and the people had saved their land, even when the rivers had risen to such a level that they ran high above the solid land, by building what they called dykes.

Father came home and began to build dykes and I helped him. What it meant was that you shovelled some of your good soil, which you could ill spare, into a high bank all round your island and banged it as solid as you could to make a rim.

It was heavy work, different from any we had ever done before, and soon we were so stiff that we could hardly move. Father said it would wear off if we kept at it, and for him it did, but not for me. The pain in my back grew worse and worse and one morning I couldn't get up from the bed at all. I asked Father to give me a hand and he began to pull me and then it hurt so badly that I screamed; and he looked at me and said, "Your face is all swollen. Have you been passing water properly?"

I hadn't, for two days; so he said I was to stay still and he went out and gathered some brooklime and bruised it in the mortar and poured boiling water on it and stirred it well, and when it was cool enough I drank it. In two days I was better; but as soon as I started to shovel again the pain came back and the swelling and all the other things.

Then it started to rain and Father said, "I shall never do it alone. You'll have to go to Withy and ask somebody to come and help me."

He drew with a stick on the ground to show me which way I must take where the waters joined, because I had never been to Withy. There was more water in the river than I had ever seen, and it seemed to be moving more, which made it easy for me going downstream but worried me about getting back, for ours was a big heavy boat and I wasn't feeling very strong. However, I went and I took all the ways that Father had shown me and I found Withy, *I think*. There wasn't any island, just the thatched tops of four houses sticking up out of the water, and a cat standing on one of them, yowling. I was able to get the boat quite close to the houses, the water was so deep and our boat so flat-bottomed. I called to the cat and it ran up and down the roof as though it was mad and then made up its mind and jumped.

I yowled, too, on the way back; what with the disappointment, and the sorrowful sight of the drowned houses, and the pain in my back and the water running so strongly against me.

When he saw me back, alone with a cat, Father went kind of crazy. "That's *just* what we needed!" he said, and seized the cat and wrung its neck and threw it into the water. Then he went back to his shovelling and banging, working like a crazy man; never stopping so long as there was light to see, and when it was dark coming in too tired to eat. I told him, "If you go on like this you'll kill yourself." And that is just what he did do.

It was evening, dark with rain. I'd felt better again that morning and helped him until the pain came back. Then I'd crawled to the hut and sat down, looking out. I could see that no matter how he drove himself he'd never do it, the water was rising too fast. Mons would drown, just as Withy had. Presently I got up and, bent over to ease the pain, went to where he was working. I said the water would get us in the end, why not give up and go away? He said:

"Go where? Don't stand there blathering."

I saw how wild and thin he looked; terribly thin; his ribs stood out like the wands of an eel trap, and inside you could see his heart banging away like a bird just caught. I thought how little he'd eaten lately, and I made up my mind to kill a pig. It wasn't the right time, the later you could leave it the better, and you never killed until there'd been a frost; but I thought the smell of the meat would tempt him—and where was the sense in saving up a pig to be drowned?

So I killed it, clumsily because my back was so lame, and slowly, stopping for rests, I gutted it and singed and scraped it and cut it up. The nicest, tenderest piece of loin I hung on the spit over a good fire of bog wood. Bog wood isn't like peat, though you often find the two close together; bog wood is trees that have somehow got in the marshes and been buried. It is as hard as iron and burns very clear.

Soon there was a very toothsome smell, and I realised that I was hungry. It grew darker and I lighted the dips and put the salt and the knives and the bread on the table. Then it was real dark.

He didn't come and at last I went to the door and shouted, "Father." He didn't answer; and as I stood there by the door I knew that he wasn't working, because I couldn't hear him. In fact, for the first time in my life, I was aware how quiet it was. Just the patter of the rain and the secret sound of water, creeping. I shouted even louder. And still he didn't answer. So I set out towards where I had last seen him working.

Dark is dark, and inside the hut you light dips and everything outside seems black. When you are out in it, even on a night when there is no moon or stars, nothing but rain, you can still see enough to find your way. At least, I could, then. . . .

Father lay, face downwards, not straight out, but huddled up. The spade lay beside him. He'd been sick, I knew that by the smell, and I was puzzled how that could be, for he'd last eaten at dawn light, and then just bread.

It took me quite a long time to realise that he was dead. The trapped bird of his heart had battered itself to death against the cage of ribs.

In Baildon, and I suppose everywhere else in the world, they talk a lot about love. Men love women and women love men; mothers love their children and children sometimes love their parents. On Mons I had never heard the word. If, say, on that dreadful day in Ely somebody had said to me, "Do you love your father?" I shouldn't have understood what they meant. Now, at the moment when I am thinking over my life story, I am using, I know, a great many words which I have learned since I came to Baildon. Love is one of them.

That night on the island that was drowning, when I found my father dead, huddled beside his spade, I didn't think—I loved him! I thought about how he had given me brooklime and told me to stay in bed when I was ill, and how I hadn't helped him much. And I thought how alone I was now. I cried, just as I had cried coming back from Withy that day with the cat. I also thought that if he had taken notice of what I said about going somewhere else he'd still be alive. I didn't think in these words, of course, I just thought.

And then I could smell the pork. I thought of all the work I'd done; first of all the great effort of deciding to kill the pig so much before time, and then the killing and the lifting and the chopping, and all with my back hurting so badly; it did seem a shame, in the end, to waste the good food. I went back into the house and ate and ate until I was filled. Then I slept.

In the morning the loneliness was there waiting for me and I cried again. Nowadays I get a sour amusement when somebody says, "I was lonely" or "I can't bear to be alone." Most of them don't know what it means. Father and I had never talked much because talking wasn't a thing that we did for the sake of doing it; we only spoke when it was necessary to say something, but without him the silence was different. The remaining pig and the two sheep made their usual noises, and so did the birds, and the water, if anything, was noisier than usual, but the main bulk of the silence remained untouched. It didn't frighten me, exactly, but it made me uneasy; and I thought to myself that even if the water suddenly started to go down and Mons was safe, I shouldn't like to live there by myself. Also I didn't feel able to do the buying and selling in Ely when next the time came round; and even if I found another place like Withy where animals were for sale, it would be quite a time before I could do as Father had done—carry them over the marshy piece between the boat and the dry land. No, it was plain to me that I must go and find a place—not Ely—where people were living and where I should fit in. It never struck me that I should be casting myself on their charity; my back would soon be well and then I could work; anybody would be glad to have me, I thought.

But first I must bury Father. I could just remember my grandmother's death. Father had dug her grave in the peat ridge, but that was swamped now. Before he covered her he had put some bread and fish and a handful of peas on her breast. He had also said some words, but I didn't know them. I couldn't dig, so I laid him flat, put the offering of food on his breast, and then pulled down part of the dyke over him. Just where he lay he hadn't had time to bang it hard, so the soil moved easily. I said, "Goodbye, Father," just as I had done on the days when he had left me to go to Ely or Withy. Then I was ready to go.

I didn't much like leaving the animals to starve or drown, but I couldn't get them to the boat; so in the end I went away with nothing except Father's fowling piece and our stilts, the Touchwood, a few crocks and what was left of the bread and the cooked meat. I turned in the Withy direction and began to row.

Rowing started my back aching again and I had to rest often. I knew that between Mons and Withy there was no inhabited place so it was not until I was past that island—where the roofs only just broke the water's surface now—that I began to look about for signs of people. I searched for places where reeds had been cut, or fish traps laid, or for smoke going up. I'd found nothing by the end of the first day, but I wasn't worried; I hadn't come far. I drove the boat into a reed bed until it was steady, lay down and went to sleep. The next day was exactly like the one before, and I did become a little anxious because I was getting to the end of my food. Also the pain was bad, and touching my face I thought it was swelling again, swelling with the water which wasn't passing out in the usual way. I kept a sharp lookout for brooklime, thinking I could chew it and get some good that way, but I saw none.

On the third day I thought I was mad, for suddenly Ely towers came into view and I'd turned away from Ely at the very beginning. It couldn't be; I must be dreaming. But it was Ely right enough! A day later I should have been glad and made my slow feeble way towards the place I hated, but I hadn't at that moment yet reached the end of my tether, and as soon as there came a choice of two ways I took the one that led away from the towering town. I was even, after the first shock, relieved to find that I had somehow taken the wrong way and come so close to the town; my mistake accounted for the fact that I had not yet found what I was looking for. Now, on the right way, I soon should! But that day ended and I was still alone. I had come to the end of my food, too, and saw how foolish I had been to leave home as I had. I should have baked a fresh batch of bread and cooked much more of the pork. I was angry with, not sorry for, myself. In our small world people who were rash and silly did often come to grief, and self-pity was not encouraged.

The next day was the worst yet; my face was so swollen that I could see my own cheeks bulging out under my eyes; the pain in my back grew worse and worse. The only good thing about it was that it made me feel sick, so I wasn't hungry. I didn't drink either; I thought maybe I could dry myself out that way.

I remember pushing the boat into a reed bed that evening, and drawing in the oars, and touching the Touchwood and lying down flat, and immediately feeling better. After that nothing is very clear. I slept in a way, but not the restful blank sleep that I had always slept before. I was doing all kinds of things and whatever I did I was in a terrible muddle. I roasted some pork and it fell off the spit and I had to pull it out of the fire, all covered with ashes; and I set an eel trap, with the openings so wide that a young pig could have got through; then I was burying Father again and the dyke was so hard I couldn't get even one shovelful of soil out of it. I was in Ely, trying to sell the bird paste, but nobody understood me; they just jeered. I was in Withy, where I bought a young pig, but I couldn't carry it, I couldn't even lift it for the pain in my back. And so it went on and on. In between the silly or annoying things, I would wake up and know I was in the boat; I could feel it under me. Once I was terribly thirsty and I thought—I must drink no matter how I swell; so I found a cup and dipped it over the side and drank. The water, like everything else, was just that little bit wrong; it tasted nasty. More than once I woke up and thought— This won't do, you must row, you must get moving. But every time I tried to sit up the pain took hold of me so hard that I had to lie down again. So I went back to my muddling sleep, and when one of the things that happened was that I was still in the boat and it was moving, quite swiftly, without my rowing, I wasn't surprised; it wasn't true, it was like trying to carry a pig. I was still in the boat; I could feel it under me. And in the morning, I thought, I should feel better.

Then there was the time when I wasn't in the boat. I was truly frightened then, and even more frightened when I had my eyes opened and saw, just above my head, some dark boards. I'd somehow managed to turn the boat over and I lay on the soft ground under it. It was a heavy boat, I should never be able to lift it and get it afloat again. Of all the muddles I had been in lately, this was the worst. The pain was better, though; better than it had been for a long time. I'd manage somehow, I thought. And I took hope from the fact that I wasn't lying in the complete dark, so the boat must be a little tilted. I could crawl out from under it. I turned to that side and found myself nose to nose with an old woman. She looked to me like my grandmother, whom I could *just* remember, and that cheered me very much for it seemed to indicate that I had

managed to find a Fen island after all. Or some Fen islanders had
found me. I smiled. She said:

"Well, are you back with yourself? I thought I heard you stir."

She didn't speak like a Fen woman, but I understood her; it was
a strain, but I understood.

I said, "Did I find you or did you find me?"

"Eh?" She turned her head a little and looked puzzled. I repeated
the question in a rather louder voice. Then she shook her head and
backed away.

I cried out to her, "Don't go. Don't leave me," and at the same
time raised myself to see how she got out from under the boat,
because if she could, I could. Then I saw that I wasn't under the
boat. I was in a tiny room, not a quarter the size of our hut, and I
was lying on a bed on a shelf. I rolled off, very carefully, and stood
on the narrow piece of floor. There was another shelf above the
one I had lain on, and it was the boards of that shelf which I had
mistaken for the boat timbers. In the wooden wall opposite the
shelves there was a small round window, and under the window a
chest. That was all. And the whole room was moving gently up and
down.

Quick as a lightning flash I remembered, not the exact words
but the meaning of what Father had said when he buried my grandmother; it was something about faring forth on a journey to the
happy place. And the food—I saw the value of that now—it was
food for the journey. So I had died, and the old woman was my
grandmother, and she'd gone to fetch Father and tell him I was
here.

I'd have gone after her, but I still wasn't feeling strong, though
the pain had gone, and the room moving up and down made me
feel strange, so I held onto the top shelf and waited and presently
the door opened and she came back with a mug held between her
hand and her body and a plate in her hand, which left the other
hand free for opening and closing doors.

I said, "Are you my grandmother?" but she didn't understand.
She gave me a little push with her free hand and then patted the
bottom shelf. I understood her and sat down. She put the plate
beside me and handed me the mug. It was full of milk, which I
had never seen before; but I was willing to try it. I took a little sip
and it was worse than the funny-tasting water which was the last
drink I could remember. I held it away from me and looked at the

old woman. She took the mug, drank from it, put on an expression of pleasure and handed it back to me.

"Good," she said. I tried again. If this was what they drank in the happy place I must learn to like it. Then I looked at the plate. It held bread and pork belly, the thin fat and lean striped part that you always salt and keep. That was good. Between mouthfuls I kept trying to talk to her, but she merely looked puzzled, and then I thought I understood. Hearing varies very much in fish, and in birds; maybe it was the same with people. Perhaps she couldn't hear. I spoke louder and louder, and then she looked distressed and started to give me little soothing pats. When I had finished the food, and with a last shudder of distaste drained the mug, she took the mug and the plate and went away again. This time she was gone only a minute and when she came back there was a man with her. He was old too and wore a knitted cap pulled low over his ears and a thick sheepskin coat, not unlike the one of Father's which I had brought to protect me from the cold.

The old woman said, "See if you can understand her, Job. She sound foreign to me."

"She's from the Fens. There was stilts in the boat," he said. He turned to me and asked:

"You feeling better, now?"

"Quite well, thank you."

"Eh?"

"Quite well, thank you."

"I think she says she's well," the old man said, addressing the old woman.

Using my hands, pointing to myself and to the old woman I asked:

"Is she my grandmother?" He thought this over for a while. Then he said, "Grandmother. Did you say Grandmother?"

I said, "Yes," and nodded my head.

"No."

Of course what he said didn't sound to me like the "no" I used myself, or that I was accustomed to hear from Father, but it was near enough. Later on, when I talked about this episode with Edward and Mr. Flowerdew and Christopher, Christopher said I understood people who couldn't understand me because I was naturally intelligent; Mr. Flowerdew said that might be true but it was also because my ear hadn't been blunted, I'd lived in great quiet and so my hearing was keen and my mind wasn't blurred by any preconceived notions about how people *should* talk.

For whatever reason, I understood that the old woman was not my grandmother. So then I asked was I dead and in the happy place. That made the old man, who had managed to understand the one word "dead," laugh.

"No. You ain't. You might have been if we hadn't found you. She leeched you."

It would be tedious to give in detail every conversation between me and Job Briggs. Bit by bit, a word here and a word there, I learned that just after his ship, *Pretty Amy*, had cast off from Lynn dock, it had almost run down my boat. Job and one of the two men who made up his crew had hauled me abroad, and Amy Briggs had given me her bed and nursed me.

When I knew that I was on a ship, I thought that after all I had, in a fashion, found an island, for what is a ship but a floating island; and I hoped very much that they would let me stay. Between the time when I came to my senses and the day that we put in at another place, called Bywater, I did my best to make myself useful, though there wasn't much that I could do. Even the cooking was different. On Mons there was a big open fire and to roast meat you hung it on the spit and to boil anything you hung the pot on a hook; bread you baked in an iron oven. You first made a huge fire, bog wood was best, but peat would do, and when it was all red hot you took a hoe and made a hole in the middle, set the oven in and dragged the fire back over it. If Mrs. Briggs had had a fire such as I was used to I could have cooked and shown her what I could do. But she had only a little round iron stove with a long pipe instead of a chimney to take off the smoke and a lid on top which when you lifted it left a round hole, just large enough to take a pot. She never roasted anything and she never made bread, and the only time I tried to help her by boiling something I mistimed it because her pot, set close down to the fire, boiled so much more quickly than my pots, slung over the fire. And one thing she cooked often I had never seen before. Potatoes. Job Briggs, who by the time we reached Bywater I could understand quite well, said that they were the most wonderful thing anybody had ever found to eat; they stored easy, he said, in a sack, and they'd keep for months and they stopped people on ships getting some illness called scurvy. They were very costly, but getting cheaper every year because they would grow anywhere and more and more people were trying them; and another way in which they were of special benefit to ships was that they took the place of bread.

I have, to this day, no fondness for potatoes; they haven't any taste for one thing, and they are connected, for me, with the shame I felt when, trying to help Mrs. Briggs, trying to make myself indispensable to her, I undertook to boil the potatoes, and not allowing for the quicker cooking I boiled them to nothing. When I took the pot from the stove and removed the lid, instead of the lumps of no taste of which Mr. Briggs thought so highly there was just a kind of mush, like onion broth but thinner.

Their kind of cooking I couldn't do, and the other things I was useful for, like setting snares, fishing, beating reed beds to start birds and feeding pigs, you couldn't do on a ship. So I was no good to them and at Bywater I had to go.

Job didn't say that it was because I was useless; taking great pains to make himself understood he explained that it was lack of space. There was nowhere for me to sleep. Now that did puzzle me. Ever since I came back to my senses and knew that I had been sleeping in Mrs. Briggs's bed—they called it bunk—I had insisted upon sleeping on the floor, between their bunks and the chest. It was just wide enough for me.

I was so immensely simple, or innocent, I never realised that my being there was awkward for them. And when, picking our way through the maze of words, Job and I reached the point where he had managed to tell me that three in a small cabin was one too many, I said then I'd sleep with the men. Oh no, he said, no and again no to that. So long as I was aboard the ship I must sleep on the floor, near them; and when we reached Bywater he would find me a place.

"A place for sleeping?"

"A place where you will work."

"Not here? Not with you?"

"No. I've been telling you; we've no room."

Mrs. Briggs opened her chest and took out two dresses and stood looking at them, and at me, rather sadly. I realise now, much too late, what a sacrifice it was for the poor woman to spare me one of her two decent dresses. At the time I wasn't thankful. I was afraid of the place we were bound for, thinking it would be like Ely, and I couldn't see any reason why I couldn't stay aboard the *Pretty Amy*

—except that I wasn't useful enough. So I was sullen while she fitted the dress on me, and stitched away, making it smaller. She made me a petticoat, too. Under them, when they were finished, I wore the short tight breeches made of monk's cloth. They were my only underwear for a long time.

Bywater, when we reached it, seemed quite as big as Ely, though it had no towers. Mr. Briggs waited and helped to unload the cargo which the *Pretty Amy* had carried, and as soon as he had done that he came and found me and indicated that I was to go with him. I almost cried when I said goodbye to Mrs. Briggs. We then went ashore and walked a little way and turned in at the door of what looked to me to be a fine big house—it was an inn called *God Save Mariners*, but I didn't know that, never having seen an inn before; it just seemed to me that there were a lot of people in this house. I was just as shy as I had been that day in Ely, though now I was properly dressed and my hair had just been washed. Mrs. Briggs did that as soon as we put in at Bywater and she knew she could spare the water. My hair was very pale, almost white, and I always wore it tightly braided, and because the braid was so long and might catch on something, I turned it up and tied it with a strip of cloth as a rule; but after Mrs. Briggs had washed my hair she went to her chest again and found a piece of ribbon. Except that my face was as brown as a smoked eel there was nothing outlandish about my appearance that day; but I still felt shy and didn't like facing people.

Mr. Briggs led me straight through the room where so many men were and into another where the fattest woman I have ever seen sat at a table on a stool. She was rolling out pastry for a pie. There were two girls with her; one was chopping onions and the other was cutting a small animal, or several small animals, into joints. They were rabbits, and unknown to me; rabbits don't live in the Fens.

She gave signs of pleasure at the sight of Mr. Briggs and asked after Amy and did they mean to come to supper with her. And then she looked at me and said:

"What have we here?"

He said, "An orphan." To me that was a new word, and though I understood most of what he said that left me puzzled.

The fat woman said, "Dear me. Where'd you pick her up?"

Then he told her what he had already told me, about finding

the boat adrift; and he told her what I had told him, with such difficulty, about the island being flooded and Father dying. And he told her what he had told me about there being no room for me on the *Pretty Amy*. He said he hoped she would have me.

"A pair of hands is always welcome," she said. And then she looked at me and said:

"Can you scrub?"

Scrubbing was unknown to me because there was nothing on Mons to scrub. At least, I suppose I could have, should have, scrubbed the table off which we ate; but scrubbing wasn't amongst the things I had ever seen Father do, or had been shown, as I grew older, how to do myself.

I said, "No," and shook my head.

The fat woman said, "Where did you say you picked her up? She don't talk English, do she?"

Mr. Briggs said, "In her own way. That was 'No.'"

"Oh. Well, she'll soon learn. Is she biddable?"

He said, "Yes," very quickly. And then she said:

"Modest?"

He said, "Yes," while I puzzled over these unfamiliar words.

Modest, of course, I was not, or at least not in the sense the fat woman meant. I was just ignorant; ignorant in a way peculiar to my circumstances. On Mons our animals were bought very young and eaten before they were fully mature, and the reproductive processes of birds and fish are very unobtrusive. The other source of information was closed to me, too; I had never had a conversation with any other female in my life.

The fat woman looked me over again and said:

"Well, she's no beauty—not that that's any guard. All right, I'll have her. Two pounds a year and her keep. That all right? Oh, and shoes. I don't let none of them run about barefoot; give the place a poor look."

Job Briggs looked at me with something of the same expression his wife had worn when she looked at the two dresses. Then he said:

"I'll see to that."

I was without any real sense of obligation; partly because money had only the vaguest meaning for me, and partly because I would so much rather have stayed on *Pretty Amy* without shoes.

In this manner I became maid of all work at the *God Save Mariners* in Bywater.

The inn belonged to the fat woman, who ran it quite efficiently without taking more than twenty or thirty steps a day—not counting the descent and ascent of the stairs. Her name was Meg Towler, and a relative of hers called Ted Towler looked after the taproom and the parlour and the yard. She did the cooking and, with the help of four, sometimes five girls, ran the house. She made up for her extreme physical lethargy by being crafty and unexpected in her ways, and by a careful fostering of jealousies amongst the girls. Her main weapon was our healthy appetites. All day long in that kitchen she plied her undoubted talent for cookery; we helped her to prepare the food and we served it. But our "keep" was meagre, so we were always anxious to please her in order to be rewarded by a slice of pie, a cut from the roast, a chicken leg to gnaw. She had another method, too. There was a sweet red wine of which she was very fond, and at intervals she would invite one girl or another to drink it with her, and then ask questions which almost invariably led to trouble for some of the others. Even I was not exempt from this treatment, despite the fact that in all the time I was in her house I don't think she understood anything I said except "yes" and "no," and then only if I nodded or shook my head. But she pretended to the other girls that she could understand me if she bothered to try, and often told them I had said things which I had never thought of. I couldn't defend myself to them, because they didn't understand me. They called me Dumb Ethel.

I was far from happy at the *God Save Mariners*; but I was learning all the time. Soon I knew all about scrubbing, and polishing furniture with beeswax, and making up beds with sheets. I learned this new way of cooking. With regards to bread making there wasn't so much difference; in the inn kitchen the oven was built into the wall and you put in a faggot and lighted it and closed the door and the bricks of the wall got almost red hot; then you raked out the ashes and put the bread in. Roasting was done exactly as it had been on our island; but cakes and custards, jams and jellies were all new to me.

I learned the facts of life, too. We girls all slept in one room which was neither upstairs nor downstairs. It was over the cellar where the ale and wines were stored; the cellar was ten stairs down from the kitchen, our bedroom was six stairs up. One door led from the kitchen to the stairs which went up and down, and that door Meg Towler always locked herself before she went to bed, she didn't trust even Ted with that job. But the room had a window which was within easy reach of the ground. And Bywater was a sailors' town. . . .

Meg Towler knew perfectly well what went on; but she ignored it. Of every new girl she enquired, as she had done of me, "Is she modest?" Or, "Is she well behaved?" And the parent or the Poor Law authority always said, "Yes," just as Job Briggs had said it of me. Then the door to the stairs that led to the bedroom was always locked, "With my very own hands, anybody can tell you that," so for whatever happened Meg Towler could not be held to blame. Every now and then, after some girl had sat down with the red wine—and I knew how it worked, making you feel dizzy and happy —there would be a row. "Dirty little bitch," Meg Towler would say, hitting a girl with the rolling pin or a wooden spoon or a ladle. "Filthy fornicating little bitch! I can't watch you all the time, I'm not your mother, thank God. But mind this. Get yourself in pup and off you go, with no back wages."

The one simple remedy, a bar at the window, she seemed never to think of.

In a very short time my elementary ideas about the differences between men and women, concerned only with the amount they could lift and carry, and their method of passing water, were extended comprehensively. The knowledge brought me nothing but disgust.

In a way I suppose I was fortunate. I wasn't pretty, I was intensely shy and my nickname hinted at an infirmity; I came to be regarded as a kind of joke and on the rare occasions when I was forced to go into one of the public rooms, the nearest anyone came to being familiar with me was to tug at my turned-up plait and say "Ding-dong; ding-dong!"

Infirmities and lack of attractions are, however, relative things, and working in the yard as an ostler there was a man genuinely afflicted; he had a stoop, so that his hands hung far below his knees, and he had a horrible squint. He looked the worse to me because he was the first misshapen person I had ever been close to; it made me uneasy to look at him, and yet he was the one creature who showed me any kindness. On my first day he showed me how the well worked. I'd never seen a well before; on Mons we dipped water, on the *Pretty Amy* it had been in a cask. Wall Eye, as he was called, not only showed me how to draw water but when I had my two buckets filled he carried them as far as the kitchen door for me. He was very strong.

Then, while I was still finding my way about in this strange new world, there was Christmas. It was all new to me, though I thought the rooms looked nice, all hung with green leaves; and there were geese to cook and special puddings. Meg Towler gave each of us girls a roll of cloth; she had bought the rolls a month earlier from a pedlar; two were blue and one was red and one was a no-colour, greyish brown. We chose in the order of age of service and, being the last-comer, I had the one nobody else wanted. All day the other girls talked about how they would make their dresses, or have them made. I couldn't sew and had no money to pay anyone to sew for me, so I felt out of it; and the other girls all had presents in addition to the cloth. I told myself fiercely that I didn't care; that their presents were really like the rolls of cloth—a kind of wages; that on Mons we had never had any presents of any kind; but I did care, partly because most of their gifts were pretty, strings of beads, bows of ribbon, shoe buckles.

Halfway through the afternoon one of the girls, Phyllis, came giggling to me and hit me on the shoulder. They none of them could realise that just as their not understanding me didn't make me dumb, neither did it make me deaf, so she shouted, "Wall Eye! At the back door. He want you."

I wouldn't have gone, for I avoided him whenever I could, but she began to push me, and then the others came laughing and pushing too.

He'd got something white in his hand, tied up with a red ribbon; and he offered it to me.

I kept my hands by my sides and shook my head and said: "I don't want it."

The girls giggled and jeered; I think now not ill-naturedly; it was for them a festival and we had all had a very good dinner.

Wall Eye said angrily, "You be off, all on you. 'Tain't for you. 'Tis for Ethel." And again he offered me the little bundle and again I refused to take it.

He fumbled with the red ribbon, and shook out the bundle, which uncurled and showed itself to be a pair of white stockings.

Now the truth is that you can, if you are used to it, walk about barefoot in comfort, but if you wear shoes, particularly shoes hastily made and at the cheapest price, such as mine were, you *need* stockings because there are rough places inside the shoes which rub and chafe your feet. I'd been wanting a pair of stockings ever since I had the shoes. And I thought of the no-colour cloth which was of no use to me; so I said:

"Wait!"

All these weeks I'd been using my ears as well as my eyes, and though as a rule I didn't bother, had in fact taken a kind of refuge in seeming dumb, I could by this time say a good many words, particularly short simple ones, just like anybody else. My "Wait" came out as clearly and ordinarily as anybody else's.

The girls laughed again and said that I could talk to Wall Eye, seemingly. I turned and ran up the six stairs into our bedroom and snatched up the roll of no-colour cloth. Back at the door I thrust it towards him.

"Breeches," I said. And then I took the stockings.

Wall Eye said something about a bargain, and a bargain should be "sealed with a kiss"; but I backed away and shut the door in his face. The girls gathered round, shouting that Dumb Ethel wasn't dumb, she was a cheat. Then I lost my temper, and forgetting to speak carefully, said:

"I'm no cheat. I gave him the cloth to make him a pair of breeches. What did you give in exchange for the presents you had?"

That they didn't understand, or chose not to understand. I went up into our room, holding the stockings by their tops, and then all at once I didn't want them any more and knew that I should never wear them. He'd looked at them with his squint eyes; he'd handled them with those great dangling hands, and his giving them to me on this particular day had held some meaning. I dropped them on the floor and hastily washed my hands in the little basin that served us all.

From that time on Wall Eye became a nuisance to me; I was as wary and careful as a water hen, but I was bound to go and hang linen on the line, or shake mats, or carry rubbish to the dung heap, or fetch water, and almost every time, before my errand was done, he would be there, leering, trying to fumble me with those clumsy hands. The girls, whose lives held little pleasure and that mainly coarse, were very greatly amused, and Meg Towler, to whom once, in despair, I tried to complain, affected not to understand me. I began to think seriously about running away. One of the girls, named Hattie, had once been maid to an old lady and all the things she had hated there and mocked at sounded delightful to me. I was sure that I could find a place to which I was more suited, a place more suited to me; yet I was timid about leaving what shelter I had found; I might very well encounter someone like Wall Eye and have no place to run. So I waited, managing from day to day.

I don't know whether what happened next was accident or planned as a joke. Hattie and I, the latest comers, always did the laundry, of which there was a great deal, for the *God Save Mariners* was a clean inn. There was a washhouse at the back of the house, with stone troughs on two sides and a hearth where we heated the water. At the back was the drying yard, with several linen lines, a patch of grass for bleaching and some gooseberry bushes upon which articles that were not flimsy could be spread. On a fine day we left the washing out as long as possible, collecting it at dusk. On this day, Hattie put off the job until it was almost dark and then, when we were halfway across the yard on our way to the drying ground, carrying the big empty basket between us, she stopped, and by shouting and making signs to me, showed that I was to go on and begin taking down the washing and that she must run back to the house but would come and help to carry the basket in. What makes me suspect that what happened was by her connivance was that Wall Eye must have been in the washhouse; for I had my back to it and was reaching up, unpegging a sheet, when he came behind me and put his arms round me. There was a horrible moment when his hands were on my breasts and his face buried in my neck, like a pig's muzzle in a bucket. He was breathing hard and saying, "Little dear!"

I was little; I have never been very big, but the life I had led had made me tough and sinewy. Even so I was no match for him. So I behaved as a bird does when taken by hand; I went limp and still, dead except for the wild thump of my heart. He began to turn me to face him; and then I braced myself and pushed free and ran like a mad thing, screaming at the top of my voice. I didn't even notice that Wall Eye wasn't running after me. I ran straight into the kitchen, slammed the door behind me and put my back to it and stood there, screaming, until Meg heaved herself to her feet and hit me. Fortunately she had nothing in her hand at the moment, for she hit me with all her force. You would hardly have thought that her fat, cushiony hand could have dealt such blows; my teeth rattled, my eyes seemed to pop and for a moment the kitchen was all blackness, shot with dancing lights. Then, as things settled again, I heard the end of a sentence:

". . . quite terrified."

Meg said, "Girls!" in a voice of deep disgust. "You hev to be firm, don't you'd hev them in hysterics twice a day. That was just a tap to bring her to her senses. And it did, didn't it?" To Phyllis she said:

"You want one? Hand me them cloves and the rolling pin."

I could look about me by that time. Sitting on the kitchen table with his mouth agape was a little boy of about six years old. Standing close to him was an elderly man—a person of some dignity to judge from his wig and clothes. Phyllis was over by the spice cupboard holding something in the cup of her hand; when Meg spoke she shot forward and laid two cloves on the table, reached for the rolling pin and stood away. Meg smashed the two cloves and said, in an unfriendly way:

"There you are. That's what you asked for, *sir.*"

The man said, "Thank you, Mrs. Towler," and picked up the fragments in his long thin fingers and placed them in the boy's mouth.

"That should cure it, Thomas. Close your mouth now. Can you count? Then count ten for every finger and thumb and by the time you've finished it should be easier." But even as he spoke to the boy he was glancing at me, a little concerned, a little curious.

He was in a predicament; not on his own ground, in the kitchen indeed to ask a favour; and any mistress was well within her rights in striking a maidservant. For all he knew I might have been a silly girl frightened by a spider. Maybe that thought occurred to him, for he asked in the most civil way:

"Could we hear what caused this particular fit of hysteria?"

"You'd be no wiser," Meg said. "She don't talk like us. She've been here four months. Took her in as a favour to an old friend I did, *and* regretted it. Make it very awkward, not understanding what she say."

"Is she a foreigner, or . . . afflicted?"

I drew in my breath and said, "I'm not dumb. I'm a Fenwoman. And I was in the drying yard . . ." I told him what had happened.

The words that I had learned at Bywater, drying yard, laundry, Wall Eye, I pronounced as everyone else did. Phyllis understood; I saw her turn to the spice cupboard to hide her face; her shoulders shook with mirth. I ended by saying bitterly, "Everybody is against me."

"So now you know," said Meg with heavy irony. "And I hope you're satisfied, because I want to use just that bit of the table where the boy's bum is."

The gentleman accepted this brusque dismissal.

"Come along, Thomas. Thank you for the cloves, Mrs. Towler."

But before he turned away he looked at me again, kindly.

As they went through the door the little boy said:

"My name isn't Thomas. That's my brother. I'm Willie."

My face is thin and my cheekbones stick out, so between the bones and Meg's hand what flesh I have there was heavily bruised. I looked a sight and was not allowed to carry anything into the dining room that evening. I was washing the supper dishes, Meg was almost asleep in her chair, when the gentleman tapped on the door. She called a cross, sleepy "Come in." When he did so, she asked in a voice so weary as to be offensive, "What is it now?"

"I would like to have a word with you, Mrs. Towler. About this girl. Could she leave us for a minute?"

"She's busy. If you want to talk about her, what matter? Not that she'll know what you say."

"Very well, if it must be so." He sounded put out. He raised his voice to be sure that I could hear. "I don't wish to sound as though I were bargaining for something in the market. It occurred to me, Mrs. Towler, that you don't place a particularly high value on this girl's services, and she doesn't seem to have fitted in very happily here; and I think she may well have some information which would be invaluable to my brother-in-law, who has some interesting theories about the Fens. So I wondered whether you would—for a consideration, of course—allow me to take her away with me."

Meg laughed, the chesty, rumbling laugh of a fat woman.

"So thass it!" She then said one of the truest things she ever gave tongue to in her life. "I never was one to stand betwixt a man and what he wanted."

I dared not look round.

"You mistake me, Mrs. Towler, but never mind. Is the girl bound to you in any way?"

"I hired her for a year. To oblige a friend, as I told you. And the last four months thass been like heving a heathen blackamoor round the place, smashing and spoiling. Cost me plenty, one way and another, I may tell you. And she's just got round to being useful."

"Despite your not understanding her, or she you. I see. Would a guinea reimburse you, Mrs. Towler?"

"No," she said bluntly. "Two might."

I heard him give a little sharp sigh. Then he said:

"She should be consulted first."

Meg laughed again.

"I never said she was crazy. Nobuddy but a crazy girl would want consulting whether to be slut of all work or an old man's darling!"

The phrase meant nothing, good or ill to me, I had never heard the word "darling" before. My ears noted it, my mind stored it, that was all. But he was angered.

"That is a damned insulting thing to say. And not the first. I admit that I am under a certain obligation . . ."

"So you should. You feel insulted! You go and work it off, Mr. Flowerdew. Walk round Bywater and find some other place where when a ship come in two, three days early, your snivelling, piddling little boys'll be took in and kept and looked after till you come fetch 'em. Find another place where they'll be welcome with their 'Can't eat this' and 'Don't like that.'"

"You've always been paid."

"For beds grown men could've slept in, and food sensible chaps'd enjoy. Don't you come the schoolmaster over me, Mr. Flowerdew. If you want the girl and she's worth two guineas to you, hev her, but leave me to say what I like in my own kitchen."

I heard the chink of coins. He said:

"I take it that I may speak with the girl?"

"You can do what you like, sir."

Washing up mattered, so the place where it was done was well lighted by an oil lamp fixed on the wall. Mr. Flowerdew came over and stood near me and said:

"I don't know how much of that you understood."

I said, "Nearly all."

He said, "I'm sorry. Most of it meant nothing. What is true is that my brother-in-law, Canon Hatton, is deeply interested in the

Fens. He used to live in Ely. Can you understand what I am saying?"

"Yes," I said.

"Where did you live—in the Fens?"

"On an island called Mons."

"Mons?"

"Yes."

"He will be so pleased. It fits in . . . but we won't talk about that now. Did you understand that Mrs. Towler has . . ." He sought for the correct, unhurtful word.

"Turned me loose," I said. And I realised that if, when he had asked if I could leave the room she had consented and I had gone, and been recalled to be told that in future I should work for him and not for her, all would have been well. I should have been so happy, so grateful. Actually I was happy, I was grateful; but it was all slightly smeared over, not by Meg Towler's cynical words but by the bargaining. A dog, a horse, passing from an unkind owner to a kindly one, recognises only an advantageous change in circumstances, of price it knows nothing. I knew my price, and it was two guineas. And it must be remembered that although Job Briggs had saved my life and then handed me over into slavery I had, for the first fifteen years of my life, enjoyed a freedom that few people ever know. No people in the whole wide world, so far as I can see, were ever as free as the people on those lost drowned islands in the Fens.

"Given me permission to engage you," he corrected me. "There will be a good deal of work . . . but you will be quite safe from the kind of thing that happened here earlier this evening."

I said, as fervently as I could, "Thank you very much, sir. I'll work hard and try to please you."

He smiled and said that he would be ready to start at eight in the morning.

Meg seemed to be asleep again. I waited and made certain, and then, because she had struck me and spoken rudely to Mr. Flowerdew, I went quietly about doing damage to things which she would use after I was safely away. Salt, grated from a block and rolled into smoothness with a rolling pin, was always kept in a big blue jar, sugar in a brown one. I hoped that she would not discover that I had changed them over until she had sugared a meat pie or salted an apple one. I made a tiny, imperceptible but fatal hole in every stretched bladder or layer of mutton fat with which her preserves were sealed.

Afterwards, in the bedroom, all the talk was of me and my going away. It was lewd, and within a few minutes I learned what Meg had hinted at when she said "old man's darling." My instinct told me that it was not true; Mr. Flowerdew was kind; my reason replied that Wall Eye had been kind at the beginning. But I thought that if this was the way of the world, then far better Mr. Flowerdew than Wall Eye. Four months at Bywater had taught me that much fortitude.

II

Mr. Flowerdew drove a kind of light wagon. I know now that it was shabby and comfortless, the horse which pulled it slow, but to me it was wonderful, the first conveyance I had ever ridden in. I sat on a board seat in front with him; the little boys, muffled to the eyes, sat on the floor at the back, with their great clothes chest between them. It was a cold morning and I was glad of Father's sheepskin jacket.

I was shy at first, but Mr. Flowerdew chatted away, dividing his attention between me and the boys. I had to keep alert to follow what he was saying. He said, for instance:

"We keep a school." I had never heard that word before. But I kept quiet and went on listening and in the end made some meaning of it. It was the same with "homesick." "Poor boys, they're homesick," he said. They certainly looked miserable enough, though Willie said his toothache was better. When I understood the term I realised that it was an affliction from which I had been suffering ever since I left Mons. The little boys had good reason to be homesick for they came from a place thousands of miles away across the sea; Bombay it was called.

"Most of our boys come from overseas," Mr. Flowerdew said; and he laughed a little, not as though anything was funny, a sad laugh, really. "Twenty years ago or more, I thought I was going to start a school that would be famous for its scholars, and I've ended up with one that's famous for its handling of little boys from abroad. The parents in such places all know one another, you see, and talk things over and say, 'Send him to the Old Vine at Baildon; he'll be happy there.' They are happy, as far as any boys can be happy at school. It seems hard to believe but within a fortnight Thomas and William will be as cheerful as grigs." He half turned his head towards them and said, "Saberton is at school, you know. He'll be a friend for you. Francis Saberton, he came last year, from Bombay."

A voice from the rear of the wagon said, "We don't like Francis. He pulled our monkey's tail."

"He called our bearer a rude name."

The hardest listening, the most close attention didn't enlighten me as to what was a monkey, or a bearer. I realised that all the learning I had done up to the present, on board the *Pretty Amy* and in the inn, had been easy because it was all to do with things which could be seen and handled. I now had learning of a different kind to do.

We stopped at an inn by the roadside to give the horse a rest and to have dinner. The food was very bad and made me see why Meg Towler never bothered to make herself agreeable to her customers. She gave them good food and clean beds, so there was no need for her to smile and smile and stand rubbing her hands and saying "sir" as this woman did.

By the time we reached Baildon it was black night and from the top of the hill the town looked like a piece of starry sky that had fallen, there were so many lighted windows. We didn't go into the town but soon turned into a yard and Mr. Flowerdew said, "Well, here we are." He sounded tired and glad to be home. I'd noticed during the drive that he was afflicted, or misshapen; his right arm was fixed to his side and he could only move his hand, which made driving awkward for him.

Four big boys—whom I was to learn to call monitors—must have been listening for the wagon, for they came running out, bringing a lantern. They knew exactly what to do; one began to unharness the horse, one took charge of the little boys and two began to lift down the chest.

Mr. Flowerdew said, "Now no fooling about! Remember how *you* felt on your first night." To me he said, "Come with me, Ethelreda."

We went into the house and I smelt, for the first time, the smell of school. It is so special that to this day if I were blindfold and led into twenty different buildings, one of them a school, I should know at once. I do not know what makes it, but it is fixed, and is the same in summer when all the windows are open and the boys swim several times a week, as in winter. It is a sad smell, and yet to call it the odour of misery would be unjust to Mr. Flowerdew, whose chief aim was to make the boys happy. He succeeded in most cases, and to this day men will arrive at the house, saying somewhat shamefacedly that, as they were in the neighbourhood, they thought they'd like to revisit the place where they were schooled.

On this night, mingled with the school smell and growing stronger as we neared a door, was the scent of fresh-baked bread and something very savoury being cooked.

Mr. Flowerdew opened a door and there we were in a kitchen, bigger a good deal than the one at the *God Save Mariners* and in a state of clutter which would have shocked Meg Towler. There was a hearth at each end, a stone trough for washing, an enormous dresser, and down the centre a long narrow table. One end of it was heaped with the fresh, sweet-smelling bread; halfway along it an old woman in a great white cap was mixing oatmeal and water in a big black skillet, and at the other end a younger woman, rather finely dressed, was mixing something else with dainty careful movements. A third woman, old and dressed like a servant, stood at the trough swilling dozens of wooden bowls and spoons.

Entering a place with three strangers in it made me shy again, so I stood with my eyes looking down. I heard Mr. Flowerdew say:

"Oh dear! Does that mean a bad day?"

"As bad as I remember. Two days alone with that rabble is really more than he can stand. I offered to take charge of the young ones, but you know how obstinate he is." She had a peevish voice.

"Surely Edward helped. He promised to."

"He had no intention of keeping his promise. He's had his foot on a stool all day, but I'm not deceived."

"Poor Edward; poor Christopher; and poor you," Mr. Flowerdew said. "Well, I'm back now. Chris can have a good rest tomorrow. And look what I've brought with me—another pair of hands."

The two servants had already—I knew without looking up—stared their fill at me; the lady, intent upon her mixing and her complaints, had not yet noticed my presence.

"This is Ethelreda," Mr. Flowerdew said. "She comes from the Fens and I thought Edward would like to ask her some questions.

And she wasn't very happy in Bywater, so I thought she could come and help Ellen and Bess." He put a finger under my chin and raised my head. "Don't be shy," he said, speaking kindly, in the slow, distinct way he used to me. "Nobody here will be anything but friendly, I promise."

The lady said, in a light, mocking way:

"Surely I once heard somebody say that in a boys' school every maidservant should be at least thirty years old."

"There were circumstances," Mr. Flowerdew began and I was afraid that he was going to tell the whole story to these three unfriendly people. For he was wrong about nobody being anything but friendly. The two old maidservants were looking at me with hard cold eyes; the lady's light reference to age had been made in an unwelcoming way. Her gaze moved over me, from the scraped-back hair to the clumsy shoes, and upwards again. Then she said:

"I agree. In this case there is no danger, no danger at all."

Mr. Flowerdew said, "Henrietta!" in a pained way.

She was pretty herself; or at least she had once been, or might still have been. Her hair curled and was a glossy blue-black in colour, her skin was white and unblemished, her eyes, though too prominent, a clear blue; but the whole face was scored over by worry, discontent, impatience. As though you took a pretty picture and folded it and creased it and then smoothed it out again.

By this time I knew what I looked like, for there was a bit of looking glass in the room I had shared at the inn. Too much of my face was forehead, high and knobbly, and of the rest my mouth took up too much space. My eyes were not as green as gooseberries—as Hattie had once said—but they were greenish; and four months of working withindoors had changed my smoked-eel brownness to something more the colour of porridge. My cheekbones stuck out and bore, when Henrietta Kentwoode first looked at me, the bruises left by Meg Towler's heavy hand. Her remark was fully justified, but I held it against her, always. I held against Ellen and Bess that they looked pleased and amused.

Ellen, the one who was making the porridge, said:

"The Canon wouldn't eat until you come, sir. There's a brace of pheasants from Mortiboys and I'm doing my best to keep 'em hot and not dried out."

"He shouldn't have waited. But I'm ready, I'm ready. Bess, would you just show Ethelreda where . . ." He made a gesture with his hand. "A long journey," he said.

The maid who was washing the bowls withdrew her hands from the water and rubbed them on her apron.

"This way," she said, and led me through a door and into a short passage at the end of which was a privy. As we left the kitchen I heard Mr. Flowerdew say that he was going to put on his slippers and would be ready for supper in two minutes.

When I came back into the kitchen, exactly at the moment that I opened the door to the passage, the main door at the far end opened and a man entered. I saw him and was shy and looked down. The one glance showed me that he was handsome, tall, very thin, little more.

I heard the lady say, in yet another voice:

"Chris! I thought you were in bed. I was just making this to bring you."

He said, "I want something *to eat*. Damn it, Henrietta, I *cough*. I know, you know, everybody knows; but I cannot live on slops. I'm a man with a cough and now and then the man demands a little attention. Ellen, what have you handy?"

"I'm dishing the Canon's supper, sir. Roast pheasant."

"I never," he said, "eat pheasant on Thursdays. Have you any cheese?"

"Cheese," Henrietta said, "always makes you cough. I was bringing you this . . . honey and cider and bread soppets. I thought you were in bed."

"And I thought you were in the parlour. Ellen, I'll have that cheese."

"Dearest, the doctor said . . ."

"I know, I know. Beef tea and gruel, eggnog and custard. Henrietta, I need something to eat. Ah, thank you, Ellen."

She said, "I *try* to look after you," in such a piteous way that had she not remarked so unkindly about my looks I should have felt sorry for her.

He said, "You look after my cough, my dear."

Ellen said, "Here you, what's your name? Pick up that tray and follow me."

She set off at a brisk, flat-footed trot.

We crossed two large rooms, one set with benches and flat-topped tables, the other with benches and tables with sloping tops. We went along a short passage and into a room well lighted and very warm and even more cluttered than the kitchen. Near the heaped fire there was a table, spread with a fine cloth and set for two. On one side of it was my friend, Mr. Flowerdew, now without his wig, and on the other a plump, pink-faced gentleman with small bright eyes. There was something piggish about him, about his skin, that was just like that of a pig that has been scalded and well scraped, and about those small, bright alert eyes. People who have never had to do with them think pigs are stupid, interested only in food, but that is not true, pigs are very intelligent.

Mr. Flowerdew said, "Edward, this is the girl I was telling you about, Ethelreda."

The little bright eyes studied me, and curiously I did not feel shy.

"You come from the Fens, Ethelreda?"

"Yes, sir."

"You and I will have a lot to talk about then. I lived in Ely for many years." He looked away from me to the dishes which Ellen was unloading from the tray she carried, and from mine. "I don't think," he said, "that the meal has suffered from the delay."

"You shouldn't have waited, Edward. Bread and cheese would have served for me."

"Nonsense. You need a proper meal after that long journey. What about this child? Has she supped?"

"I don't suppose so," Mr. Flowerdew said. "Ellen seems to have put her to work at once."

"And that is what I wish to do. Questions I cannot wait to ask. Antony, if you have no objection . . . Girl, run back to the kitchen and fetch another plate and what you need. You can make a meal and answer my most urgent questions at the same time."

I was still, even after my four months in Bywater, so unused to the ways of the world that I saw nothing so very extraordinary in the invitation. I simply hoped that I should be able to answer the questions satisfactorily. But as I followed Ellen back to the kitchen I saw, or sensed, that she was outraged.

"We're going to sup in the study," she said to Bess, who understood that the use of the word "we" was ironic.

"Oh, are we indeed," she said. "Then I think we should take our coat off. The Canon keep his study proper warm. Last time I was invited there to eat roast pheasant I broke out into a rare owd sweat."

They both laughed unpleasantly. It was, indeed, the start of a jealousy that lasted as long as I worked with them.

Canon Hatton talked all through the meal, asking me questions about our life at Mons; answering them made me, like the little new boys at school, homesick, and spoiled my appetite for the delicious food.

"You lived on an island, I understand. What was its name?"

"Mons."

"How far from Ely?"

"I don't know. My father could go there and back in a day."

"Did you ever go?"

"Once."

"Did other people ever visit you?"

"No."

"Not at all? Tell me, what would you have done if a stranger had arrived at Mons?"

"I think I should have hidden myself in the reeds."

He laughed delightedly. "There you are. That's what they all did, the real Fen people. Wild as the birds they snared. The only ones you could get near—except by accident—weren't Fenmen at all. Antony, I think you've found a treasure." He twisted his bulk in his chair and reached something from a table crowded with small objects. "Do you know what this is?"

I recognised it at once; it was a lamp, exactly like one we used at home on the rare occasions when we had a little pig fat to spare. It was made of thick reddish pottery and shaped rather like a sauce-boat, but the lip was closed in, leaving only a small round hole through which you pulled a piece of cloth to act as a wick; the handle was at the other end. The advantage of a lamp over a rush dip was that it gave rather more light and could more easily be carried about.

"It's a lamp."

"It's a Roman lamp, and it was given me by a Fenwoman." He began to tell a story about how he was once called to a sick parishioner who could only be reached by boat, and how a fog came down and he was lost. By chance he had come across one of the secret islands—it might have been Mons, but was not—and there he and the boatman had entered a hut to await the fog's lifting. He had seen the lamp, and some crocks which he thought were

Roman, and heard for the first time the real Fen speech, which he described as being like that of boys who have had a few Latin lessons and then amuse themselves by speaking English as though it were Latin.

"I was convinced then, and I remain convinced," he said, "that some Romans took refuge in the Fens. But further evidence was hard to come by. I never again found a group of people who had not been in touch with modern civilisation."

A great deal of what he said was at that moment far beyond my understanding; but by speaking instead of asking questions he gave me a chance to attend to my meal. I was startled when he snapped at me:

"Where did you learn that pernickety manner of eating?" I did not know the meaning of the word, but the tone he used made it sound unpleasing, which puzzled me, for I was eating as I had learned from seeing my father eat and I knew, from watching others, that my way was less gross, noisy and clumsy than any I had yet seen.

"It's all right, Ethelreda," Mr. Flowerdew hastened to say. "It only means dainty, nice. I told you, Edward, she has lived in Bywater for several months."

I looked down at my plate and said sullenly:

"They weren't dainty there. They'd lick their fingers and then put them in the salt, and they'd talk with their mouths full and wipe their knives on the cloth."

The Canon said, "Antony! Do you hear an echo?"

"An echo?"

"Listen. Say that again, my girl."

I did so, wondering.

"Well, I recognise it, if you don't. That and her name, Benedict. I smell monk!"

"It's my breeches," I said. "They're made of monk's cloth." And because what I had learned in the bedroom of the inn had no connection, in my innocent mind, with a nicety—or a nastiness—about skirts and petticoats, I lifted my hem and showed them the good cloth, still strong and sound after uncounted years.

They both laughed and the Canon said:

"Well, my friend, even if you haven't brought me conclusive proof, you have brought a curiosity, there's no denying that."

He then asked me if I had brought anything away with me when I left the island.

"A few crocks, but I gave them to Mrs. Briggs, because she had been kind to me. All I have now is my Touchwood."

"What is that?"

I explained its use as well as I could and told him that it was in the kitchen in my coat pocket.

He wanted me to fetch it there and then, but Mr. Flowerdew said:

"Let the child have her supper, Edward, and get on with your own. There'll be another day tomorrow."

When at last I went kitchenwards I carried one of the trays. In the kitchen the fire was almost dead under the black porridge pot, Ellen had gone and Bess sat, almost asleep, by the table. She grumbled about the length of time she had been kept waiting and sent me back for the other tray, saying words that I was to hear many, many times, "Your legs are younger than mine."

When I showed my Touchwood the Canon said in an astonished voice:

"Why, it's a Crucifix! Of immense antiquity . . ." He turned it about in his hands, gloating. "Tell me again, exactly how you used it?"

He went on asking questions until Mr. Flowerdew said:

"We've had a long day, Edward. And God bless me, nobody's done anything about a bed for her. How very remiss of me!"

"She can sleep where you put your barking boys."

"The Cough Room? An excellent suggestion. Come along, Ethelreda."

What he called the Cough Room was a small chamber next door to his own; it was used, he explained, for any boy who had a cough or some other complaint likely to make him an uneasy bedfellow for those in the dormitories. "And if they want anything they can rouse me. I sleep very lightly nowadays. I wonder how young Watson's toothache is. I'll just slip along and see if all is well. Good night, Ethelreda."

III

For me the change from the Bywater inn to the Baildon school was entirely for the better, despite the fact that Ellen and Bess never liked me and put upon me as much as they could. I entered upon this new life with certain advantages, some of my shyness had worn off and I had learned to make myself understood; I found Ellen and Bess easier to live with than the girls had been, they were both respectable women and too old to take pleasure in teasing or playing pranks.

The work was hard; the two new boys brought the school's numbers to forty-two, and forty-two boys took a deal of feeding and clearing up after, even though some of them, old enough to be responsible, were called sewerers and helped with the serving of the food and the clearing away of empty plates. In addition to the boys there was the Canon who must be waited upon, coddled indeed, in his study, and, on the other side of the house, Mr. and Mrs. Kentwoode in the parlour. Only Mr. Flowerdew, claiming no privileges for himself, took his meals with the boys in the dining hall and had no room save his sleeping chamber for his own.

As I settled down and observed this and that, and listened to the talk between the two old servants, I realised that in some ways the Old Vine was a troubled house, and that it was only Mr. Flowerdew's determined cheerfulness and unfailing good nature that preserved its peace.

To begin with Mr. Flowerdew and Mr. Kentwoode were often at odds with one another. Mr. Flowerdew held that merely to be young entitled you to be silly and made you pitiable: "poor boy" was a phrase constantly upon his tongue. Mr. Kentwoode held that, being young, you were naturally silly and the sooner the silliness was knocked out of you, the better. He was never deliberately unkind—that Mr. Flowerdew would never have tolerated for a moment—but he was strict and hasty-tempered, and what Mr. Flowerdew, for all his cleverness, failed to see was that it was because Mr. Kentwoode was there and known to be stern, that he himself could be so indulgent without too much disorder resulting. Once the boys were well behaved Mr. Kentwoode was prepared **to** treat them as grown up, and he was always noticeably interested in any boy who was musical. There was one named Saunders, for whom he obtained permission to use the organ in St. Mary's Church; and another named Callard who used to make fearsome noises on the violin. Mr. Kentwoode, who played the instrument wonderfully well himself, must have suffered more than the rest of us did from the screeches and squawkings, but he persisted, and in the end he had Callard playing recognisable tunes.

I learned from Ellen's talk that some years earlier there had been a war. It must have been in my father's lifetime, but if, on his rare visits to Ely, he had ever heard about it, it had made so small impression upon him that he never mentioned it. Ellen mentioned it often, timing everything, "before the war," "since the war." Before the war everything was better, prices were lower and food more flavoursome, kitchen girls worked harder and boys were better behaved; even the weather had deteriorated since the war. The restoration of the King, ten years before I came to Baildon, hadn't righted things as it should have done, though Ellen was all for the King.

In this war Mr. Flowerdew and Mr. Kentwoode had fought on different sides; Mr. Flowerdew had fought against the King—the old one, not the new—and had taken a wound which had left him with a stiff arm; Mr. Kentwoode had fought for the King, and slept in damp clothes and so gotten his cough. Perhaps in these later days, when they differed over how boys should be treated, they were, in their minds, refighting their old battles, though Ellen, one day, when she was peevish with Mr. Kentwoode, said:

"He might bear in mind that but for Mr. Flowerdew he wouldn't hev a roof over his head. Them that fought for the old King weren't allowed to own nothing after they was beat. It was Mr. Flowerdew being here and heving friends on the winning side, saved the place. Come to that Mr. Flowerdew saved him twice. It ain't everybody would hev taken him back, after he'd flung off and left and then made a mess of his business and got hisself married. And landed us with the Canon round our necks for the rest of our days."

"I never got that straight in my mind," Bess said.

"Nor did I, nor did anybody else. All I know is that as soon as the mistress was dead, poor soul, the Canon come along and took over Mr. Kentwoode's share, and he went off. I ought to hev gone too, and I would if I could hev seen what a greedy old sod we'd landed ourselves with. Bone idle, too. He was supposed to *help*, he was younger then, and he could of, but no, then we must hev ushers."

The ushers were hired schoolmasters, and according to Ellen they were all either mad or drunk; there was a quiet one who got up one night and hanged himself in the stable, and one who had a crazy fit and caned everybody, even Mr. Flowerdew who went to wrest the cane away.

"May I drop dead, with this spoon in my hand, if that ain't sober truth. I can tell you, the morning Mr. Flowerdew come in here and say to me, 'Ellen,' he say, 'Mr. Kentwoode's coming back to us,' he had tears in his eyes. But then, of course, he wasn't reckoning on *her* with all her airs and graces."

It was the serving of separate meals in the study and the parlour which, as Ellen said, "stuck in her craw"; it certainly made a great deal of running about for me, on my young legs, but I was used to running about and did not resent it. The Canon always had some pleasant, cheery word to say, and his food was a never ending source of interest and mystery to me. Into the house came a constant flow of presents from old friends and relatives who must have known that the old man was a glutton and the school fare very plain. It was a rare day, and for him a doleful one, that failed to bring him some special and delightful dish. In the parlour Mr. and Mrs. Kentwoode ate the ordinary school food, supplemented occasionally by some delicacy which Ellen or Mrs. Kentwoode thought would be good for the cough. Mr. Kentwoode was never grateful for these attentions. Had I liked Mrs. Kentwoode better I should have felt sorry for her. She knitted him a woollen comforter to wear in the classroom, which was always chilly; he despised it and passed it on to Mr. Flowerdew, who wore it gratefully. She was always being told not to fuss; and once I heard Mr. Kentwoode say in a most bitter tone, "Can't you forget for one moment, day or night, that you're married to a wreck?"

She had a rooted belief that wine was bad for a cough and held it against Canon Hatton that occasionally, when he had a present of wine, he would invite his nephew in to share it. A curious thing happened one evening when I had not been very long at the Old Vine. It was after supper, and when the dishes were washed Bess saw the Canon's log basket standing empty in the kitchen.

"I forgot his wood," she said, "you fill it and take it along."

Even for me, strong as I was, that was a heavy load and on my way I had to set it down once or twice. One of my resting places was just through the classroom door, at the end of the passage leading to the study. It was a short passage, lighted by one candle on a shelf opposite the study door; I staggered through the classroom door, set the log basket down and stood bent over catching my breath. I could hear laughter, very merry and rather excited, coming from the study. Then, as I straightened myself and took a breath before lifting my load, I saw that I was not alone in the passage; Mrs. Kentwoode was walking up and down outside the door in an agitated way, her hands clasped at the level of her bodice's edge.

When she saw me, she stood still and when I reached her she said:

"I'll take it in. It'll be a good excuse . . ."

I said, "Madam, you couldn't lift it; it's as much as I can manage."

She said, "Rubbish. Open the door for me."

I had, anyway, to set the basket down and open the door. She bent down, took hold of the handles and attempted to lift it; she could as well have lifted the floor on which it stood.

"You . . . take . . . one handle," she gasped. I obeyed and we went awkwardly through the doorway.

My months in the inn at Bywater—much as I had kept to the background—had introduced me to the facts of drunkenness; I'd heard drunken men shout and laugh and quarrel, I'd caught glimpses of them, and I'd done a lot of cleaning up in the morning. The Canon and Mr. Flowerdew and Mr. Kentwoode were all a little drunk, but not quite in the manner of the customers at the *God Save Mariners*. They just looked happy, all their differences forgotten. Mr. Flowerdew was saying something in a strange tongue which I didn't then know was Latin and they were all laughing; when he finished, Mr. Kentwoode said about three or four words in the same tongue and the laughter increased tenfold. And then the inflowing cold from the open door and the sound of our entrance drew their attention to us and all was changed.

Mr. Kentwoode stood up and said:

"Henrietta, what d'you think you're doing?"

She said, "I'm helping Ethelreda; this basket is too heavy for her."

"And since when have you cared how much Ethelreda or any

other wench carried? How did you even know? You were spying again! All right, you've found what you were looking for. I've been drinking. Uncle Edward and I, with a little help from Tony, have disposed of two bottles of the best port wine it has ever been my privilege to taste. *And what have you to say to that?*"

As soon as we were inside the room she had lowered her side of the basket, and since I had loaded it high, and was a little behind her in lowering my side, the topmost logs had begun to fall off. I made a grab to recover them.

"Shut the door!" Canon Hatton bellowed, and at the same time Mr. Flowerdew took Mr. Kentwoode by the arm and said:

"Steady, Chris. Mind your tongue!"

I shut the door. And having done that I heaved up the basket and took it to its usual place, within reach of the Canon's chair. As I did so Mrs. Kentwoode was saying what she had to say.

It seemed to make nonsense of all her tender care and fussing, for it sounded as though she hated him; he drank to spite her, she said, because he knew that it worsened his cough and he knew that she couldn't bear him to cough. She claimed that his cough would have cured itself if he hadn't drunk so freely while he was in the wine trade. She said several times that she did her best to look after him and that he ridiculed her efforts and then brought them to nothing by indulging in orgies like this. She also said that what made everything worse was that she loved him; and she made her love sound like some kind of debt, or burden.

It was embarrassing for everyone, but most of all for me, who should not have been there at all. But when she started to speak she had taken a stand just in front of the door, and if, having deposited the wood basket, I had departed, as I should have done, I should have been obliged to push past her, asking to be excused, and interrupting the flow of her tirade. So I did what I could to make myself inconspicuous, first placing some logs on the fire very gently and then standing aside, in the shelter of the Canon's big chair.

When, at last, she stopped for breath, or because she realised that she was repeating herself, Mr. Kentwoode said:

"Gentlemen, the voice of love!"

Mr. Flowerdew said, "Don't mock, Chris. That is exactly what it is. I'm sorry, my dear. We were celebrating my birthday."

Canon Hatton was quick to back him.

"That's what it was, Henrietta. And I blame myself for opening the second bottle; but one amongst three—on a birthday, too—did seem a trifle meagre. And despite his boasting, Chris hasn't really drunk his full share; how could he, with two old rogues like me and Tony here outpacing him?"

She was on the verge of tears.

"It isn't just this once. It's everything. I try and I try and he won't even wear a hat when he goes into the yard!"

Mr. Kentwoode burst into a roar of laughter.

"Of all forms of humour," he said, coming to the end of his mirth, "I find the non sequitur the most appealing. My sweet, you love me, or rather my cough, and to pleasure you I swear I will wear a hat which you shall knit for me."

Mrs. Kentwoode then began to cry and say, "Oh, why did I marry you?" and "How could I have been such a fool?"

Canon Hatton lost his good humour and said, "Oh, for God's sake go and conduct your marital squabbles elsewhere!"

Mr. Kentwoode took his wife by the arm, turned her about and opened the door. I was about to slip out behind them but Canon Hatton called me back.

"You take that stool, Ethelreda," he said, "and tell us some more about your happy pagan life on Mons. It will take the taste of that out of our mouths."

Mr. Flowerdew said, "Poor Henrietta. She can never see that even sickness can't turn a hawk into a turtle dove."

Canon Hatton replied, "One has only to know Henrietta to realise why God in His wisdom gives most women a baby every year." He then turned his attention to me.

All too often during those early days he would catch me like that, and hold me, while my weary bones cried out for bed. Sometimes he showed a childish excitement about the things I told him; often he made notes in a big book. He had poor eyesight, the reverse of shortsightedness, so that when he wrote he leaned away from the page and when he read held his book at arm's length. Many of his remarks were clean out of my understanding; when I told him about the Beltane Fire, for example, he said that it proved that some people even older than the Romans had made their way into the Fens, Phoenicians, he called them. And he said that our ceremony of Pleasing the Waters was an offering to the tutelary spirit of the stream. Father had never used the word "spirit"; he spoke of Pleasing the Water and went out and did it as best he could. Maybe it was already too late for me to learn to understand about spirits; and that was a drawback to me in the next stage when, the Canon having asked me every question he could think of, he decided to teach me instead of questioning me.

It began one evening when he and Mr. Flowerdew were talking about slaves—black people taken from their homes and made to work in the sugar islands and on the tobacco plantations in Virginia. Mr. Flowerdew, naturally, pitied them extremely and said that he had doubts whether English people who used the sugar and smoked the tobacco were doing rightly. The Canon said:

"Slavery brings them one advantage which they would not have known in their natural habitat; they come into contact with Christianity." He looked musingly at me. I'd been there in the room, talking to him, when Mr. Flowerdew entered, and some remark I had made about the complete freedom of the real Fenman's life had led on to the discussion about slavery.

"I've often wondered," he said, "how it's done. Converting them, I mean. The Catholics claim great success in Mexico and such places. Take Ethelreda, she's as much a heathen as any Indian in Mexico, or any slave in Virginia. Would it be possible to convert her?"

Always over-ready to accuse himself, Mr. Flowerdew said:

"I grieve to admit, Edward, that the thought had never occurred to me. Very remiss. But then," he smiled at me, "Ethelreda never struck me as being any more of a heathen than anyone else."

"Instructing her would be an interesting experiment; and I propose to begin at once."

I should have preferred to go to bed in the evenings, but it would have been out of my place to say so, and I soon made the discovery that I learned easily. My mind was still somewhat like an empty bucket; it held everything poured into it and spilled nothing. Everything the Canon told me, or gave me to learn by repeating after him, I remembered, and he was delighted with me, but none of it meant anything in the way that touching the Touchwood had meant in the old days. I was mystified almost from the first when the Canon began by telling me the story of the Garden of Eden and the Fall of Man. Why, I wondered, did God put the tree there in the Garden if He didn't want Adam and Eve to eat the fruit?

And mystified I remained, even when we came to the story of Jesus and His life and His teaching and His horrible death. He was being punished for the sins of the world, and that didn't make sense to me.

Nor did it make sense that, having learned by heart the Ten Commandments, the Creed, the Sermon on the Mount and the Lord's Prayer, I was, in the Canon's opinion, sufficiently a Christian to be baptised. I went to St. Mary's Church for this ceremony hoping that after it I might understand, feel some change. But nothing happened. I was no different. I still believed the simple things that my father had taught me.

I hoped that once I was baptised the Canon would lose interest in me and then I could go to bed as soon as my work was done, and the hours in the study—about which Ellen and Bess were so sour—would cease. But no! Almost immediately he had thought of something for me to do, something which annoyed them even more. He had never allowed either of them to do more in the study than take away the accumulated ash from the fires and occasionally brush the carpet; he now decided that in the evenings, working under his eye, I could be entrusted with the thorough cleaning of the room. It was filthy from years of neglect and the only way to clean it properly would have been to move everything out, open the windows and work vigorously with brooms and cloths and mops; instead I had to move gently around him, careful not to raise a dust which would make him sneeze, careful not to make a noise. It took me weeks of evenings.

Most of my other work was in the kitchen, and there I did learn, very thoroughly, the art of providing plentiful and tasty food at the least possible expense. Mr. Flowerdew naturally wished to feed his boys well and wished them to enjoy their food, but money was short so there was a good deal of contrivance. We always bought the cheapest kinds of meat and these were made into stews, with vast quantities of vegetables and dumplings; or the meat was minced, mixed with herbs and onions and enclosed in thick pastry covers which the boys called coffins. Fish, except when intended for the parlour or the study, was never simply boiled or fried, it was cut into thin slivers and dipped in thick batter and then fried, or it was boiled and flaked and mixed with rice or bread crumbs, or thick onion gruel. Always over one hearth was a great cauldron of simmering marrow bones; the liquor was made into soup, the bones were split and the marrow, well salted and peppered, spread on bread. Ellen also made a dish which I had seen Meg Towler make for a guest who arrived late or had a delicate stomach, beaten eggs cooked until they thickened; the only difference was that at the Old Vine the eggs were added to an equal amount of flour and water, so the result was a more solid and satisfying dish, and paler in colour. The boys called this "cowshit" but ate it greedily all the same.

Perhaps Mr. Flowerdew's interest in and anxiety to do well by his boys showed most plainly in the great pickle barrel which stood in the corner of the kitchen. In the early days of his schoolmastering he had noticed that boys delighted to eat very sour young apples, unripe gooseberries, even sloes from the hedges. He decided that their stomachs craved the sour as well as the sweet, so he started the pickle barrel. We chopped up and boiled, with vinegar and peppercorns, anything that happened to be plentiful at the moment, onions, apples, cabbages, unripe plums, pumpkins, beans, young walnuts. As soon as each potful was cold it was tipped into the barrel and stirred in. The mixture, sour enough in good truth, was served at supper on Sundays and Thursdays and was very popular.

It was while I was working in the kitchen that I could hear Ellen and Bess talking. Ellen had been longest at the Old Vine; she could remember when it was an inn, though it sounded a very different place from the *God Save Mariners*. She spoke often of the mistress, the woman who was Mr. Kentwoode's mother and Mr. Flowerdew's wife; Ellen had held her in high esteem. "She had a way with her," Ellen said. "You can believe it or not but twenty or more men'd bed down here of a night and not one of 'em would spit or swear."

"She sound like a Tartar," Bess said.

"No, you're thinking of the one afore; her they called Madam. I never knew her, only heard tell, but by all accounts she was fearsome. She had the evil eye and they say the Devil come for her on her deathbed." Ellen gave me a sly look and went on, "Wouldn't surprise me a bit if she still walked; you want to look out, Ethelreda, one of these nights when you go off to bed so late, you might meet more than you bargained for."

I saw that Bess shuddered and the gooseflesh came up on her plump arms. I was spared from fright by my ignorance; ghosts were unknown on our island.

The days grew longer and the weather warmer. Being so busy and doing the same thing day after day seemed to make the time go fast. Twice during that late spring and early summer Mrs. Kentwoode went away to make visits; she had relatives of her own, and there were Hattons scattered about all over the countryside around Baildon; she was in great demand in the various houses because of her skill at dressmaking; she could turn an old gown and furbish it up so that it looked like new. Before each visit she would come into the kitchen and give Ellen special and careful instructions about airing Mr. Kentwoode's shirts and making him what she called "dainty little dishes." Ellen would say, "Yes ma'am, yes ma'am," and then when Mrs. Kentwoode had gone, say, "If you ask me a mite of neglect wouldn't do him no harm." Despite her snorting she was ready to keep all Mrs. Kentwoode's rules, and to make some of her own.

While Mrs. Kentwoode was away I was excused from my slow labours with the cleaning of the study because Mr. Kentwoode spent his evenings there and the three men did often make merry together, without, so far as I could see, any harm coming to Mr. Kentwoode. Once they fell out, though, over the supper table and, when I went to clear it, were in the thick of an argument about caning boys. Mr. Kentwoode had apparently caned three boys that day and Mr. Flowerdew, over supper, had protested. Just as I entered the room with my tray, Canon Hatton said:

"You make too much of it, Tony. They probably deserved it, and if they didn't today, they certainly will in the not so distant future."

"It's when I think of the future that I can't bear to hurt them now. When you think of the troubles and sorrows that are bound to come . . . and then they'll die."

"So shall we all," Mr. Kentwoode said, "and a damn sight sooner! God help you when I'm gone, that's all I say. They'll ride over you roughshod then, you old fool."

"I must agree," the Canon said. "Once start treating everybody as a potential corpse and there'd be no justice, no order at all. Where would you stop? You'd catch a pickpocket with his hand in your pocket and think—Poor boy, one day he'll die!"

"I probably should," Mr. Flowerdew said, but he didn't speak with his usual mildness. There was something savage and resentful in his voice. "You speak glibly about dying, but you don't *realise*. I once did. A flash of realisation, a long time ago, at a burying. And it ruined my whole life! Old fool, eh? That comes well from you, Chris!"

By that time I had the table cleared. Going back along the passage and across the two great rooms I wondered what Mr. Kentwoode meant by "when I'm gone." Did he expect to die soon, or was he planning another move? It was a bright evening, but the light seemed to fade as I thought of the Old Vine without him, whatever the reason.

Shortly after that evening something happened in my life, something new to me in that I myself had a hand in it. Hitherto I had been rather like a leaf being carried along by the flow of the river and lacking all choice of direction; this turn I chose.

IV

It was one of those hot still days when to make any kind of effort, do any kind of work, is wrong, an insult to the weather, which comes so rarely, and to something deep inside oneself. On Mons, on such a day, Father and I would have fed the animals and had our breakfast, lain in the sun until we were hot, plunged into the cool clear brown water and stayed until we were cool, slept in the hut's shadow, waked, basked and bathed again and so idled the day away, until it was time for supper, and that we should have eaten at leisure, watching the sun go down behind the willows and the reeds. A timeless, happy day of the kind that comes less than a dozen times in a whole year.

At the Old Vine we made black currant jam in addition to doing everything else just as usual. It was so hot that when the boys went out in the afternoon they were quite quiet, content to lie in the shade of the sweet-smelling elm trees and be idle, or play marbles. They came in again for their evening lessons and in the kitchen, having sealed down the hot jam, we began to prepare for supper, and then, almost comically, along came the man who supplied the house with firewood, wanting to know if Mr. Flowerdew had an order for him, "against the cold weather," he said, sweating as he spoke. Ellen told me to run fetch the master.

To reach Mr. Flowerdew, who had all the younger boys at the

far end of the classroom, I must pass Mr. Kentwoode, who had a few of the older ones about him near the foot of the great staircase. I think he had been reading to them, for as I entered the room and was level with them, he closed the book, saying:

"*The Purple Island*—by Phineas Fletcher."

That was all. I passed on, gave Mr. Flowerdew the message and went back to the kitchen, taking with me the words *Purple Island*.

The word "island" to me was almost the same as "home," and I had been thinking of my island home all through that long hot day; also there is a season when there is about the willow wands a purple look. No separate one is actually purple, but standing together they sometimes seem to have trapped a purple mist among them. I remembered that look with a feeling of piercing homesickness; and then my thoughts took a leap. All that meaning, all that calling up of lost things, lay in two words, lay in some black scratchings on white paper. I thought of the book which Mr. Kentwoode had closed with a little snap, and it seemed to me to be a treasure chest to which I had no key.

Then it was suppertime and I carried the tray to the study. As I was on my way to the door Canon Hatton said:

"And what is going to have the benefit of your attention this evening, Ethelreda?"

I said, "I finished yesterday, sir. Down to the very last book."

That had been one comforting thought, all through the day; the work in the study was done at last, and this evening, as soon as the supper dishes were washed and set away and the new jam put on the store cupboard shelves, I could go to my little room and strip and lie naked on my bed.

"Dear me," he said, almost peevishly. "I didn't notice. Well, if it's done, it's done. You made a very good job of it, too. I shall give you a present. What would you like?"

The whole sentence came into my mind, clear and solid as though it had been carved on wood or stone—*I'd Like to Learn to Read*. But he meant something that cost eightpence or a shilling.

"Come now," he said, "don't be shy. There must be something you'd like. A new hair ribbon, or a pair of stockings, eh?"

I still had no stockings, for I had so far not drawn any wages. I could ask for stockings without looking a fool. I could ask for stockings without seeming to be above myself. I swear I opened my mouth to say, "I'd like a pair of stockings, sir." I even thought—

Not white, they'd remind me of Wall Eye. But I didn't say what I meant to. With a feeling of shock I heard myself say:

"I'd like to learn to read, sir." I waited for him to be shocked, too. The best I could hope for, I thought with the blood banging in my ears, was that he should laugh and think it a joke. A kitchen slut, wanting to read!

He said, as though to himself, "I could have thought of that!" And then, to me, very kindly, "So you shall, and you'll find it easy, I'll warrant. You had the Creed by heart in less time than anyone I ever knew. I'll teach you, right gladly."

I began to thank him but he interrupted me by laughing and slapping his thigh.

"Ha!" he said. "That would be a prime joke!"

I thought he meant that teaching me to read would be a joke and all shyness fled away under the prick of anger; I raised my eyes and gave him a furious look and was about to say that I would sooner not learn than be taught on such terms.

"Not you, my touchy Fenwoman! Friend Flowerdew. One of those little chaps—he came about the same time you did—is still stuck in his first hornbook, C A T, cat. I'll wager a guinea that I'll have you reading first, despite his head start. That's the joke. That'll put them on their mettle."

"But I wouldn't want anyone else to know that I was learning."

"In Heaven's name, why not?"

"They'd think I was getting beyond myself."

"Not Flowerdew. He believes, he really does, that everybody should learn to read because those who can't miss so much pleasure. You wouldn't mind his knowing?"

"No," I said, doubtfully, "but please, nobody else."

"That slummocky couple in the kitchen. Who minds about them?"

"I do, sir. And the boys. And . . . and Mr. Kentwoode." That again was a thing I hadn't intended to say, not out loud.

"Oh, come! He'd see the joke. He'd want to have a bet on it too."

"He'd laugh."

"You know, Ethelreda, this horror of being laughed at is a sign of a very primitive nature. Dogs share it. Properly civilised human beings are far less sensitive, how else could they survive the jokes, the lampoons, the caricatures? You mustn't mind being laughed at, or you'll never amount to anything." I saw by the expression of his face that another thought had struck him. "Still, just as you wish, a secret between the three of us, eh? But in return you must do something for me."

"I'd do anything I could, sir."

"You must bring me presents, Ethelreda."

"Oh," I said. "But you must know, sir, I can't. I haven't had any wages yet, and when I do I shall . . ."

"You don't understand. Listen. And remember that this also is a secret. . . ."

He was very frank with me. He told me that years before he had "scraped together," as he put it, enough money to buy the Old Vine from Mr. Kentwoode when he was anxious to go and try his fortune elsewhere. "It was an act of charity; for a far smaller sum I could have bought a more comfortable house, in better condition; however, I enabled Mr. Flowerdew to keep his school and Mr. Kentwoode to prove he had no knack for business. The loan was never repaid, and once you lend money on those terms you're in danger of being asked again. So I never admit to having a penny; I am indeed very poor, but not so poor that I must eat school fare, thank God. Those presents that arrive so unfailingly, Ethelreda, are presents I send to myself—all but a few from Hattons here and there. In future it will be your duty to organise them for me. At the moment young Saunders does my errands when he goes for his organ lessons; he obliges me because I give him a shilling now and again to sweeten the Choirmaster. I was wondering what I should do when he leaves, as he does, I believe, this summer. To teach you to read instead of giving you a shilling at odd times will suit me very well, because, as I said, I am a poor man."

I said I would gladly do his errands. I already did the marketing for such things as could not be bought in large quantities, and it was easy enough to go to the stall and choose a fine fat hen which was a present from an old friend named Mr. Bishop, or the whole ham which a former parishioner at Ely had been thoughtful enough to send. I came to look upon the whole business as a game, and as the reading lessons went on and he praised my progress, I would search the market for something that would please him and bring that thing home as well as whatever he had thought of for himself that day. Whenever I did that he was delighted with me, saying that surprise added zest to a dish. His remark about being a poor man puzzled me a little; whenever he gave me money he seemed to take the needed amount from a whole handful of gold and silver.

In addition to arranging for the presents, I carried letters to the post stop, and sometimes brought one back. The postboys used the *Hawk in Hand*, an inn which belonged to some people named Webster. The letters I carried were always for London, and all the ones I brought back came from there. London was one of the first words I learned to recognise at sight. The Canon never opened one in my presence, but I could tell, from his look later on, whether the contents had pleased him or not. Once he was so extremely pleased that he gave me a guinea all to myself.

Wonderful as the gift was it put me in a painful position. I longed to buy a new dress, having worn the one Amy Briggs had given me every day, without change; but I also needed shoes, my own being worn through at the toe from all the kneeling I was obliged to do. I also needed shifts, and longed for stockings and a new hair ribbon. I fretted away for a week or more, trying to decide how to spend my guinea, and then one day, while I was still undecided, Mr. Flowerdew met me in the bright sunshine in the yard when I was bringing in water and looked me over in no very flattering way and then, confused and abashed, said:

"You poor girl, I never paid you! You should have reminded me, you know. The others always do." He fumbled in all his pockets and adding coin to coin counted out eleven shillings and a four-pence.

"That's all I have at the moment," he said, "but I'll make it up, I'll make it up."

He didn't say when, or to what amount, but I was so pleased to have anything, and at the same time so sorry for him, that I just said, "Thank you, sir, thank you!" And then I could truthfully tell Ellen that I had been paid and hoped to have a new dress.

"Not afore you needed it," she said, unkindly. "The one what you're wearing now'd stand alone with grease and muck, I should reckon." But she went on to say that if I bought some stuff her sister would sew it for me. Her sister lived in Bridewell Lane and had very poor health, sewing was all she could manage. So I bought some stuff, a greenish blue, the colour of young reeds, and Ellen's sister made me a dress which fitted me badly until she thought of running a drawstring through the neck and then, all suddenly, it was very becoming. I wore it for three days straight off while my old one was washed and ironed and aired, and then I kept it for best. I was also able to have a pair of new shoes, two shifts and two pairs of stockings. I felt wonderfully well provided.

Keeping the reading lessons secret from everyone except Mr. Flowerdew wasn't easy. Telling the Canon about life in the Fens, being prepared for baptism, cleaning that long-neglected study, had all been reasonable excuses even though they were the cause of unkind and jibing remarks. "Trying to save your soul, is he now?" Ellen said. "Funny thing, I been here all these years and all he ever cared about me was how I cooked."

I pretended that once the supper dishes were done and the preparations for the next day made I went straight to bed; but one night, just as she was going to bed herself, Ellen remembered that the sweep was to come in the morning, and she padded along to the Cough Room to tell me that I must be alert to let him in. I wasn't there; and in innocence, or from malice, Ellen raised a hue and cry which ended only when I was discovered in the study.

The Canon was quick-witted; he said that he had called me down to sew a button on.

"I thought she was the one as couldn't sew," Ellen said.

"She's learning. She's learning," he said, and laughed and looked sideways at me, sharing the joke which Ellen couldn't even guess at.

Then there was an evening when, unknown to me, Ellen had gone to visit her sick sister. I thought she'd gone to bed, as she sometimes did, leaving the last jobs to Bess and me. I went to my room, having said good night to Bess at her door, and I washed my hands because I had learned that washing up left a greasiness which transferred itself to the paper and made the ink run. The Canon insisted that I learn to read and write at the same time, he said one helped the other. I put on my green-blue dress, as I always did, and brushed out and rebraided my hair, not from vanity, but because the lessons meant so much to me; I dressed for them as people dress for churchgoing.

Coming down the back stairs I met Ellen coming up, and she demanded of me, as she had a perfect right to do:

"Where you off to at this hour?"

I could smell the ale on her breath.

"I've just remembered something that I promised to do, and forgot."

"And what might that be?"

I was a poor liar, but then lying, like other things, needs practice. In the first fifteen years of my life I had never told a lie. What was there to lie about? If Father had asked me had I fed the beasts and I said I had when I hadn't, their blaring would soon have made the truth known.

"The Canon asked me to make some flour and water paste to stick back a loose page in a book," I said.

"Oh." She pushed her face forward and looked at me hard. "Loose pages you can stick back," she said, "but there's things that once they've gone can never be put back, and a girl's maidenhead is one of them things. Outside of the kitchen where you go and what you do ain't my business, but I'm warning you, friendly, see? A dirty owd man is a dirty owd man, whatever his age and call him Canon or Mr. or Sir Tom Noddy. So you mind what you're up to."

The word "maidenhead" had never figured in the girls' talk and I had no very clear notion of its meaning. I recognised the look in Ellen's eyes, however; it was just like that which had greeted the news that I was going away with Mr. Flowerdew, and it filled me with the same anger and disgust. I was handier with words now than I had been when I left Bywater; besides what the girls said or thought didn't matter any more since I was leaving them. Here I must live and I must face Ellen every day.

"I'm not up to anything with Canon Hatton, nor he with me; and you should be ashamed to think such things, leave alone say them." I remembered that Ellen was a good Christian and always went to Church on Sunday evenings. "Jesus Christ the Lord bear me witness and strike me dead on this stair if that is a lie," I said.

She evidently had deep suspicions and thought I might be struck and she share my doom, for she stepped back hastily and so clumsily that she had to catch the handrail. I had a flicker of doubt myself, since "up to anything" might, just possibly, cover the giving and receiving of lessons. Nothing happened however, and after half a moment she said:

"Well, don't say I never warned you . . ." and pushing past me, went to her bed.

There was another evening when I was almost caught by Mr. Kentwoode. The Canon and I had a sign. If he expected Mr. Kentwoode in the study after supper, or if he himself didn't feel like being bothered with me, he would say, as I cleared away the dishes,

"Good night, Ethelreda." Then I knew. On this evening he had not said good night to me, so when all was done and I was clean and tidy I went along and the Canon set me my copy. Mr. Flowerdew was there, and before he went to bed he leaned over my shoulder and looked at my work. He said nothing directly concerning it, but over my head addressed the Canon:

"Young Watson is the most *determinedly* stupid boy it has ever been my misfortune to handle."

"But he's young; and it is well known that the capacity to learn decreases with age. You're how old, now, Ethelreda?"

"Sixteen, sir."

"And a girl, to boot."

"She has the benefit of your undivided attention, Edward."

"So she does! And when? At the end of a hard day's work when she's half asleep."

"If she writes like that when she's half asleep, Heaven knows what a pretty page she could turn out when fully awake."

He went off to bed and silence fell on the room. I was at the writing table, my back to the door, the Canon sat half dozing in his chair by the fire. The cold weather was on us again.

I jumped when the door opened.

"Ha, Chris!" the Canon said. "You look cold. Come in and warm yourself."

I opened a drawer and slid my paper into it. Then I opened another and closed that too. I was so startled and confused that though I was pretending to look for something, had I been asked I could not have given the thing a name. Canon Hatton said:

"Can't you see it, Ethelreda?"

"No, sir."

Mr. Kentwoode went to the fire and stood warming his backside.

"What have you lost?" he asked.

"My seal. It's probably under my nose. I really think I must make an effort and get myself a pair of these newfangled spectacles. The only thing is, I suppose their price is exorbitant."

"If they improve the sight they are beyond price," Mr. Kentwoode said, but he was looking hard at me as he spoke. Had I, as I occasionally did, got ink on my fingers and transferred some to my face? Or did he share Ellen's suspicions? I felt the hot blood begin to mount from the edge of my dress and rush up to where my hair began.

"May I go now, sir?" I managed to ask.

"You may not. I asked you to find my seal, Ethelreda. When you've found it you may retire and not before."

I opened two more drawers, holding my head down, waiting for the blush to subside.

"It's probably in your pocket," Mr. Kentwoode said.

"Bless my soul, I never thought of that. You were right! Here it is. All right, Ethelreda, away to your bed!"

Next day, of course, this made an amusing story for Mr. Flowerdew.

"Your pupil," the Canon said, "doesn't look like a thief caught in the act if anyone enters the room."

"My pupil," Mr. Flowerdew retorted, "writes as though he'd been caught and was manacled."

The year moved on; the weather was exceptionally cold. Soon there was talk of Christmas, and one evening the Canon said:

"Now, my dear fellow, about this test. I could use a guinea, you know. Christmas is a very expensive season."

"I could use a guinea, too. The cold so early has played havoc with the woodpile."

"I thought they'd been sparing with the logs lately. I'll see if they can send a load in from Mortiboys. Now, about this wager. When can we settle it?"

"At the rate we're going now it looks as though Willie will be sixteen before I dare risk it."

"Is he one of those who're going away for Christmas?"

"Yes. The Watsons have an aunt in Ipswich."

"Well, I want to be fair to you. He'll come back having forgotten all he ever knew, whereas Ethelreda here, slowly moving her finger along the lines as she goes, will probably have covered three pages."

He gave me a sly look. I no longer used my finger to guide my eye, but it was part of the joke to pretend that I was less able than I was.

"I was an ass to wager on such a matter," Mr. Flowerdew said. "And it serves me right. I thought I was safe. I'm experienced, which you are not, and I'd reckoned without Ethelreda's unusual application."

Canon Hatton laughed quietly to himself.

"I still contend that I took the greater risk, but then you know what we Hattons are. Though what my father would have said to see me laying evens on such a childish game I shudder to think."

The test was to be made one afternoon when the boys were in the yard, running about and shouting hard to keep themselves warm. Mr. Flowerdew had asked Mr. Kentwoode to leave a book, suitable for young readers, open at any page he chose. It lay on the high desk nearest the great window so that we had the advantage of the last daylight.

"Now we must toss to see who is to lead off," the Canon said. "Heads, it's Ethelreda, tails, it's Watson. Agreed?"

It came down tails.

Now I know that some people, wise ones maybe, believe that everything in our lives is ordered from the beginning, that there are no accidents to blame for what happens to us, that we have no real choice, no will because our way is already decided. Others hold that we shape our own fates. I do not know. I can look back upon that grey winter's afternoon and see the course of my whole life shaped by the chance falling of a coin; but I can also see that a few minutes after it had fallen I did have a choice of actions and that I chose deliberately.

Mr. Flowerdew said, "You begin, then, Willie. Take your time and do the best you can." He spoke in no very hopeful tone of voice, but kindly and supportingly.

Willie stood behind the high desk and began. He read very badly. "Once . . . upon . . . a time . . . there . . . was . . . a poor . . ."

"Spell it," Mr. Flowerdew said patiently.

"S h e p . . ."

"Shepherd," the Canon said quickly. "All right, we'll give you shepherd."

We gave Willie every word of more than four letters, but each failure unnerved him a little more and soon he blundered to a stop and looked up and said piteously:

"I can see 'hut,' sir, and 'log,' but that's all."

It was a moment to show Mr. Flowerdew at his very best.

"You made a good try, Willie," he said. "Before next Christmas we'll have you reading the lesson in Church. Run along now and have a game."

"Go on from where Watson left off," said my teacher.

I took the book. The letters were very black and clear, the paper much whiter than that of some of the Canon's books in which I had read. The hardest word on the page was the "shepherd" over which Willie had boggled. I could have read it away back at Michaelmas. But as I looked it over I remembered the way they had joked about the guinea; on the Canon's side it was a joke; he had plenty of them. He had a soft leather purse with a brass ring round its neck, and out of it he would shake the money for the oysters and the port wine, the young chickens and the fat hens, the partridges, the venison. To him a guinea meant very little; to poor Mr. Flowerdew it was a load of fire logs, badly needed. . . .

It broke my heart to do it, for I was inordinately proud of my reading and the speed with which I had learned, but I stood up on the little platform and I read worse than Willie Watson; I boggled over three-letter words.

To tell the truth, I hadn't fully realised how much this meant to the Canon. It had started as a kind of joke, and all the talk about it had been gay and teasing—save for the remark about the fire-wood. If I had known that he would be so angry I don't think I should have dared to do it. Making out that I couldn't read "B E D, bed," I looked at the Canon with as near an imitation of Willie's piteous look at Mr. Flowerdew as I could manage, and I saw a face black with fury. He was too angry to speak, and it was kind Mr. Flowerdew who put an end to the performance by saying:

"Shall we call it quits, Edward? In any case it couldn't be a real test because we neglected to provide that essential thing—an impartial judge." And with those words and a smile for me he went hurrying off, leaving me and the Canon in a room which felt unusually large and chilly. He spluttered a little before he could speak; then he raved.

"You . . . you . . . you jenny ass! You silly female fool! There wasn't a word there that you didn't know by sight. Look what you've done, you wriggling, fatuous little blockhead! For years Flowerdew and I have argued about the best way of teaching young idiots, and I know I'm right. Then, just when I'm on the point of proving it, and taking a guinea from him, you go and lose your head. You could have read it in the study. Just because you're out here and have one extra listener, you must turn coy and shy and disgrace us both."

His black, displeased look had frightened me; if he had turned

away without a word I should have felt disgraced and stayed frightened and somewhat ashamed; but the loud, angry words roused
something in me which quelled my fear. Also, because shyness was
a thing I suffered from, I resented being accused of it when I had
felt no shyness at all. I said:

"I did it on purpose. I didn't want to win."

His pink face went purple-red and swelled, his eyes bulged. He
reached out and took me by the shoulders and began to shake me.
For one so old and stout he had surprising strength, he shook me
as I might shake a duster. My teeth rattled and I turned dizzy.

It was all over in a minute. The violence eased him. He stopped
shaking me, but keeping his hands hard on my shoulders he said:

"Now are you sorry? Say you're sorry! You naughty, naughty
girl, say you're sorry!"

There was a change now; I could feel it in his hands, hear it in
his voice. Swift and frightening as the violence had been, this was,
somehow, more alarming. It was only one step, one small step,
away from being handled by Wall Eye.

Dragging in some breath I gulped out:

"I'm sorry, sir. I'm sorry."

"So you should be," he said, and let go of me, suddenly and
with a little push, so that I staggered and hit my elbow against a
corner of the desk. They call that particular spot on the elbow the
"funny bone," but there is nothing funny about the agonising pain
a sharp blow there can cause. I yelped like a dog whose tail has
been trodden upon, and then began to cry. I also began to run,
ignoring the Canon's call:

"Come back here! Ethelreda. You've dropped your hair ribbon!"

Upset as I was, I still had some part of my wits about me. There
were five exits from the big classroom; one led to the passage where
the Canon's study was, one opposite to a similar passage which
ended in the Kentwoodes' parlour. There was a big door into the
yard—if I ran out that way I might meet the boys coming in; and
there was a door that led to the kitchen quarters. I *might*, going that
way, be lucky enough to gain the back stairs without being seen by
Ellen and Bess, but it was a chance I was unwilling to take. So I
ran the one remaining way, up the big main staircase which was
only used by the family and—greatly coveted privilege—the monitors. I held my elbow with my hand as I ran, and the long braid

of my hair slapped at my back, unplaiting itself more with each swing.

The staircase did not go straight up; ten steps—I know the number for it was one of my jobs to polish them—ran up to a landing upon which stood a chest and two chairs; from the landing, eight more stairs rose to the upper floor, going in the opposite direction. By this time it was nearly dusk. I didn't expect to meet anyone on the stairs and I didn't see Mr. Kentwoode coming down towards the little landing. Whether he saw me coming up I don't know; if he did he would naturally expect me to stand aside and allow him to pass. As it was, scuttling along with my head down, I ran full tilt into him just as I gained the landing. Being lighter than he, and moving more quickly, I bounced and might have fallen backward down the stairs had he not taken hold of me. The jolt loosened the last link of my braid and my hair fell all about me.

This is a thing incapable of being put into words or even into orderly thought. It is such a wordless thing that even now if someone told me such a tale, or if I read it in a book, I should doubt its truth. Words played so little part in it. He swore as we collided; then, holding me he said, "What is the matter?" and I said, "Nothing, nothing." That was all. He kept hold of me, I thought with intent to comfort, and that surprised me, for he was, I should have said, the last person in the house to feel compassionately towards a blubbering kitchen wench. But any comfort was welcome at that moment, so I leaned against him, and he moved one hand, putting it behind my head, pushing his fingers into my mane of hair. And leaning there against him I knew the truth of something the girls at Bywater had often laughed about, and used lewd words for. To me it was amazement and pity and longing, all in one.

The longing got the mastery of me because I had no defence against it. I was a wild Fenwoman, born and bred. Putting shoes on my feet and a pen in my hand didn't alter my nature. My father had gone down to Withy one day and seen a woman who roused longing in him, and he took her; I have no doubt she felt for him in the same way or she would not have let herself be taken. Free unions of that kind were my heritage. Animal in a sense they may be, but at least they are clean and real, not cluttered up with questions of dowries and parental wishes and class distinctions. In the Fens we were all free men and women and to the best of our ability we satisfied all our appetites as simply and as directly as possible.

So now I hungered for Christopher Kentwoode. I'd lived in the ordinary world long enough to know that ordinary people never admitted to a feeling so stark; they dressed it up, they called it love, they tried to explain it to themselves; or, on the other side, they joked about it, as Hattie and Phyllis and all the others joked. I didn't dress it up, and I didn't joke. I faced the truth. From that brief contact on the stairs I knew that I wanted him, that he wanted me. But we weren't on some lost island, we were in the world, more than that we were in a small world within the world; and he was married. All day we went our ways, exposed to dozens of watching eyes; at night I went to my lonely bed and the bedroom door at the other end of the passage closed on him and his wife.

It looked like one of those wasteful, pointless things to which those who live close to the earth become accustomed—the clutch of eggs so carefully brooded over, the young birds so laboriously fed, one swoop of a hawk and there's nothing to show for it. This longing in me, so sharp that it came between me and my food, me and my sleep, me and my work, could be as meaningless as the yellow pollen that is blown by the wind into the sterile water.

And then, soon after Christmas, Mrs. Kentwoode went off on one of her visits.

That night my little room was icy cold, and so was the water, but I washed myself all over and put on a clean shift. I loosened my hair and combed it out so that it fell like a pale silky veil to my knees. Then, carefully shading my candle and moving with barefooted softness, I went along to the room where he was. . . .

V

Women, if they escape death in childbed, are indestructible; and in their old age they sit about, talking over their pasts, saying, "I was married for four and twenty years," and things of that sort. In their company I match my talk with theirs, but I never tell the truth. My marriage lasted for a fortnight, and that was twice as long as I had counted on, the frost being too hard for Mrs. Kentwoode to travel back at the end of the week as expected.

She came back, and I should have felt worse about it had there not immediately begun some talk of a Hatton wedding at Mortiboys before the start of Lent, and an urgent invitation for her to go and stay and help with the making of the dresses. There would not be, I thought, over-long to wait, just time to remember and to look forward.

And then, twelve days of the waiting time being gone, the thing which Hattie and the rest of them were always dreading happened to me. Late with my female benefit.

In the days of my chastity I should hardly have noticed or, noticing, been glad, for those were weary days, hard on the back with all the scrubbing and polishing to be done; a day's delay would seem a day gained. But now, with the secret which I had prepared to hug so joyfully suddenly assuming another shape, a day late, two, four and I knew how a trapped bird felt.

There was not a soul in the world to whom I could turn for advice, or for the small relief of speaking about my fear. I wished that I had listened more carefully to the talk in the cluttered bedroom, but while I was there the whole matter had seemed something that Ethelreda Benedict could afford to ignore; nothing of that kind would ever happen to *her!*

A week, and no doubt about it now. And above all things the thought that *he* must never know.

Once, in a fury, Canon Hatton called me an animal. I didn't relish it at the time but there may be some truth in it. Animals know certain things, about weather, about the moods of their owners, without being told. And I knew a great deal about Mr. Kentwoode, things he never guessed I knew, things that were never said. One of those things was that he was bitterly ashamed of his weakness for me. I was young and ripe and eager and I had, in very truth, forced my way into his bed; and once the candle was out, whether my face was pretty or not didn't matter. There was my body, and my hair. If he could be said to have loved anything about me, it was my hair. But he was a sick man, a man whom life had defeated and it did nothing to help his self-esteem to be, almost against his will, seduced by a kitchen slut. He would never, in all eternity, have made a move towards me. I knew that, but I didn't mind at all. What mattered to me was what I wanted. "Love" is a word that I still use cautiously. I suppose that for some time I had been what people call "in love" with him—always contriving that it should be I who carried in the parlour trays, always aware of his "good" or "bad" days; taking pleasure in cleaning his shoes. I hadn't wanted him to know that I was trying to read and write, for fear of mockery; and that moment on the stairs had roused in me a hunger that must be appeased. Love? Maybe. Two things I do know for certain; in all my life no other man ever roused even a passing lust in me; and in my fearful situation during that cold January I wanted, above all things, that he shouldn't know and be involved in the squalor of it. If all that adds to love, then I loved him.

Bereft of all other props I had to fall back upon only the beliefs of my childhood—that by Pleasing the Water one might have good luck. I lay awake at night puzzling over how to get hold of a bird. It was cold weather and, with a few crumbs and a little honey to act as birdlime, I could have caught a half-starved thrush, but that would have cost me nothing and wouldn't count. I could have gone and raided a neighbour's fowl house—the sacrifice there being the risk of being caught and set in the stocks; but I might be caught before I had time to give the bird to the Water. In the end I saw that my only hope lay in the Canon's greed.

He'd been very huffy with me after the reading test, and on the next market day when I asked him if there were any errands, he had said, "No," very crossly. But Christmas was coming, and just before the festival he sent for me and said he had decided to forgive me, so between his genuine presents and those I arranged for him he had a fine Christmas. And ever since things had been as usual.

On the ninth morning of my worrying, which was a Wednesday, I asked him, "Any errands, sir?" and he said:

"I think it's about time my old friend Thomas Bishop sent me a nice fat hen, don't you?"

"High time, sir," I said.

"Go to Mrs. Scratcherd's stall first," he said, and put eighteen-pence into my hand.

Before I left the house I laid my fingers on the Touchwood. That and putting on my father's old sheepskin coat made Mons seem very near for the moment; then I remembered and it seemed a long way away, part of another life.

Ordinarily I did my house shopping first and then added whatever "present" the Canon had ordered, but on this day I did differently. I went to Mrs. Scratcherd's and bought the best hen she had for sale. It was roughly plucked, but there were still some reddish-brown feathers about the long limp neck; it was nicely fat and, judging by its feet, not too old.

Carrying it, I went through a tall stone gateway into a place which the people of Baildon always called "The Ruins." It was a desolate spot, with low, broken-down stone walls standing amongst weeds and little self-sown trees. In the summer, looking through the gateway, I had seen children in charge of geese or goats moving about, but on this wintry morning I had the place to myself. At its farthest end there was a stream, narrow and sluggish and evil-smelling. I walked over the frost-stiffened grass, lifted the fowl from the basket and threw it into the water, saying, as I had heard my father say:

"Be pleased to take this offering; be mindful of our needs."

On Mons that had simply meant a good season, plenty of eels to smoke, plenty of fish to eat and plenty of birds to make into paste. But my need was the restoring of my female benefit; and it was for that I asked as the hen fell into the water.

The water moved so slowly, in such a thick kind of way, that I was afraid it was going to nudge the fowl against the bank and leave it there. But under the surface some current was moving and after a moment it took the fowl and, turning it over and over, swept it away. Never, even the year when Father gave Flumen the black cockerel, had the omen been better. Much heartened I turned away, went to the stalls and finished my shopping and then, with the laden baskets, trudged home, so full of faith and hope that I expected to feel the pain before I was withindoors. When I reached the Old Vine without anything happening I thought—But of course not, I haven't yet made the sacrifice, the price is still to pay.

The price was facing the Canon in his study and telling him that there would be no fat hen for supper.

"I put it in the stream, to Please the Waters," I said, and waited for him to strike me. I'd thrown away his eighteenpenny hen, and I had made nonsense of his missionary work; surely he would hit me.

"Oh," he said, "did you? With what object?"

I had been prepared for anger, not for questioning.

"What particular favour were you asking?"

"Oh, just for good luck through the new year," I said, as lightly and infuriatingly as I could.

And still he wasn't angry.

"I'm afraid you're a backslider, Ethelreda. We must talk about this. In the meantime you will return at once to the market and buy another fowl." He gave me the money.

Perhaps Ellen would be angry when I told her that I must make another outing, but she let me go with the general remark that girls grew lazier and more forgetful every day.

The short day darkened. Perhaps, I thought, the Waters had, after all, rejected my offering as soon as I turned away. Or maybe it was only the Flumen which accepted offerings and granted wishes; my clear brown river between the reeds, gold-flecked in the morning sun, rose-red at sunset. . . . And then the truth struck me. I hadn't performed the whole ceremony; the sacrificial bird should have had its throat cut! How could I have overlooked that vital detail?

Hope was dead in me when I carried in the steaming white fowl and a dish of parsley sauce.

"Boiled?" the Canon commented.

"Yes. Ellen said it was too old to roast."

"I suppose the one you presented to the town ditch was a younger and altogether superior bird?"

"Yes, sir."

He laughed.

"You're a worthless baggage, Ethelreda, but you have the charm of the unusual! So you are forgiven. Come back after supper and practise your reading."

I couldn't face supper at all, I was too wretched.

While Bess and I washed the dishes Ellen said:

"I'm just stepping over to my sister's. She was poorly, Sunday. You, Bess, can make the porridge for once, and Ethelreda can split the marrow bones."

I was squeamish for the first time in my life. On Mons I had killed a pig; now the very thought of marrow bones nauseated me.

"It'll make me late," I said.

"Late for what, in the name of goodness?"

"Something the Canon told me to do after supper."

"Ho!" Ellen said. "Happen he want another button sewed on!" She laughed coarsely. "If you knew what was best for you, my girl, you'd sew him into his breeches altogether!"

She went off laughing; and Bess laughed too, until Ellen was gone, and then, as she often did, she changed sides.

"You marn't take no notice of Ellen," she said. "She don't mean half she say."

Perhaps she had meant nothing, either tonight or on the occasion of her former warning; but to me, in my confusion and distress, it was as though, in a strange place, on a dark night, I had caught a gleam of light.

All the time I was splitting the bones and scraping out the marrow I was thinking.

The Canon had always shown a partiality towards me and it had been innocent enough up to the day of the reading test when he had shaken me, and his anger had been polluted by another emotion. But for what had happened immediately afterwards on the stairs I should probably have given that incident a great deal more thought. I thought about it now. I remembered how, when he had said that he had decided to forgive me, he had patted me on the shoulder, how afterwards whenever he gave me money for shopping he would close my fingers over the coins, how once when I was mending his fire and he was talking he had taken hold of my looped-up plait and pulled my head round and said, "Are you listening to me, my girl?"

All these things added up. There was a vast difference between us in age and state, yet Ellen thought ugly thoughts about us, and it wasn't as if marriage came into the question. All I wanted to do was cover my tracks. . . .

When the work was done I washed and put on my best dress. I dared not let my hair flow, in case I met somebody, but just outside the study door I removed the ribbon and loosened the loops so that I had only to shake my head to set it all tumbling. My face was plain, but my hair was beautiful.

VI

I contend to this day that I did Edward Hatton no wrong. He enjoyed me in his greedy, fumbling old man's way, and was both pleased and proud of his prowess. I was inclined to think that Ellen's suspicion was near the mark and that only the fear of being repulsed, either with screams or laughter, had restrained him so long. In any case, my conscience is unlike that of more civilised people; I simply did the best I could in unfavourable circumstances, as my people had always done.

I was the one who was hurt by what I did, hurt and forever soiled. I was so ignorant at that time that I didn't know what a whore was; now I do, and I am one of the few people who pity those who bear that name. To accept a man for whom you have no taste, no longing, does violence to something at your self's very root, and the wrong is a little deepened—if that be possible—when the man for whom you do long is only a passage length away.

It was during these few weeks that I developed a nervous habit of washing my hands. It was senseless, I knew, I was no cleaner for all my washing, but it would afford me a momentary relief. I do it to this day; always there must be a bowl of water ready, and sometimes as many as a dozen times a day I must wash my hands. In the whole of the Bible the words which mean most to me are in the Gospel of St. Mark—"Pilate," he says, "took water and washed his hands." When I read that I knew exactly how he felt, and I knew, too, how hopeless was the attempt to cleanse one's mind by the washing of hands.

As soon as I dared—it was February and snowing hard—I mentioned my condition. I didn't cry; only pretty women can weep without being disgusting. I went sullen and silent, so that he must ask me:

"What is the matter?"

And it was rather like opening an eel trap; in a moment you'll know, a good haul or nothing.

A good haul for me at that moment would have been for him to accept responsibility; that, honestly, was all; I didn't think about money, about where or how I should bear the child or what its name would be, nothing like that at all. I hadn't lived in the outer world long enough to consider these things of importance. There I was, and I was going to have a baby; and there was Mr. Kentwoode who had been to bed with me. I didn't want him to be blamed, or to go blaming himself. If Edward Hatton had repulsed me, I should have had to try one of the men in the yard, and that would have taken longer, because I was on no terms of any kind with them.

Now, when he asked me what was the matter, was, I knew, the most dangerous moment of all. He might very well repudiate me altogether, say he was falsely accused and have me driven from the house. But, even so, my story would leave a little doubt in some minds. In Ellen's, in Mr. Flowerdew's: he had remarked once how late I went to bed and looked at me in a manner that made me uncomfortable. I was not fully covered, but neither was I fully exposed. And wherever the baby grew up, if he looked like Mr. Kentwoode that was easily explained by my story, which would present them to the world as cousins.

I said in a sulky, injured voice:

"The matter is that you've got me with child."

He just stared at me; here and there in his pink face the colour ran away, leaving white patches the size of a groat.

At last he asked, "Are you sure?"

"Of course I'm sure. Why should you look so astounded?"

"Dumbfounded," he corrected me. "At my age one would hardly . . ." He broke off and laughed. I was afraid that the laughter was the first move in dismissing my tale as nonsense; the queasiness that had threatened me all day grew worse, became almost unmanageable. "Don't look so downcast, Ethelreda," he said.

"I don't see anything to laugh about."

"No, my dear, you wouldn't. But I do." And then it was my turn to be dumbfounded, for he said, "And so will a lot of other people. We must get married, at once, Ethelreda. My child must be born in wedlock."

Interlude

The wedding, though somewhat hurried and—because of the groom's age—quiet, was properly celebrated in St. Mary's Church. Ethelreda wore her first silk gown and, upon her thin, work-worn finger, a golden ring. None of the Canon's faithful old friends was invited to the ceremony, but several sent generous presents and there was a feast for everyone under the Old Vine's spreading roof.

Afterwards, almost as though the wedding had been a marker between two periods, a blight seemed to set in. To the outside observer financial difficulties explained much; the gradual decay of the house which, amongst its neighbours, seemed already very old; the close, shrewd marketing; the lack of labour in the kitchen. Those within the house sensed deeper change; after all, the school had never been prosperous, but it had worn its poverty with a cheerful air. All cheer had now departed, even from Mr. Flowerdew. He was still kind, still anxious to see everybody's point of view, but it was an effort now, and the strain began to show. There was first, in moments of agitation, a slight tremor of the head and hands, each attack lasting longer until the condition became chronic, and finally no longer slight.

Everyone understood why Ellen left; her sister's health remained poorly, and it was natural for her to resent the obligation to address one who had been a fellow servant as "Mrs. Hatton" and "ma'am." Ellen and those who enjoyed the privilege of being her gossips were not at all surprised that Ethelreda's baby was so prematurely born that it took even its mother by surprise; according to Ellen the old man and the kitchenmaid had been carrying on for almost a year. Canon Hatton and Christopher Kentwoode, not having the benefit of Ellen's inside information, viewed the matter differently. Christopher Kentwoode had but a short time to brood over his possible guilt; the Canon lived on, a doting and indulgent father to as handsome and engaging a child as ever gladdened any man's heart. The old man appeared to be fond of his young wife, too; but when, six months after Ellen's departure, Bess, who had said all along that the work was too much for her, proved it by dying as she washed the breakfast bowls, it was not the Canon who was concerned by the fact that Ethelreda was now alone in the kitchen, it was Mr. Flowerdew. And there was little that he could do, poor man, save to bribe boys to take turns at menial jobs like washing dishes; and there were a few parents who disapproved of paying fees in order to have their sons turned into scullions. For this reason or that the number of boys who left school each year exceeded the number of newcomers, yet Ethelreda remained overworked. The gold ring became too big for her finger and was laid away with the silk dress, awaiting what?

Now and then an old boy would pay the school a visit. Those who came back were roughly divided into two classes, boys who had been nonentities during their schooldays, but had prospered in the world and came back to show themselves off, and those who had found the world lacking in kindness and remembered the Old Vine and Mr. Flowerdew with nostalgia. One of those who came back during the year 1679 was Oliver Stanton.

Part Six

OLIVER STANTON'S TALE

Circa 1679

I

Life for me really began when, at the age of twenty-four, I had my first and last row with my father. That it hadn't come sooner is evidence of my weak and pliable character; but in contact with my father one must be weak and pliable or die.

Father was one of Cromwell's original Ironsides; sometimes I think they derived their name from him. He honestly believed himself to be in close daily communication with the Almighty; therefore any opposition to his will was blasphemy, no less. The death of his idol, Cromwell, and the restoration of the monarchy were to him the literal fulfilments of the prophecies in the Book of Revelation, the start of the rule of Anti-Christ which was to precede the end of the world. The first flicker of doubt which ever enlightened my mind came when I wondered why somebody like Father, so sure that the entire world was rushing to destruction, should be so deeply concerned with the amassing of money and property. It seemed somewhat inconsistent.

Father had done well out of the Civil War and the peace which followed. At the beginning he had been rather more than a yeoman farmer, for he owned five hundred acres and a substantial house. After the war he had been able to buy, very cheaply, twelve hundred acres and two big houses, the property sequestrated from Royalists. The restoration hit him a little, for one of the owners returned and claimed his house and about three hundred acres of land. Thereafter Father regarded him as one of the beasts of the Revelation who would eventually be cast into the bottomless pit.

Father married late in life and I was the eldest of the four children my mother bore him before, being insufficiently weak and pliable, she succumbed under his iron régime. My aunt Elizabeth, Father's sister and his female counterpart, brought us up. The motto was—Mortify the flesh; subdue the will. It worked out, in terms of common living, that if you liked fat you were given lean, if you liked lean you had fat; if you liked to read you were idle and must go and cut nettles, if you enjoyed cutting nettles you were idle and must go and read. We were not, in actual fact, so positively miserable as one might imagine; children are very resilient, we had no other way of life with which to compare our own and we made the most of any small, chance pleasure, and—as we grew older—any chance to outwit those who ruled us. Oppression from above welded us into a close entity, intensely loyal to one another. We grew up to be quiet, industrious, and entirely undemanding.

When I was ten years old Father decided to send me to school and chose the Old Vine because it was not too far away, just over the border, in Suffolk. For me this was a fortunate choice, for there, from Mr. Flowerdew, I received a kindness and tolerance unknown at home, and my five years there were very happy. I was studious, and Mr. Flowerdew spoke hopefully of my passing on to Cambridge; however when I was fifteen Father said that it was time for me to return to Witherfield and take my share of work on the estate. In my case that meant doing all the reckoning. My brother Cromwell, one year my junior, had had no respite at all, he had been put straight to work in a practical way. It was Father's idea that we should make a team, live at home and work for him until he died. I have no doubt that we should have done so if he had not —in direct disobedience to the Scriptures—one day taken thought for the morrow and announced that it was time I was married. He had chosen a wife for me, Lucy Newton.

I had nothing against her; she was young, quite pretty, as far as I knew, amiable, and certainly of unimpeachable character, having been brought up much as we had been. If the idea of marrying her had arisen in my own mind I should have thought myself fortunate to be accepted. And again, if Father had reached his decision a bare four months earlier, I should have said, "Yes, Father," and counted myself lucky that he hadn't chosen Dorcas Stokes, who was very plain, poor girl. But it so happened that when, halfway through the month of September, Father issued what was to be his last order to me, I was already deeply in love. Deeply and hopelessly, for the girl I loved was Marie Garland, daughter to the Royalist who had come back and in my father's opinion cheated him of a house and three hundred acres. We were, in fact, Romeo and Juliet in homely guise. The Garlands were Papists, and Marie had been, since the age of twelve, betrothed to a member of a Westmorland family, also Royalist and Catholic. They were to be married at Christmas, and in May, when our paths crossed, the stuff of her wedding gown was already chosen.

During that summer we met nine times, once by accident, eight times by assignation. We never did more than kiss one another, and each time we parted we knew that it might well be forever. Our upbringings, so different in ritual and theory, were alike in result; we were both aware of what sin was and anxious to avoid it. So the Puritan youth and the Catholic maid met, held hands, bemoaned their hard fate and wished things otherwise. That was all, but enough to change my life.

When Father returned from hobnobbing with Mr. Newton over a harvest supper and told me what he had arranged, I said simply:

"But, sir, I don't love her."

He gave the nearest thing to a smile that his grim face could manage and said:

"That is of no account. What matters is that Newton's land marches alongside ours, and she is his only child."

Something happened to me then. I'd borne his iron rule, his fierce cold piety, his harsh treatment of me and Cromwell, of Prudence and Charity without a whimper on my own account or a protest on anyone else's. I'd worked for nine years without a penny in wages, taken what food he provided, like a dog, and been fresh shod when he thought I needed it, like a donkey, and never once even questioned his right to treat me so. But when I heard all that I felt, all that promise of joy and tenderness and all the importance of the one chosen person dismissed as of no account, I was suddenly as much shocked as he would have been had he caught me drinking brandy or playing cards.

"I won't do it," I said.

Perhaps that shocked him; perhaps he realised, for the first time, that I was, in age at least, a man and not a boy. He began to argue, to try to persuade me.

"I promised Matthew Newton," he said.

I retorted, "Then you had no right to promise such a thing!"

and was aghast at my own daring. Ordinarily he would have raged, never having been spoken to thus by any of his children.

"But what have you against the girl?"

"Nothing. Except that I don't love her."

"You said that before. Love. You don't know what you're talking about, boy. Idle fancies, lusts of the flesh. I didn't lust after your mother; but God looked with favour on our union and blessed it with offspring. No man can ask more."

"I can. I do."

"You'd better take time and think this over," he said, reverting to his grim manner. "And mark this. I'll brook no defiance. You either do as I say or you're no son of mine. 'If thine eye offend thee, pluck it out!' And I will pluck you, Oliver, out of my family, out of my home."

To be quite honest, I gave this threat little heed. He too would have time to think things over, and he must surely see that I was too useful to be so lightly thrown over. His acres were scattered about in several parishes; he had no trust in bailiffs; he wasn't getting any younger. He could keep his promise to Matthew Newton by letting Cromwell marry Lucy. I should go single to my grave.

I reckoned without taking into account his conviction that, under God, his will was holy. Two days later he said to me:

"Well, have you decided to do as I said?"

"I can't marry Lucy Newton."

"Then you can go. A man must be master in his own house. Your brother Cromwell will marry Lucy and will henceforth be my only son."

It dawned on me then that he meant it and my belly seemed to fill with ice-cold water. For a moment we looked one another straight in the eyes; his were pale blue and hard as stone. I remember thinking that if I gave in now I should never be able to look him in the eye again; the slavery into which I had been born would be mild compared with that into which I should, of my own free will, be selling myself.

"I'll go," I said, and I wished the words hadn't sounded so breathy.

"There's the door," he said.

It stood open to the golden September twilight. I swung about, walked down the steps and into the avenue where the first curled yellow leaves of autumn lay. It had all happened so quickly that I was stunned. I couldn't think or even feel much. Where the avenue joined the road I turned left and had walked a full mile before I realised that I had chosen rightly; this road led to Colchester and so to London, and it was in such places that work was most easily found.

Twilight came and deepened. Suddenly, through the quietude, there came the sound of a horse, ridden at full gallop. I moved to the side of the road. The horse came on, shot past me, was abruptly halted and turned. Astride it, without saddle or bridle, riding with only a halter, was my brother Cromwell. For one wild moment I thought that he too had rebelled and had come to share my exile.

"Can't stop," he gasped. "I'm supposed to be racking up the bullocks. Brought you this." He slung towards me a saddlebag, full and heavy. "I wish I could have laid my hands on some money. I put my watch in."

I was so touched that I almost burst out crying. Our watches were the only things of value that we had ever owned, and they were given us because Father was a stickler for time. Every so often we were obliged to check our watches by his, so that there should be no excuse for a moment's unpunctuality.

"I can't take it, Cromwell. He'd never forgive you."

"You'll need it, Olly. I'll make some excuse."

I opened the bag and began to fumble amongst the hastily crammed-in clothes.

"I can't stop. Anyway, I'm grateful to you, Olly. I like Lucy. If you'd had her, I'd have got Dorcas. Goodbye. God keep you!" He touched the horse with his heel and was gone. It says something for the force of my father's personality that I walked along for some time worrying not about what was going to happen to me, but about how Cromwell was going to explain the fact that he was now without a watch.

Just before full dark I found a field from which the corn had not yet been cleared. I pulled some sheaves from a stook and made myself a bed. It was a warm night for the time of year and lying out was no hardship, but I couldn't sleep. My thoughts drifted away to Marie, whom I should never see again; to the recent scene with Father, so short and so final, and to events in the past which should have warned me that he always meant exactly what he said. Presently, thinking of the past, I came to remembering my school-days, and Mr. Flowerdew.

Always, when a boy left school, Mr. Flowerdew would say, "Let me know how you get on. I always like to know what happens to my boys." Sometimes, when there was something in a boy's circumstances to warrant such words, he would say, "Let me know if there's ever anything I can do for you." He hadn't said that to me because my father was well to do and my future seemed assured. To me he had said that it was a pity about Cambridge, and mind that I didn't stop reading. I had kept reading as much as shortage of time allowed. I never had a new book, of course, but there were plenty in the house, for my mother's father had ended his days there. He'd been a clergyman.

Lying there under the stars and the wheeling moon, I decided that it might be a good plan to go to Baildon and see Mr. Flowerdew. He might make some helpful suggestion about employment; he might give me a testimonial of some kind, something which I could show to any potential employer.

I reached the Old Vine just at midday of my second day in exile. In the nine years since I had been in Baildon the town had grown considerably, reaching out into the country; a stretch of road along which we had walked between hawthorn hedges on our way to the river on summer afternoons was now a street with cobblestones between the new-built houses and the roadway.

When at last I stood outside the remembered house all my resolution drained away. In the cornfield I had remembered only Mr. Flowerdew's kindness; now I visualised his surprise at seeing me, his possible disapproval when he heard my story. I also remembered, uncomfortably, some old boys who had come back during my schooldays and it seemed to me that they had come back, mainly, to show off their clothes, their horses, their maturity. I was coming back as a beggar.

I walked past the house, walked as far as the old crumbling archway which in ancient times had been the town's gateway and then in desperation turned back. When I reached the Old Vine again I noticed a change in the appearance of the place. Surely it hadn't been so shabby in my time. Or was it that I was now regarding it with an eye accustomed to looking at my father's properties? He tolerated no ragged thatch, no slipped tiles, no unhinged gates; prompt repair, he held, saved money. It was plain that there had been no repairs done at the Old Vine for many a day; the woodwork had a grey paint-starved look, there were broken panes in some of the big windows, flaked plaster left ugly patches and a place in the roof where the tiles were all awry showed where damp had crept in and rotted the timbers below.

Then, and only then, did I remember Mr. Kentwoode, who was Mr. Flowerdew's stepson and his partner. I stood there and thought —Mr. Kentwoode would never have let the place fall into such a state. He was a good manager and very strict about how things looked. I'd never liked him, though many of the older boys did. I was always a bit frightened of him and I think he sensed it and despised me. I now remembered that he had been a sick man, with a terrible cough. Maybe he was dead. Quickly there followed the thought that maybe Mr. Flowerdew was dead, too. He was getting old in my day and nine years, at that end of life, is a long time. . . .

Finally I plucked up enough courage to open the gate in the low wall and walk up between the overgrown rosebushes and ring the bell. In my day the big front door had been used on Sundays when we went to Church and on other days reserved for the family, visitors and the monitors; it still awed me and perhaps I gave the bell too gentle a pull. Nobody answered. I pulled again, and this time the iron knob, shaped like a fir cone, at the end of the chain, came away in my hand, the link that held it had rusted through. It then occurred to me that I might have made this detour from the Colchester road for no purpose. The Old Vine might be uninhabited.

A voice behind me made me jump. It said:

"That door is never used now, sir. Everybody goes to the side."

I turned and found myself face to face with a tall, gangling boy, all wrist and ankle and elbow, the way boys are in their teenage.

"Does Mr. Flowerdew still live here?" I asked.

He did not immediately answer but stood looking at me and then smiled shyly.

"You're Stanton. I remember you. I'm Watson. Watson Minor."

"I remember you, too." He'd been a very homesick little boy, much troubled by the toothache until Mr. Flowerdew had taken him on the Market Square and paid the travelling tooth-puller to attend to him.

"Mr. Flowerdew is here. Not Mr. Kentwoode. He died."

I said, "I'm sorry to hear that." A lie which would count against me on the dreadful Day of Judgment.

"Mr. Flowerdew *will* be pleased to see you. We're just sitting down to dinner."

We went round to the side. I dropped my bag in the passage and breathed in the school smell which hadn't changed at all. It took me back nine years to the time when I had been happy.

Most childhood places revisited seem smaller than one remembers, but the dining hall looked larger because there were fewer people in it; only one of the tables was in use. Mr. Flowerdew sat at its far end, and just as I entered the kitchen door opened and a maid whom I remembered, Ethelreda, carried in a large tureen of soup. One of the sewerers followed with a platter of sliced bread.

Mr. Flowerdew looked at me without recognition, almost with apprehension. He had aged very much, grown shrivelled and small. Palsy shook his head and his hands, and everything about him sagged, even his lower lids, which gave him the look of an old, melancholy hound. Not, I thought, as I walked towards him, a man to bring one's troubles to. I must pretend that I had come on a visit and get away as soon as possible.

I said, "I'm Stanton, sir. Oliver Stanton. I was passing and thought I would like to call upon you."

He brightened instantly.

"My dear boy. How very pleasant! I'm delighted to see you. You must forgive a moment's blankness; you've changed a great deal."

He pressed his hands on the table's edge and half rose; holding his stiff right arm awkwardly he tried to take my hand and then, unable to support himself with the left alone, dropped back into the chair. "Old age," he said, "the ailment that catches those who escape all others. You haven't dined, have you? Rayner, find a chair for Mr. Stanton and put it here by me. Ethelreda, my dear, could we have another place?"

She sent a boy running and went on ladling the soup into the wooden bowls. She had changed very little. I remembered her well because she was the only young maid we had ever had at the Old Vine. Her arrival had caused some curiosity and amongst the oldest boys some half-bawdy talk. Nothing came of it because she was not only plain but very prim and shy. One boy, Wilcox, said that she'd be beautiful if she didn't scratch her hair back in such an ugly way. But he'd been left at school too long. I wondered what he would have said now, for the only changed thing about her was that she wore a huge plain linen cap which hid every bit of her hair.

I was ravenously hungry; all I had had to eat since leaving home was a lump of cold porridge which a farm wife was about to throw into her pig pail. The Bible says that the sins of the fathers shall be visited upon the children, so perhaps my father was to blame for the lack of charity which I had met with. Father never gave anything to beggars even when they were old soldiers and could say exactly when and where they had fought and been wounded. Father believed—I think sincerely—that God could be trusted to take care of His own; after all he had taken care of Thomas Samuel Stanton, with only one small oversight in the matter of the Garland property; and if men were deserving they wouldn't be begging on the road. As soon as hunger drove me to beg I found that a surprising number of people appeared to share his views. Even the woman who gave me the porridge would clearly have preferred to give it to her pigs.

The bowl of soup, with shreds of onion and carrot and cabbage in it, pleasantly salted and hot, went down well, and I remembered that at the Old Vine, on the days when the soup had no meat in it, it was always followed by another dish.

"Let me see now. You went home to help your father. Wither-field. You see, I *do* remember. You should have gone to Cambridge; one of my most promising boys. Your father . . . still alive and well?"

"Very well, sir."

"Are you married?"

"No, sir."

"Well, all in good time." He rambled on a bit, recalling this boy and that, muddling his times a little, but showing, in those cases of which I had some knowledge, a remarkable memory for individual characteristics. Finally he began to tell me about some boy who had come back to show off a pretty wife and a fine fat baby.

"About your age, but the name for the moment eludes me. Untidy chap. Ethelreda, my dear, what was the name of our last visitor?"

It was then that I realised that Ethelreda had not returned to the kitchen after serving the soup, but had taken the seat at the other end of the table.

"Would it be Johnson?" Her voice had a kind of weary patience, as though she had been asked the same question, or one very similar, too many times.

"No, no. Years apart. Still, it's of no importance. Now, if everyone has finished, we'll have grace, Watson, please."

So that was the end of the meal. The food, never very good, had deteriorated since my day; and so had the discipline, for when the old man said, "You may disperse," there was a wild, disorderly rush for the door.

He ignored it, and taking me by the arm, said:

"You must just look in upon the Canon. Sorry change there, you'll notice. Greatly aged. Very poor sight nowadays, the worst thing that could happen to a studious man. We read to him when we have time to spare, but it isn't the same."

To my eye Canon Hatton seemed to have worn the better of the two; he was still plump and pink, and though he might no longer be able to read his sight still served at a distance, for having greeted me, he said:

"Well, I'm glad to see that *you* haven't become a young man of fashion, Stanton. Quinton came back a real jackanapes."

"That's the name I was trying to remember. I thought the change was all for the better. Wife's influence, I expect."

The remains of the Canon's meal were still on the table, the scent of it on the air; he'd eaten jugged hare. Some of his old friends were still alive, and faithful. I could remember the study meals being a matter of mouth-watering interest, in my day.

There was a little three-cornered conversation to which I failed to give my full attention. In a few minutes I must decide whether to be frank with Mr. Flowerdew and ask his help, or pick up my bag and move on. I even wondered whether Canon Hatton, with his wide circle of friends, might not be the likelier man to help me —though less easy to confide in.

"Now, Edward, you must take your nap," Mr. Flowerdew said. Outside, in the passage, he asked a little wistfully:

"I suppose you're anxious to be getting on, Stanton?"

"I'm in no hurry, sir."

"Oh, good. Good. We'll go into the parlour. I use it nowadays. You knew about Mr. Kentwoode?"

I felt rebuked for not mentioning him.

"Watson told me. I'm sorry, sir."

"Still a young man. Tragic. There were things upon which we didn't always agree, but I miss him. Yes, after eight years. Little I thought he'd be the first to go. And I don't know . . . I'm not the manager he was. Things seem to go from bad to worse. Fewer boys, more expenses, worse conditions, fewer boys. Vicious circle, that's what it is."

We reached the parlour which I remembered as the sanctum of Mr. and Mrs. Kentwoode—I should ask about her, perhaps. I had never been inside the room but on one or two occasions, bidden to report at its door, I had looked in. It seemed unchanged, a pretty, womanish room. The violin which Mr. Kentwoode used to play still lay upon the cushioned window seat.

I made my enquiry about Mrs. Kentwoode.

"Oh, poor Henrietta. She left us. Went to live with relatives; she never cared for school life. . . ." He seemed to brood for a moment. "There again," he said, with something of vexation in his manner, "I couldn't let her go away empty-handed, could I? But you didn't come here to hear about my troubles. Let's have a nice cheerful chat about the old days. Not," he said, with his old smile, "that you yet need the comfort of looking backwards. All your life before you."

I drew courage from the smile, and from the memory of how sympathetic he had always been over a headache or a hacked shin. I said:

"I really came to ask you to help me to find work, sir. I'm looking for a job as a clerk and I need a testimonial."

"But your father . . ."

"We've quarrelled," I said, and told him how and why. He dismayed me by looking so dismayed.

"Dear me, dear me! How rash. Look, my boy, I don't want you to think that I don't feel for you. I do. And I might advise differently if there was a hope of your getting the girl you want. You say there's no such hope, so I think your best course would be to go back, make your peace with your father and do the best you can with the girl he chose. He's a rich man. He can't live forever."

This was the man who had so many times, in my hearing, in a subtle way, decried the purely material approach to life and too much devotion to money.

"Apart from all else, sir, I can't do that because it is too late. My father is not the man to waste time and my brother Cromwell has a fancy for Lucy. But I wouldn't, in any case, go back. I've got myself free at last and I will stay free, even if I starve."

"Starve," he repeated thoughtfully. "Starving isn't the only thing, maybe not the worst thing lack of money can bring you to. Be hard up long enough and you lose your . . . integrity. True, my boy. No matter how you start off, no matter who you are. Even the King said he'd do anything sooner than go on his travels again. He *knew*. And I know. I can see myself getting less and less scrupulous every day. If there's a letter to be written I get Ethelreda to do it, even my name, so it shouldn't look old and shaky. I'm always telling parents that a new master is due any minute, young and very scholarly. I tell the butcher new boys are on their way and when they come I'll pay his bill. That's what it's done for *me*, and I'm old and my needs are small." He put out his tremulous hand and laid hold of my arm.

"Don't think I'm dried up and cynical. I'll tell you another thing. Marry a woman you love and she can hurt you as nobody else can, and if she dies you're maimed forever. You're over the worst now, you've lost your first love and I think you might well have a very happy life with the second best."

"You won't help me?"

"Of course I will. But not till you've counted the cost. You could get a job in a countinghouse. Or in a school. Damn it, I'd employ you myself if I could afford ten pounds a year, but I can't. I don't make ends meet as it is."

"I'd come for five."

"Nonsense. As though I'd take advantage of you!"

"Five pounds, *one* pound a year, of my own, would seem riches to me. I've worked nine years for my keep alone."

"Then in addition to all else you're chucking away nine years' hard labour. While you worked for your father you were working for your own ultimate good."

"That can't be helped."

He sighed.

"Oh, I can remember a time when I'd have advised differently. Stick to your principles; all for love and the world well lost. I'm wiser now and I'm sure the kindest thing I can tell you is—Make friends with Mammon; he always has the whip hand. I'm sorry, my boy, but that is true."

Silence sagged between us. He looked at me almost apologetically, and I looked back at him. A brave old man whom circumstance had almost defeated; a kind old man to whom life had been cruel.

"May I stay till Christmas, just for my keep? It'd give me a chance to see if I preferred teaching to bookkeeping. It'd give me some experience and I could earn a testimonial perhaps."

"You put me in such a quandary. It'd be such a good thing for everybody but you. There's such a variation in the ages. D'you know, now and then when we have had a new boy, I've had to ask poor Ethelreda to teach him his letters, and God knows she has enough to do without that. I can't overlook their free time properly—remember how I used to take you out to swim in the river, and those Nativity plays? None of that lately. There's no doubt a young, able-bodied man would be a Godsend."

I said, as lightly as I could:

"Perhaps God did send me, sir."

"The Devil more like. Just to see how low I could fall. No, it wouldn't be right, Stanton. This is a sinking ship. Nobody else must come aboard."

"Till Christmas, sir. The autumn is a bad time to look for work of any kind. And after the kind of life I've lived at Witherfield, I'm not really equipped . . ."

"All right," he said quickly, "stay till Christmas and then we'll see. Maybe the tide'll turn."

I said, "Thank you very much, sir. That suits me most admirably."

II

Settling down was easy so far as the house and the timetable were concerned. There were some changes—all for the worse, I thought; and I had one or two surprises.

The first came on the afternoon of the day of my arrival. I was to sleep in a room which in earlier days had been occupied by four of the older boys. I was putting the contents of my bag into the chest when the door opened and Ethelreda came in, bed linen piled in her arms. Seeing me she backed away in her old shy fashion.

"I'll come back later," she said.

"No, come in. I've just finished." I lifted the saddlebag from the bed and she came and laid the linen down. I said:

"It seems strange to me, being in this room. I always wanted to be one of the four, but I didn't stay long enough to qualify. It's almost as though I had never been away. You, for one, haven't changed a bit, Ethelreda."

She looked down at the heap of linen.

"I don't think you should call me that now. I'm Mrs. Hatton."

The truth never even brushed my mind.

"You're married. Well, that is one change." I used the voice one does when speaking in a friendly way to servants. "Fancy your having the same name as the Canon."

"I'm his wife," she said, and went away and closed the door, leaving me to my amazement.

Marriages between young girls and old men are common enough, both in real life and in stories, but as a rule there is money or some other worldly advantage involved. What on earth could have brought about a marriage between this plain, shy little kitchenmaid and an elderly clergyman so poor that he lived under his brother-in-law's roof and only ate well because his friends were charitable?

Almost at once a possible answer suggested itself; if things were as bad as Mr. Flowerdew had hinted, labour in the kitchen would be hard to find and to keep; Ethelreda married could neither leave to better herself nor demand a wage. I had a fleeting, irreverent vision of the two old gentlemen concocting a scheme to retain Ethelreda's services, perhaps debating which one should marry her. Then for a moment, because I was in love myself, I thought it a heartless trick; but one must not be sentimental. With her plain face and painfully shy manner she might not have got a husband at all. And hadn't there been a certain pride in the way she had told me her new name and said, "I'm his wife"? Females set great store on being married and by her own standards the girl had probably succeeded beyond her wildest dream. Maybe I should have congratulated her.

My next surprise concerned Watson. I went into the yard where the boys were having their free time, and despite their depleted numbers making ten times the noise we would have dared to do, and seeing him standing there, went and stood beside him. He said:

"You still here, Stanton?"

I returned the smile and said, I swear in a friendly manner:

"Yes. And I'm going to be here for quite a while. It'd be better, I think, if you didn't call me Stanton in front of the others."

His face assumed a sullen, hostile look.

"You mean *you're* the new master there's been so much talk of?"

I nodded.

"Oh," he said.

I thought I understood. I'd been one of the boys, now I'd gone over to the other side, joined the watched-for, the guarded-against, the enemy.

"Mr. Flowerdew tells me that you are a monitor," I said cheerfully. "I'm glad of that. I shall look to you for a lot of help while I'm learning the ropes."

"Yes, sir," he said; but it wasn't a promise, and the look of disgust, almost of anger, remained on his face.

When the free time ended the school reassembled for the presupper session of lessons. We had been accustomed to line up at the door, walk quietly to our places and remain standing until our master said we could be seated. Mr. Kentwoode had been very strict about order at such moments, saying that this was a school, not a cattle market. Mr. Flowerdew was less particular but having formed disciplined habits we behaved whichever master was in charge. Now boys strolled or pushed in just as they fancied and sat down at once.

Mr. Flowerdew mounted the platform with me, but made me take the place behind the high desk. He then made a speech which reddened my ears, saying that I had been one of the best scholars he had ever had and that I had come back after nine years' experience in Essex, which was true in a way, but not as he made it sound. He said they were all good boys at heart and he would leave me to get acquainted with them. Then he shuffled away.

I began by learning their names, and remembering what disproportionate mirth is caused by any boy being called by the wrong name, did my best to associate some distinguishing feature to each name. Ears stick out. Breathes through his mouth. Pale, looks ill. Eyebrows meet over his nose. There were only twenty-one boys now and the state of the school could be judged by the scarcity of young ones. Amongst these there was one whom I should have no difficulty in remembering, I thought. He was extraordinarily handsome, not with the almost girlish look which some young boys retain until they are ten or eleven, his wasn't even a childish face, but it was remarkable because every feature was so clear and firm and in proportion. He had an air, too. Every other boy had either remained in his seat or half risen and muttered his name as though it were something to be ashamed of. This boy stood up as straight as a wand and said, "My name is Rupert Hatton."

As with Ethelreda, no hint of the truth reached me. I imagined that some branch of the Hatton family had been loyal to their kinsman's establishment or chosen this school, as my father had done, because it was not too far away.

At supper—onion dumplings and very welcome—I found my place again laid by Mr. Flowerdew's. I asked him if he would prefer me to sit halfway along the table.

"No need," he said. "Poor little devils, they never play tricks at table nowadays. Too sharp set. Well, and how did you get on?"

"I learned their names. I notice there's a Saberton still."

"No relation to the one who was here with you. He did have brothers but they went . . . elsewhere." He spooned up some food clumsily. "Word gets about, you know. Only one master, one foot in the grave, forgotten all he ever knew; poor food—though Ethelreda does her best, miracle of the loaves and fishes every day of her life; no servants. New schools growing up like mushrooms, too. Notice how few youngsters there are?"

"Well . . . yes. I noticed a very handsome young Hatton."

"Ah yes. Ethelreda's boy." He scowled at his plate. Then, lowering his voice, he said, "Outrageously pampered. I cannot make his father see that a boy is either in school or out of it. He'd be far better elsewhere, but there again, money! He's a clever boy and he can be charming—and otherwise. If ever you have trouble with him, Stanton, do nothing. Refer him to me. I know how to deal with him."

"Compared with some he seemed mannerly, sir."

"I daresay."

"I didn't know about Mrs. Hatton. I called her Ethelreda. I'm afraid I offended her."

"Unlikely. She's too intelligent to take offence at a natural slip. I'm sorry. I didn't realise that you'd left before . . . We made quite a feast of it, you know. Two sucking pigs and a huge plum cake."

The last two sentences had a triviality, a false cheerfulness that set me wondering. It was as though the marriage was a thing about which Mr. Flowerdew didn't feel quite easy, so he took refuge in the thought of it as a festive occasion. It might be that he disapproved.

"A long time ago, now," he said, as though to himself. "The boy's eight, no, bless my soul, nine. Then it's nine years I've been on my own." He turned and blinked at me. "But you said this morning you'd worked nine years for your father, so you should have known about Ethelreda and Edward."

"I was speaking in round terms, sir. I left school ten years ago this coming Christmas."

"Ah, then you just missed the wedding. Pity. We had a whole holiday."

There it was again. Almost as though he were anxious to assure himself that the thing had been done properly.

Well, strange match as it was, and whatever lay behind it, as my father had said of his own marriage, God had favoured it and blessed it with offspring. What more could any man ask?

III

My remark that I was sorry about Mr. Kentwoode's death had been perfunctory: in a matter of hours I found myself genuinely regretting that he was not there to walk in with a scowl on his face and a cane in his hand.

I was prepared, of course, for the inevitable bad time that every new master must endure, the testing to see how far he can be baited without retaliation. Life with Father had taught me self-control and I bore my trial with patience and some semblance of good humour, hoping that things would improve. They did not, and soon my patience frayed. Also my Puritan conscience began to bother me. I was employed to teach and how could I do that if the boys never obeyed me, and wasted their time in attempts to make me look a fool?

Their methods were sly and slippery; they were too ready with excuses, too eager to side with one another, much too free with their "sirs."

I'd find a boy working on an exercise far easier than the one I had set him.

"Sir, I'm afraid I didn't understand you, sir. I was sure you said page ten, sir." He'd look round, rallying the support which never failed to come.

"Oh, sir, I've done the same, sir."

"Sir, I thought you said page ten."

Or I would say, "Ashe, I told you and Meadows never to sit together again."

"Yes, sir, I know, sir. But, sir, Meadows has the Lexicon and I just wanted . . ."

"Return to your place. Meadows can pass you the book."

Meadows did so, careful to start the book off in such a direction that every boy must handle it before it reached Ashe. Delighted grins followed its roundabout progress. There were dozens of similar incidents, trivial but irritating, and each one proof of my failure.

Mr. Flowerdew and I had had a long session, dividing the school into two groups, seniors and juniors. Vague and muddled as he was over some things, he showed a shrewd and comprehensive knowledge of each boy's abilities and weaknesses. "Phipps, now; he's ten, but clever and well grounded. Father taught him, parson with a very small parish, nothing else to do. He'd better be a senior." Or, "Ah no, poor old Hedgely. Tries hard, no memory. He'd better stay with the juniors till Christmas."

He chose the junior class for his own. "Always had the youngsters in the old days; get on best with them. And the older ones will appreciate somebody lively, nearer their own age."

While he was actually teaching he seemed to have his class well in hand. He had an ability to interest, a kind of charm which worked well on small numbers and at close range. It was far from being the complete authority of Mr. Kentwoode, whose cough on the far side of a door could bring the whole school to order; still, it was more than I had.

After about ten days of it, one evening in the parlour after supper, I said:

"I expect you have noticed, sir, that I'm making no headway. My morning class is very unruly, and when I'm in charge before supper the young ones are just as bad."

"Have you tried handing out a few hundred lines?"

"Thousands. They're either not done at all or done so badly that it is a mockery. What I need is Mr. Kentwoode's cane."

"Oh no. Mustn't say that. I'm against caning; always was. That was one of the things poor Chris and I disagreed about. In all these years I've never caned a boy."

I thought—No. Mr. Kentwoode took care of that for you, and look at the state of things now.

"You'll find that most boys are open to reason and persuasion, Stanton."

I said, "Sir, I find it a bit difficult to reason with a boy who is sticking a pin into another boy's behind, or with twenty boys who're all trying to shove through a door at once."

"Well, there is one punishment that you can apply," he spoke reluctantly. "If a boy is downright defiant tell him to forfeit his turn at dishwashing. Maybe you hadn't noticed, we have dishwashers now as well as sewerers." The ghost of his old humorous smile gleamed out. "Heard of a rod in pickle, eh, Stanton? Well, that's just where I put it. In the pickle barrel. Pepper, cloves, spice, all very expensive, couldn't afford to serve pickles regularly any more, couldn't afford help in the kitchen. So I compromised. Two boys wash dishes after each meal and take a dip in the barrel. They hate to lose a turn. And it's not a penalty to be too freely inflicted because I am certain that school food, even at its best, leaves *some* craving unsatisfied." He gave me a little tap on the wrist. "You do that, my boy. Make a couple of them lose their pickle turn, and they'll soon come to heel."

My inner irritation remained unsoothed. I felt that he might have armed me with this frail weapon when I started and saved me ten days' muddling misery. Now that I had it I was determined to use it in the most effectual way.

They played into my hands.

I had endeavoured to re-establish the old, orderly way of entering and leaving the classroom and of standing until given permission to sit. My mentioning of the way I liked things done had up to now simply rebounded on me, giving more chance for petty disobediences; never yet had I seen an orderly entry or a time when somebody didn't sit before I gave the word.

There came a Wednesday evening when everyone lined up in orderly fashion, walked to his place and stood. I was still such a novice that I thought I had won, and with no little feeling of achievement said:

"You may be seated."

Nobody moved. I had one of those moments of self-doubt. Had I actually said the words this evening? Had I spoken loudly enough?

"You may be seated," I said.

They sat down like one boy. Wonderful, I thought. Then Ashe, that bad boy, politely raised his hand and asked for permission to speak. Even more wonderful.

"Sir, have I permission to give this knife to Meadows?"

I was so elated by the change in my class that I would have given him permission to stand on his head. He rose, passed my desk holding a pocket knife across his palm, laid it down before Meadows and came back, halting by my desk to say, in a pleasant, conversational way:

"Sir, that was a bet. I lost. I bet Meadows that *you* never repeated yourself."

I had reproved them, earlier in the day, for the over-use of "sir" and told them there was no need to repeat themselves. Now they all roared with laughter, the exaggerated, almost hysterical laughter of the schoolroom; they rocked to and fro slapping their own knees and the shoulders of their neighbours. I waited, forcing myself to maintain an amiable expression. When I could make myself heard, I said:

"Very funny! And now everybody will lose a turn at dishwashing."

It sounded the most ludicrous punishment ever named, but Mr. Flowerdew knew boys. They were instantly sober and Ashe said, in a hurt way:

"Sir, it was only a joke."

"I recognised it as such. I said, 'Very funny.' No dishwashing is *my* joke. I hope you find it funny."

I saw Watson, who all this time, so far from being helpful, had been one of the leaders in the Stanton-baiting, nudge Swann, the other monitor, and whisper something.

"You have some comment, Watson?" I spoke pleasantly.

He went red in the face and rose clumsily to his feet.

"Sir, you see, we . . ."

"Go on. I'm listening."

"Sir, somebody has to do the dishes. Mrs. Hatton can't manage alone."

"I can wash dishes; and naturally I shall do so. I shouldn't dream of upsetting the household arrangments because you happen to be a pack of fools. And I'm warning you all now. Nobody will have the privilege of washing up again until I am satisfied with the general behaviour."

It was the quietest evening session I had ever held, the quietest, I guess, that there had been in that classroom for a long time. Some subdued boys went to bed, with Watson and Swann, for once, making some attempt to act like monitors. Free at last, I ran down to the kitchen, took off my jacket and rolled up my sleeves. Ethelreda was in the kitchen mixing the water and oatmeal for the breakfast porridge.

"I'll wash up, Mr. Stanton," she said, almost peevishly. "I must just get this over the fire before it dies down."

"I wouldn't dream of giving you an extra job, Mrs. Hatton. I can't see how you manage as it is. Two women used to be in this kitchen, at work all the time."

"Three."

"Well, yes." I was embarrassed.

"There were more boys then. And the parlour to serve as well." As she spoke she lodged the spoon against the side of the pot, crossed to a bowl of water that stood on a slab and washed her hands. Then she went back to her porridge and I began to wash bowls.

"The boys do far more work about the place than they did in your day," she said, as though defying me to feel sorry for her.

"I know. And I'm sorry the punishment had to take this form; but I'd tried everything else. I've worked it out. No boy will wash up until Sunday. And please, even if at any time I should be detained, don't touch the washing up. This is strictly between me and the boys."

"It's time somebody took them in hand."

"I've made a start, at least." I told her of the evening's incident. I could hear her beating the lumps out of the mixture, and then the rattle of the pot's handle as she hung it on the hook.

"Mr. Flowerdew," I ended, "is very kind and the boys are fond of him, but fondness doesn't always lead to good behaviour. I've reached the point where I don't care whether they like me or not,

so long as they do what I say. In fact, for the time being I'm model-
ling myself on Mr. Kentwoode rather than on Mr. Flowerdew."

I heard the swish of water and turned my head. She was washing
her hands again. It was the first time that I had noticed her fanatical
cleanliness, but I was to notice it again and again. Before a job,
after a job, sometimes in the middle of one, over to that bowl she
would go and solemnly, almost ritually wash her hands.

On this occasion it seemed a waste, for her next job was none too
cleanly. She went into the larder and brought out a brace of partridges, tied together by their heads. She spread a piece of sacking
across her lap and began to pluck the birds quickly and expertly.

Tomorrow's dinner for the Canon, I thought. He still ate well
and Rupert shared his meals. Ethelreda always ate at the school
table, and I wondered how it felt to cook such savoury-smelling,
succulent dishes and then sit down to such dull fare.

We worked away in silence and I had almost finished my task
when the door opened and Rupert Hatton entered. He walked to
his mother's side and said in an abrupt, arrogant way:

"Father is still waiting for his port wine. He reminded you when
you cleared the table."

"Oh dear! I forgot." Neatly she shook the feathers into the centre
of the sacking, folded the edges inwards and laid it and the birds
on the table. Then she fumbled under her apron and brought out
some keys on a string. With one of them she unlocked a door beside
that of the larder, reached in and produced the wine.

"Will you take it in to him, darling?"

"He said you were to. He has something to say to you about
being so neglectful."

The words and the tone in which they were spoken horrified me.
I suppose I was bound to be a little sentimental about mothers:
my own had died so long ago that I could not have told you her
colouring, shape or size, but I did remember her as someone gentle
and soft-spoken who had sometimes tried, ineffectually, to stand
between Father and us. That a boy should speak to his mother as
though she were a careless servant shocked me.

Ethelreda hurried away; her son came and lolled against the
dresser where I was stacking the bowls.

I said, "Do you often speak to your mother in that fashion?"

Very civilly and as though genuinely interested in the answer, he
asked:

"What fashion, sir?"

I then, because I was ruffled, made a mistake.

"As though she were a servant," I said.

"But she is. Didn't you know, sir? I thought everyone did." He wore a look of innocence; innocence with something else very sinister behind it. It was a look I'd seen somewhere else though at the moment I couldn't remember where.

"There," I said, as crushingly as I could, "you show your ignorance, Hatton. Your father is a dignitary of the Church, and when he married your mother he made her his equal."

"You mean that my mother is now a dignitary of the Church, sir?" His please-inform-me way of asking the question was infuriating.

"You know very well what I mean, Hatton."

"I know that I delivered the message just as my father gave it to me. I always do."

As though that were the end of the matter he turned to the table and pulled open a drawer and took out a wooden spoon with a long handle. With this he delved into the pickle barrel and brought out an onion.

"Would you care for this, sir? After all, you did wash up, didn't you?"

Angered as I was I was compelled to admire the insolence, the superb timing of the gesture. I had rebuked him, he had put me in my place. I did not then know, I was far away even from dreaming, that one day I was to make my mark as a playwright. I had never seen a play, knew nothing of the craft in which one calculated action can be more eloquent than a thousand words, but I recognised a kind of perfection in his action. The devil of it was that I did, very badly indeed, *want* that pickled onion. Ten days of school food had reduced me, as it did everyone else, to pickle hunger.

The desire to hit him, the *need* to hit him, was so strong that I could only control it by turning away and busying my hands with the unrolling of my sleeves and the donning of my jacket.

Later on, when I was calmer, I thought about his cleverness and the budding schoolmaster in me reflected that such intelligence, properly directed, might be turned to good account. And then I found myself wondering about that innocent-sinister look which I had recognised but failed to place. My memory gallery of faces was limited and nowhere in it could I find one which wore a look which said I-wouldn't-harm-a-fly overlaying another look which said I'd-kill-anyone-who-stood-in-my-way.

It came to me, as such elusive things often do, when I was on the very verge of sleep. It was a face in a picture which during my school-days used to hang near the foot of the big staircase which only the family and the monitors used. One summer day I had an unseasonal cold and couldn't go with the rest of the school to swim, so I mooched about the classroom, miserable and unoccupied, noticing things which on ordinary days were so much part of the background that they were not observed. I saw how beautiful the staircase was, each step inlaid with a pattern in different woods, and how elaborately carved the banister rails were. Then I paused by the little picture. It was the portrait of a child, a girl, in old-fashioned clothes. She was pretty and I stood for a moment admiring her; then, behind the prettiness I saw something else, something that made me uneasy, made me aware that I was alone in that part of the house and that the afternoon was too quiet. As soon as the other boys returned I naturally forgot all about the picture and so far as I could remember never looked at it again.

Now, however, I felt that I must see it again, so I lighted my candle and made my way downstairs. It was no longer there, but a darker oblong upon the panelled wall showed where it had once hung.

Some little time after this, when the weather was wet and chilly, Mr. Flowerdew had a heavy cold and was obliged to keep to his bed. After supper I carried a hot drink to him and stayed for a while, dredging up what bits of interest the day had provided. Just before I left him he said, "Light me another candle. That one is about done and I shan't sleep yet." With the new candle alight, the old one not yet dead, the room was brighter and I could see, on a piece of wall that had been in shadow, the little portrait hanging. I exclaimed:

"Oh, there she is. I wondered what had happened to her."

"To whom?" he asked huskily.

"The little girl in the ruff. She used to hang downstairs."

"Oh, that."

"Do you mind if I look at it, sir?" I took the new candle and went close. I had remembered aright. There was the surface innocence, the seemingly candid blue eyes, the sweetly shaped pink mouth; and there was the other thing.

"It's Rupert Hatton to the life, isn't it? Allowing for the sex and the clothes."

Mr. Flowerdew said testily, "What's so remarkable about that? The picture belonged to my wife, and she was a Hatton before she was married."

"Who was the little girl? What happened to her? Do you know?"

"How could I? She was dead long before I ever came to Baildon."

He sounded so cross, so unlike himself, that I said:

"I'm sorry, sir. It's such an interesting face, as well as a pretty one, I thought she might have had a story."

"Everybody has a story, if you like to think of life in such terms."

His cold had made him irritable, I thought.

Having instilled some sort of order into the boys, I set about trying to get on good terms with them. I decided to start with Watson and Swann. Watson, though more attentive to his duties, remained unfriendly, and Swann, a nonentity, copied him faithfully.

I sold my own watch, retaining Cromwell's because of the vague hope that I might somehow, sometime return it to him. From the proceeds of mine I spent a lavish eightpence on slabs of gingerbread and a jug of cider.

I liked cider, both for its own sake and because it represented one of Father's few defeats. Essex is corn-growing country and, being flat and open, ripens its harvests all at the same time, so there is always much competition for the extra casual labour upon which farmers depend for hay and corn gathering and for sheep shearing. Men often come from a distance, sleep rough and are paid with food and drink as well as money. They like ale, and everyone except Father provided it. Father was sternly set against any intoxicant and pooh-poohed Mr. Newton's argument that home brew could be as harmless as barley water. Father provided his own infusion, nettle and mint leaves, well bruised and steeped in water and sweetened with honey. As a result, the best of the itinerant labourers avoided him and sometimes his harvesting suffered. Even so he would not sacrifice his principles to the extent of providing ale, but eventually he managed to persuade himself that cider was comparatively innocuous. Even so Cromwell and I were forbidden to touch it, but of course, out of his sight, we drank cider with the rest, and found that it had a heartening quality which the infusion lacked. Enough of it made one cheerful and lightened the weariness of long hours of unremitting labour.

I set out my small feast on the table in my bedroom and asked the boys to come there when all the others were in bed. For the first five minutes they wore wariness stiff as armour and answered me, "Yes, sir," "No, sir," in voices that rejected my friendliness, but the food and the cider took effect and when I asked Watson about his brother, Thomas, he answered me normally.

"He went back to India last year. He's a clerk in the East India Company's office. You have to start at the bottom if you go in straight from school, but my father has influence and Thomas is clever. He'll soon get his umbrella."

"His umbrella?" I asked.

He gestured above his head. "They're carried out there to keep off the sun. Mere clerks aren't allowed them, so the first step of promotion is called getting your umbrella."

"There was a year between you, wasn't there? I suppose you'll be going soon."

The expression of angry disgust returned to his face.

"I should have left in the summer by rights. I shall stay here till I grow a beard and young Phipps'll come back and tell me to call him sir!"

"So that's what you've been holding against me," I said.

He said, sullenly, "Not you so much. Everything. Just because I'm bad at lessons. Lessons aren't everything. Keeping me here is like keeping somebody in prison because he can't sing. Outside he might be a very handy carpenter or something."

"That's right, Watty," Swann broke silence to say.

"It *is* right. What's more it shows intelligence. I wonder why you are bad at lessons."

"I try," he said, "but I can't get interested and I can't care. I don't care why Caesar went to Gaul, or when, or what he did there. He's dead and it's all over and done with. It's the same with congruent triangles and all that stuff. If you ever had two triangles and wanted to know whether they were congruent or not you could put one on top of the other and you'd soon see."

I laughed. "But suppose they were triangles of land."

"Sir, did anyone ever want to know if two triangles of land were congruent or not?"

"I doubt it. Tell me this. Who stopped you from leaving when you should? How would the Company know, at this stage, whether you were a good or bad scholar?"

"Mr. Flowerdew wrote to my father. Father sent the letter back to me—that took a year! It said it would be a small kindness to toss me into the world unfledged."

"Watty showed me the letter, sir, and he . . ."

"You shut up! I'll wring your arm off!"

"I was only going to say what you said about Mr. Flowerdew."

"And that was true! He didn't want me to leave. I was a good monitor. Anybody didn't do what I said, he knew about it later on in the yard."

"Clouts," Swann explained, through a mouthful of gingerbread, "or your arm wrung."

"Anyway, I kept some sort of order, and he didn't want me to leave. Then you came back, and I sort of realised how I was wasting my life and I wanted to spew."

"I can understand that. And I promise you, Watson, that if you'll try to give your mind to your lessons from now to Christmas, I'll help you all I can, and I'll speak to Mr. Flowerdew about your leaving."

After that the atmosphere became cordial and we fell into gossip about the school. Presently Rupert Hatton was mentioned.

"There's nothing to be done about him," Watson said.

"Show Mr. Stanton your finger, Watty."

Watson held out his left hand, the little finger of which was lumpy and crooked.

"Canon Hatton did that to me. One day I gave Rupert a clip of the ear, in the yard, and he went and blabbed. The Canon sent for me and just sat there, talking. He didn't seem angry. Then suddenly he lashed out with his stick and broke my finger. I never touched that little wretch again."

"It was him . . ." Swann started and stopped.

"He thought up that trick to make you say something twice over. But don't let him know we told you, sir. He'd get his own back somehow. He's a little rat."

Swann said, "Watty says that but for him Mr. Kentwoode would still be alive."

"Oh, come," I said, "Mr. Kentwoode died of his cough."

"In the end he didn't," Watson said seriously, and rather as though dying were a long-continued process. "He died through picking Mrs. Hatton up the day she fell downstairs and nearly had young Hatton right there on the floor. I know. I was there. Mr. Kentwoode strained himself and had a hem . . . a hemma . . ."

"Haemorrhage?"

"That's it, sir. He coughed his lungs up." Watson spoke with all a young male's delight in gruesome details. "Mrs. Hatton nearly died, and so did young Hatton, because he shouldn't have been born so soon. And then Mrs. Kentwoode went hysterical; you could hear her all over the house, screaming and blaming Mrs. Hatton. We didn't do any lessons for three days and we lived on bread and cheese and then bread. A boy called Robinson said he didn't intend to starve and just went home."

After that evening I had the monitors on my side, and a few days later I made an attempt to win over the rest of the boys. I was out in the yard on a dry but chilly afternoon and I remembered how often during my schooldays, on just such an afternoon, we had enjoyed a game of football with a blown-up pig's bladder. Once indeed we had had a proper leather ball, but someone had aimed ill and broken a window at the back of the house and Mr. Kentwoode had been angry and confiscated the ball.

I'd reintroduce the game, I thought, and leaving Watson in charge, went into the house to ask Mr. Flowerdew's permission to send a boy into the town, and also to ask which butcher enjoyed the school's custom, for since bladders made such handy containers for lard it was useless to ask for one except from the regular butcher.

The house was very quiet. Mrs. Hatton, accompanied by the boys whose turn it was to carry the baskets, had gone into the market; the Canon was asleep in his study; Mr. Flowerdew I expected to find in the parlour, huddled in his woollen shawl, for he did not allow himself a fire there. I was halfway along the parlour passage when I heard, very faintly, the sound of a violin.

Mr. Flowerdew, with his stiff arm, was incapable of playing and the only other person who could possibly be in the house, apart from him and the sleeping Canon, was young Hatton, and even in my ignorance I knew that this was not the playing of a child of nine years old. In fact the only person I had ever heard play like that was Mr. Kentwoode himself. At that thought I felt a cold trickle between my shoulder blades. All through my schooldays, stories had been whispered in dark dormitories; the house was haunted, the boys said. There was a bedroom where knockings were heard, and downstairs in the dining hall there was a ghost who danced and played a tambourine. For one weak, superstitious moment I wondered whether Mr. Kentwoode . . . Then I called upon the sturdy common sense of my upbringing and moved forward and tapped on the parlour door.

"Just a minute, there. Just a minute," Mr. Flowerdew called.

I waited. There was a click and the door opened about four inches, enough to show a section of Mr. Flowerdew's face and his hand, pulling aside a fold of heavy dark curtain.

"If anyone opens the door when the curtain is drawn it strains the rod," he said. "There, come in."

Rupert Hatton sat at the table, his legs hooked round those of a chair, his hands tucked into his armpits as he brooded over a chessboard. One of Mr. Flowerdew's wraps, which had been over his knees, lay on the floor by his chair; he wore another over his shoulders, but even so his face had a bluish tinge.

I stated my errand, but as I did so, I looked toward the window seat where the violin had lain. It wasn't there.

Mr. Flowerdew said, "Rupert, run outside and jump about for a bit, warm yourself, get some air into your lungs. You can come back in ten minutes." As the door closed behind the boy, he said to me, almost accusingly, "You heard?"

"That child?" I said, unbelievingly.

"Very gifted. Not that I'm much of a judge. Never been caught yet, but I hadn't taken you into reckoning." He went back to his chair and wrapped himself in his shawl. "I shall have to ask you, Stanton, not to mention this to anyone, anyone at all. Be the most unholy row, and I don't want to start quarrelling with my oldest friend at this late date. You know how crotchety old men can be, and he absolutely forbade the boy to touch the violin again."

I suppose my bewilderment showed on my face, for he went on:

"To tell you the truth, I think it's jealousy. I appreciate music, though I know very little about it, and Edward is tone deaf. I think it irks him that there's something I can share with the boy that he can't."

It sounded a childish reason, but it was none of my business, so I said:

"Well, sir, I hope that doesn't apply to everything, because I propose one day, if I can get young Hatton out, to teach him to play football."

"Oh no, no. Just this one small quirk. So you won't speak of it, will you? Thank you."

I had not, however, sworn myself to secrecy. He had answered himself, and I reserved the right, one day when sufficiently provoked, to take Master Hatton by his neat little ear and say, "Any more of this behaviour, young man, and your secret's out." I had no notion then that such a silly-seeming thing could be so potentially dangerous.

IV

After Christmas, the really wintry weather began, and we all lived closer, because the only warm place in the house after suppertime was the study, where the Canon made me welcome. His nephew at Mortiboys had sent him a load of logs, each so long and thick that it took two boys to carry it indoors. I was glad enough to sit by his fire and get warmed through before going to bed, for the school-room fire was dead by suppertime and the dining hall was nowadays completely unheated. It was nothing to hear a boy's teeth chatter against the rim of his mug. We all developed chilblains on our fingers and toes; unlucky ones had them on their ears and noses as well.

I changed my mind about Canon Hatton; I had imagined that Rupert's attitude towards his mother had been inculcated by his father, but seeing husband and wife together, I could no longer believe this. True, the old man demanded a good deal of attention; sometimes, indeed, I wondered if he fully realised that there were no longer any maids in the kitchen, but his manner towards Ethelreda was fond, almost doting. He always addressed her in affectionate terms and seemed unable to keep his hands off her. I revised my notion about it being a marriage of expedience and concluded that ten years earlier he had felt a last flicker of lust and married her against—now why should I think this?—against Mr. Flowerdew's wish. Mr. Flowerdew appeared to think highly of Ethelreda, yet whenever the three of them were together in the room there was something not quite comfortable. . . . Often when Ethelreda went near enough and the Canon put out his hand and touched her, Mr. Flowerdew would look quickly away as though the display of uxoriousness embarrassed him. That it embarrassed Ethelreda was plain in the way in which she tried to evade the caressing hand, or, when it fell upon her, stiffened and jerked away.

Her last job, every evening, was to help the old man to haul himself to his feet and mount the stairs. It was some long time before I noticed, one evening, that when he said, "Well, my dear, I'm ready," she braced herself and compressed her mouth as she extended her hands. I realised then how remiss I had been. She was small, and when you looked closely, frailly built for all she was so active, and he weighed all of sixteen stones by this time. And by nightfall she must be exhausted. I laid aside the book I was reading and jumped to my feet.

"Sir, let me help you."

"That's very kind of you, my boy. Very kind. But I don't think my wife would care to be usurped. Thankless as the task is, she likes to help me, don't you, my dear?"

She said, "Yes."

"You don't sound very sure. Shall I take advantage of Stanton's kind offer?"

"No. I'll help you." In another woman the reply would have sounded gruff and grudging, but she always used the fewest possible words.

I persisted. "You could lean much more heavily on me, sir. I'm very strong."

"Mrs. Hatton is stronger than you might think. I've been leaning on her heavily for a long time, now, and she's never yet broken down. Have you, my dear?"

"I can manage," she said. He was in no way infirm, he just moved ponderously. When they had gone their slow way I noticed, again for the first time, that he had left his massive, silver-knobbed stick leaning against his chair. Stupid fellow, I thought, why hadn't he taken it in his other hand and put some of his weight on it?

Noticing such trivial things was, I supposed, a sign that I was moving out of my self-absorption. I was a little like someone who has passed the crisis of an illness. Christmas had been agony. It was all very well to tell myself that I had known my love to be hopeless from the start; resignation didn't put imagination to sleep. A small extra turn of the rack was administered by the fact that I did not know the exact date of the wedding. Marie had said, "I'm to be married at Christmas," so there were a series of mornings when my first thought was—Maybe this is the day! Nights when my last thought must be—Perhaps this very night! But it was over at last; she wore another man's ring, bore another man's name, and my feet were set on the road which would lead me to old age. I should never marry; I should remain faithful to my first love.

Meanwhile I had an interesting and rewarding job. All my ideas and improvements had worked out well, and some of the boys who went home for the Christmas holiday must have carried a good report, for we had three new boys, unexpected, in January, and the promise of six more after Easter.

One of my new ideas had been the division of the whole school into two teams, Blacks and Whites. I let Watson and Swann choose their members, turn and turn about, and the teams were now in fierce competition for the marks I awarded for good work and good behaviour. Then, in addition to playing football, I tried to employ their leisure time usefully, and we had set ourselves, this year, to reclaim part of the neglected garden and grow some vegetables.

In February, as soon as the frost had broken, we began to dig, and one evening, after an afternoon spent working first with one team, then with the other, I was so tired that I fell asleep in the study. I was awakened by the movement of Ethelreda hauling the Canon from his chair. Mr. Flowerdew had already gone to bed. I yawned, jumped up to open the door, wished them good night and then turned back to pick up the book which had slipped from my knee as I slept. Just at that moment the log on the fire burned through, fell inwards and broke into lively flame. I sat down in the Canon's chair and held out my hands. Then I must have leaned back and fallen asleep again. When next I woke it was after eleven o'clock and the candle had burned down almost level with its holder. I took it up and made my way to bed, shivering as I crossed the icy classroom. I had my foot on the lowest stair when a sound above made me look up. What I saw made me, in my dazed state, wonder if I were fully awake. No one could have believed that the mere letting down of her hair could transform such a plain young woman into something of almost unearthly beauty, but it was true. It was simply Ethelreda, with her hair down. But such hair! It rippled down, silver-gilt and shining, almost to her knees; it softened and altered everything, so that what had seemed the opposite of beauty, the high forehead, the sharp cheekbones, the wide mouth, became the very essence of loveliness.

She came on down the stairs, holding her candle, the cloak of hair shimmering. She wore a long white shift, and thrown over it the old sheepskin coat in which she did her marketing in cold weather. My mouth was dry, and when I spoke my voice sounded unlike itself.

"Did you want something, Mrs. Hatton? Can I fetch it for you?"

She said, in her ordinary, matter-of-fact way:

"My husband can't sleep. I'm going to make him a warm drink."

I took my foot off the stair and stood aside to let her pass. And something woke and began to raven in me, something new to me, in no way akin to anything I had ever felt for Marie.

"Can I help?" I managed to say, sounding as though I were being strangled.

"You could work the bellows for me if you liked."

I followed her into the kitchen.

"It's dead, I'm afraid," she said, with a glance at the heap of ash under the porridge pot. But when I stirred it there was a pink glow, a little outgiving of warmth. I laid some dry sticks on the glow and used the bellows, carefully at first and then vigorously. When the flames leaped she came and held over them a little skillet of milk.

I was shocked by what her nearness did to me. When I had said to Father that I loved Marie Garland he had dismissed it as a lust of the flesh and presumably he had known what he was talking about, but I hadn't. Now I did. I had such a powerful desire to take hold of her, to bury my face in her hair, to kiss her roughly and take her breasts in my hands, that to master it I had to step away from her. I thought wildly of the times when I had been alone, in a hidden place, with Marie, how almost reverent my kisses had been.

I should have retreated then, and saved myself much subsequent trouble, but she said:

"Would you hold this, please? I've forgotten the cinnamon."

I moved forward and took the skillet's handle. She reached up to the shelf over the fireplace. The loosely slung coat slipped aside and the sleeve of her shift slipped down so that her arm to just above the elbow was exposed. I saw, with a kind of disbelieving horror, a mass of small, isolated bruises, some new and black, some old and turning greenish yellow.

The words jerked out of me. "What on earth have you done to your arm?"

She took hold of a little box, lowered her arm and shook down her sleeve.

"I often knock myself," she said. "I'm very clumsy."

She opened the box, took a pinch of brown powder between her finger and thumb and scattered it on the mixture in the skillet. She did not return the box to the shelf. Perhaps the same thought had occurred to her as to me—the part of her arm that was bruised was the soft, pale, inner side, and no woman, however clumsy, could bruise herself there, twenty times in a few days.

She brought a covered cup, took the skillet from me and poured the steaming mixture. As she put the lid on the cup she said:

"Thank you for your help, Mr. Stanton. Good night."

I stood there by the fire and thought about the two revelations which had been made to me in the course of a few minutes; my own capacity for lust, much as it startled me, was a personal matter, between me and my conscience; the evidence that Ethelreda had been subjected to unkind treatment merited more thought. I understood now why she avoided the touch of the Canon's hand with those fingers like little pink sausages, why she had to brace herself to help him up to bed, why he had rejected my offer of help. Under pretence of caressing her, he nipped and pinched. Why? And why did she so meekly submit to such treatment from an old man, half immobile and purblind?

V

Nothing in my upbringing had prepared me to handle the emotional situation in which I now found myself. The strongest influence in my life, so far, had been my father's, and he was a true Puritan, his attitude towards sex, as towards God, stark and simple. Men and women were made as they were so that within the bond of marriage children should be born. All else was sinful. I had already deviated by falling in love, in a romantic and sentimental way, with Marie Garland, and I was still, at this point, committed to that love. My feelings towards Ethelreda Hatton were thus doubly damned, by my father's standard, and by my own.

There was no one to tell me what is true—that every man is capable of entertaining romantic feelings towards one woman and carnal feelings towards another, or a mixture of both, in varying degree, towards a number of women. Ignorance and my carefully inculcated tender conscience combined to make me feel much ashamed. I was still enough of a Puritan to believe that if I wrestled with my illicit emotion I should be able to overcome it.

My wisest course, I knew, was to avoid Ethelreda, and that would not have been difficult for, except for the brief meals, the only time when we were flung together was in the study after supper. Then, with the rest of her work done, she would busy herself with mending. Each day I made up my mind to retire early, yet every evening found me in the study, alert and watchful. Sometimes I thought wryly that any unwitting observer would have thought that Canon Hatton was a rich relative from whom I expected a legacy. "My dear, my candle . . ." he would say, and up I would jump to snuff or replace it. "My dear, the fire . . ." and there I was laying on a new log. Now that my eyes were opened I saw that his unremitting demand for small attentions were like the regular flips of a whip, such as an inconsiderate carter gives to a horse which is already pulling its hardest.

I renewed my offer to help him to bed, this time with such insistence that he was obliged to accept; but even as I saved Ethelreda from a few nips and pinches, I realised the futility of my efforts; presently they'd be in the bedroom, with the door closed, and she'd be at his mercy. The thought sent a pitchfork through my bowels, one prong pity, the other lechery.

Sometimes, brooding over the way I had been deceived by a few affectionate terms and gestures, I marvelled that Mr. Flowerdew, that kind man, should still be so blind to the truth. Sometimes I wondered if it were my duty to enlighten him. Would he believe me? He was fond of the Canon; and the old man's methods were subtle. One evening I learned that he could inflict verbal wounds, too.

The school day always ended with a reading from the New Testament and the repetition, in unison, of an evening prayer, "Lord, be Thou our guard through all the hours of darkness . . ." The boys took turns to read, only a few, too young or too stupid to read intelligibly, being omitted. Rupert Hatton, though young, read very well and liked to show off. On the evenings when it was his turn he would present himself at the supper table and forgo whatever delicacy was served in the study.

One March evening, when he was due to read next day, he spent some time preparing his passage. Presently he stood up, took from a shelf another Bible, and having found the place in it, bumped it, without warning, into his mother's lap, saying:

"Hear me read."

She was sewing and had not had time to lift her hands. They stayed pinned under the book and making no attempt to free them, she said:

"You've broken my needle."

In a more insolent manner than he generally used in the study, he said:

"Never mind that! Hear me read."

Quite sharply, Mr. Flowerdew said, "Rupert!"

The boy stood back, lolling against his father's chair, looking innocent and ill done by.

"I only wanted her to hear me read."

I got up and lifted the book. The pointed end of the broken needle was driven deeply into the heel of her thumb.

"Of all the clumsy, inconsiderate things to do," Mr. Flowerdew said.

The Canon said, "My dear, you can get another needle; there's no need for all this fuss."

Mr. Flowerdew turned towards him angrily and said, "You . . ." and then in his ordinary, mild voice, "But of course you can't see the damage. Ah, that's right, Stanton."

I had taken the broken end between my finger and thumb and with a firm tug pulled it out. A bead of bright blood welled up, ran sideways across her wrist and splashed on the white thing she had been mending. Another followed.

I longed, I *ached* to put my arms round her, comfort her, kiss her. I remembered, for the first time in many years, how my mother used to say, "Let me kiss it well." Strange to think of her, now.

"It must have gone in quite deeply. Poor Ethelreda. Here . . ." Mr. Flowerdew pulled out his handkerchief and with his unsteady hands tried to swaddle it around the puncture. "You do it, Stanton.

And hold her hand *up*. Blood always runs downwards. Once, I remember . . ."

It was some story of a boy bleeding. I didn't pay any attention. I wrapped the handkerchief and knotted it and then took hold of her wrist to hold her hand up, as directed. The smallness astonished and moved me. Her bones were like a bird's. A curious thought flashed through my mind. So frail, so meek, she would inevitably be attractive to anyone with a cruel nature. But then, she was attractive to me. Had I a cruel streak?

"Pour it carefully," Mr. Flowerdew was saying. "That's right. Now give it to your mother and say you're sorry."

The boy came forward with some brandy in the Canon's own glass and said, "I'm sorry."

Ethelreda said, "I know you didn't mean to hurt me, darling. I'm all right now."

I realised that I was still holding her wrist and with an effort loosened my fingers.

Canon Hatton said, in a pleasant, conversational way:

"My dear, had you still been on your island you could have given the Flumen your blood. I'm sure it would have Pleased the Waters more than any number of fowls."

Mr. Flowerdew said, "Edward, this is hardly the time . . ."

"Time? Time for what? I was merely remembering. All those interesting details about Beltane Fires and Touchwoods and Pleasing the Waters. It's a long time, isn't it, my dear, since you entertained me with your stories? And such a lot has happened since then, has it not?"

There was something forceful behind the question. Ethelreda said nothing. As though speaking for the sake of preventing the silence being noticeable, Mr. Flowerdew said:

"We've all grown older, alas. Let's not think about it."

"Rupert, too, has grown older. I think he has reached the age where such oddities would interest him. After all, it isn't every boy who has a pagan for a mother. Rupert, do you know what a pagan is? No? Then suppose you tell him, my dear."

"Let him look it up, Edward. Experience has taught me that boys remember things better if they have to ferret them out for themselves."

The words, ordinary enough, added to the tension in the room.

"Books are a poor substitute for firsthand experience." The Canon's eyes were bright with malice. "Come along, my dear."

In a dull, quiet way Ethelreda said:

"A person who has never heard of Christ."

"A good definition, as far as it goes. But there are many pagans who *have* heard of Christ. Consider the missionaries who preach to thousands and count their converts in tens." His mellifluous voice changed a little. "Of course the missionaries may be at fault. I have to admit that my one attempt at converting a heathen was not outstandingly successful."

I said, "With all due respect, sir, there were some *good* pagans. There was a Roman corn chandler who said that if you put in at Ostia with a ship full of corn and knew that other ships were just behind you it was your duty to tell the people that more corn was on the way even if it meant not making such profits as you might have done. That man had never heard of Christ, because Christ wasn't born then."

With an air of pleasure, and relief, Mr. Flowerdew said:

"Fancy your remembering that, Stanton. It must be twelve years since I told that tale. A boy named Witherspoon carried it home, and his father—an Anabaptist—removed him and wrote me a *very* abusive letter."

As though a little displeased by the distraction, Canon Hatton said:

"As an ordained priest, I should be failing in my duty if I did not point out the fallacy in that argument. No one would deny that there were good men in the pre-Christian Era, all the patriarchs, all the prophets. The threat of damnation fell upon those who, coming later in time, heard and failed to believe."

"Well, I've always found it difficult to believe in damnation on the ground of wrong beliefs, Edward. I maintain that the nub of the matter lies in how you behave to what Christ called little ones—always remembering that that includes everybody except yourself."

"My dear man, what arrogance! Everybody little, except yourself. That surely is pride, one of the cardinal sins."

"I don't think I ever overestimate my size, Edward; and any pride I had was knocked out of me, long ago. And if you start talking about cardinal sins, you'll be suspected of a leaning to Popery. Look at that child, yawning his head off. He should be abed."

Rupert said, "I'm waiting for somebody to hear me read."

VI

Before Easter I began looking about for a job I could do in the evenings. Watson and Swann, armed with the power to award marks, and each feverishly anxious to catch a member of the other's team committing some misdemeanour, were now good monitors, capable of seeing the school to bed. I reckoned that if I skipped supper and walked quickly I could be in any part of Baildon by a quarter to eight.

I did not mention my plan to Mr. Flowerdew because it would have seemed as though I was drawing attention to the fact that I was still working without wages. The money I had obtained for my watch was all spent; I had been obliged to have my shoes cobbled, and to buy a warm jerkin to wear under my jacket. Cromwell, when he clawed a few of my things together on a warm September evening, hadn't thought of the winter. I was penniless, and my shoes were falling apart again.

I suffered some humiliation. To find work of any kind in a strange town is not easy, and the hours I could offer were awkward and seemed always to have to be explained. I approached in turn three men who had businesses in which my experience of reckoning might be of service; one was a miller, one was a wool chandler, and the third a tanner. In two places I was smartly rebuffed, there was no work of any kind; the tanner said he could employ me if I could start work at seven in the morning and was willing to unload hides and work in the tanning pits. I explained—for the second time— that I was already employed by day, and was walking away when he called after me:

"Hi! What about Webster? Have you tried him?"

"No. What is Mr. Webster's business?"

He laughed. "That'd be hard to say. He keep an inn, the *Hawk in Hand*, up Baxter Street, just off Cooks' Row. But it didn't do too well, so he's trying out all sorts of new notions. How long you bin in Baildon?"

"Since September."

"And never bin to Webster's. Not even to his Christmas Pantomime. Man, you missed a treat! There was a female, well-shaped one, too, mother naked, 'cept for a tail. Talk of the town she was."

It sounded like one of those so-called entertainments against which my father and his kind railed so furiously, and nothing much to do with a serious keeper of accounts.

"You could stand at the door, like, and take the money. Thass the only job I know hereabouts that start when all else is stopped."

Somewhat reluctantly I found my way to Webster's. Had I possessed any money at all I would have gone into the taproom and drunk a mug of cider and tested the atmosphere of the place; but I had nothing, so I went in at the side, through a vast, deserted yard, and to the kitchen door. It stood ajar and before I tapped on it a woman's voice called:

"Who's there? Come in, whoever you are, and show yourself."

She sat in a chair which looked as though it had been made for her, one of the fattest old women I ever saw. She wore a garment shaped like a tent, but made of good green velvet. Gold earbobs hung from her ears and there were rings embedded in the flesh of her fingers. She looked good-natured.

"You lost your way? Taproom's through there."

"I know. I just wanted to speak to Mr. Webster."

"Well, he's there to be spoke to. Go in."

"I hardly like to. He might think I was a customer. And you see, I haven't any money."

"Poor sod," she said, not without sympathy. "All right, open the door a bit and I'll give him a shout. John! Come here a minute."

The man who came into the kitchen momentarily reminded me of Mr. Kentwoode, perhaps because he scowled and looked impatient, perhaps because he was about the same build and was obviously fastidious about his linen.

He greeted me more amiably than his look had led me to expect. I told him why I had come, ending by saying, "I'm very quick at figures."

He gave a laugh in which there was no amusement, and which again made me think of Mr. Kentwoode.

"So was the last chap I had on the door. So quick he got away with one night's takings! It's true, I could do with somebody honest and reliable now and then. You say you have a job. What is it?"

"I'm a schoolmaster."

"At the Grammar School?"

"At the Old Vine."

The scowl returned, more deeply scored.

"Oh, that lot. Well, we don't want any doings . . ."

The old woman, who had been following the conversation, cut in:

"John, let bygones be bygones. Don't miss a good man on account of whass all over and done with. They took their sign down I dunno how many years ago."

"After it'd hung there long enough to ruin us. Sign or no sign, trade once lost never comes back. You know that as well as I do."

"That way you sound just like your father. You can't blame the Old Vine for the bloody great coaches that can't turn a corner, nor for the post shifting to the *Rose and Crown*."

"All right, all right. Let's say the Old Vine never did us any good." He turned to me and said, half jokingly, "You may think me a superstitious fool, but it'd be asking for bad luck. The stage'd collapse or something. I'm sorry. You look just the sort of man I'm needing. I aim to bring in the respectable people before I finish." He said the last words with a kind of violence.

"You will, boy, you will," the old woman said soothingly. "And him, here, he's just what you want. And after all, he only work there. You think it over."

"I'll do that. Yes, I'll do that. There they go!" His voice and his expression turned savage as somebody in the taproom began to bang on the table. He went quickly to the door and the noise stopped. He turned and reverting to his pleasant manner, asked:

"Would you like a drink? What'll you have?"

Astonished at my own daring I said that I would like a mug of ale.

"My usual," the old woman said.

When he had gone, she said, "You mustn't mind him. He's touchy tonight. He don't like the taproom. He weren't reared to it for one thing; and that is a bit irksome when what you like doing don't pay and you must depend on what you hate for your living. You like your job?"

She never heard the answer to that, for John Webster opened the door and handed to me a pewter mug and a glass. I gave her the glass and she said:

"Thank you, my dear. Now sit down and drink comfortable. Wish you good health and good luck. Speaking of health, how do they feed you? Pretty poor, eh? I've heard talk. Scrag ends and bones, and them not paid for."

She was kind and cheerful and I liked her, I had no intention of snubbing her, the words came out far more stiffly than I intended.

"About that I wouldn't know. I only teach there."

She laughed. "You eat there, too, I suppose. Still, I like that. No complaining. You're a gentleman, thass what you are. I can always tell. Them that ain't go round licking their sores, saying, 'Pity me, pity me.' Proper people don't. They say, 'This is my sore, ain't it a beauty? Pity me and I'll kick your teeth in.'" She sipped her brandy and went on:

"You know, talking about food, even scrag ends and bones, make me hungry. Most anything'll make me hungry. Be so good as to open that door there. Now, can you see a brawn on a blue dish? Fetch it out. You and me'll hev a bite. John ain't much of an eater, never was. There's bread in the crock on the floor and butter there by your elbow. You like pickles with your brawn? So do I. Bring the cheese while you're at it, it'll save you getting up again."

She had managed, without leaving her chair, to spread a cloth over one end of the table and to lay out knives and forks.

Just before she started to eat she looked over the table with great contentment and smiled.

"Them that live longest see most. You remember that, young man, if ever you're down on your luck. I've had a funny life, times when anybody'd have thought I'd be better off dead, times when I thought it myself. But I set myself to live and take care of my boy and I done both. Yes, I done it, and now I enjoy myself. What you wait for taste very sweet when it do come."

I was extremely hungry; I realised that I had been hungry for months. My appetite delighted Mrs. Webster, who kept pressing me to help myself again.

"I like to see somebody eat hearty," she said. She ate heartily herself and had acquired the art of eating and talking at the same time without being in any way disgusting. What with the ale, the food and the talk I grew a little dazed and when she began to talk of Mrs. Kentwoode it was a minute or two before I realised that she was talking, not of my Mr. Kentwoode's wife, but of his mother who had afterwards married Mr. Flowerdew.

"She was the plucky one. The old one, Madam they called her, she was a Tartar. And a witch. She'd ill-wish you as soon as look at you. But Mrs. Kentwoode managed to live with her when she was rich, and when she was ruined she turned to and helped her, which there was no call for her to do. That was when the Old Vine hung out its sign and did us damage. Somehow I never could feel any spite agin Mrs. Kentwoode, and I was glad when Mr. Flowerdew come along to look after her. Poor dear, she didn't make old bones though, even so."

I remembered Mr. Flowerdew saying that when a woman you love dies it maims you for life.

"Was she pretty?" I asked.

She gave a fat woman's chest-rumbling laugh.

"If I told you the truth, you wouldn't believe me, because the truth is, yes, she was, and as much like me, we could've passed for sisters any day. First time I saw her, I felt queer, that was like looking in the glass. She'd even got *this*." She touched a mole on her face. "I was pretty, too, in them days, believe it or not."

"I believe it easily. You have beautiful eyes."

That was no flattery. Her eyes, the colour of a newly husked horse chestnut, were as bright and clear as a girl's.

"You're a nice lad. And I'm going to bear you in mind. I can talk John round if I set myself to it. He's moody, but he's had enough to make him. This ain't what I meant for him, this ain't what he was cut out for. But what with one thing and another, and then the war . . . But there, you'd be too young to remember that. Have a bit of cheese."

I walked lightheartedly part of the way home, cheered by the food, by the old woman's kindness and her promise to speak up for me. Then my spirits declined. I still had no evening work, I still had no money, my shoes still needed mending, and behind these mundane matters which could be remedied with any luck, there was the thing for which there was no cure at all—my longing for Ethelreda. Longing and pity. I must hurry now, or that old devil would take advantage of my absence; he'd pinch the arm he leaned upon, throw all his weight on those frail shoulders. I began to run.

Easter came and went. I heard nothing from the *Hawk in Hand*: old Mrs. Webster had forgotten me, or had failed to talk her son round. To the further detriment of my shoes I went on searching for evening work and word must have got around, for one day there was a message left at the door to say that a Mrs. Manning would be pleased if I would call upon her at her house in the Salt-gate. I set off, full of hope, but what she wanted was a tutor for her son, a typical widow's son, "too delicate for the rough and tumble of school life." She offered me fifteen pounds a year and my keep, which was generous. "I keep a good table," she said, "and it wouldn't be all work, either. There are many occasions when a respectable woman needs an escort. Not," she said, with a toss of her elaborately curled head, "that I am lacking in that respect, you understand; but in a town like this, a lady has only to take the same gentleman's arm twice and there is talk."

She gave me a look so coy and suggestive that I was sickened. Sex on the rampage, and all the more disgusting to me because, in my situation, I had no right to be disgusted. It was like meeting, when you yourself are sneezing and snuffling, another sufferer from cold in the head. I told her that I could not possibly leave the Old Vine and she said that she had been misinformed about me.

After that I gave up all hope of finding extra employment and began to lie in my bed and, amidst sinful thoughts about Ethelreda, to plan a crime. Admittedly the man I intended to rob was my own father, who owed me nine years' wages, but it was stealing nonetheless. One plan I considered was to go back home and whistle a horse from the pasture—there were two, at least, who would come to my whistle—slip a halter over its head and take it to Bures or Sudbury and sell it. The other, more risky, was to waylay Father on his way home from market and snatch the leather bag in which he carried his money.

But I had already left it too late. Both plans involved walking back into Essex and my shoes were now in such a state that one more mile would find me barefoot.

The morning came when I decided that, no matter how awkward it might be for both of us, there was nothing else to do but face Mr. Flowerdew and ask him for just enough money to buy a pair of shoes. After all, I reminded myself, the new pupils had arrived. I'd ask him that evening.

At midday there was a note for me, an invitation to go to supper at the *Hawk in Hand* and talk things over.

The evenings were growing lighter and it was scarcely dark when I reached the inn. Mrs. Webster was on her feet, moving cumbrously about; the table was set and there was a good smell of roasting meat.

"He've been altering the place," she said. "And a bit pigheaded, but I talked him round. He's across there now, in the barn. Damn it, Assembly Room we call it now. You go over and don't get talking, tell him supper is ready. Mind now, admire everything. He've done the most of it with his own hands."

It had been a barn, much like our own at Witherfield, built of oak and solid as rock, the crossbeams as thick as a child's body. The walls had been plastered and painted in such bright colours against the whiteness that, although there was only one lantern alight, down at the far end where John Webster was working at the top of a short ladder, the whole place seemed light and gay, lighter and gayer than any place I had ever been in. At the end near the entry the floor was raised and set with padded benches; below, on the flat floor, the benches were like those in the schoolroom. At the other end, beyond where John Webster was working, long dark curtains hung from one of the crossbeams. The whole place smelt of fresh plaster and paint, with, underlying these scents, the not unpleasant one of ancient hay.

He heard me and called, "I shan't be long. Just putting the finishing touches."

I sat down on a bench, thankful to ease the pressure of my feet against the damp, uneven soles of my shoes. He worked on in silence for a few minutes and then came down from the ladder.

"I'll look at that tomorrow. I think it's all right, but by lantern light it's hard to tell."

The lantern was a good one, with sides of glass, not horn, and it burned whale oil instead of a candle. As we moved towards the door he swung it from side to side and I could see that the walls on both sides were painted to represent a series of archways, through each of which one seemed to look at a piece of scenery. One was a street full of water upon which floated some strange boats with prows like the necks of swans; the houses along the street had balconies, with great masses of coloured flowers tumbling from them, all reflected in the water.

"That's Venice," he said.

"You mean it's a real place?"

"They're all real places. Places I went to, after the war; I was a sailor for twelve years. There's the Bay of Naples, with Vesuvius in the background—I never saw it in eruption but somebody who had told me how it looked. There's Tangiers—a hellhole, if ever I saw one. And that's the Guinea coast, slaves going down to the stockades. Don't they look like real places? Maybe I should have stuck to nymphs and shepherds and St. George and the Dragon?"

"Oh no. These are very beautiful; it's just that I . . . well, I'm ignorant, and they're all so different from anything I've ever seen, or imagined."

He halted.

"Different. That's what I aimed at. Tell the truth, now. How did it strike you when you first stepped in?"

"I thought how clean and gay."

"And decent? Decent and respectable?"

I had not thought in those terms, but I gave him the answer he wanted.

"My trouble is that I started off on the wrong foot. I'd no money, just this barn, doing nothing. I had to do what I could, cheap. Cockfights!" He spoke with scornful disgust. "Ever seen a cock-fight?"

"I've seen cocks fight in the yard at home."

"That's natural. In the business they stive them—keep them very warm and cram them with corn—and then fix bloody great spurs, that long, on their legs. And the people sit round, with blood lust and money lust on their beefy great faces, till one is dead and the other too far spent to crow his triumph. I soon gave that up. Then I tried wrestlers, acrobats, conjurers. Sometimes I made money, but only the riffraff came, and that's what I aim to get away from now."

"Mrs. Webster said not to be long."

"No. We mustn't keep the food waiting." Nonetheless, instead of walking straight across the yard he led me to the side and showed me where the hard ground had been broken and young trees planted.

"They're limes. When they're about eight feet high you stop them and let the side branches spread out till they join. Hung with little lanterns they're a pretty sight. I want to have tables and benches, with refreshments served in a decent way." Then he sighed and added, "But a bad start takes a lot of living down. The name too, Webster's Wonderland they call it. . . ."

He talked in this fashion, now hopeful, now despairing, all

through the meal. His plans were ambitious. Troupes of players who had hitherto stopped short at Colchester were to come to Baildon. There were to be Musical Evenings, too; he had ordered a harpsichord, and spoke of engaging a violinist who was the rage of London. "Ten guineas for one night; and his fares. One minute I think it's well worth it, because ladies in London will have written to their friends and relatives hereabouts, spreading his fame, and the next minute I think it's money chucked away because men, on the whole, don't care for music, and it's the master of the house who decides whether a thing is worth harnessing the horses for."

Mention of horses brought him to what he wanted of me. With the help of a hired boy I was to see to the disposition of the horses and carriages; I was to take money at the door; I was to see that everyone was as happy and comfortable as possible, help with the serving of refreshments during the intervals and throw out any undesirable characters.

"There're some who still hanker for the cockfights and the wrestlers; if they can force me back to them by wrecking what I'm trying to do, they will. So you must keep a sharp lookout. And half past seven's no good. Seven at the latest."

I said I thought I could manage that.

Mrs. Webster said, "Well, now. After all what he must *do*, tell him what he'll *get*."

"I was coming to that, Mother. I thought a shilling a night and one per cent of the takings, for a start. If it works . . . if say by Michaelmas we look like making any headway, then I'll pay more."

Before I could say that this suited me very well, the old woman said:

"And a good bite of food afore you go back, of course. I towd John here that you was the chap for the job. And I reckoned to myself that you want the extra to save up and get married. Was I right?"

"Far from it. I need the money for . . . well, shoes most of all." I thrust one foot out for her to see.

"You'd be as well off barefoot. John, give him a week's money now. If you've spent all yours on paint and stuff, you can take it outa my pot."

"No. This is my venture and I'll pay for it. If I come to grief I don't want you to be worse off. You've had your lean times,

God knows." He patted her shoulder with one hand while with the other he felt in his pocket.

Next day, choosing my moment, I told Mr. Flowerdew that I had managed to find some spare-time employment. I hoped he would not ask me what it was. He looked stricken, almost comically contrite.

"I swear I didn't forget, my boy. Often, in the middle of the night, I've thought about what I owed you. The truth is, I'm so damned used to people demanding money . . . Why didn't you *ask?*"

"I thrust myself on you, sir . . . and I've had my keep."

"You'd have fared better at the Poor Farm! You should have reminded me, instead of going out and selling yourself into slavery. Why didn't you ask?"

"I didn't want to bother you. I only mention the matter now because I must have your permission to leave just before seven. But I think the monitors . . ."

"Of course. And I'll busy myself. Had a very easy time lately. What work did you find, Stanton?"

I told him, carefully emphasising Webster's intent to make the place attractive to better-class people. To my relief he made no comment upon the suitability or otherwise of the job. His face assumed the old man's reminiscent look.

"John Webster, eh? I remember his mother. Her name was Emma." He spoke as though she had been dead for years.

"She's still there. In fact I think I owe the job to her. Webster himself seemed to think that any contact with this house would bring him bad luck."

"That I understand. When I first came to Baildon this was an inn, you know, and being better run, and in a better position, took some of Webster's trade. And there's an older story still, going back to when this place belonged to a wool merchant who put a wool-dealing Webster out of business. You know how old stories and old grudges are handed on? How does she look nowadays?"

I remembered Mrs. Webster saying that she had seen Mrs. Kentwoode and it was like looking in the glass. Had Mrs. Kentwoode, after she became Mrs. Flowerdew, ever mentioned that meeting, that likeness? Was there, at the back of Mr. Flowerdew's question, a wonder as to what time might have done to his wife, had she lived to make old bones? I didn't say, "Very fat." I said:

"She's good-looking still, plump, with beautiful eyes, especially when she smiles."

"I remember her smile. Husband was a surly brute. He died. Well, Stanton, I only hope working at two jobs won't prove too much for you. I must help you more. And look, here's a guinea, on account, just to be going on with. Take it, take it, it's little enough, God knows. And remind me, sometime, that I'm still in your debt."

VII

All through that summer the converted barn which people still called Webster's Wonderland offered amusements of varying quality and kind. The little lime trees came into shining leaf and there were evenings when the kind of people Webster yearned to attract sat at the table and sipped wine and ate ratafia biscuits. Then he would be jubilant, full of plans for the future—comfortable chairs to replace the benches in the expensive part of the house and even the serving of something he called ice cream, though that, he admitted, would be a little difficult since it called for the making of an ice-store where pond ice could be kept all through the summer. There were other evenings when the audience was of the kind to bring its own refreshments—apples crunched noisily through the most touching scene, young onions with their lingering odour. Then Webster would turn surly, swear that there was a curse on everything he ever planned, that he was doomed never to prosper and might as well resign himself to innkeeping.

We found out gradually what things were popular and what were not. Comedies were always acceptable, even by ladies, though some were so bawdy that I was bound to wonder whether my father's opinion of plays and playgoers hadn't some justification. Tragedies were acceptable so long as they were on the large scale, concerned with the sack of Troy or the sorrows of the Queen of Carthage. Plays in which ordinary people came to grief never did well, they made the ordinary people in the audience too conscious of their own vulnerability to misfortune.

It was amazing how the word seemed to spread. We didn't open on Monday, Tuesday was the test night. If the audience, however scanty, went away pleased on that evening, on Wednesday the place would be full of people from Baildon, on Thursday of people from a wider circle and so on until by Saturday people would be coming in from as far away as Nettleton, which meant staying overnight with friends. It was indeed due to Webster's Wonderland that some of the richer country families began to hire or buy houses in the town where they could stay the night without imposing upon their friends' hospitality.

On evenings when people came from a distance I had to be extremely active. Then when the yard was cleared I must go into the kitchen to hand over the money and to have the meal which was part of my wage. I began to drink regularly, on a good night to celebrate a success, on a bad one to soften a failure. "Come on, man, I can't drink alone," Webster would say. There were times when I went home a little tipsy. I always knew when I was because at such times I was quite sure that I could write a play as good as, or better than, the one I had just seen something of. I'd walk along arranging the scenes, building up the characters and composing the speeches. I'd invent situations so comic that I laughed as I walked, or so tragic that I almost wept. I never gave a thought to what would happen to these superb plays of mine when they were written, they were enough in themselves, a kind of mental exercise, and the characters were company for me in my lonely walk. In the morning the charm would have vanished, what had seemed so comic was no more than a schoolboy's joke, the sad scenes too much contrived. I was sober again, back in the real world, with real work to do and real problems to face.

Ordinarily I came back to a darkened house with the back door left unbarred for me. Often, as I approached, my tipsy, play-making mind would see everyone in the house, every apartment, as though the walls were made of glass. The boys asleep in their hard beds, even the naughtiest seeming innocent and pitiable; Mr. Flowerdew, victim of Time, so changed and depleted, sleeping his light, old man's sleep or lying wakeful with his memories; and in another room the Canon, lying bulkily beside the girl he hated and subtly tormented, and she with all that silver-gilt hair spread out on the pillow.

At such moments I would shape scenes in which she and I were the chief actors; scenes in which I would snatch off her ugly linen cap and spread her hair and bury my face in it and say, "I love you." And Edward Hatton, being an old man, would die so that we could live happily ever after.

In the morning I'd see that this was all nonsense, too, as far removed from reality as the other things I had imagined on my walk home; I would become uncertain about the word "love" and remind myself that what I felt for Ethelreda was a combination of lust and pity.

One evening in September I came home with ale in me, and found the kitchen door open, the kitchen lighted and occupied. I went in and found Mr. Flowerdew, Ethelreda and Phipps. The boy sat by the table, his face screwed up with pain, holding a roasted onion against his ear. Ethelreda, wearing one of the Canon's old night robes hitched about her waist with a girdle, was washing her hands, Mr. Flowerdew was watching the boy but as I entered he glanced at me and said:

"Hullo, Stanton," and then, to Phipps, "Is it easier, yet?"

Phipps hesitated between the truth and the lie which would please and said:

"A little, sir, I think."

Ethelreda turned; the streaming hair threw its beauty about her and I looked quickly away.

"It takes time," Mr. Flowerdew said soothingly. "My dear, I think he'd better have a dose of poppy syrup."

"I'll get my keys," she said, with patience, but with the utmost weariness. I looked at her again and saw her sleep-weighted eyes, the sag and droop of her shoulders within the voluminous robe.

"Can I fetch them for you, Mrs. Hatton?"

"If you would. No. I hope my husband is asleep again. You might wake him."

"I wouldn't have disturbed you," Mr. Flowerdew put in, "if I could have found the onions."

"It couldn't be helped," she said, in that same weary way.

"I'll go. I'll move like a thief. Where are they?"

"On the chest just inside the door. Don't take the candle in, Mr. Stanton, stand it on the floor outside."

"You come along, Phipps. I'm going to put you in the Cough Room, next to me, then if you sleep on in the morning you won't be disturbed. Perhaps Mr. Stanton will be good enough to bring the dose there."

I lighted them upstairs and then went along to the room where the Canon was peacefully snoring. The keys lay just where Ethelreda had said, clear to see because they lay on her white cap. I picked them up carefully and ran downstairs.

The fire had been revived to roast the onion and still gave a flickering light. She sat on a stool, crouched low, holding her hands to the warmth. It was, in some way that I could not find words for, an attitude of grief, of despair as though all that was left of comfort in a ruined world was the small sensuous pleasure of feeling warmth on her hands. Outlined against the firelight they looked small and thin, almost transparent.

The sight of her combined with my unsober state to make me lose my head, I crossed the kitchen swiftly, knelt by the stool, put my left arm round her and took both those piteous hands in my own. It was almost as I had so often imagined it, except that it was much more gentle and less demanding. I was indeed astonished at myself. Lechery was there, but it was not master, yet. I kissed her mouth and her sleep-heavy eyes; I put my face into the shining hair so that when I said, "I love you," the words were muffled and sounded gentle rather than passionate.

She didn't speak or repulse me, nor did she respond. It was as though despair and weariness had left her too limp, too drained to make any move at all.

I said idiotically, "I'll look after you. I'll take you away," and I put my arm further about her, so that my fingers touched her breast. Pity lost ground then, and lust gained. I let go her hands and pulled her towards me, letting her know my need.

Then she did stiffen and stir. She put both hands against my chest and pushed, with a surprising, sinewy strength. And she spoke, as an adult might speak to a child.

"Don't be silly."

"I'm not silly. I'm in love with you, Ethelreda. I have been for a long time."

"Ever since you saw me with my hair down."

Taken by surprise, I said:

"How did you know?"

"It's something my hair does to men." Her voice was flat, matter-of-fact; she might have been speaking of the way the wind affected a smoking chimney. "It's nothing. You'll get over it."

Saying that she stood up. I was still on my knees and I reached out and took hold of the worn greasy velvet.

"I shan't get over it. I tell you I love you."

"I don't love you. And even if I did there's nothing to be done about it. I'm married."

"And he treats you vilely. You owe him nothing, no scrap of loyalty, no . . ."

"You know nothing about it. Where are those keys?"

I'd dropped them, and feeling ridiculous, asking myself had I been too easily repulsed, I was secretly glad of the excuse to get up and find them. When I handed them to her she unlocked a door beside that of the larder, reached in, then unhooked a cup from the dresser; she poured something into it and handed it to me.

"You're very kind," she said, "and I'm grateful for what you do. But you shouldn't be sorry for me. Everything that happens to me I've brought on myself. And this," she moved a hand and flipped back a great fold of the cloak of hair, "is a trap you're well out of. In my cap it's quite harmless and tomorrow we'll forget all this. Now, Mr. Flowerdew will be waiting. . . ."

She swung away from me towards the basin of water and began to wash her hands.

I sometimes wonder whether life isn't simpler and easier for people who have never learned to read: and that, for a man who spends his days teaching boys the art, is a sombre thought. But there it is, if you can read you attribute a certain power to words, and you spend some part of your life in a make-believe world. In that world, the world of words and books, it would have been impossible for Ethelreda and me to have gone on living side by side as though nothing had happened. In the real world we did so. I came down, a little thickheaded, renewing my vow never again to drink mug for mug with John Webster, and there was Ethelreda ladling out the breakfast porridge. It didn't seem possible that I had told her that I loved her and that she had told me not to be silly. In books rebuffed lovers kill themselves, or pine away and die; in real life, God pity them, they eat their porridge, wishing there were more of it, and go on with their work, even finding time to ask, "Phipps, is your earache better?"

Life went on, both at school and at Webster's. Soon came the week when we learned that Shakespear, of whom John Webster thought highly, was stinking fish in Baildon. Despite the activities of the Crier for the benefit of those who could not read, and of large bills for the enlightenment of those who could, Tuesday's audience for *The Merchant of Venice* was so sparse and its applause so perfunctory that it was a painful evening for all concerned. The company was the best and quite the most expensive that Webster had ever engaged, and they had been enthusiastically received in Chelmsford and in Colchester. After the first performance Portia wept in the inn kitchen and refused to eat her supper; Nerissa, a pretty redhead, used language to which even the old inn was a stranger and Antonio, who also owned and managed the company, relieved his feelings by abusing John Webster, saying that he had been brought to this outlandish and barbarous place on false pretences.

Webster, already in the depths of depression, said:

"I can't see what you're grumbling about. You'll get your money."

"That is the kind of remark one would expect from a Baildonian! Money, money. Are there no other considerations? What of our feelings? Our hearts?" He flung out his arms in a gesture too wide for the room. "To be unappreciated, to have one's offering scorned, that to an artist is a little death. Poor sweet, poor sweet Portia, let us mingle our tears!"

And he did weep with her, like a girl, while Mrs. Webster, over the good beef pudding, said things might be better next day.

"Don't count on that," John Webster said harshly. "For every one who didn't like it tonight, having seen it, there'll be twenty who'll loathe it tomorrow without having seen it. Sheep, bloody sheep, that's all people are."

I then had my idea, I drew him aside and suggested that I bring the boys the next evening.

"They couldn't pay, of course, but they'd fill up the benches and make the place look better. And they'd clap, I promise you."

"Let 'em come," he said bitterly. "Free seats for all. That's what this town is waiting for. That or cockfights."

Mr. Flowerdew took kindly to the idea of the boys having an outing.

"I'd come myself, gladly, but it wouldn't be wise. Less I'm seen nowadays the better. People think—Him, run a school! The old dodderer, can't even keep his head still! Edward now, he used to be a great playgoer and he still sees fairly at a distance. Problem is how to get him there." He felt in his pocket and seemed mildly satisfied with what he found. "We'll hire the carriage that takes him to Church."

The idea of the Canon, so clumsy and slow-moving, accompanying us had not occurred to me, but I welcomed it. If he came Ethelreda might, too.

"It's very civil of Webster," the Canon said, "but I think I'm a trifle old to go patronising Wonderlands, don't you? And it certainly isn't the place to which a respectable woman should go without her husband's escort."

"Webster has made it into a most respectable place, sir. And I shall be there, and all the boys."

"If I may say so, Stanton, you betray at times a certain rusticity. Are you unaware that, except when with her husband, a lady only appears in a public place accompanied by a gentleman of her own standing, a female older than herself, or a stout servant. I don't know into which category you would place yourself, but in my view you are in none."

"You allow Mrs. Hatton to go to market."

"The two things are not comparable and if you can't see the difference you are excessively stupid. Also you are mistaken in saying that all the boys will be there. Mr. Flowerdew may please himself about the other youngsters, my son's theatregoing days will begin when he is twelve and not before."

In that he was mistaken. Exactly where or when Rupert joined us I didn't see; I only knew that I set out with twenty-eight boys, all scrubbed clean and wearing their Sunday clothes, and that when I counted them onto the benches there were twenty-nine. Seeing Rupert I imagined that his father had relented and sent him to catch us up.

The paying audience was as scanty as it had been on the previous evening, but the atmosphere was entirely different. The boys were so touchingly enthusiastic that other people caught the glow. At the end of the performance Portia came before the curtain and smiled and threw kisses in all directions, and every boy who was not already in love with her succumbed then.

Mrs. Webster, bless her heart, had sent across a great dish of pastry strips dotted with currants that she called "Fat Jacks" and they kept the boys busy while John Webster and I reckoned the miserable takings and doused the lights. Then we set out for home and since young Hatton had no partner I fell in beside him.

I said, "So your father changed his mind, eh?"

"My mother, sir. She said I was too young, but my father said she couldn't be a judge in such matters."

The fact that Ethelreda had rebuffed me, had in fact made me feel ridiculous, had not hardened my feelings towards her and I was shocked afresh at this new evidence of the Canon's malice.

I said, "Are you sure of that? This morning your father himself told me that he thought twelve was the age to begin theatregoing."

"Then perhaps he changed his mind, as you said, sir."

"I think perhaps he changed his mind without telling your mother. And if he'd said earlier that you were not to come she would be bound to agree with him."

"Anyway, I was allowed to come, and thank you very much for arranging it, sir. I did enjoy it, particularly the music. I thought it silly of that girl to say she was never merry when she heard sweet music. I think the music was the best part."

We walked a few steps, then he said:

"Do you think Mr. Webster will ever ask us again? We did clap, didn't we?"

"Everybody behaved very well. As for asking you again, I don't know. Sometimes every seat is taken; and sometimes there are plays which would be too hard for boys to understand."

"What I want to see isn't a play at all."

"Oh, what is it?"

"It's a Musical Evening. There was a bill about it just inside the door. I read it while we ate the cakes. It was a yellow bill, with a black violin at the top. That made me notice. Do you think it possible that Mr. Webster would invite us for that evening, sir?"

"Nothing is less likely. Danielli is a very famous violinist and he will be there for one evening only. The place will be full, and people standing around the sides, I hope."

"I'd stand. I don't take up much room." He spoke in a manner which in any boy would have been humble; in him it was touching. "Would you ask? Please, sir?"

"I'll think about it." I could, if it came to the point, buy him an entry. "In return you'd have to do something for me."

"Oh, I would, I would. I'd do anything in the world. What do you want me to do?"

"I'll tell you another time." Raising my voice I called, "Swann, unless you step out a bit, we shall all be late for breakfast."

Laughter rippled along the line.

For two days Rupert tagged after me like a dog, at every turn there he was, waiting to be told what he must do in order to get to the Musical Evening. Heaven knows what he thought I was going to demand; he looked positively disappointed when I said that all I wanted was to see an improvement in his manners, particularly towards his mother.

"Is that all?"

"It's very important. I admit that you're in a difficult position. Your father is getting old, and old men are inclined to be forgetful. The other night I expect he forgot to tell her that he had changed his mind about letting you come with us, so you can't be blamed for thinking she was against it. I daresay the same thing has happened a great many times and you think you get your own back by behaving rudely. I don't like to see it. I'm here to teach you manners amongst other things and properly brought up boys treat their mothers with respect and affection."

"And their mothers are fond of them."

"So is your mother fond of you, otherwise she would not tolerate your behaviour."

"If she was so fond of me she would have stood up for me when I . . ." He broke off and stood biting his lip.

"When you what?" I asked, in a more friendly voice. He didn't answer and I lost patience again. "There you are, you see. You are unmannerly. It is rude not to answer when someone older asks you a question. Not that it needs answering. I suppose you hold it against her that she didn't stand up for you over playing the violin."

His face went the colour of bleached linen and his eyes darkened till only a hairline of blue showed.

"Did Mr. Flowerdew tell you that? He promised. He *promised*."

I knew a moment of remorse, accusing myself of being cruel, in a way, to a child whose life had not been easy or straightforward. I thought of my own childhood, it had been bleak, but plain sailing, there'd been no conflicts between adults to confuse us. This poor boy . . . even I was trying to use him. Before I could speak a reassuring word he tossed back his hair and lifted his face like somebody walking into the wind.

"Tell on me then! I don't care. I'm tired of trying to hide it and only being able to play once or twice a week, with the door shut and a curtain hung over it. I won't have anything else to do with any of you. I'll run away before he can break it, and I'll play in the roads, all day long."

He swung away and would have run from me, but I caught him by the shoulder. He had his mother's frail, birdlike bones.

"Don't be silly. I'm not going to tell anyone, and no one told me. I guessed, that day when I came to the parlour. I thought that for your age you played exceptionally well."

He said insolently, "What do you mean by 'for your age'? Can you play? Do you know anything about it?"

"You won't get to a Musical Evening by speaking to me like that, you know."

"Like what? I only asked because I want to know the answers. I wanted to know what you meant by 'for your age' and whether you could play, and if you knew anything about it."

"I'll answer you. By 'for your age' I meant that when I heard the music coming from the parlour I couldn't believe that it was you playing. I do not play the violin or any other instrument, but I have heard people play. You play better than any of them, except Mr. Kentwoode."

He drew a deep breath, flattered, satisfied.

"It was his violin, you know. One day, years ago, I found it in the parlour. Mr. Flowerdew was reading so he told me to take it and go and find Callard—he was a big boy. He could play. He used to play in the loft where he couldn't disturb anybody. He knew about ten tunes and he taught me some. It was going to be a surprise for everybody. Callard didn't go away for Christmas, his home was in India, so when the goose came in we were going to play. Father was there—you know how it is at Christmas—and he said, 'Stop that wailing noise.' And he said if ever he saw me with the violin again he'd smash it to tinder. I cried, I was very young then. And after a little while Mr. Flowerdew said I could play sometimes in the study. But Mother never spoke up for me at all."

I thought of my own mother as I said, "I expect she knew it

would be no good. On the whole women have to agree with their husbands. Did your father give any reason for not wanting you to play?"

"He called it a fiddle and said fiddling was for oafs. That isn't quite true, you know. Purcell plays the violin as well as the organ. It said so in a Newsletter. I began to read it out to Father and he said he didn't wish to hear anything about it."

"It's a pity. Anyway, you shall come to hear Danielli. I'll buy a seat this evening to make certain. And it would be as well, wouldn't it, if you began to make a habit of coming to school supper, and keeping to the ordinary bedtime? Otherwise your absence from the study is going to be noticed and I shall be in trouble."

Apart from its results—one of which I see every time I look in the glass as I shave—that Musical Evening would stand out in my memory as something special and apart. It was John Webster's dream come true, and I was by this time sufficiently fond of him to share his joy. People had come in from miles around, the hard wooden benches were packed with silk skirts and satin breeches. To hear Danielli people had been prepared to visit a place called Webster's Wonderland, and they found it wonderful, to judge from the comments they made as they walked round during the intervals, admiring the painted wall, and asking who had drawn the pictures. The harpsichord—not yet fully paid for—was another centre of attention, the first that many people had seen. Ladies with dainty jewelled fingers touched its keys admiringly. John Webster's cup was full.

And so was Rupert Hatton's. I caught a glimpse of him now and again as I went about my duties. I'd bought him a seat on the cheapest bench and he had been pushed to the end, to the last favoured, most neck-cricking place, but he sat there in a trance of happiness. When the lesser items of the Musical Evening were being performed he sat with his eyes half closed, but whenever Danielli was on the platform he stared at him unblinking, watching every movement, listening with his eyes as well as his ears.

Seeing the crowd, I knew that I should be busy for some while after the last note had died away, so I told him to go to the kitchen and wait for me there.

"Will *he* be there, sir?"

"No, Mrs. Webster has opened the parlour in his honour."

"Of course," he said, with a smile, "I should have known that."

When at last I staggered, half dazed, into the kitchen I did not immediately notice that young Hatton was not there. John Webster seized my arm and pushed a glass into my hand:

"Drink to Wonderland that has lived down its name," he said. He was already a little drunk, so were the flautist and the harpist for whom Mrs. Webster was setting supper upon the table. When, having done this, she turned to the spit where a young fowl was roasting for the great man's meal, his manservant, standing by, said in a lofty manner:

"It must be jointed here. My master has a delicate aversion to being served with a *body*."

John Webster took up a knife.

"I'll carve it for him. If he had a delicate addiction to cannibalism he could have my right arm. He's made me!"

The harpist said, through a mouthful of pie:

"I must say I never heard him play better. Thomas neither, come to that."

Thomas played the harpsichord and had been invited to sup in the parlour.

I had been running about, crying, "Mr. Drury's carriage," "Sir Evelyn Fennel's horse," and trying to keep some degree of order; I was thirsty and gulped at the glass Webster had given me without much noticing what it held. Whatever it was went down smoothly and then seemed to make an explosion in my stomach. I drank again, and within a few minutes my dazed feeling lifted, and everything seemed unusually sharp and clear. Then I looked round and saw that Rupert Hatton was missing. Little wretch, he'd gone home without me! The schoolmaster in me was affronted by this direct disobedience—I'd have something to say to him in the morning. I also felt uneasy about his entering the darkened house alone. I was used to it, and knew exactly where to put my hand on the candle; he'd go blundering in and make a noise and give the game away.

I asked Mrs. Webster if he had come into the kitchen at all.

"There was a little boy come in, hanging onto Mr. Danielli. Seemed to be begging, but he went off. What a night, I don't know whether I'm on my head or my heels. You h'ain't had your bite yet."

She pushed a piece of pie at me and I'd taken two bites when the outer door opened and there was Rupert, lugging his violin. He was completely breathless and the sweat ran down his face like tears. He looked for and found me and spoke as though we two had been alone in the room.

"He . . . said . . . he'd . . . hear . . . me play . . . sir," he gasped. Skirting the table he reached the parlour door and shot through like someone pursued.

Soon I heard and recognised the tune that had reached me in the passage outside the study on that autumn afternoon.

The flautist and the harpist stopped chewing for a moment and held their heads in a listening attitude.

"Not bad, not bad at all," the flautist said.

"They're often good at that age, on the violin. Ever hear an infant play the harp?"

"Or the flute?" They laughed together, deeming themselves superior.

"Your boy?" the harpist asked me, returning to his pie.

"God forbid," I said.

"If he was, I'd give you a word of warning. Dozens start off like that and then, poof!"

Mrs. Webster said, "John, ain't you going to eat at all? Bad nights I can excuse you scorning the good food, but tonight I should have thought . . ."

"Presently," he said, and went on drinking.

In the parlour the music stopped and then started again. It was the same tune, with a difference.

"That's him, now," said the flautist. "You can tell blindfold, can't you?"

The music stopped again and then the parlour door opened and Danielli stood there, all plum-colored velvet and frothing cream lace. He had removed his wig, and his white close-cropped head looked curiously small and poor. It was easy enough at that moment to believe what was said of him—that he had been born plain Daniel Sims and run barefoot about the streets of London, and that his Italian-sounding name, like his airs and graces, had all been acquired.

He looked at me and raised his hand, beckoning with a long bony finger. I followed him into the parlour and closed the door.

"Meester Stan-ton? Ze boy tells me you are his master. You know the parent, the father of heem? You weel gif heem a message from me, from Danielli?"

"Not if it concerns his playing the violin. He has been forbidden to play. I brought him here tonight as a special favour, and there'd be trouble enough if that were known without any messages." I turned to Rupert and said angrily, "You must have gone crazy. Suppose you'd been seen, carrying that. You know what would have happened."

Danielli seated himself at the table.

"Zis I do not understand. Zis boy has talent of the most extraordinary—genius perhaps, it is too young to say. But dedicate. Somezing of which any parent should be proud and encouraging, no?"

"His father calls a violin a fiddle and says fiddling is for oafs." How had I dared to say that, in such company? But he was beyond taking offence from me.

"Zen he is mad; many are in zis world, and running loose. Zis is a boy should have a good teacher, the best to be found; and he should practeese and practeese every day. Six hour, no less. Presently more."

The man who played the harpsichord was stolidly eating his supper, the manservant stood behind his master's chair. Their attitude announced that they were accustomed to, tired of, such scenes, but their remoteness was nothing compared with the boy's. He had given me one glance when I snapped at him, and then looked away again. He stared at some point high up on the wall; he wore his tranced expression and that look of being blown on by a wind from far away.

I said, "As long as his father lives he will not be allowed to play, I'm afraid. He has threatened to smash the violin."

"Zis beautiful instrument? Zen he is worse zan mad. Wicked."

Why I should stand up for the Canon I could not tell, but I said:

"No. He's just an old man with fixed ideas, used to having his own way."

"Zen he must wait—ze boy I mean—until he is of age to please himself. Is not the best way, is waste of good time, but not fatal. Myself, I am twenty year when I begin."

Rupert jerked back to life and let out a strange little puppyish noise, and then said in a rush:

"Don't send me back! Don't send me back. Please, Mr. Danielli, take me with you. Teach me. I'd do everything you told me. I'd . . . I'd work for you. I'd be your servant. Please, please take me."

"But zat is impossible. The way I lif, everyzing. Dear child, so despairing do not look. When you are twelff . . . Every year, one time I shall come back, and when you are twelff, eef you practeese well, zen maybe I visit your father and we talk, eh?"

"I can't wait. I wouldn't be a bother. I can look after myself. I wouldn't cost you anything. I'd play in the streets . . ."

He'd moved to the table and stood there, gripping its edge with both hands and looking into the man's face with something too passionate and forceful to be called pleading. Danielli felt the impact, and under it seemed to collapse, not into acquiescence but into plaintiveness.

"Please," he said, looking at me and then at his servant with a curiously helpless expression. "Please, too much, ze journey, ze performance, and now zis . . ."

The manservant said, "Eeere naow." I cut him short.

"Hatton, you're making an exhibition of yourself. Thank Mr. Danielli for listening to you, and come away at once."

I don't know about musical genius but he had *something* equally rare in a child of his age. He took his hands from the table and straightened up.

"I'm sorry, sir. I didn't intend to bother you. Thank you for listening. And for playing so beautifully." He lifted his violin and, though cumbered with it, made a graceful little bow.

We were now very late and I stepped out briskly, ignoring the shortness of his legs, so that every now and then he had to take some running steps to keep up with me. Into Cooks' Row and out onto Abbey Square, past St. Mary's Church and into the Southgate we hurried, all without a word.

I was angry with him, feeling that he had taken advantage of the favour I'd done him, and that trouble might well result. Below the anger, however, other feelings stirred. The dignity of his last words and his exit had impressed me. Danielli was a great man and famous but at the end the boy had, in theatrical parlance, "stolen the scene," and painful as any rebuff must be to his arrogance, and one concerning his music especially, he had shown fortitude. I was reminded of the way his mother had shaken her sleeve over her bruises. I'd never before seen him so clearly as her child.

When I spoke, just as we hurried through the broken archway, I used a cold tone.

"I suppose you realise that now your secret is out. Sooner or later word of this evening's doings will get back to your father."

"It couldn't be kept secret forever. Just so long as he doesn't break the violin. If I can keep that safe I shall be glad for him to know. Then I can practise properly."

There was sense in that. It set me wondering why Mr. Flowerdew had been so furtive. Why hadn't he stuck up for the boy openly and told the Canon not to be ridiculous? I made up my mind to take that line if the news leaked out and the old man accosted me.

"Can you keep it safe, that is the question?"

"I don't know. I shall have to find a lockup place. I'll think about that tomorrow. He can't know tonight, so it will be safe in the parlour until then."

We turned in at the entrance.

"Move very quietly," I said. "I'll go first and make a light."

I then opened the door—not upon the darkness that I expected, but upon a scene so bright that it was a little like the stage at the Assembly Room when the curtain was pulled aside. There was the square back hall and near the foot of the stairs Canon Hatton, wearing a dressing robe and a nightcap. He sat on a kitchen chair and had his stick planted in front of him, his hands resting one on top of the other upon its knob.

At the sight of us he said, "Ha. Exactly what I suspected." Raising his voice, he called, "My dear, the prodigal has returned." Ethelreda had heard us and came from the kitchen; she was still fully dressed in her working clothes and her face was the colour of milk cheese. She made a move as though to come to Rupert but the Canon reached out and took her by the wrist.

"Well," he said, "and what have you to say for yourselves?"

There was in fact nothing to be said. Yet I found myself fabricating the most unlikely tales; I even thought of claiming the violin as mine, entrusted to Rupert to carry.

Rupert said, "There was a Musical Evening and Mr. Stanton took me. I persuaded him."

"We guessed that much. A few enquiries elucidated the fact that you had been seen to leave in Mr. Stanton's company. But for that we should have been very anxious, should we not? That occurred to neither of you, I suppose?"

"I am responsible for the secrecy, sir. It was a musical programme and I knew that you were not in favour . . ."

"You *knew* that. Yet you took him. Will you be so good as to tell me why?"

"I believe in encouraging any boy's interests."

"And you would extend that to, let us say, bullbaiting, in which every boy in school would be avidly interested, I am sure?"

"Harmless interests," I amended.

"Exactly. With *you* as arbiter. You see no harm in encouraging the boy to deceive me? I shall have more to say about this, Mr. Stanton. Rupert, I see that you have your fiddle. Did you contribute to the programme in Webster's Wonderland?"

"No, Father."

"No? You surprise me. Did you then carry the instrument out for an airing?"

"I ran back to fetch it, after I'd heard Danielli play. I asked him if he would hear me play one tune and then tell me whether I'd ever play properly."

"And what was the verdict?"

"He said I had talent, he said perhaps genius but I was too young for him to say, yet."

"How very gratifying. Well, it's much past bedtime. Perhaps you would bolt the door, Mr. Stanton. You'll understand that I feel disinclined to accept your assistance this evening. Good night."

He was displeased with me, but nothing like as angry as I should have expected, and he appeared to think that his son's offence merited no more than a few sarcastic words. I went up the stairs thinking that on the whole we had escaped lightly. I was halfway up when I heard him say:

"Go ahead, Rupert. We're slow." Then there was a scuffling sound and a cry. I turned. The Canon now had the violin in his left hand and Rupert was pinned against the wall with the ferrule of the stick in his stomach. He wriggled and lunged, crying, "Give it to me. Give it to me."

"You'll do yourself no good." The Canon's voice was a trifle breathless. "I don't want to strike you, but I shall unless you go over there and stand quite still." He must have sensed my presence on the stairs and without looking at me said:

"I have bidden you good night, Mr. Stanton. This is a family affair and we can dispense with your company."

I said, "Sir, apart from all other considerations, the violin is of value . . ."

"Thank you. I am aware of its value, both sentimental and otherwise. *Good night!*"

Rupert made one more attempt at rescue; the Canon drove the stick into his stomach again.

"I'll kill you, if you break it," the boy said in a shrill, shaking voice.

"I'm far more likely to kill you, my dear boy, if you offer me any more provocation. And I will smash this thing forthwith unless you go away, Stanton, and leave us to settle this as it should be settled, between ourselves."

I looked at Ethelreda; her pallor had taken on a greenish tinge, but she seemed calm, and with a tiny movement of her head she signed to me to go away. I went, slowly, taking some small comfort from the thought that if the old man had really intended to break the violin he would have done it the instant he snatched it from the boy.

I reached my own room, set down my candle and removed my shoes. Then I thought—If he isn't going to break the thing what is there to settle? And why this insistence upon the family theme? I was curious, and at the same time concerned for Ethelreda. Even in his seemingly good-natured moments he could be unkind to her, what might he not do in his present mood?

I stole to the top of the stairs, and keeping to the curve of the wall, went down as far as I could do while remaining in the shadow. From this position I could not see Rupert at all, and I concluded that he had obeyed the order to stand away. Canon Hatton was on his feet, and the violin lay behind him, on the chair he had occupied; his stick lay there, too. For a second I imagined that he was leaning upon Ethelreda, and then I saw the truth. He had her in the playground bully's grip, and was twisting her arm. Just as I realised this he said, through his teeth:

"You will, you will. Smash it, I tell you, smash it!"

He wrenched her arm higher until her hand was almost at the nape of her neck. She didn't cry out but I heard her gasp.

My stockinged feet made no noise on the stairs. I was there before any of them knew. I broke his hold with another playground trick, knuckling. He resisted me strongly; it was surprising what strength lay under those layers of fat. As his hold on her relaxed

Ethelreda staggered away and leaned against the wall, holding her wrenched arm with her other hand. I said:

"Are you all . . ." Then something hit me smack across the nose; there was a great pain and some sparks, a voice saying, "Damn you! Damn you!" and then nothing.

VIII

There was pain again, grinding and rending as though my whole face were being torn off. I groaned.

Mr. Flowerdew said, "I've almost done. I had to set it before it swelled, otherwise it might have been four or five days and you'd have a crooked nose for life."

His hands, for all their tremor, were purposeful and gentle. There was another grinding pang, then a slight easement. Presently I ventured to open my eyes which I had held screwed up against the pain, and that hurt, too. Mr. Flowerdew, with one of his shawls pinned round him, was just straightening up and reaching for something on the table by the bed. I was in my own room.

"Drink this," he said. "Can you hold it?"

I was aware, even then, that his tone lacked the full warmth of sympathy which as a rule he extended to any sufferer of pain. I raised myself cautiously and several hard heavy objects seemed to bang about inside my skull. I took the little mug. Its contents were syrupy and sweetish, but under the sweetness was another taste, faintly bitter and mouth-wrinkling.

"Is Mrs. Hatton all right?"

"Of course she is, apart from being upset. It's him I worry about, poor old man, such a shock at his time of life, and not being able to see well. He thought you were dead!"

I was about to say, "Small thanks to him that I'm not," when it struck me that Mr. Flowerdew was on the Canon's side. Why? Because he hadn't been told the truth. I was curious to know just what tale the Canon had concocted to explain the situation, so, feeling that the truth could keep awhile, I said:

"I don't seem to remember very much."

"I don't suppose you do. The fall seems to have sobered you, but you must have been very drunk."

"I was *not*."

"Oh, come now. You reek of brandy. But we won't discuss that now. Go to sleep."

Protests formed in my mind; I wanted to say that though perhaps Ethelreda might have reasons for bearing ill-treatment in silence nobody was going to break my nose and get away with the pretence that I had had a drunken fall, but a wave of lethargy washed over me. I could not make the effort to speak again. I fell asleep.

When I woke I was conscious that someone was in the room. I resented the disturbance and for a moment tried to burrow back into sleep. Then I heard Ethelreda's voice:

"Mr. Stanton, I've brought you some bread and milk and some more medicine."

Painfully and with difficulty I opened my eyes as far as I could and, through the slits between my swollen lids, looked at her. She held the covered cup in which, on that memorable night, she had made the Canon his hot posset, and a small mug.

"Mr. Flowerdew says it would be best if you stayed in bed so that the boys don't see you."

"He thinks I fell down because I was drunk," I said bitterly. "I'm going to tell him the truth. All of it."

She put down the cup and the mug and linked her thin fingers together, twisting them in agitation.

"I know it's a lot to ask, but I do beg you not to. He'd be so grieved. There's nothing so out of the way in a young man getting tipsy and stumbling on a stair. He won't hold that against you for long. The truth would break his heart. He's very fond of my husband. He'd be so upset."

"I'm upset. Look how I've been treated. Not that that matters so much, one isolated incident; but look how you are treated. Last night, suppose I hadn't been there . . . The old brute would have broken your arm."

A curious expression, almost a smile, shifted the planes of her face.

"Oh no! I couldn't cook with a broken arm."

The simplicity of that remark, and all its dark implications, moved me almost past bearing.

"I don't know what's behind all this, but it shan't go on," I said, with a vehemence which sent knives of pain through my head. "If he touches you again he'll have me to reckon with."

"Please," she said, "can't you believe that nothing happens to me that I can't bear and that I don't deserve? I'm sorry you were hurt —but you would interfere. If you feel you must tell the truth about your own injury, say he hit you for taking Rupert out. Don't mention me or what . . . or anything about me. Please, if you want to help me, the best way is to ignore it all. I must go now. I brought you a double dose of the medicine; take half now, after the bread and milk, and the rest tonight."

"I don't want to make work for you. I'm not hungry. I shan't want any more food today."

She slipped away without answering me.

My watch, though unwound the night before, was still ticking and I saw by the time that the boys would all be in the classroom, so I slipped down to the privy in the yard. My shaving glass had shown me a hideous and curious sight. My nose was enclosed in a kind of tent made of linen, stiffened with something—flour-and-water paste, I guessed—and held in place by a piece of wood with a fork in it, like a cut-down linen peg. My eyelids and the tops of my cheeks were puffy and discoloured.

When I came back I looked at the bread and milk with distaste and left it untouched, but drank what I judged to be half the contents of the mug. For the rest of the day I slept, or drifted about in the half-world between sleeping and waking. I finally woke to find the room grey with twilight, and Rupert Hatton standing by my bed. He was regarding me with a cool, assessing eye, and he looked as neat and self-contained as a tom kitten.

The effect of the dose had worn off, I was in pain again, so I said, pretty shortly:

"What are you doing here?"

"I wanted to see how you were, sir."

"Well, you see. I hope you're satisfied. It was your fault."

"Also I wanted to thank you for saving my violin."

"That was unintentional. I wasn't, at that moment, concerned with your violin."

"But you did save it. Another twist and Mother would have done it. Not that you could blame her. If you've ever had your arm twisted . . ."

"I wonder you didn't go to her aid, for the violin's sake if nothing else. You could have swung on his arm and impeded him a bit."

"You didn't see me, did you? He'd given me a whack across my belly. It made me throw up."

"I see. What happened then? After your father hit me?"

"Oh, Mr. Flowerdew came. He came slowly and Father made Mother take the chair and the violin into the kitchen. He said if we breathed a word he'd smash it. He told Mr. Flowerdew you fell down drunk and he came down to see what the noise was about. Sir, I swear I would have told the truth, but I daren't because of the violin. May I sit down? It still hurts." He held his stomach with both hands. I nodded and he seated himself carefully at the foot of the bed. "Sir, I see now that when you said forgetful you were being polite. My father is a liar; but I can't give him the lie because he has my violin."

"Oh, for Heaven's sake stop talking about that violin! Who got me to bed?"

"We did. Mother and Mr. Flowerdew and me. We dragged you mostly. This morning Mr. Flowerdew said you had a touch of fever. Swann made a collection and went out to buy you some oranges, but there weren't any."

"It was true to say that I was feverish. You often are with a broken bone."

"Broken. . . ?" He put his hand quickly and protectively to his own nose. "You mean your nose is broken? Oh, how horrible! And it was my fault. But what else could I do? It was my one chance to find out. All these years," he spoke as though he were fifty, "there's never been anyone who really knew. Callard with his ten little tunes, and you saying I played well for my age, and Mr. Flowerdew who can't play at all but is kind, and my father whose one idea is to smash my . . . I had to *know*. I'm truly very sorry that your nose is broken, but I am not sorry that I did what I did."

"You will be, eventually, I'm afraid."

"I know. He has it now, and he'll hold it to keep Mother and me from telling how he hit you. But later on . . . Sir, you heard what Danielli said, didn't you? He said I had talent and should practise. The one person I ever met who could play said that to me. And now I can't practise at all."

He spoke with extreme pathos. I remembered how Danielli had said, "And dedicate." I should have pitied him more had I not been in such pain.

"Hand me that mug," I said. "I'm going to take my dose."

He stood up and moved to the table.

"Oh, poppy syrup. I once had a spoonful for toothache. You aren't going to drink all this, are you, sir?"

"Your mother poured me two doses and I've had one. Naturally a man would have a larger amount than a boy."

"It's very dangerous. Did you know that? If you drink too much, you die. Mother keeps it locked up."

"I know. Give it to me."

He peered into the mug before relinquishing it.

"It doesn't look dangerous, does it, sir?"

I drank it, with a little shudder as the bitter astringency reached me through the sweetness.

"It tastes dangerous. Ugh."

"When I had mine I already had a clove in my mouth, so I didn't notice. Is it very horrid? Shall I fetch you a clove?"

A little touched by his solicitousness, I said:

"No, don't bother. It's not so bad."

"Couldn't it be mixed with something tasty? Then you wouldn't notice, would you?"

"That would be making a fuss about nothing. But that reminds me, Hatton. Today I haven't wanted anything to eat, but tomorrow I may be hungry, and I still shan't be fit to be seen. You bring me something to eat, will you, to save your mother running up and down."

He nodded. "I'll try to find you something good. And if you have to take any more medicine I'll mix it with something. What do you think would cover the taste well? Port wine?"

"For Heaven's sake, don't go meddling with wine. You're in trouble enough as it is. Just bring me a bit of whatever comes handy."

"Yes, I'll do that. Good night, sir. I hope you'll feel better in the morning."

Soon the dose took effect and I did feel better. I ventured down to the yard again, meeting no one; came back, ate the cold bread and milk, wishing that it were something more savoury and substantial, and composed myself for sleep again. Mr. Flowerdew hadn't been near me all day, sure sign that I was in dire disfavour.

Once in the night I woke and thought I heard a sound of movement somewhere in the house. I listened but all was silent and I decided that I had been dreaming. I slept again and woke to find someone gently shaking me by the shoulder.

"Wake up, Stanton. Wake up!" It was Mr. Flowerdew's voice, thin and urgent.

"I am awake. It takes time to get my eyes open." I helped the process with my fingers. In the grey morning light Mr. Flowerdew's face seemed almost without substance, a soiled muslin face, much creased. He wore his breeches and one of his shawls.

"Are you unwell, sir?"

"No, no," he said irritably. "Edward, taken ill in the night. He's very poorly, very poorly indeed."

"Oh, in what way?" I asked, with a marked decline in sympathy.

"Vomiting, purging, delusions. An inward chill, probably. He clings to me, like a child, so appearances must go hang and you must get up and take charge."

He began to shuffle to the door; there he turned, and with his head trembling violently said:

"I've been thinking. I'm to blame. If I'd paid you properly you wouldn't have had to go near taverns. Don't overdo yourself, just keep them quiet. That's the main thing, quiet."

I went to my glass and with delicate fingers touched the peg on my nose. It lifted away clean, bringing with it the stiffened linen, shaped exactly to my nose. I looked little better without it, there was so much bruising and swelling, and in one place, where the skin had broken, some dark, clotted blood. The lower part of my face bristled and glistened with two days' growth of beard and my cheeks seemed to have fallen in. Washed and shaved I might look a trifle less villainous but still somewhat extraordinary for a fever victim. Still, there was no help for it.

I was forced to use a little pressure in washing away the blood, and I heard a click, felt a pang of pain. It was not until later that I realised that I had undone all Mr. Flowerdew's careful work and unset my nose. By that time it had set itself, with a hump and a dip and a twist, so that I looked like a prize fighter.

To encourage myself I donned my new shirt, the first I had ever had that was frilled; despite this I went to face the school with considerable trepidation. The boys seemed pleased to see me, and if any one of them thought it strange that fever should result in such disfigurement, he gave no sign. I was grateful and resolved to maintain the quiet for which Mr. Flowerdew had asked by means of promises rather than threats. I said that if their behaviour throughout the morning satisfied me I'd take them out on to the Common to play football in the afternoon.

By eleven o'clock, when there was a short break so that the boys could go out and stretch their legs and relieve themselves I was beginning to hope that there would be noise so that I could retract this promise. My nose and face hurt and I viewed with dread the walk to the Common with every step sending a jolt of pain through me. I saw the boys out and then, coming back, halted by the kitchen door. Ethelreda was there and I thought I would ask her for another dose of the pain-killing medicine.

There was a smell of ham boiling and I thought—He can't be so ill if he's going to eat ham. It occurred to me that he might be foxing, pretending to be ill in order to make sure of Mr. Flowerdew's sympathy. He could be sure—because of the violin—of Ethelreda's silence, and of Rupert's, but he couldn't be sure of mine, and he knew Mr. Flowerdew's aversion to physical violence.

"How is the Canon, now?" I asked.

"He seems easier. I'm making him some gruel."

"I'm sorry to bother you at such a moment, but could I have a dose? I'm in agony."

"You'd have been better in bed." She pulled out her keys and opened the cupboard, looked in, stepped inside, came out again, empty-handed and looking puzzled, and said:

"That is strange. I'm positive I put it back. I'm always so careful . . ." She looked about the kitchen.

"When did you have it last?"

"Yesterday morning, when I poured your double dose. And I was sure . . ."

"Did you overlook it?"

"You look. It's a wooden bottle, about so big," she showed me with her hands.

The cupboard was quite uncluttered. The Canon's little store of wine was there, the bottles lying on their sides, and there was a small cask of ale or brandy. No wooden bottle.

"I must find it. It's poison, and you know what boys are." She began to move things on the shelf over the hearth.

"Did you have it in the night, for him?" I asked.

"Oh no. He couldn't have kept it down. It was yesterday morning and I could have sworn . . ."

She moved to the dresser and began to move things about there. I went to help her and once we both reached for the same pile of wooden bowls, stacked inside one another. Our hands touched, and wretched with pain as I was, an undreamed-of hunger leapt in me. I drew my hands back as though the bowls were red hot; they tottered and she caught them cleverly.

"There it is," she said, in a wondering voice. "How in the world could it get there?"

The bottle lay on its side at the very back of the dresser.

She set the bowls down and lifted the bottle, weighing it in her hand.

"There's hardly any left. It was almost full. . . ."

"Lying on its side it leaked," I said. "May I have what is left?"

It eased my pain and made me sleepy again, and because I could not sleep I passed into a peaceful, dreamlike state in which nothing seemed quite real. I remember thinking that I had been wrong about the ham, for it was served for dinner. No dumplings, no batter, no peas, no makeweight at all, plain bread and meat, the best meal I had ever had at any time under that roof.

I remember finding myself on the Common with the game in full swing, but I had no memory of walking there. And then the afternoon was gone, the crisp, chill scent of an autumn evening came floating up on the faint mist, and we were walking home again.

I thought of the ham. It was certainly one of the Canon's presents and for Ethelreda to have cooked it and let the boys eat it was proof that she believed him to be dying. If he died I could marry her and look after her forever and ever. I'd work up the school and make it prosperous, so that we could have help in the kitchen. And I'd so arrange things that I could go on working for Webster for a while, so that I should have money to spend on her, on the silk dress and the earbobs women set such store by. Above all I'd treat her so gently that she would forget these years of misery, and open out and laugh and talk gaily as a young woman should.

By the time the evening session started the pain was with me again, a little lessened but bad enough to make my bed seem desirable and a long way away. I must have been less than usually observant, for I did not miss Rupert Hatton until I heard footsteps on the stairs and looked up and saw him coming down. He came between the benches and stood at the edge of the platform.

"Sir, I have a message from my mother. She says will you please serve bread and cheese for supper. It is a round cheese on the top shelf."

"What news of your father?" I asked.

"He was bled again, and he has had some physic."

It was an answer, but not to the question in my mind.

He took his place and sat down, his head in his hands, his eyes downcast to his book. I noticed that he did not turn a page. Twice he looked towards the stairs and seemed to listen. The pity I sometimes felt for him even when he was being exasperating came upon me again; apart from the matter of his violin playing his father had always been kind and indulgent towards him, he was probably feeling some anxiety now. After his second glance at the stairs I said:

"You may be excused, Hatton, if you wish." But he stayed where he was.

Just before suppertime I put Swann in charge and went into the kitchen. I found the cheese and began to cut it, not without a fleeting feeling of respect for Ethelreda who every day, sometimes twice a day, divided something into neat and fair portions. I was hacking away when the door opened and Mr. Flowerdew, supported by Ethelreda, came staggering in. I ran to offer my arm, but she said:

"Pull out the chair." I pulled it out from under the table and brought it along to the end nearest the door. She lowered him into it. He put his arms on the table, laid his head down on them and sobbed. I looked at her and without speaking aloud asked my question; she replied with a slight nod of the head. I stopped cutting cheese and stood still, thinking how awkward it was to witness such distress and not to be able honestly to share it even in a small degree. I think she felt the same. After a minute she put her hand on his heaving shoulder and said:

"Try not to grieve too much. It happens to us all."

He sobbed on, beyond all comfort, utterly broken down. A man crying, even an old man, is somehow more pitiable to watch than any woman can be. We stood there helplessly until I caught Ethelreda's eye and nodded towards the liquor cupboard. She looked relieved, drew out her keys, crossed the kitchen and came back with a cup in her hand.

"Mr. Flowerdew, try to drink this. You were up all night, you know. And you've had nothing all day. This would make you feel better."

The smell must have reached him, for he said in a terrible voice, "Poor Edward's brandy," and sobbed harder.

"You're the one person in the world he would wish to have it. Please try."

She went on coaxing him, like a woman persuading a child. To anyone unconversant with the circumstances it would have seemed a strange scene, the widow so calm, so set on easing the old man's misery. Finally he took the cup in both his trembling hands and put his lips to it.

"Drink it all. You need heartening," she said. Then she stepped back a little and lifted her hand and twitched the linen cap from her head and threw it aside. I never saw a more eloquent and final gesture. She ran the fingers of both hands through her hair and the flattened waves sprang into crisp life.

Mr. Flowerdew said suddenly, in a thick voice:

"Nobody knew how good Edward was. He lent me money. Almost all he had. At least he *gave* the money to Chris, but it was a loan to me, really, to keep the roof over my head. If he hadn't bought the house, which he didn't want, that'd have been the end of my school. I never paid him back."

"Not in money, but in other ways. He always had a comfortable home, and the pleasure of your company."

"We always got on well. And I kept hoping things would improve so I could pay him back. But they never did. And he never complained. And now it's too late." He seemed determined to lacerate himself with remorse.

"He had nothing to complain of," Ethelreda said patiently. "You mustn't think like that, it makes you feel worse."

"He impoverished himself for me; and now, God help me, I don't see how I can give him a decent funeral."

I said on impulse, "Perhaps I can help. I have a few shillings, and a watch that I could sell."

"You're a good boy," he said dolefully.

Ethelreda said—and her voice had changed, grown brusque, almost rough:

"You're not to worry about such things. Would it comfort you at all to know that he was not poor? He was rich. Rich." She repeated the word with a kind of anger. "He had fifteen thousand pounds that I *know* about. Probably more."

Mr. Flowerdew looked at her as though she had gone demented. "You don't know what you're saying. How could he have anything like that amount?"

"I know he had. I've helped with his affairs ever since his sight failed."

What that information did for Mr. Flowerdew I don't know; I know what it did for me. It explained why Ethelreda had submitted to such outrageous treatment. He was old; he had fifteen thousand pounds.

"But, my dear girl, where did he get it?"

"He gambled. I don't mean with dice or cards. With money. Investments. He once told me that all Hattons were gamblers and that was his way. You buy things called stocks and shares when they're cheap and nobody wants them, and then sell them when they're valuable. He did it again and again."

"Then why did he always act so poor? He . . . he wore my cast-off slippers."

"He was mean," she said, with no more vehemence than if she had stated that he was bald.

"Now, now," he said, with mild but definite rebuke in his voice. "You mustn't say things like that. He's dead."

Distressed again, he lifted the cup and took a tiny sip and pressed the back of his hand to his mouth. After a little silence he said:

"I think I understand. Poor Edward. He didn't look on that as spending money. It was like the counters in a game; and he never knew when the game might turn against him. Yes, that would explain."

From outside came the muted voices of boys trying to be quiet. Class was over and it was almost suppertime. I began to cut the cheese again. Ethelreda went to the basin and carefully washed her hands, preparatory, I thought, to helping to cut the bread.

Mr. Flowerdew said, "We must let people know. The family at Mortiboys, of course. And all his old friends. He had a lot of friends. I'm not sure where they all live, though. Do you, my dear?"

"No. No, I don't."

"There was a Mr. Bishop—I've heard Edward speak of him, and

one of the Drurys, which I don't know, and a Canon Fawcett. We must look amongst his papers."

She came back to the table, twisting the towel in her hands.

"None of them ever visited him," she said.

"His friends would be as old as he was, or older."

It was a cool evening, but I saw the sweat spring out on her forehead and lip.

"I don't want to tell you this, but I can't let you go writing round to people whose names he just used. He didn't *have* any friends. All those presents! He did have some presents, from Mortiboys, and at Christmas some wine from a place in Colchester, but the rest he bought for himself. You see, he wouldn't admit that he had any money; but he couldn't bear to eat what the rest of us did."

There was a silence. I pulled the loaf towards me and began to slice it. The knife going through the crust made a squeak which sounded extremely loud.

"You forced me to tell you," she said at last.

Mr. Flowerdew had assimilated and transmuted the rather ugly fact.

"Well," he said, "at least he was always very generous about sharing what he had. Almost every evening he pressed me to sup with him."

I almost laughed. I thought—It is necessary for Mr. Flowerdew to think well of people, therefore he does. Think well. Thinkwell. Mr. Thinkwell. For the first time in my life a play character sprang into my head when I was cold stone sober. He was based upon Mr. Flowerdew, but carried to extremes, and he was revealed to me, whole and complete, with all his deliberate blindness, his endearing stupidity. He was to be the most talked-about, most quoted-from character in any play I ever wrote, and the most misunderstood; for I wrote of a Mr. Thinkwell who could be deceived and exploited, even cuckolded, and still find some kind excusing word to say, and to me he was a tragic as well as a comic figure. The London playgoers found him irresistibly funny and for several months it was the fashion to ask, in any dubious situation, "What would Mr. Thinkwell say?"

I had finished slicing the bread and went to the dresser for a dish. The movement called Ethelreda's attention to me.

"Thank you, Mr. Stanton. I think it would be as well if the sewerers didn't come in here this evening." She bent over Mr. Flowerdew. "I'll make you a milk posset, and tomorrow we'll have some real food. Even the poor boys shall have meals to remember in their last weeks."

Mr. Flowerdew's head jerked.

"Last weeks? What do you . . . Ethelreda, you're not thinking of closing the school?"

"Of course. You need peace and quiet now. And I want the house as I once heard Ellen describe it, before it was an inn, even."

"But the boys. We can't break faith with the boys, and their parents."

She said, "But for me you would have been obliged to break faith with them long ago. No one else would have cooked and cleaned and managed and contrived, all for nothing. I'll take any blame there is, and I'll write to the parents. As for Mr. Stanton, he's never been properly paid, has he? We must make up the arrears and give him a quarter's salary in lieu of notice and a testimonial that will ensure him another post by Christmas."

I thought of all the plans I'd made about being kind to her and saving my shillings to buy her a silk dress.

I was just about to tell her that she could keep her testimonial and her money, when the sound of music came into the kitchen. It came from the depths of the house and increased in volume as it came nearer, a violin playing a flaunting, merry tune, a musical crow of triumph.

Ethelreda, moving with light, free steps, longer than women generally take, went to the door and flung it open so that the music seemed to leap into the kitchen dragging Rupert Hatton with it as a kite drags its tail. He came in like a sleepwalker and began to move around the table.

She closed the door and said, "Stop! Rupert, stop that noise!"

He obeyed her. The music broke off abruptly and he stood with his bow poised, regarding her with surprise and reproach, as though she had wakened him too roughly.

"You don't mind, do you?"

"That's no way to play, with somebody dead in the house."

"But that's why I can play. He's *dead*."

Too many things rushed into my head in one second of time. The boy's obsession; his interest in the poppy syrup, the accessibility of those keys; the almost empty bottle, and the crazy triumph of the music which was echoed in those words, "He's dead."

One second in which to suspect a child of murder.

It took about so long for Mr. Flowerdew to put his right hand on the table and lever himself up and with his left to strike two flailing blows which seemed to meet their mark by chance, one on each side of that handsome little face.

"He was a good father to you!" he said, and the way in which he spoke offered me more enlightenment than I could, at that moment, accept.

Rupert, his eyes gone dark and the red marks leaping out on his cheeks, turned to his mother and she swooped forward and put her arms about him.

Mr. Flowerdew collapsed again and said with a groan:

"I never hit a boy before."

I heard the boys, slightly less quiet now, begin to form the line upon which I had insisted at the outer door. It was suppertime. One certain thing in an uncertain world, I thought to myself. One secret plan may come to fruition, another be blown away like thistledown; the seesaw that is life may tilt in fantastic, unpredictable fashion, but mealtimes come round and people must be fed.

I took up the platters of bread and cheese and walked out of the kitchen, out of the scene in which, without understanding, I had played my little part. I was free again and ready to begin anew.